PEN[...]

GOING MAD [...]

'A wonderfully engaging odyssey, and a great tribute to the late Lindsay Anderson' – Alan Bates

'*Going Mad in Hollywood* gives a continual insight into the dynamics of a partnership which saw each man at his outlandish best ... a record both of a time when anything seemed possible (but probably wasn't) and one when all looked hopeless (but might not be). Sherwin feared the complete diary "an out-of-control-monster" but this version leaves one avid for more' – Christopher Hawtree in *The Times*

'His story has been rocky but hardly dull and he tells it with a breezy self-deprecation ... whether sleepwalking naked in strange hotels, whispering paranoid messages to Harold Wilson into a dictaphone or silencing a restaurant with a piscatory dance emulating a tankful of tropical fish. It must have been tough on the remonstrating girlfriends and wives, but it's fun for the reader' – Helen Osborne in the *Spectator*

'This diary of "not a normal person" but of a man who was once "one of the most sought-after scriptwriters in the country" is ... far from self-pitying but, instead, spritely and effervescent' – Gerald Kaufman in the *Sunday Telegraph*

'This book continues the battle against prosaic conformity which David Sherwin and Lindsay Anderson fought so brilliantly in their films together. It is a unique diary, filled with rich and comic portraits' – Julie Christie

David Sherwin went to Tonbridge School and was briefly a scholar at New College, Oxford. He has lived in the Forest of Dean for twenty-five years. His chief passions, apart from the movies, are his family and flying vintage model aircraft on the Malvern Hills.

David Sherwin

GOING MAD IN HOLLYWOOD

and
Life with Lindsay Anderson

PENGUIN BOOKS

PENGUIN BOOKS

Published by the Penguin Group
Penguin Books Ltd, 27 Wrights Lane, London W8 5TZ, England
Penguin Books USA Inc., 375 Hudson Street, New York, New York 10014, USA
Penguin Books Australia Ltd, Ringwood, Victoria, Australia
Penguin Books Canada Ltd, 10 Alcorn Avenue, Toronto, Ontario, Canada M4V 3B2
Penguin Books (NZ) Ltd, 182–190 Wairau Road, Auckland 10, New Zealand

Penguin Books Ltd, Registered Offices: Harmondsworth, Middlesex, England

First published by André Deutsch 1996
Published in Penguin Books 1997
1 3 5 7 9 10 8 6 4 2

Printed in England by Clays Ltd, St Ives plc

For my beloved Monika, Skye and Luke
and
All Lindsay's Friends

The author would like to express his deepest thanks and gratitude to Charles Drazin, without whom this book would never have appeared in its present form.

Foreword

by Malcolm McDowell

David Sherwin was right at the centre of one of the most influential and creative periods of British cinema. His screenplays for *If . . .* , *O, Lucky Man!* and *Britannia Hospital* are enough to put David in the screenwriters' hall of fame. His collaboration with the late, great Lindsay Anderson is wonderfully documented in this book, and brings back fond memories for me.

I am very proud to call David Sherwin my friend, as he has been for the last twenty-eight years. He wrote me the greatest entrance into film that any actor could dream of – my opening appearance in *If . . .* , disguised in his father's Royal Navy demob coat and scarf. I shall always be grateful for that.

Great work lies ahead for David. As Lindsay Anderson always told him: 'ONWARDS!'

Ojai, California

Acknowledgments

My thanks to Plexus, to the *Guardian* for permission to reprint my article 'Picking the bones of Social Security' and to everyone who helped in the creation of this book.

David Sherwin
January 1996

From *Crusaders* to *If...*

10.50 a.m., Oxford. The Cornmarket. A Great Revelation suddenly hits me, and seconds later my friend from Tonbridge School, John Howlett . . .

. . . It happens like this. We're up at Oxford, but both committed to the same ambition: we will go to Hollywood and make films together. This is the only noble goal in class-rotten England. We're both just 18 and have the boring business of finishing our education to get through. We haven't given that much thought. What we are giving a lot of thought to is this Hollywood dream of ours. We are trying to write a script. Our script must be so perfect that Hollywood will beg us to direct. Orson Welles is our hero. Our film must be popular – a Western, of course. We go to all the Westerns showing in Oxford's six cinemas, from *Stagecoach* to *Gunfight at the O.K. Corral*.

But we can't get a new angle. For six months we've been walking up and down the High Street and Cornmarket trying to work out our Western's original story. But we haven't any new, different plot. All plots have been done. We are stuck.

And I'm personally in trouble. I went up to Oxford wearing an English scholar's long black gown, but found I had to study not Shakespeare, or the great Romantic poets, but three foreign languages: Latin, Anglo-Saxon and Mediaeval Chaucer. I found them incomprehensible, and after my first tutorial with Tolkein spent the day vomiting, and then dropped out.

At the end of the second term I was one of three undergraduates out of 567 to fail their first exams.

Total disgrace.

Both my parents are Oxford Classics dons. My father had to be faced first: author of the classic *Roman Citizenship* and favourite to become the Camden Professor of Roman History.

'Pa, I've failed . . .'

Shattered, standing in his beloved rock garden, he makes a desperate gesture, smiting his hands. 'Oh, Christ . . . well . . . that's it,' he mutters. 'You're on your own now.'

So I need to get to Hollywood fast.

... Then, at last, at 10.50 a.m. in the Cornmarket, Inspiration Strikes.

'John! I've got it.'

I'm so excited, it all comes out in a rush.

'Remember what Wordsworth said: "Poetry is experience recollected in tranquillity." We've got to write from experience. And the only experience we've got is that Nazi camp – Tonbridge – our schooldays!'

'Jesus, you're right!' says John Howlett. 'And it's never been done. Not the real truth. The torture! The keen types!'

Immediately we buy ten Oxford writing pads and three bottles of ink. Since my disgrace I've received a letter from Oxford's Vice Chancellor, in Latin, expelling me from the city limits. My mother, who also loves the movies, lets me – illegally – use her spare room. We move in, and begin ...

For three days and three nights, John and I talk non-stop. Write and rewrite. Our story is about two friends, Mick Travis and Johnny Knightly. After the euphoric freedom of their summer holidays, they return to their boarding school for the winter term. Immediately they experience the torture of Tonbridge. Nightly beatings and buggery. No mother. No father. A diet of cabbage and watery stew – 'Dead Man's Leg'. Insane punishments for having your straw hat at the wrong angle, or the wrong blazer button undone. One terrified new boy seeks sanctuary in the school chapel. He is dragged from the altar by prefects to be flogged until he bleeds.

But the worst thing for our heroes is the complete absence of girls – pin-ups are forbidden. Mick Travis rebels by having an affair with a pretty boy; Johnny Knightly by watching *Rebel Without a Cause* in the town and seducing a café waitress. They are both caught, flogged and expelled.

Unable to tell his parents he slept with a little boy, Mick says farewell to Johnny and runs away to sea. Johnny takes the café girl to a fun-fair. They climb on to a wall of death, and circle happy together for eternity ...

9 May 1960

My girlfriend, Gilda, types out *Crusaders*. Gilda is another problem. She is built like Bardot, is sweetly compliant in the double 'love' seats in the back row of the cinema. She is obliging in every way, but definitely not in love with me.

'God you look like a gangster with that fag in your mouth!'

'I'm trying to look like a gangster.'

'You just look ugly . . .'

Still, she types and binds five copies of the script. We send one to the only film producer I've met, Lord Brabourne, the son-in-law of Lord Mountbatten. Lord Brabourne makes quality English pictures like *Sink the Bismarck*. A second we post to a London agent whose name I've found in the 1959 *Writers' and Artists' Yearbook*: Margaret Ramsay. She sounds human. She is the only agent who doesn't have 'Limited' after her name. Then, as a long shot, we post off a copy to Nicholas Ray, the cult director of our favourite film, *Rebel Without a Cause*, starring our favourite actor, James Dean, whom we constantly imitate with buddy-buddy talk and pretend knife-fights. We address it to Nicholas Ray, Esq., c/o Warner Brothers, Hollywood, USA.

17 May 1960

Margaret Ramsay writes back. She is fascinated by *Crusaders* and would like to meet us. Since John is still at Oxford, determined to get his degree, and I'm 'available', I take the train to London and find St Martin's Lane. I climb bleak stairs to Margaret Ramsay's office. I knock on the door. A woman shrieks, 'Enter!'

Margaret Ramsay sits alone, swivelling violently on her office chair, in a tiny room crammed with scripts and files and her small mechanical typewriter. It turns out she represents almost all of Britain's great playwrights from Robert Bolt to Joe Orton.

She is forthright. *Crusaders* shows talent but will never make a film, except perhaps a documentary. But it's a good thing John and I write together. Film companies like teams. We must write something else more acceptable. Plot, she says, is 75 per cent of a script. Dialogue is the icing on the cake.

I tell her I need a job.

'Oh. The trouble is you're not pretty enough for the theatre, but oddly I did have an enquiry from some engineering firm who want a writer for their industrial film unit.' She rummages amongst a mass of papers and scripts and produces a letter. 'Perkins Diesels' of Peterborough. 'Give them a ring. Say I recommend you and you know all about diesels.'

21 May 1960

A letter from Lord Brabourne. Will John and I meet him to discuss *Crusaders*? Again I take the train to London. The noble lord is straightforward. *Crusaders* is the most evil and perverted script he's ever read. It must never see the light of day. I visit another well-heeled producer, Ian Dalrymple, who had been head of the Crown Film Unit. He says we should be horse-whipped.

22 May 1960

John and I sit on the roof of Christ Church Cathedral amidst the dreaming spires while we contemplate the rejection of our master-piece. I suggest we throw ourselves on to the spikes below. We'll never beat the establishment. The world is, and always will be, run by school prefects. We might as well die young like James Dean.

'No. No . . . We must never give up.' We swear a solemn oath.

So we climb off Christ Church Cathedral, go to the crummy city bus station and leave our last copy of *Crusaders* in the drab waiting room. I write 'GREAT FILM AVAILABLE' across the cover. We leave it beside the yellowing bus timetable. You never know, Lady Luck may strike. We get drunk in the 'Lamb and Flag' pub.

25 June 1960

Kiss Gilda goodbye, and travel to Peterborough for my first assign-ment as an industrial writer for Perkins Diesels. Brian Eldiss, the film unit's cameraman, shows me the mysteries of the huge factory and explains the essence of every Perkins film script.

'It's simple: Perkins Diesels are the best in the world. The best in the Arctic, the desert, the Atlantic.' We drive to Grimsby to go trawl-ing with the fishing fleet for three days.

28 June 1960
The North Sea

My job is easy. I just have to take stills and make notes of life on the boat. Brian Eldiss's job is hell. Tied to the mast, he has to focus through the camera and get a steady shot. He is sea-sick for three days. Every hour thousands of fish are trawled up from the sea, flap-ping and gasping, and plonked in the hold, where they writhe and die. I take a lot of photographs of dead and dying fish, all with their eyes open.

2 August 1960

Writing the script for Perkins Diesels is simple. Brian knows every word. He just wanted company as his wife has left him. That is why he wrote to Margaret Ramsay. He picked her name out of the *Writers' and Artists' Yearbook*, as I had.

11 April 1962

Disaster. Perkins Diesels are taken over by the tractor manufacturer Massey Ferguson. Massey Ferguson have their own industrial film unit. Brian and I are redundant. Brian says he'll emigrate to Australia. Start a new life. Wipe out England.

'And you, Dave?'

'Oh, I don't know. I still have this mad dream of going to Hollywood.'

'See you at the Oscars,' says Brian.

We shake hands on it – and part for ever.

17 April 1962

Hollywood is 8,000 miles over sea and land, but Earls Court and Gilda are only sixty-five miles and a twelve-shilling rail ticket away. Gilda's career has taken off. With her Bardot figure and Garbo face she's become a very successful model. When I arrive back I find every escalator in the London Underground is lined with framed posters of her in a Slix Swimsuit, smiling happily.

Hearing my predicament, Gilda insists I stay at her Earls Court flat, and, provided I do the vacuuming, share her bed. Sadly, 'share' is exactly what she means, because she has another lover, Billy Bottoms, who lives in the flat below. She tries to work out a sensible rota system – 10 p.m. to 3 a.m. in bed with me, and 3 a.m. to 8 a.m. with Billy Bottoms – but my share is ruined by Billy howling endlessly from his room below like a mad dog. 'O Gilda! O Gilda!'

23 May 1962

Gilda is worn out. Her face ravaged. Her looks, on which she relies to pay the rent, gone. I do the noble thing: 'OK, Billy Bottoms can have you. I can't bear to see you suffer so.' Later Gilda tells me Billy is training to be an actor at RADA.

24 May 1962

I phone round old friends for shelter. To my surprise, someone I hardly know offers me the whole front room of his very large Holland Park flat. This is Mark Shivas, whom I briefly knew at Oxford, where he was one of the founders of *Movie* magazine. Mark is now a trainee producer at Granada TV in Manchester. He's away most of the time. His front room is large, carpeted, but furnitureless. Mark apologises. He only had enough money for the lease and his bed. Do I mind sleeping on the floor? Of course not. He reads *Crusaders* and likes it. He gets me a job as a reader at Granada at £3 per book. The only work I recommend is Daphne du Maurier's *The Birds*. Philip Mackie, the head of drama at Granada, says it's 'silly' and turns it down. Alfred Hitchcock thinks differently.

3 June 1962

Gilda's looks and generosity return. She has a good job, a swimwear commercial in Antigua. She buys me a Nikon F camera and gets me a job as a photographer's assistant in a Knightsbridge studio.

15 November 1962

A letter arrives from Hollywood. Thin airmail paper with the heading 'Nicholas Ray' in blue print. He writes that he will be in London all November. He'll be staying at the Grosvenor House Hotel in Park Lane. He would like to meet me to discuss *Crusaders*.

'This is it,' I breathe to Mark. Then panic sets in. I daren't phone the god.

'Just do it,' says Mark.

The phone is answered immediately.

'Is that Mr Ray's secretary?'

'No . . .' – long pause – 'this is Mr Ray, I'm afraid. (He DOES sound like a god. A voice that is omniscient, but with no solid personality.) 'Yes, David. *Crusaders*. Come and talk to me if you can spare the time – tonight at the hotel as I'm having to leave urgently tomorrow for California.'

I put the phone down, shaking.

I take the lift to the top floor of the Grosvenor House. Windowless corridors branch in all directions, each corridor with the same carpet and aluminium lights. I am accosted by a valet who at first thinks I am a hotel thief, then shows me Nicholas Ray's suite. I press one of the four buttons on the suite door. There is a very long pause. The door opens. Nicholas Ray himself stands before me. He is tanned, tall, silver-haired. He stares at me blankly. Which messenger-boy this time?

'It's er . . . David . . . er . . . David Sherwin.'

He leads me down a short corridor with bedrooms off it – one open and lit – and then into a lounge area. There are no windows. The walls are wood-panelled from top to bottom, the carpet midnight-blue, the chairs crimson. A sweaty, shiny little man in a black suit sits on a chair looking terrified of Ray. I sit in a corner while they finish their conversation.

The shiny man pleads: 'Nick, sign any letter you want. I will alter it to just how you want – take out anything, put in anything. Your total fee is two million dollars. But just sign, because I must have something to show *them* . . .'

Mr Ray does not answer, but stares quizzically at the letter, then cruelly at the round, sweating man. The telephone rings in one of the bedrooms. Ray goes to answer it. The sweating man turns to me: 'I hope I'm not keeping you from important business with Mr Ray.'

Mr Ray can be heard talking to some young children, his own. He comes back and reads the letter in silence.

The sweaty man says, 'Nick, I wish you'd talk to me like you talk to your children.'

Another long Ray pause . . .

A blonde suddenly runs into the room in a bathrobe and curls up on a sofa. She looks like Carroll Baker in *Baby Doll*.

'Why, Mrs Ray, I have not seen you in bare feet before,' says the sweaty man, unable to help himself. 'They are very – er, you have lovely feet.'

Another long pause.

The man gets up and Nicholas Ray hands him a mackintosh and places it neatly and patronisingly over his shoulder.

Ray stares quizzically at me after the scared man has left. 'Well, why don't they want to make your . . .' – a long Ray pause – 'film?'
I explain Lord Brabourne's reaction. 'It's England.'

Ray tells me he is too American to make the film himself, but I have a great future in Hollywood.

God, I think, I'm almost there.

Then the phone rings and Ray disappears again. Mrs Ray and I talk. She is very American and very young. All her emotions are on the surface, and in one shriek she breathes them all out: 'I HATE!!! phony plays. God I HATE them!!! I don't go for that phony *Taste of Honey*.'

Ray, as he returns from his phone call, says in a fatherly voice, 'But, honey, you haven't seen *Taste of Honey*! Perhaps that's why it's . . .' – a long pause – 'phony?'

'I just hate all phony plays,' she screams.

We have some cheese and wine. Ray tells me to write a new script as soon as possible and send it to him, and maybe I wouldn't mind being his personal assistant on his next film – *55 Days at Peking* with Chuck Heston?

The dream is coming true. 'I'd love it.'

Then he asks me to do him a very special favour. As he has to fly back to California tomorrow, could I ring the British Film Institute to tell them he won't be able to give his lecture.

7 December 1962

I'm over the moon. I'm going to work for Nicholas Ray. I'm going to be a successful Hollywood writer. Mr Ray said so. He knows about these things . . . I take a lot of colour photographs of hedgerows and rivers in the winter light. I forget about *Crusaders*, idiotic film script.

24 February 1963

I'm twenty-one. My mother sends me a £5 note, and I buy a book of plays by a young German revolutionary who died tragically young, aged 24, in 1837. Georg Büchner.

One thing bothers me. I should have heard from Nicholas Ray by now and be starting that Hollywood career he said lay waiting. I ring the production office of *55 Days at Peking* in Madrid. 'I'm Mr Ray's personal assistant. When can I come out?'

'He's no longer directing the picture.'

I'm dumbfounded. It turns out he's had a nervous breakdown.

28 February 1963

I'm downcast until I read Büchner's plays *Wozzeck* and *Danton's Death*. I discover the epic world: comic, surreal, human, pitiful and tragic. Büchner wrote one other masterpiece. As he lay dying, he willed this play to his young fiancée. She thought it disgusting and pornographic and, as she lay dying, ninety years old, had the only copy burnt in her grate. Büchner's two surviving plays and his heroic revolutionary life are what John Howlett and I were really aiming at when we wrote our script. John is likewise fired up. We post *Crusaders* to a director we both much admire – the Ealing Studios rebel, Seth Holt.

10 October 1964

The 'Bunch of Grapes' pub, Knightsbridge, London.

'Are you famous? Should I know you?' Seth eyes us mischievously when we introduce ourselves. Orders whisky all round. He loves our script, but he's never been to any school in his life and is entirely self-educated. He doesn't feel he's the correct person to direct, but he'd like to produce *Crusaders* and find a director, come hell or high water.

Well, it takes a lot of whisky, and a lot more water . . .

September 1965

At last I fall in love again. Val works for the Bursar of Jesus College, Oxford. She is funny and highly neurotic – two qualities I adore. She also loves *Crusaders*. Tonbridge is just like her school, where she had to polish the prefects' bedsprings. She types drafts for me in my father's rooms at St John's. She adds her own poetic touches to the story.

She also teaches me how to make love: 'A woman's body is like a musical instrument,' she constantly reminds me. One day, after making love in my father's study at St John's, we draw back the curtains to see Dirk Bogarde. We are being filmed in a shot of Losey's *Accident*.

Our favourite place is the cosy cockpit of my MGB GT at sunset at the end of the runway at RAF Abingdon. Our music crescendoes as just a few feet away Blackburn Beverleys thunder into the skies. It seems it will go on for ever, but Val is neurotically adamant that she wants no marriage and no children. I want both.

10 July 1966

I am shooting the still sequences for a Hovis film – 'Flour Piece' – in the middle of a sodden wheatfield. It is pouring with rain. I am supposed to be creating a picture of an angelic little girl dancing through sunlit ripe wheat.

The little girl, who is an exceptionally tough child model, her ambitious mother, the director Antony Short and I have been waiting for sunshine in this rotting field for five days. We are desperate.

An urgent message from our hotel. It's Seth on the line. He tells me I must meet Lindsay Anderson tonight about *Crusaders*. I only know of this Lindsay Anderson as the director of a British film I'd seen three years ago, *This Sporting Life*, which had made a star of Richard Harris, 'Britain's Brando'. It was almost as good as a Hollywood picture.

I tell Seth I've got to stay in this rainy wheatfield in the middle of Bedfordshire until the sun shines.

'Forget sunshine,' Seth growls. 'Lindsay's read *Crusaders*. He's the man for the job. Anyway, you can always see the sunset in England. Just wait and then shoot fast. We're meeting him with John at the 'Pillars of Hercules' pub in Soho. 8 p.m. sharp.' I curse this Lindsay Anderson, but the sun does shine briefly at sunset.

The tough little girl dances and twirls her huge translucent multi-coloured umbrella which symbolises the goodness of Hovis bread. I even get a rainbow, striking through the umbrella and turning the wet wheat golden. Click, click, click . . . Amazing! This is the climax and close of my photographic career.

8.30 p.m. The 'Pillars of Hercules', Soho.

I arrive late. All I'm thinking about is a pint of beer. Seth is sitting and smiles like a friendly lion, John looks serious with his spectacles perched on his forehead like a real movie writer, and Lindsay Anderson is standing up asking me if I'd like a beer.

I remembered Richard Harris beating up Rachel Roberts in *This Sporting Life* and expected someone big and aggressive, but Lindsay

Anderson is like a young gnome. He has an odd but humorous smile, and seems intelligent in spite of his first bantering words: 'Well, the script is very bad.'

'No, it's brilliant,' I reply.

'Oh, is it? Good?'

It dawns on me that this man has read *Crusaders* seriously. I warm to him. The version John and I wrote six years ago he thinks is too sentimental. He adds that most of the boys and masters are only thinly sketched. They need to be truly imagined, and with more humour. The script needs to be freed, to be more poetical.

'Have you read Georg Büchner?' I ask the gnome.

'Yes.'

'It should be like *Wozzeck*.'

'Yes. Poetry is the key.'

'And the epic.'

'Exactly.'

With this mutual flash of understanding my and Lindsay's destinies change . . .

Seth Holt speaks for the first time. He proposes an agreement between the four of us. He himself has got lucky again and landed a big assignment directing Bette Davis in *The Nanny*. He wants John to write his next commercial film after this, a thriller called *The Velvet Well*. He will pay him £100 a week. He wants me to give up photography and start writing *Crusaders* afresh for Lindsay. He will pay me £20 a week. So I become a real scriptwriter.

12 September 1966

I show Lindsay my new notes for our film. He likes them. They are poetic, but need organising. He has to go to Warsaw for two months to direct (in Polish) John Osborne's play *Inadmissible Evidence*, and then his own documentary poem about a Polish Dramatic Academy, *One Two Three*.

All the time he is away we keep in touch, phoning each other through the Iron Curtain. He sends me a letter about our work:

HOTEL EUROPEJSKI
Warsaw

Monday November 6, 1966

Dear David
Thanks for the phone call: and also for the new selection of notes.
As I think we agreed, the problem with them seems to be the lack
of organising principle in them: and also a somewhat *literary*
quality, which makes them excellent often on the page, genuinely
poetic and suggestive, but sometimes in a way that doesn't trans-
late into images or drama: I will try to be more specific about this
later . . . But I do think that writing them has been valuable if only
because they do suggest the opening of a more poetic, less axe-
grinding, and I think less sentimental attitude to the subject. But
plainly, the time has come to consider *form* a bit, not conclusively
of course, but as an 'organising principle' – to see the bits, not as
isolated fragments and observations, but as complementary, parts
of what in some way must eventually be a whole . . . i.e. who are
the characters in the story; how do they relate; what is happening
at the beginning, middle and end; what are the main incidents?

(Maybe to you these notes do have some kind of relationship: I
don't find it very clear!)

I have read again the two scripts I've got. Interesting. The first
(dated 1960) is understandably a bit . . . shall we say immature:
bad on construction, and very romantic – sentimental in a touching adolescent sort of way. But some of its scenes are good material – funnily enough I prefer the scene with Mr Stewart and
Garibaldi, to Mr Stewart and Carlyle (that Carlyle prose is
practically incomprehensible to me).

In the most recent script there is obvious improvement in construction; but I think we're agreed that too much was lost in order
to achieve a tight narrative involving really only Mick and
Johnny: and of course there remains the basic flaw of Glenda; a
bit less indulged than Judy and Johnny; but still entirely sentimental in conception – and having become the basic subject of the
whole story – plus the somehow unresolved question of Mick's
relationship with Bobby Phillips . . . Some good scenes and valuable inventions in this script also, though!

It seems to me that the film should start at the school, and in the school; because that is the world of the film; not coming into it with scenes in the 'real' world first. For instance, the titles could be over shots of the empty school, details of chapel, desks, gym, passages etc. with at the end a jump cut (for instance) from a deserted corridor to it suddenly full of boys, shouts, trunks being dragged etc. . . .

Now what about the notes? Well . . . the page headed 'Term flowed on' for instance is delightful; but are you considering these as items for incorporation, or what? On the page they make a very interesting design: and I can see that kind of thing forming the basis of a kind of impressionistic short film. But can you find a way of incorporating them into a larger design? If so, how?!

Well, there are other bright ideas, lines, possibilities: but undoubtedly these intuitions were related to *something*: shall we say a progression of events, and a list of characters, rather than a *plot* . . . You have (excuse me writing like a school report) a fecundity of imagination, but it seems to operate rather without organic sense: like a series of prose poems: or jottings for a script. Sometimes a whole idea is valuable, sometimes a couple of lines, sometimes nothing.

What is really wanted, if not a tidy 'skeleton', is some idea of the progression: and some key scenes – instead of a plethora of peripheral imaginings . . . For instance, do Stewart and Mick ever talk together? You remember you thought of using songs as some kind of linking device: I expressed scepticism: have you still a place for the school song? What about the speech, or Founder's Day celebrations, with the visit of the corporation members who provide an opportunity to demonstrate the social foundation and implication of the school?

Who are the principal characters? Warden; housemaster; wife; chaplain; what masters? Stewart – who else?

Mick: Johnny: Wallace: Peanuts: Stevens: Bobby Phillips: Barnes: Denson etc.

The Girl.

I think the houses should be separate: I suppose because they were at Cheltenham: but it seems to make it clearer.

I mentioned the idea of a Wallace who was after Bobby Phillips: I imagined Mick hearing a noise at night – going to see what it was, and finding Wallace with Bobby – (I don't know what Bobby feels about all this) – maybe telling him not to be a fool – sending him back to his own bed. Maybe he (Mick) would kiss Bobby before going . . .

The under-housemaster playing Mozart on his gramophone.

I haven't mentioned, and am not sure if I should, what is the *theme* of this film . . . Maybe it can't be put down on a postcard . . . The image of a world: a strange sub-world, with its own peculiar laws, distortions, brutalities, loves . . . With its special relationship to a perhaps outdated conception of British society . . . Its subjection of young minds to disciplines hardly related to the contemporary world; and to the domination of often freakish or deformed or simply inadequate 'masters' . . .

From the two scripts, and from the notes, I find it difficult to get an absolutely consistent picture of MICK, whom I take to be the principal character. I suppose I see him as a lively, independent, anarchic character; who arrives at the end at an act of violent, poetic protest . . . But what precipitates this act? Has it something to do with the expulsion of Wallace (if you accept this idea)?

I am not quite sure where we are now with the Johnny–Mick relationship . . . because Johnny is made a prefect: is this still a basic feature?

It may be: but then be careful that the story doesn't get diminished into a conventional personal struggle between Mick and Johnny.

An early scene, first working day maybe, should show the music master teaching the new boys the school song. 'The New Boy' should be a character: what is his name?

I don't very much like the juxtaposition of the naked HM's wife with the military footsteps: isn't this a rather heavy symbol? (Maybe it depends 'how it's done': not heavy, aggressive tread.)

'Field Day': some misdemeanour here might precipitate a beating for Mick. Anyway a funny and significant sequence is possible with this material.

I think Bobby Phillips's mother still has a place. Perhaps he's showing her round the empty house when Mick meets them.

I don't know if all this is of much use: what is necessary now is to be CONCRETE. The TRUTH is always interesting. And an overall conception, integrating detail with 'theme', 'story' or 'pattern', whatever you like to call it.

I won't start about Poland: which is not a vital, exciting,

temperamental place, but a sluggish, drab, egocentric place, strangled in bureaucratic red-tape, with personal initiative and responsibility practically unknown ... Everything takes an age: no one is paid enough: in other words, what is known as an 'interesting' experience. Since talking with you, the production date has been changed to December 7th: I shall try to insist it is not put any later. Enough is enough.

I feel (one always does) I've been away an age: no word either from Seth or my agent. I'm not surprised about my agent, in fact quite pleased, since it gives me a motive to leave him! But I should like a word from Seth. The really universal problem in the world now is time. No one has time any more to do anything; let alone achieve the sustained concentration necessary to achieve something in terms of art. That is certainly true in Poland.

My best to John and to you,
Lindsay

December 1966

I get so carried away by this letter that I produce a script which is complete rubbish.

Christmas Eve 1966

Lindsay tells me the script is awful. I have failed. 'Go away and write simply. Remember Georg Büchner,' he says.

Spring 1967

Val and I labour long and hard and finish the new draft in April. In trepidation I post it off to Lindsay. He rings me at the crack of dawn to say it's brilliant. But John and Seth don't like it. 'It's too TV,' says John. Seth thinks the young scum (junior), Jute, should become the main character.

April–May 1967

Now it's Lindsay's turn to do some work. I drive him every weekend in my MG Bluestreak to his mother's house, Fuchsia Cottage, Sea Avenue, Rustington, West Sussex. Lindsay's mother is one of the great women of this world.

'She's called Mrs Sleigh, not Mrs Anderson,' says Lindsay by way of introduction. Mrs Sleigh looks after me. After supper, at 7 p.m. sharp, she watches *Coronation Street* and forbids Lindsay from making me do any more work. 'Don't work Peter so hard,' she tells him. She often calls me Peter.

We settle into a routine. After breakfast I go to my room to work alone. Then I show the scene to Lindsay and rewrite it. Thesis. Antithesis. Synthesis. Our work is also physically gruelling. Lindsay insists on two walks a day around Sea Avenue, a kind of South African suburb with total apartheid from the working class, then along the stony beach and into – JOY! – a wonderful seaside pub called the 'Broadmark'. Here in the public bar we play the jukebox and listen to the Beach Boys. If I've been a good writer, Lindsay allows me a second glass of barley wine, which warms and tastes like Christmas. Then we walk back, examining every house and car on Sea Avenue.

One scene comes whole and perfect out of my head in a split second. The housemaster's wife, Mrs Kemp, leads the terrified new undermaster, John Thomas, up a narrow staircase to his lonely room in a turret at the top of College House.

MRS KEMP: The central heating doesn't come this far, I'm afraid. But the room itself is quite warm.

The chapel clock chimes and she unlocks the door to reveal a small, dingy room.

MRS KEMP: It's a little bare, but Mr Britton made it very snug. The marvellous thing is you're completely quiet up here. You can see the chapel spire when the leaves fall. Have you a shilling?

Mr Thomas puts down his suitcase and fumbles in his pocket.

MR THOMAS: Oh yes.

He gives her one and she puts it in the empty meter with a metallic clatter.

MRS KEMP: Do come down and see us if you're at all lonely.

MR THOMAS: Thank you so much, Mrs Kemp . . .

He sits on his bed, disconsolate and lonely.

The staff suffer just like the boys.

Another scene I find it impossible to finish – the gym scene where the scum have to leap a wooden horse. I can't think of how to get them out of the gym. I'm stymied for two days while Lindsay, eyes closed, waits for 'the obvious answer'. Finally he gives up on me. 'It's so obvious!' he says. 'Just "UP! UP! Get back to your houses." '

'Why couldn't I think of that?'

'You haven't developed a dramatic sense, yet.'

I do, however, have one dramatic idea. The Chaplain in the Drawer. It happens like this. I am lying on the floor with a pad and Lindsay is walking around the large wardrobe. We are running through the scene where the Crusaders are being 'punished' by the Headmaster for 'murdering' the Chaplain. And I blurt out: 'Cut from the screaming Chaplain as Mick bayonets him to the Headmaster looking solemn.'

'HEADMASTER (to Crusaders): "Now I take this seriously, very seriously indeed. The Reverend Woods might have been very seriously hurt. Now I want you to apologise to him." Now, Lindsay, at this moment the Headmaster slides open the large chest of drawers and there is the Chaplain! He sits up and the Crusaders each shake his hand one by one. Then the Chaplain lies down and the Headmaster shuts the drawer . . .'

'Shuts the drawer with his back to the drawer,' says Lindsay.

We go down to the 'Broadmark' to celebrate with barley wine and the Beach Boys on the jukebox.

15 May 1967

Our draft of *Crusaders* is finished. Lindsay is pleased and goes off to bed. The next morning I burst into his room in floods of tears. 'The script is rubbish,' I weep. 'Every line is exactly the same as every other. I've just read it from cover to cover. It's hopeless drivel.'

Somehow Lindsay manages to calm me down. I drive him back to London in Bluestreak. It's such a cosy car, this MG, with an interior like a plane's cockpit. As always Lindsay says, 'I wish I had a car like this.'

Every film company turns us down. We trudge round Soho, getting meetings with the likes of Alan Ladd Jr (then an agent), who winks at me behind Lindsay's back and says, 'God, it's shit.'

29 June 1967

Lindsay is making a carpet-sweeper commercial to try to make ends meet. He has cast me as the carpet-sweeper to get me some cash. We are walking down Wardour Street, downcast about *Crusaders* when suddenly there's a shout from an upstairs window. 'Lindsay!' It's Albert Finney. We go up to the cutting-room where he is editing the first film he's directed, *Charlie Bubbles*, written by Shelagh Delaney. Albert hopes it will look like the kind of film you see at the Odeon. But at the moment, he says, it looks like the kind of film you'd never see anywhere. Lindsay sympathises and mentions *Crusaders*. Suddenly Albert says, 'You're serious about this, aren't you?'

'Yes.'

'Send it round to Michael.'

Michael Medwin, who has been a successful actor (*The Army Game*), now runs Albert's film and theatre company, Memorial. He had been to public school, so understood and liked our script. *Crusaders* becomes a Memorial production.

5 August 1967

CBS agree to finance *Crusaders*. I wander round Memorial's offices looking at wall-to-wall sheets with scene numbers, characters and shooting dates. After seven years it's really happening.

17 August 1967

Lindsay's old school, Cheltenham College, have given us permission to shoot in their buildings. But we daren't show them the *Crusaders* script, so I'm typing a cod script for the headmaster. I can't think of a title for this false version, so I ask Daphne Hunter, Albert's secretary, if she can think of something really old-fashioned and corny.

'You mean like Kipling's *If* . . . ?'

'Daphne! That's the title for the film! You're brilliant. How does it go?

' "If you can keep your head while all about you
Are loosing theirs and blaming it on you,
You'll be a man, my son," ' says Daphne.

And so *Crusaders* becomes *If* . . ., thanks to Daphne Hunter and the great Kipling.

3 September 1967

CBS Films pull out of the production. *If . . .* is off . . . Paramount in London also turn down *If . . .*

11 October 1967

Luck again. Charles Bluhdorn, billionaire owner of the oil conglomerate Gulf and Western, buys Paramount. Albert Finney is in *Joe Egg* in New York. Mrs Bluhdorn is a great fan of Albert. A word from Mrs Bluhdorn to Mr Bluhdorn. A phone call from Mr Bluhdorn to Paramount in London. *If . . .* is financed by Paramount and neither of the Bluhdorns ever read the script.

3 November 1967

Val has a brief affair with her mother's fragile lodger, Pierre, who, her mother says, 'won't make old bones'. I am so shocked I set my guns on the prettiest secretary in my agent's office, Gay – all long legs and blond hair. I'm determined to fall in love with her and make her my wife.

1 January 1968

Casting

'Do you want to be a star!?
Boys 12–19: THIS IS YOUR CHANCE!'

Our ads in *The Times*, *Telegraph* and *Melody Maker* draw over 5,000 boys from the length and breadth of Britain to Marylebone Town Hall. Each hopeful reads for Lindsay and Miriam Brickman, our casting director, Britain's greatest. Each hopeful is photographed holding guns and books. But only one part, that of Peanuts the maniacal star-gazer, is cast. A 15-year-old with diabolical pointed teeth: he is a savage mated with a scholar.

Lindsay is gaga after face number 5,323. We still have to cast the hero Crusader, Mick, plus the vicious Whips. Lindsay decides these will have to be professional unknowns.

David Sherwin

The Best Audition in the World

The scene. A revolving slapstick stage in the Jimmy Edwards Comedy Playhouse, plus props. This audition is make or break. No room for error. A script can be rewritten, a shot repeated a hundred times, but the wrong actor and the film will die. Our struggle for perfection will be down the drain.

The revolving stage is still. Lindsay chats, relaxing the hopefuls. They are to play the most demanding scene in the film – the scene in which Mick makes love to the greasy spoon café waitress. The first girl is late, and the second girl is called. She steps forward from the wings, small, dark-haired – a touch of gipsy. The actor who is auditioning for Mick calls out that someone's nicked his script and he hasn't had time to learn his scene.

'Why not?' asks Lindsay acidly.

'I only heard of the job yesterday.'

'A script, for God's sake, someone.'

There aren't any scripts. We could only afford to get fifty printed. I climb up on to the stage, and give him mine. He says thank you blandly – he's obviously too smooth for the part. No chance. Poor chap.

The nobody quickly scans his scene, then walks on to the stage still holding his script. He explores Jimmy Edwards's props with suddenly intense eyes. His movements are precise, yet natural. He approaches the girl, who stands behind a table, our pretend café counter. He raps the table hard, still reading from his script. He ogles her as she mimes pouring coffee. Then, without warning, not looking at the script, he grabs her round the neck, pulling her across the wide table, and kisses her hard and long. He looks at her, smirking, as she lies half off the table.

The actor picks up his script to find out the next action when, without warning, the girl rears up and smashes him in the face with her fist. He reels across the stage, hurt and shocked. What's happening? He studies his script again, and goes to a bookshelf and works it like a jukebox.

'Go on, look at me,' says the girl. 'Look at my eyes. I've eyes like a tiger. My eyes get bigger and bigger . . .'

The actor smells the girl. They are animals. What's happening? Bites, blows, bodies thumping on the boards. Struggling on the floor, he tries to turn the next page to see what's coming next. The girl tears into him, tugging out his hair, ripping the script in two. Maddened, he retaliates, wrestling, breaking the girl's bra under her sweater.

'The jukebox has finished,' Lindsay calls to break the battle. The actress gives a final blow and a shriek of laughter. The actor rolls in pain. I go on to the stage, pick up my shredded script and call across to Lindsay: 'I wouldn't bother to go on auditioning. You've got Mick and the girl.'

'Oh, you wouldn't bother, would you, Sherwin? That's a brilliant way to cast a film. Piss off.'

I repeat, 'They're brilliant.'

'Then fucking well tell them. Their names are Malcolm McDowell and Christine Noonan.'

Christine has vanished, but I ask Malcolm McDowell how he acted the fight so brilliantly.

Malcolm replies with his James Cagney grin: 'Oh, I'd only looked at my lines – typical actor. I didn't know I was going to get knocked out just for kissing her. I was absolutely stunned, and then I thought, right – I'll give it her back!'

And so a Star is Born!

After casting Malcolm and Christine, Lindsay, Miriam Brickman and I rush back to Memorial's offices. The last vital character has to be cast by this evening: Robert Rowntree, the sadistic Head of House.

Lindsay and I go up in one lift, Miriam in the other. She never arrives.

'Do you realise, David,' says Lindsay, 'this is what making films is all about. Miriam Brickman trapped in Albert Finney's lift – perhaps for ever.'

Sunday 28 January 1968

The night before shooting starts at Cheltenham College. Lindsay calls me round to his flat in Greencroft Gardens. He admits to me point-blank that he's terrified. Lost. He doesn't even know where he's going to put the camera. We drink a whisky and listen to the Beach Boys one last time before the battle begins.

Tuesday 31 January 1968
Cheltenham

I watch the first set-up: the juniors playing rugger. Mirek, our brilliant Czech cameraman, knows exactly where to put the camera. But one thing is dreadfully wrong: the keen-type, Bobby Phillips, isn't nearly beautiful enough. When I tell Lindsay, he orders me to drive to every public school in England, and be back by eight to-morrow morning with someone more beautiful.

7 February 1968

Lindsay is shooting the exit from Chapel. The junior boys have shoving fights as they run down the Cloisters with their school books. The young actors don't understand. I immediately volunteer to demonstrate with Michael Medwin, who also knows about shoving fights. The first assistant director, John Stoneman, throws us both off the location as non-union stand-ins.

28 February 1968

We watch the rushes at Cheltenham's Odeon cinema. Christine Noonan roars with hysterical laughter when she sees herself for the first time on screen. Lindsay keeps bellowing 'SHUT UP!' but she takes no notice. Her laughter destroys the pomposity of film-making.

2 March 1968

The rooftop battle scenes. The Crusaders' sten guns keep jamming, requiring take after take. The roar of the guns can be heard all over town. And the jamming.

17 March 1968
Merton Park Studios, London

We are filming the scene under the school stage where the Crusaders find their hoard of ammo and guns.

'Do you realise,' Lindsay says, 'that from this point on there's not one line of dialogue between the Crusaders? They say nothing for the rest of the film. Sheer laziness on your part.'

'It's called poetry, Lindsay – the poetry of cinema,' I say.

Floored, he attacks Jocelyn Herbert, our art director, instead.

Shooting starts. Mick explores the relics in the darkness. He comes across a shelf of medical jars, and picks up one containing a preserved human embryo. Mysteriously, silently, Christine comes up behind him, gives him a look, and gently replaces the embryo.

Suddenly one of the electricians hits me and curses violently. 'You're evil! You must have an evil mind to use a child's embryo! You evil bastard!'

It turns out his wife lost her child last month. Lindsay advises me to leave the studio fast and not come back.

5 April 1968

A late-night summons to Lindsay's flat. The art department have failed to come up with any pin-ups for Mick and Johnnie's studies. And the scenes are being shot in the morning. Luckily Lindsay has a huge collection of *National Geographic* and *Paris Match* magazines. We snip pictures of tigers, war photographs, advertisements, pin-ups of Charlotte Rampling and Marilyn Monroe, pensive gorillas, the Queen in her Royal Coach, young Communist soldiers, golden retrievers . . . We work through the night, arranging the pictures in different patterns on the floor, until finally we have highly charged collages for our heroes.

28 July 1968

My last contribution to *If* . . . Lindsay is dubbing the sound for the cadet corps' field day battle. He needs more orders from officers. I remember my field days and yell, 'Rabbit crawl, man, Rabbit crawl!'

I leave the dubbing theatre thinking everything in my life is over. Rabbit crawl, man . . .

23 November 1968

On this bleak November day Gay and I get married. John Howlett is my best man. After the reception we all go to the cinema to see *Invasion of the Body Snatchers*.

27 November 1968

Lindsay has completed his final cut of *If*... Paramount are so shocked by what they think is madness that they try to sell it to an American art-house chain. The art-house chain think it is madness too. *If*... will never be shown.

December 1968

Lady Luck again. Paramount are told that they haven't fulfilled their Eady quota for the year. The Eady quota is a brilliant idea which Harold Wilson had when he was very young and at the Board of Trade in the Attlee government, to help the always struggling British cinema. A certain number of films shown in cinemas must be British films, and ten cans of a British film stand on a shelf in Memorial's office.

Paramount also have a huge flop on their hands at their West End cinema – *Barbarella* starring Jane Fonda as a sexy superwoman. The week before Christmas is always dead. So they decide, 'Hell, take off Fonda, and shove in that crap.' And so *If*... opens. Two nights later I walk along the queues winding all the way from the Paramount Plaza, round St James's, almost to the gates of Buckingham Palace, half a mile away. It's a phenomenon. Malcolm McDowell, the star of the film, my wife Gay and I spend a happy Christmas just watching the queues. Even Lindsay is impressed and joins us. Michael Medwin is a happy man. He promises Daphne Hunter £200 for thinking of the title, and Malcolm, who was only paid £750, a share in the profits. Naturally, he forgets.

6 March 1969
New York

Malcolm and I arrive in New York for the opening of *If*... next Sunday. We are here to help publicise the film. The air fares alone cost £298 each, but we haven't a cent in our pockets. A very pretty girl from the publicity office meets us, but she can't find our driver. The driver is asked on the public address system to present himself at the BOAC desk. After two appeals he appears. His feet slop forwards over the marble as if he were trudging through mud in heavy army boots. He is completely drunk.

During the drive to our hotel the pretty girl tells us our schedule.

Morning screenings for magazines and newspapers, chat shows on the radio. It's not going to be a holiday. But if there's anything we need, the pretty girl will be on hand. She wears the tiniest mini-skirt Malcolm and I have ever seen. Her name is Margot and she's married to Keir Dullea, the star of Kubrick's *2001*. I can tell Malcolm is smitten, and I, newly married, try not to be smitten too.

In the hotel Malcolm picks up the phone to order champagne and a cup of tea. A giant spark shoots out from the mouthpiece to his chin. Our porter, the 'Captain', tells us it's static electricity from the wall-to-wall nylon carpeting. Whenever we touch door handles, the TV or phone, sparks shoot out. The Captain advises us to lift one foot off the ground before touching anything. Malcolm pours the tea, hopping on one foot. We have no money, so we order everything on room service. It's three times as much – whisky costs fifteen dollars instead of five in the shops.

Over champagne and tea I tell Malcolm my idea for a story called *Manpower* – the story of a young man, perhaps an out-of-work ballet dancer. He works as a char doing different jobs on different days in different people's homes. He practises leaps while dusting.

Malcolm has also been working on a story about a character starting life at the bottom of the pile; something autobiographical and in some ways, he says, similar to mine, but before he can tell me we are interrupted.

The doorbell rings. A weirdly dressed 'family' enters. There are three sons who seem about thirty, very pale faces, black plastic macs or jackets and black rubber boots. They hold cheap plastic shopping bags containing Instamatic cameras. They take Malcolm's photo and ask for his autograph. With them is a tall old lady in a mackintosh whom they address as 'Mother'. One of the sons tells Malcolm, 'She's English. She's a dame, she's a real dame from England. But with a small "d" coz she's no lady. A dame, see?' They leave. Who are they? Journalists? Queers? How did they know we were in the hotel? We'd only arrived an hour ago.

Malcolm pours out another round of champagne and tells me his story, an idea he has been working on since he finished *If . . .* It's called *Coffee Man* and starts in a coffee-making factory in Liverpool. The story follows the ambitions of a trainee salesman, which Malcolm once was. There is no proper training and he has nothing to do all day. He wanders aimlessly around the factory floor with a clipboard for notes, chatting to the roasters, blenders and coffee-packing girls. Then one day he is suddenly sent off to Yorkshire in a battered van to replace a salesman who has vanished without notice. The hero ends up in London giving his life savings to a music teacher, a con man who promises to make him into a pop star. *Coffee Man* seems much more real than *Manpower*. Also Paramount, to whom the *Manpower* idea has been put, are only prepared to pay £1,000 for the first draft, and it will be a couple of years' work. Malcolm asks me to work on *Coffee Man*.

9 March 1969

A press screening of *If* . . . Marion Billings, in charge of publicity and Margot's boss, tells me there is one very important man in the audience whom I must be nice to. The film critic of *The Midwest Times*. He's seen the film three times and is a masochist.

'What kind of masochist?'

'Beating . . . Just be nice, you understand?'

'I understand.'

Marion, Margot and I wait anxiously in the foyer of the Paramount screening theatre for *If* . . . to finish and the masochist to emerge. Once again I hear the finale's explosion of gunfire, then the sudden eerie silence and the Sanctus . . . and then, amazingly, applause.

The masochist, who has a stutter, is exceptionally benign. 'Tell me,' he says with a beam, 'did Malcolm McDowell have any protective padding when he was beaten by Rowntree? A rubber pad?'

I'm beginning to get the hang of this publicity game. 'None whatsoever,' I reply. 'Lindsay Anderson is a great realist. Malcolm's pain was real – it took fifteen takes, and his tears after his beating were real tears.'

'Wonderful,' breathes the *Times* critic, and the next week he gave us a rave review and five stars.

Hollywood, here I come

11 March 1969
New York

I stare at the story in *Variety*, not quite believing that it is true:

SHERWIN WINS BRITISH WRITERS' GUILD AWARD

London, March 10. In the Film section of the Writers' Guild Awards for 1968, David Sherwin has won the prize for the Best British original screenplay for his script of *If* . . .

The phone rings. It's Tom Gries, calling from Hollywood. Will I fly over to discuss this great idea he had for a film while in Spain? 'I've got a terrific title. I'm going to call it *Castle on Top of the Hill*.' I instantly agree. I can't believe my luck – it's like a fairytale.

I remember Gries very well. I met him last autumn at a showing of his film, *Will Penny*, an unusually realistic Western starring Charlton Heston. I'd taken to Tom immediately. He was surprised by the success of the film and very modest. His other oddity is that he has a completely bald head. In *Will Penny*, Charlton Heston, for the first time ever, looks frail, frightened and human. Tom Gries found the great actor hidden in Charlton Heston.

The phone rings again. It's the star Maximilian Schell, famous for playing Nazis. He's about to direct his first film, Turgenev's *First Love*, and wants a writer. Can I come round to his suite at the Pierre Hotel in ten minutes? He'll send a limo. I feel a shiver of adrenalin. I'm H-O-T . . .

Maximilian gives me a drink and tells me he has a 'discovery' who will play the heroine: a childlike French model who can't speak English. Nor can she act, and she's crying too. But Maximilian wants to show me how he's going to coax a brilliant performance out of her. He tells the girl to go out of the room and make an entrance. Again and again the wretched girl comes in holding her script, but can't bring herself to say a word. She is struck dumb. Maximilian gets more and more angry. He yells at her to do it right. Then in a sudden fury he jumps on a marble table to curse her further. The marble cracks in two and he is trapped by the iron framework of the table, just the top of his head and his feet visible.

'Help me, I'm in agony!' he shouts. The poor girl and I burst out laughing and summon the hotel doctor.

Next stop Robbie Lantz, the Cartier of agents. Oddly, he doesn't want to take me on. Instead he gives me a terrible warning: 'You'll never make it in California. You'll be miscast. Your face won't fit.' But my mind is made up. Hollywood, here I come!

12 March 1969

I'm in *Variety* again:

SHERWIN SCRIPTS GRIES' 'CASTLE'
Writer/Director David Sherwin has been signed by Tom Gries for a joint effort on *Castle on Top of the Hill*, to be filmed in Spain after Gries finishes *Hawaii* sequel for Mirisch Corp. Sherwin arrives here tomorrow for story conferences with Gries, who will also produce *Castle*. Gries is now winding editing on *Pro* for Paramount with Heston in lead role.

I walk into the streets to say farewell to New York. In the evening light the mass of brownstone blocks beyond Central Park look exactly like the ruins of Babylon.

13 March 1969
Los Angeles

I travel to LA with Tom's wife. Her luggage comes on the carousel immediately. I have to wait an hour for mine. I'm convinced it's been left behind but don't care. The warm, dry air is instantly relaxing.

Tom waits for us in the arrivals lounge. When I try to thank him for having me over, he says, 'Don't say thank you. You owe me nothing' – an example of the American inability not so much to give as to receive. No one wants to be owed anything.

701 Alpine Drive. There's a receipt on Tom's desk for a $20,000 donation to the Society for the Advancement of Colored People, but his wife tells me you have to be very careful with coloured folk. You can't just let anyone into your home. They have a coloured maid, but the only coloureds they would see socially are professional people. The maid washes and irons all day – Tom changes his shirt as soon as it has the slightest mark on it.

He takes me for a drive around Beverly Hills. When we get back, he leaves the car in the drive unlocked.

'Beverly Hills is pretty wonderful, isn't it, David?'

It's exactly like Lindsay's home in Rustington, which I had thought was the nearest place to white South Africa outside South Africa.

I ask Tom what *The Castle on Top of the Hill* is about. He says he isn't too sure yet. He just has this image of an old castle in Spain on top of a hill. Perhaps tomorrow we should have a story confer-ence, I suggest, but Tom has a much better idea: tomorrow he and his wife will take me to my first Hollywood party.

14 March 1969

It is the Shalletts' twentieth wedding anniversary. Mr Shallett played the doctor in *Will Penny*. He is a kind, gentle man, exactly like his screen image.

I am introduced to Walter Matthau, who I thought was brilliant in *The Odd Couple*. He has never heard of *If . . .*

'Were the reviews good?'

'Yes. Very.'

'Who plays in it?'

'No one you'll have heard of. Yet.'

After an embarrassed pause, I stumble on: 'It was directed by Lindsay Anderson. Do you know him?'

'No.'

'He directed *This Sporting Life*.'

'Oh.' There is a flicker of recognition.

'Did you like it?'

'No. Seemed to me like a lot of homosexual whales pinching each other. I see it from a very – er – lofty point of view. Excuse me . . .' And he heads off.

I join Tom Gries, who is talking to a sad girl with dyed blonde hair. She is in her thirties, and wearing a loose, virginal dress that she is far too old for. Tom asks her what she does.

'I'm an actress.'

'A real actress?' Tom asks cruelly. 'Or is that just the title you give yourself?'

'A real actress. But I'm looking for work at the moment. It's hard to find the right thing.'

Later I see her talking to a young lump wearing the traditional Californian blazer. He's seven feet tall with no neck. She turns the stem of her glass round and round between her fingers. His mouth is half open, as if tasting hot spice.

'What are you going to do after this?' the lump asks.

'Go home.'

'And then what?'

'Make a milk drink.'

'And then?'

'Go to bed.'

'And then what?'

She looks down and smiles, ashamed of the transparency of their ritual.

'C'mon,' he says. 'It's too hot in here.' He propels her proprietorially out with his fingers gripping her shoulders.

14 March 1969

Perhaps we should have a story conference, I suggest at breakfast. 'I mean, we ought to know who the main characters are, when it is set, and what happens . . .'

'Oh, that may take a little time. It's no good forcing it, David. It took me a year to write *Will Penny*. You're under absolutely no pressure at all. When it happens, it will happen.'

In any case Tom has to visit the Mirisch brothers today for a pre-production conference on *Hawaii*. I come along too, but am not invited to lunch. I wait in the brothers' office, drinking coffee from a dispenser, and wonder if we will ever get round to doing any work on *Castle*.

On the way home Tom shows off in his Mustang, speeding down the freeway. 'What car do you drive, David?'

'A Porsche.'

'You mean you own a Porsche?'

'It's the best car in the world.'

'Hey! David's got a Porsche,' Tom tells his wife.

'How do you like our genuine seventeenth-century Spanish furniture?' she counters.

Their furniture would be very nice if they were living in a castle on top of a hill in Spain, but only just fits their small Beverly Hills home.

15 March 1969

Tom asks me if I'd like to go for a drive. He'll take me anywhere I want.

'The desert,' I say, 'I've never seen a desert.'

'No', he says. 'It's too hot and we might break down and die.' So we drive around Santa Monica beach instead, and watch the flaunting of bodies and cars – purple beach buggies with huge, naked twelve-cylinder engines.

Suddenly I'm transfixed. A tall girl walks nonchalantly down the road wearing a completely see-through blouse and no bra. She has huge breasts. I've never seen anything like it outside the topless Minoan aristocrats in the Ashmolean museum.

Tom notices my astonishment. 'Do you want to turn round and drive past again?'

'Yes, please.'

'Did you notice how much taller she was than her boyfriend?'

'What boyfriend?' I ask, puzzled, until I notice a little man in a cowboy hat swaggering along a few paces behind.

We pass two more girls in see-through blouses and then drive on to Paramount, where Tom is working on the final cut of *Pro* (or *Number One*), in which Chuck Heston plays an ageing American footballer. The streets round the studio are quiet and empty. The houses are in Spanish style and over forty years old. They are genteelly run-down. Paint peels from the walls. I can see why the great Christopher Isherwood likes California. It is a powerful cocktail of peace, violence, shattering noise and overwhelming sexual promise.

I watch Tom and the editor at work. Heston is playing his first all-nude love scene on a white carpet in front of a roaring fire. On the set, as he embraces the naked Jessica Walter, he has a dreadful accident. I watch it happen over and over again as Tom and the editor try to cut round the scene.

Monday 18 March 1969

Tom drives me to the airport. We still have no idea what *The Castle on Top of the Hill* is about, but as we say goodbye outside the departure lounge Tom reassures me that when it happens, it will happen.

If . . . wins the Cannes Film Festival

12 May 1969
Cannes

The British Ambassador arrives foaming with fury. *If . . .* is an insult to the British nation. It must be withdrawn from the Festival. Lindsay replies that it is an insult to a nation that deserves to be insulted and tells the Ambassador to bugger off. Anyway, the film can't be withdrawn: it is the official British entry.

I explore Cannes. Naked old men on the beach holding little dogs as they watch girls being photographed, old ladies with little dogs, androgynes with little dogs . . . Dogs are the craze. They are talked to, carried across the beach to sunbathe, and have drinks ordered, then brought to them by bow-tied waiters.

13 May 1969

Penelope Mortimer, the novelist, stands for hours in the Carlton lobby. 'Waiting for Spiegel,' she says wryly. Sam Spiegel, the producer of *Lawrence of Arabia*, has moored his huge yacht opposite the Carlton. It is the centre of attraction. In the afternoon a passenger steamer anchors alongside, making it look like a tug.

15 May 1969

Press photographs after the first critics' show of *If . . .*, then lunch on the beach. That night at the official Jury Prize screening at the Palais du Festival there's a row because no one from the Festival is there to greet us. 'Normally there's a spotlight that comes on and lights up the director,' Lindsay complains. 'We were left alone. Nothing. No one to introduce us to the audience.'

Michael Medwin's wife faints and there is no one to take her home.

16 May 1969

'Paramount Cars' take us to the Colombe d'Or, outside Cannes, where the Medwins are staying. Picasso and Manet, who often visited, paid for their meals with paintings, which now decorate the walls.

When I make some silly comment about stealing a Picasso, Gene Moskowitz, *Variety*'s Paris correspondent, shouts out, 'This is the man you're supposed to be working with, Lindsay?'

'I'm not working with David Sherwin,' Lindsay retorts. I feel desperately hurt, and say nothing.

17 May 1969

Lunch with Michael Flint, the head of Paramount, Europe. I had been dreading it but it turns out to be unexpectedly pleasant. I tell him that the success of *If . . .* means nothing – everything is still a struggle. 'I know what you mean exactly,' says Flint, but then talks non-stop about the deals he has set up. Eventually he recalls himself: 'I sound dreadful, I'm sorry.' He tells me that he refused to have a Rolls at Cannes. 'They said I wouldn't be noticed. Well, if that's the only way I'll be noticed, I'd rather not be.'

No one will give me a ticket to the Bo Widerberg film, *Adalen '31*. I stand in the crowds, watching the stars enter. Lindsay and Michael Flint pass me. I turn away so as not to be seen. They are just ahead of Widerberg and his actors. I hang on to see if there are any more famous stars. Then I hear shouts and screams from the top of the stairs to the Festival hall. A body tumbles down, crashing at my feet, unconscious. Widerberg's actors march down yelling at the tops of their theatrically trained voices. Lindsay, Michael Flint and Bo Widerberg follow.

Lindsay sees me. 'Come on, David!' Photographers and an angry official chase after us. One of the actors turns and yells at the official in a huge bass voice: 'Non! Non! Non!'

Lindsay and Flint were refused entry because they were not wearing black ties. A French official tried to explain to his colleagues that he had promised Mr Widerberg that they could enter. But before Widerberg could be consulted, Lindsay had turned at the top of the stairs in the cinema and shouted at the entering guests with his arms outstretched, 'Stop! Listen everybody. We are being treated like animals!' Soon afterwards Widerberg appeared and told all the Swedes to leave.

The President of the Swedish Academy tells Lindsay that he has been discourteous. Lindsay explains that the officials were letting men in who were wearing white polo-neck sweaters but not those in ordinary shirts. He could understand an absolute rule: black ties only, but not these subtle distinctions. 'They are beyond me.'

18 May 1969

I have coffee with Malcolm on the terrace. 'I love it here,' he says. 'This is the life! I've sold out, mate.' Sadly, we go home tomorrow. The French Paramount people have already gone back to Paris and we are left alone, penniless. Malcolm has no money to pay the $600 bill for Margot's collect calls from New York. She wants to marry him. Even Michael Flint is not sure how he is going to pay his bill. Luckily I have £5, enough for a taxi to the airport. Our fling is over.

Costa-Gavras's political thriller *Z* will win, everyone says.

27 May 1969

Our Frognal flat, London. I'm woken at two in the morning by the phone. It's a man who wants to take Gay out. He says he met her at the Playboy Club, where she now works. He will buy her a mink coat. The phone rings again half an hour later. This time a drunken voice tells us we're going to be rich. Something strange is happening. Bertie, our Yorkie, barks all night. Gay is terrified. She double-locks the front door and puts the chain up. I listen to the eight o'clock news. *If . . .* has won the Grand Prix. Joy and disbelief. We've won!

Gay gives up her horrible job as a trainee bunny.

3 October 1969

Lindsay and I have a beer with Sally Trench in the 'Pillars of Hercules'. Sally is a strapping 23-year-old, who has just written an extraordinary book, *Bury Me in My Boots*, about her life on the road with the tramps of England. It is a modern *Road to Wigan Pier*. Mia Farrow wants to play Sally in a movie of the book, which I will write and Lindsay direct.

5 October 1969

In the evening I meet Lindsay at Mia Farrow's house. The living room is full of screaming Americans. Mia Farrow and her friends were kicked out of a restaurant the day before and have been charged with obstructing the police. Some are sitting cross-legged on the floor as they explain to a lawyer what happened.

'They said I wasn't properly dressed,' says a high-pitched American. 'But I was wearing a 350-guinea suit. I tell you, there's no morality in this town. A 350-guinea suit on! No morality at all!' Meanwhile Mia Farrow is yelling on the phone to America. 'Listen, I want to fucking play fucking Mary Queen of Scots in the fucking movie!' She puts down the phone and comes across to talk to me in those generalities about art which people high on pot kid themselves is a sublime vision of wisdom. I say exactly this to her.

She curls up at my feet, looking at me with adoring eyes. 'You writers – you're like composers, you're the very beginning of life itself. You're like God.'

I tell her I'm more like a bricklayer.

At first Lindsay wants to run away, but later he has a long chat with a pop singer, who says the Americans are protesting too much. 'I've been thrown out of hundreds of places. You're thrown out of one place, you go round the corner where they like you.' He speaks the whole time in an affected American-French accent with a lisp. At first I think he is a foreigner but later he tells me, 'You know who I am of course – I'm Brian Jones of the Rolling Stones.' It's just five years since I was photographing five pleasant young boys in Mick Jagger's mum's kitchen.

I walk home with Lindsay. He tries to analyse why he doesn't like Mia Farrow and her friends. They're spoilt in some way. They make no effort to meet you halfway and find out what you think or are interested in. They lack manners in the bourgeois sense. Also they're fey – as with all stars you feel they're insubstantial, you feel they and their opinions will change overnight.

I think Mia Farrow is bonkers. There is no real centre from which her thoughts flow. Consequently, she expresses them with huge nervous energy, and you have to supply the substance. This is why she is so tiresome. She plays for effect – bad acting yet again.

Lindsay and I console ourselves with the delicious chicken liver at our favourite Viennese restaurant, the Dorice, in the Finchley Road, home to old ladies kicked out of Austria by Hitler all those years ago.

Mia Farrow didn't once mention *Bury Me in My Boots*, and that is the end of that.

Family life

17 November 1969

Lindsay comes to dinner. Gay cooks him a revolting underdone stew, which he dutifully munches.

Gay starts to lecture him about film. 'Flashbacks never work. I hate flashbacks!'

'Oh, do you? What about the flashbacks in *This Sporting Life*?' asks Lindsay.

'They ruined the film.'

Not a successful evening.

3 December 1969

A huge row with Gay. She has been going out with some mysterious friends every night for weeks.

'I want a wife who looks after her husband!' I say.

'You're a dictator. Surely the writer of *If...* knows all about fascist dictators – and the results. David, our marriage is over.'

10 December 1969

Another horrible row. Gay has dutifully stayed in all week, but playing the television very loud. I'm trying to concentrate on the pages Malcolm has written about his life as a coffee salesman.

Work is impossible. The inane babble of *Top of the Pops* maddens me. I rush into the bedroom and hurl the television through the window. We fight, tearing each other's hair, until we exhaust ourselves. Then I apologise for being an animal and we have a good cry.

19 December 1969

We decide our tiny Frognal flat has bad vibes, and move into a more spacious one up the road in Platt's Lane. It has three big rooms and a study. 'My hubby's own little room,' says Gay. 'Now everything will be all right.'

On the side of the house is an inspiring bonus: a blue memorial plaque to one of the great men of the twentieth century:

Thomas Masaryk lived here
1914–1919
Father and first President
of Czechoslovakia

9 January 1970

We find another paradise: The Falls, a little tumbledown cottage with three acres of jungle in the Royal Forest of Dean, where the foresters still dig their own coal in tiny mines. They are 'free-miners' – so named because they were the only free men in medieval England when even Dukes and Princes were bound in servitude to the divine King.

It happened like this. King Richard the Lionheart, as everyone knows, was very fond of crusades, and was obsessed with regaining Jerusalem from the infidel and killing as many Muslims as possible. But this required an endless supply of swords, double-headed axes and fancy armour, and the only place in England able to manufacture enough weapons was the Forest of Dean, with its wood for charcoal, its iron and coal. In return for ten years of working triple time, Richard gave the miners their freedom in perpetuity – a freedom which survived the nationalisation of the mines in 1945.

I love our cottage in the wilds. We even have an old mine at the top of our lane. I regard myself as an ancient free-miner. Gay loves it too. She plans to live the good life for ever with me, raising cows and goats, and breeding Yorkshire terriers.

15 January
57 Greencroft Gardens, London NW6

Lindsay has invited Malcolm and me to lunch, to gee us up on *Coffee Man*. I tell them about The Falls, and the new flat in Platt's Lane.

'Just how many homes do you both have?' Lindsay asks us.

'Two,' we both reply. Malcolm gives me a wink. He owns a mill-house.

'Two homes and God knows how many cars, and you call yourselves poor! Just greedy. Yes, you're both going the way of the world,' sighs Lindsay.

Never in my life will I dare tell him about the silver 911 Porsche with tinted glass. I've bought a little Citroën Dyane for the sole purpose of driving Lindsay to Rustington . . .

19 January 1970
Platt's Lane

The prize guests at our house-warming party are Dr David Owen, MP, and his rich young American wife Debbie. Gay works part-time for them both. David Owen is a rising star in the Labour Party and is tipped to be Prime Minister. Debbie runs a literary agency, inherited from her father, which keeps the pennies rolling in to support the good doctor's political ambitions.

'We've just seen the worst play of our lives,' says Debbie, kneeling next to me in her caftan.

'Poor you,' says Gay. 'What was it?'

'David Storey's *The Contractor* at the Royal Court. An insult to a paying audience.'

'Robbery,' adds David Owen, smoothing that famous forelock. 'I mean, who wants to spend two and a half hours watching a tent going up on stage?'

My hackles rise. I have seen the play twice. Lindsay directed. It is a remarkable piece of poetic theatre. It is about a wedding – or rather, the workmen who erect a beautiful wedding marquee on the stage, and then take it down again in tatters. It is about eternal themes – love, life, suffering, old age. 'Chekhov on the high wire,' the critic Harold Hobson has called it.

I am ablaze. 'If you think that play was rubbish, you can both leave my home this second! Go on, out! Philistines!'

'This is a democracy!' giggles Debbie. 'Everyone's entitled to express their opinion.'

'Not if it means vilifying a masterpiece. Out! Both of you.'

Gay's party is ruined, but a doctor congratulates me on my stand. 'That man makes me ill. God help this country if he should ever get into power.'

March to August 1970

John Schlesinger has started shooting his partly autobiographical film, *Sunday, Bloody Sunday*. It features the first ever kiss between gay men and is a sad, triangular love story. The script has been written by John Osborne's wife, Penelope Gilliatt. But after two weeks' filming, John Schlesinger suddenly realises her script is unshootable. Filming stops. Jo Janni, the producer, calls me in to rewrite the whole film.

Jo is a charming gentleman and a brilliant producer. He has made John Schlesinger the great director that he is today, producing *A Kind of Loving*, *Darling* and *Far from the Madding Crowd*. He teaches me everything about writing in a crisis. Whatever the chaos, he insists on making a 'scalata' every day – a little ladder, a kind of memo-cum-script outline.

Jo is nothing if not like glue. When I try one weekend to escape to The Falls, he finds me out, drives the 150 miles to admire the view and then remorselessly demands to see my scalata. I continue writing the script as shooting resumes after two weeks. I am never more than a day ahead. The stars, Glenda Jackson and Peter Finch, eye me warily as I approach each morning across the jumble of wires and brute lights with their latest lines. Usually apprehension turns to relief, but the weeks become months and our nerves are at snapping point.

'John, this scene of yours is absolute shit!' I say one night on location in a café on Oxford Street. Peter Finch, Glenda Jackson and the crew can hear every word.

'And your scene is absolute shit,' Schlesinger replies.

'You are fucking crap!' I yell back.

'And so are you fucking crap!'

'I'm quitting the picture!' I say, and walk out to catch the last bus home.

'David!' Jo calls with a look like a whipped dog. I walk up and down the pavement amidst the black cables and arc lights. No more movies – ever! I think to myself. A 2A bus approaches and halts. I'm just about to jump aboard when I think of Jo's desperate, beseeching eyes. I'm no quitter! I re-enter the café, sit at the table with John and Jo, and we return to our scalata as if nothing had happened.

5 August 1970

I type out the first twenty pages of *Coffee Man* up to the end of factory section – coffee sampling. Talk on the phone with Malcolm as to whether the scene when Mick goes into the packing room should include the line, 'Christ, the girls in that room – they reek'. Include it.

Show the twenty pages to Lindsay. He thinks it is too mini and naturalistic.

'Keep working on it,' he says, 'get it away from just being about selling coffee. Have you read *Heaven's My Destination*? It's about a Bible salesman. Quite epic. Tails off at the end, though. Why is it that writers can never write endings? It's very odd – why is it?'

21 August 1970

At Malcolm's flat in the morning. Sunny outside. We talk to and fro, trying to find the essence of *Coffee Man*, trying to make it 'epic' for Lindsay.

Malcolm says, 'I always remember Gloria Rowe, the Sales Director, who I used to talk to when I was training on the shop floor – I wasn't training – I was just walking around with a clipboard looking for something to do – she used to say to me, "Malcolm, you'll either be a duke or a dustman." And I'd always been told I was born with a silver spoon in my mouth. I always believed I would be lucky.'

I jump up –

'That's it!'

'What?'

'Luck – luck's the essence. You've always believed you'll be lucky.'

'Yes – luck – *Lucky Man*.'

'Lucky Man!' we both yell.

We drive round to 57 Greencroft Gardens fast.

'We've got the title, Lindsay. *Lucky Man*.'

He makes the inside of his cheek pop with a finger. An annoying habit.

'No.'

A tense pause.

'*O Lucky Man*, like *O Dreamland* or *Oh! Calcutta*. Much better than *Lucky Man* – it's got a ring to it. And it ought to have an exclamation mark. Where should the exclamation mark go?'

'At the beginning, after the "O",' I say.

'At the end. *O, Lucky Man!*'

23 August 1970

Malcolm rings to say that he has arranged a meeting for two o'clock to see Lindsay to discuss *O, Lucky Man!* But he can't go. He has to go to rehearse his film with Stanley Kubrick. I must go alone.

I groan. 'It'll be a disaster without you. You can recount the good episodes. You're the actor. You've got to be there. Well then, let's put it off till you can go and we can all three meet.'

'No, I've just rung him. He's in a very good mood. He's expecting you. You can talk to him better than I can.'

Malcolm's psychological warfare. He has realised that two against one would make Lindsay antagonistic.

So I drink some whisky and write out a plot. The first thing Lindsay will say is, 'What have you written? Why haven't you written anything? You're supposed to be a writer, aren't you? What do you do all day?'

Lindsay opens the door. Gives a groan, a wry smile.

'Malcolm's just been. He's quite batty. Left me a script to read. (The script of another project.) God I hate reading. Do I really have to?'

'Well, it's very easy. It's better than the book.'

'I thought it looked bad. What have you written?'

I screw up the plot in my pocket.

'Nothing.'

'What? What's there to talk about if you haven't written anything? What have you been doing with Malcolm all this time?'

'Well, we've been discussing it.'

'Discussing it!'

'We've discovered the essence, what it really should be about, and also a style which makes it more than just a story about a salesman in coffee. Coffee would just be part of it. He'd do other things.'

'What other things? What essence?'

'Well, it should be like *Heaven's My Destination* or *Amerika*. A series of things. And his character – like Candide. He believes he's lucky. Some of the time he is successful and then suddenly it all vanishes. But he thinks it doesn't matter. He's always been lucky. Something will turn up. And there's a girl – first she works for a den of thieves, the next adventure she's a chimney sweep – and . . .'

'You see, I think a series of adventures, this girl popping up – other characters popping up – it runs the risk of running away into the sands of – how can I say it? – into little sand hills – of something small-scale. What is the character really after?'

'I don't know. He just believes he's lucky. He's not like the hero of *Heaven's My Destination*. He hasn't got a mission.'

'Have you read *Pilgrim's Progress*? Perhaps it should be like that. Or what was Candide after? He wasn't after anything, was he?' says Lindsay.

'Yes, he was. He was after the Princess. That was why he was kicked out in the first place. When he gets her she's hideous and covered in VD. But he is still in love with her. But you couldn't stage that to make it believable. It's just a literary device.'

'You could stage it. You'd just have to turn the whole thing over and stand back from it, and make the ending a comment on the action – an alienation.'

'I suppose so.'

Lindsay grins. Does he really believe what he's said?

'Mind you, in *Amerika* the hero isn't after anything. He just gets shoved to and fro suffering injustice,' I say.

'That's true. I mean, our character – perhaps he should just want to be successful? I mean, to make it epic, to give it an epic quality, a view of society, it ought to be quite separate things he tries, thinking each time that this is going to be marvellous, this is the answer, then when it collapses he tries something new – so each time we see a completely different aspect of life. That would be epic. I suppose you want a whisky?'

'Please.'

'Help yourself. By the way: what about that book *The Hand-reared Boy*, what did you think of it? I mean, you didn't react to it really, did you? You don't really enthuse about anything, do you?'

'Yes, I do. I loved the book. I told you. But I thought it would be impossible to make.'

'But if it were it would make a fortune.'

'Yes, it would.'

'Then why, when you read it, didn't you say it was very exciting and would make a film? You didn't react at all,' says Lindsay, cross.

'When I read it I didn't look on it as a film. I just read it as an ordinary reader and I enjoyed it – as a normal reader.'

'A normal reader! You don't think I keep sending you these books for you to read as an ordinary reader? You're supposed to be one of the most sought-after scriptwriters in the country – you don't think I send you stuff to enjoy as a normal person. You're not a normal person.'

'Yes, but when I read it I realised it would be impossible to make it into a film. I just enjoyed . . .'

'Why is it impossible?'

'How do you as a director use small children in direct sexual actions without perverting them and exploiting them?'

'And being sent to jail.'

'And rightly.'

'Yes, that's what I thought. That's why I thought it was impossible . . .'

2 September 1970

Malcolm and I meet Lindsay, who's working at the Royal Court Theatre. We go to a coffee bar round the corner. We sit on high stools over weak coffee to finalise our plans to produce *O, Lucky Man!* We have to form a company to make and own the film. Lindsay wants to call it Manic Productions, but settles for SAM, based on our initials. The three of us will be paid an equal amount for the whole film, £10,000, and each will have an equal vote in any SAM decision. Democracy. We have all brought prototype contracts from our prospective lawyers. We pull them out. One is bound in black tape, one green, one red. They are each biased in favour of their client and against the others. After having read the others' contracts, we decide to amalgamate them into one master contract so as to be fair to all. This we do with Lindsay's red Tempo pen. We cross everything out that we don't like in each other's contracts – initialling every crossing out: three sets of initials for every crossing-out or insertion. It takes forty-five minutes. So SAM was born to produce its one and only film. We drink a toast to SAM in coffee.

20 September 1970

Lindsay, Malcolm and I walk through the Inns of Court, looking for Lindsay's lawyer's office. We get lost in the Oxford college-like quadrangles. It starts to rain heavily. We arrive ten minutes late, and drenched, to find a room full of expectant lawyers, and Lindsay's and Malcolm's agents . . .

It is apparent at this meeting that these people have different objectives from our one of setting up the film simply, without a big, unnecessary financial hassle. They are determined to complicate things as much as possible in order to make work for themselves.

Lindsay tells them that they must keep things simple. The meeting lasts an hour and a half. 'It was like directing a film,' Lindsay says afterwards. 'The amount of energy you need to cut through the financial and legal snares – if we go on this way we'll be too exhausted to make the picture.'

But, coming out of the Inns of Court, we feel like millionaires, after all the talk about percentages and profits. Unfortunately nothing concrete has been decided; we don't have a producer; we don't have a frame of film to our name, only three pages of script (*the car crash scene; the only scene to remain unaltered through the two and a half years of making the film*); no one has yet put up any money, and we don't have a deal with any major distributor.

We decide to go ahead with our development of our script without the backing – and the consequent sense of obligation – of a distributor. This was how I developed *If . . .* with Lindsay; and we felt freer that way. We also decide to wait until we have a reasonable first draft before approaching a producer. Malcolm and Lindsay each put up a modest stake and I put up my services as a writer (the only stake I have). So we got going.

26 February 1971

I pack excitedly. Best shirt, camera, tape-recorder, note-pads and barbiturates. Lindsay and I are to drive north for our first research recce for *O, Lucky Man!*

At the front door Gay unexpectedly recoils from my goodbye kiss. 'I won't be letting you back in the flat when you return. I'm changing the locks. You can go and live with your beloved Lindsay. I've my own life to lead. GET IN THE HOUSE, BERTIE!' she screams at the dog and slams the door.

I pick Lindsay up from 57 Greencroft Gardens and tell him the latest. 'She's mad,' he says calmly. 'Now take it easy. Follow the map . . .'

Lindsay and I drive to Liverpool to inspect the actual coffee factory where Malcolm trained as a salesman. It is very different from the factory Malcolm had described. It has shrunk. It is much too small. There are only four women on the packing lines.

A foreman, in a white linen pork pie hat, shows us round. He explains the intricacies of roasting, blending, gas-flushing, and why although teabags have revolutionised the tea industry, coffee in similar bags would be flat as a flute. I take down pages of notes which I compress into a three-page scene in which the foreman lectures the trainees . . .

We drive on north towards Bolton to visit Alan Price, where he is doing a gig with Georgie Fame. He is staying at Dimple Hall, an isolated stone farmhouse . . . It is Alan's regular lodging place when he is on a northern tour. Everything is uncannily quiet. Later that evening we go with Alan, Georgie Fame and their group to Bolton where they are to give a concert. We drive to the gig, huddled in their freezing van.

Our night drives in this van later gave us the idea that the musicians' van should rescue our hero, Mick, when he is fleeing from the experimental medical laboratory.

The concert takes place in a nightclub unlike anything to be found in the south. It is huge, modern, densely packed; standing room only. The crowds of smartly dressed workers are in darkness. Only the stage is spotlit. Alan and George sing their hit songs – 'Simon Smith', 'Bonnie and Clyde', and the rest as well as rock and rhythm and blues classics. Lindsay and I take photographs. In the middle of the concert, Lindsay suggests I phone Gay. 'We can't have her fucking up the film. Plead . . .' I do and she agrees to let me back into the flat.

After the concert the musicians unwind at Dimple Hall by playing Scrabble until four in the morning. Lindsay and I lose every game.

Lindsay had been planning a film with and about Alan Price after Alan had written the music for Home. *It was to be a documentary, featuring gigs, travel, digs and one-night stands. Like the old actor-managers with their travelling fitups. But when Alan teamed up with Georgie Fame the project ran into difficulties, chiefly on copyright for the material they were using. (£1,000 a minute for a Ray Charles number.) But quite a lot of the idea became part of* O, Lucky Man! *Great songs like 'Everyone's going through changes', 'O, Lucky Man!' and 'Sell! Sell! Sell!'*

28 February 1971

We spend two nights watching Alan Price and Georgie Fame, then drive back south to London. On the drive we discuss the scene when Mick meets the big businessman. Something else is needed in this scene, says Lindsay, something that will tell us the businessman's power, the way he operates. I suggest a mad inventor who is given the boot. Kicked out after forty years' service on which the company's fortune is based. Lindsay likes the idea. He thinks the inventor should commit suicide in front of Mick and the businessman's eyes – hurl himself through the window at the top of Centrepoint.

This businessman became Sir James – father of a girl, Patricia, whom Mick meets in the musicians' van . . .

1 March 1971

I return home to find a note from Gay on the kitchen sideboard: 'Working late with David and Debbie Owen. They're real live wires! Ham in fridge. Feed Bertie.'

28 May 1971

FA Cup Final day. In the middle of the hot May afternoon I get fed up writing epic lines for Alan Price and decide to watch the great match too. As I walk down the corridor, I hear Gay on the phone in the bedroom, laughing huskily from her belly, intimately, in a way she never talks to me.

'No, no, darling, it's perfectly safe. He's in his study . . .'

I realise everything in a split second.

2 *June* 1971

I get back from a talk with Lindsay to find that Gay's left the flat. She's taken Bertie and the television set.

That evening I get a phone call from her.

'I won't tell you where I am. And I'm not coming back.'

'Good,' I say, to her surprise.

I phone Lindsay and Malcolm, tell them the news and announce that the work must go ahead professionally from now on. I'll need a secretary.

7 *June* 1971

Lindsay has agreed to let me work in his flat. He has set aside his huge front room for my study. I remove from the walls the grim paintings of coal mines by David Storey as Lindsay says I can make the room just the way I like it. Therese, my new Australian secretary, arrives on the dot of ten. Her presence is inspirational and ideas flow out of me. I finish the scene early on in the film where Mick is given a magic gold suit tailored for him by the mysterious lodger, Monty. As Mick sets out from his lodging house to sell coffee to the whole of north-east England, Monty calls after him, 'Try not to die like a dog.'

At lunchtime Therese and I go out to a pub and swap our sad stories. For five years she lived with a TV director called Ric, who kept on going back to his wife, Meredith. She can't understand why Ric prefers dull Meredith to her. That's why she fled Sydney and came to England. 'Marriage is the strangest thing,' she says.

Back at Greencroft Gardens I find that Lindsay has made an inspection and put a large tick in red Tempo on the magic gold suit scene. 'VG work.'

In the evening I return to Platt's Lane. Suddenly the door crashes open. It's Gay.

'My spies tell me you've found a new secretary. What's she like?'

'Small, slim and dark.'

'You don't like them small, slim and dark. Anyway, my spies will keep me informed.'

'Are you leaving now, Gay?'

'No! This is my home.'

Marriage is the strangest thing.

8 June 1971

Therese turns up to work carrying an enormous cardboard box.

'Provisions,' she says.

The box contains cold meats, paté, cabbage, celery, radishes, onions, carrots, mayonnaise, garlic bread, a dozen large oranges, two bottles of claret and a jar of Marmite. It must have cost her thirty pounds.

As I hold her in my arms, she flutters like a bird. We make love on the carpet Lindsay's spent an hour trying to vacuum, and then we eat.

9 June 1971

I move out of Platt's Lane and into Therese's tiny Chelsea flat.

19 June 1971

Lindsay asks to see the script. I tell him to wait till it's finished. I'm going great guns with Therese. He's delighted.

1 July 1971

I ring Malcolm. I tell him I'm stuck on the section dealing with the big businessman, Sir James, who drives the inventor to suicide, and whose daughter Mick tries to woo. Malcolm rings the chairman of EMI, Sir Joseph Lockwood, whom he'd met while making the film *The Raging Moon*. Sir Joseph agrees to explain to us some of the mysteries of big business.

5 July 1971

Malcolm and I drive in his car to the EMI headquarters in Manchester Square. Sir Joseph Lockwood sees us in his huge board-room. He tells us some of the truths of business.

'The pioneer always pays,' he says. 'The first invention – no one wants to know. Look at tape cassettes.'

We ask him how he chooses an employee?

'What has he done so far? Once he's past thirty, degrees don't mean a thing. So long as he can read and write. If you've had failure you'll go on being a failure. If you've had success, you'll go on having success. Unless you go gaga. First thing a successful man in business has got to do is get rid of non-essentials. Never make wrong decisions. Good health. Sleep well. You should like to make money but not to spend it, unless it's going to make more money. No round the world trips with the wife. It's not a question of morals – not morals – it's waste. Once you allow waste it goes right down the company. You end up ruined, be you the United States or a fish and chip shop at the Battersea funfair.'

I type out this speech. It's perfect for Sir James to say to Mick in the back of his Rolls Royce.

It is shot, but cut out in the editing.

8 July 1971

A phone call from Ric in Australia. He's decided to leave Meredith and marry Therese. He's arriving in twenty-four hours.

9 July 1971

I expected a huge beer-swilling Aussie to beat the living daylights out of me, but Ric is as thin as a beanpole and gentle as a butterfly. He suggests that since we both love her we share her. I say since he's had her for five years, I want her for five months, and then she can decide whom she loves. Ric moves in upstairs.

23 July 1971

With Ric so close we've found it impossible either to make love or do any work. Therese tells Lindsay the truth. He insists I go into a rest-home to work on the script for a week by myself, and then we'll go to the seaside and work together, as we did on *If . . .*

31 July 1971

Go down on the train with Lindsay to Hythe – to spend the week-end working. On the train he reads the first draft for the first time, groaning and closing his eyes.

'It's terrible,' he says.

Then he comes to three blank pages.

'What's this?'

'It's the scene on the roof. Mick and the girl. It's a complete blank – I can't think of anything. It's totally unreal. I can't write it.'

'You'll just have to this weekend or we'll have to pack in the film.'

Lindsay has booked into a three-star hotel on the seafront where his mother is staying. I'm booked into a no-star hotel behind it. It is occupied mainly by permanent guests: old age pensioners who have made the little cold rooms into their final nests. As I walk down the long linoed corridor I can see into one of the rooms – it's crammed with potted plants, the dressing table crowded with framed photos of the owner's family. In the hall is a gong with a floor brush beside it which serves as a hammer.

There's no table in my room, so I set the typewriter on the chair by the bed. But feel so depressed about the script, and the unwritable scene on the roof, that I go to the nearest pub. Drink and read the *Daily Mirror* over and over.

That evening Lindsay phones Malcolm.

'The author's lying drunk on the floor and the script is in ruins. You'd better meet me at the flat on Monday – I think we'll seriously have to consider forgetting the whole idea.'

Malcolm mumbles, 'Oh God, I'll never work again.'

Lindsay says to me – 'Write that rooftop scene tomorrow morning.'

'It's a complete blank. Nothing there.'

'Just write something. Anything you like.'

I go back to my hotel. It is 10.30 p.m. Not a light in the place. Everyone is in their own room, trying to sleep.

2 August 1971

I wake up to the sound of the gong being beaten with the brush. I run down to breakfast. About ten very aged guests gathered at the same table shouting into each other's hearing aids; I'm put at a table by myself, away from them; in the far corner, also set on her own, is a beautiful Arab girl. Why should she choose this hotel? Anyway, I feel cheered up. Buy a newspaper and go upstairs to read about the *Oz* trial, locking the door in case Lindsay should make one of his unannounced inspections and find me reading the newspaper and the typewriter silent. I put down the paper and write the first line – he said write anything: very well . . .

Later Lindsay phones Malcolm again and says, 'Author woke up in the morning and produced some very good work in the afternoon.'

Malcolm says, 'I know it will be good. Just keep him off the barley wine.'

7 August 1971

The end of a happy and productive week by the seaside. I phone Therese, who sounds like Tinkerbell – she's happy because Ric has once again gone back to his wife. The only worry is Lindsay's mother – Mrs Sleigh has a bad pain in her stomach and can only eat ice-cream.

8 August 1971

Reunited with Therese in her tiny Chelsea flat. Happy days. Good work.

15 August 1971

A bombshell. Ric phones. He can't stand Meredith and he's going to commit suicide unless Therese returns to Australia. My girl is torn between two men, both of whom she loves. Its like *Jules et Jim*. The good work ends.

21 August 1971

Victoria Coach Station. I kiss Therese farewell. I watch as her coach slowly, so slowly pulls away. Her face is stone. She doesn't once look back . . .

The soup fight

28 August 1971
Platt's Lane

I can't eat. I can't work. I can't face the empty flat . . .

I phone Gay's barrister friend John Haines, who tells me Gay's living with some air hostesses and gives me the number. I dial and the phone is answered with a fit of girlish giggles.

'Is Gay there? It's David, her husband.'

More giggles and then Gay is on the phone.

'I know you're my husband. What do you want?'

'Bring me over some fish and chips. I can't eat by myself.'

'Have you any idea what time it is? I was asleep,' she says.

'Fish and chips. And don't bring your John Haines.'

A few minutes later the doorbell rings. Gay stands before me, dressed in her nightie and fur coat, proffering a can of soup. Beside her is a giant young man called Richard Onmeny, her old boyfriend.

'You come in, damn you,' I say to Gay. 'You get out,' I say to Richard Onmeny.

'Don't talk to your wife like that,' he replies.

'We're coming in together, or not at all,' says Gay.

I lunge past Richard Onmeny and grab Gay. Richard grabs me from behind, slips his arms round my neck and starts to strangle me. I just have the strength to bite the finger clamped across my mouth. I bite hard. He starts to scream in agony.

'For the love of God, let go, David! Stop!'

I unclench my teeth. Instantly he swivels my head and grabs my neck in the crook of his freed arm. I'm trapped. He smashes me in the face with pile-driver blows. I pass out.

When I come to, I find blood pouring down my cheeks. Richard sits opposite me, cradling his bloody finger and weeping. The police arrive and take statements.

'He's run off with my wife and tried to murder me!' I cry. 'Charge the bastard!'

But they seem amazingly unconcerned. 'It's just a family fracas. Happens all the time. Your face needs stitching up. Get someone to take you to hospital.'

29 August 1971

I look at myself in the bathroom mirror with one eye that I can open only slightly. My face is purple and twice its normal size. My eyes are like black eggs. My mouth looks like a black cactus plant, the lips split in several places and held together by stitches. I try to shave, but can't stop trembling.

Lindsay's doctor, Martin Johnstone, visits. The trembling's only shock, he tells me, but I may lose the sight of one eye. He suggests that I should stay with friends and rings Malcolm and Margot.

Malcolm comes round at once. He can't believe what he sees.

I retell the story. '. . . And all over a can of soup!'

He puts an arm round me and helps me into his BMW. He hasn't a spare room, but Margot fixes up a mattress in the study. Their dog, Alex (a present from Stanley Kubrick for Malcolm's performance in *Clockwork Orange*), senses I'm ill and never leaves me.

Lindsay arrives. He looks at me and says, 'You'd better divorce her. And as soon as that shaking stops, I want you back at work. No more of your fucking about with women.'

3 September 1971

Malcolm's flat. Back to work. Alan Price comes round and we talk about the songs.

11 September 1971

Therese rings. She loves me, she wants to come back, but Ric is being so sweet and understanding that she'll have to choose the right time. 'Trust me, darling,' she says.

Lindsay rings from Prague, where he's been trying to persuade the Communist authorities to allow Mirek Ondricek, who shot *If . . .*, to come to England to make *O, Lucky Man!* He still hasn't got a definite 'Yes'.

'How much have you written?' he asks me.

'Just a bit.'

'Just a bit? That's absolutely useless', and he slams down the phone. Half an hour later he rings back. We both laugh. The conversation continues as if uninterrupted. He thinks they will let Mirek come.

12 September 1971
Platt's Lane

I phone Therese. With her soft loving magical voice she tells me I must be patient. If she walks out on Ric he'll attempt suicide again. But she's coming back soon. 'Just be patient, darling.'

Glowing with her promise I get a flash of inspiration. I ring Lindsay. 'Wouldn't it be a good idea if Arthur Lowe, who plays the coffee factory manager, Mr Duff, also plays the black president Dr Munda, and all the other characters are played by the main actors?'

'Absurd! Absolutely silly! Arthur Lowe blacked up! It'll look like a pantomime. Another of your silly ideas! I suppose you've been phoning Therese?'

A long, long pause follows . . .

'No! It *is* a good idea,' says Lindsay. 'It will make the film! Well done. Maybe Therese *is* good for you.'

'I just hope she returns.'

19 September 1971

Lindsay rings to find out how I'm getting on with the orgy scene. 'We'll just have to think of something else,' I say.

It's based on an adventure Alan Price once had, when the manager of a five-star hotel invited him to an orgy in a shed. I confess to Lindsay that I'm finding it impossible to write.

'But you were the one who loved Alan's story so much.'

'I can't write it.'

'It's the only way to end Mick's first unsuccessful day on the road – something like what happened to Alan.'

'Well, get Alan to write it.'

'I've got a shock for you. Malcolm's coming in at six, and I've promised him he can read the orgy.'

'But I've never been to an orgy.'

'Perhaps it should be like the other orgy Alan told me about. He was in the north of England, and he looked through the window of this respectable suburban house and saw the head of police, and the mayor, and all their wives – just sitting – watching blue films.'

'All right. Hmm . . . Why is it I never get asked to orgies?'

'Because you don't look sporty enough.'

I decide that the key to the orgy must be respectability and good-neighbourliness. Mick being introduced to everyone as though it were a vicarage jumble sale. Finish it just in time. The absolute necessity of having a deadline, however artificial.

Late September, 1971
56 Greencroft Gardens

Lindsay and I work together on putting the finishing touches to the first draft. We only have the evenings and the weekend because Lindsay is directing *The Changing Room* at the Royal Court. I am going mad trying to get Therese to leave Australia without Ric committing suicide. Lindsay is also going mad trying to cast *The Changing Room*. He has to find fifteen Northern actors who look as though they could all be members of the same Rugby League team. He is absolutely exhausted. He also has to look after his mother, who is so ill she has left her home in Rustington. She is living in Lindsay's front room. It takes her five minutes to get out of bed, with my help and a walking stick. Lindsay and I take it in turns dictating from my almost illegible scrawled-over sheets while the other types out the finalised version. We drink a lot of barley wine.

15 October 1971

The first draft is completed. In the evening after supper, Lindsay composes a killer telegram to Therese. 'Script finished and brilliant. David loves you and needs you. Please return. Love, Lindsay.' If that doesn't do the trick, nothing will.

16 October 1971

Therese phones to say that she's leaving in two days. I hug Lindsay and his mother. We show our first draft to Michael Medwin as we had done with *If*... He understands and likes it immediately, and agrees to join us as a producer. Old collaborators are contacted. Many of them know about the project already: Miroslav Ondricek, our cameraman; Jocelyn Herbert, production designer; Miriam Brickman, casting; David Gladwell, editor...

20 October 1971

I go to Heathrow to meet the mid-day flight from Sydney. Therese is home. At last we can be happy . . .

24 December 1971

Warner Bros agree to back us. Budget $1.5 million. All we have to do now is make the film. Therese is decorating our little tree and hoping for a white Christmas. She's never seen snow. On Boxing Day we're going to give a Christmas party for our friends: Lindsay and his mother, Margot and Malcolm (who is now the hottest star in the world after the astounded world watched *Clockwork Orange*), Alan Price and his girl-friend Wiffle. A perfect Christmas, I think, as I watch a car pull up outside. It's Gay.

'Like to see Bertie?'

'I'd love to.'

'Get in then.'

In the entrance to Gay's flat, Bertie jumps up, delighted to see me. She runs round and round in circles and I have to calm her down. Just pleased to be back with Bertie and without another thought in my head, I follow Gay into her bedroom.

'Shall we . . . ?' she says, undressing.

Five minutes later she drives me back to Platt's Lane. I enter the bedroom to find Therese packing her enormous suitcase. She's leaving. Those stupid five minutes have cost me everything. I wash down a bottle of barbiturates with a bottle of whisky.

26 December 1971

Hampstead Hospital . . . I awake feeling elated. *O, Lucky Man!* is on. But why are there all these beds?

'What's going on?' I call out.

'A few years ago you'd have woken up with a policeman by your side,' says an elderly man in the next bed.

'Why on earth?'

'You tried to knock yourself off. That used to be a crime. Took all your pills. You nearly didn't make it. They were working twenty-four hours on you. The young lady doctor saved your life . . .'

'What day is it?'

'Boxing Day.'

'It's our party today!'

I get out of bed and find a male nurse, a young and handsome

Indian.

'So you're awake, Mr Sherwin.'

'I've got to go home. It's our Christmas party.'

'You've been pretty ill. You can't leave without seeing the psychiatrist tomorrow. But you should phone Therese O'Leary. He gives me a piece of paper. There's a telephone number on it. Malcolm's. It's beginning to dawn on me . . . I dial.

'For God's sake, David! Well done!' It's Malcolm. 'We've all had a great Christmas thinking you'd had it. I'll get you Therese – she's some girl. Saved your life . . .'

27 December 1971

Lindsay comes in early. He tells me Therese is going back to Ric. I'm to be adult for once. His doctor, Martin Johnstone, suggests I see Dr Woolfson, a very good psychotherapist. And that rooftop scene with Patricia needs more work . . .

28 December 1971

Dr Woolfson lives in a big house off Hampstead Heath. He listens to my story and says my problem is I'm not sporty enough. I should socialise more, stop being a loner. He's going to send me to a very jolly mental hospital called Springfields in Tooting Bec. I'll have my own room where I'll be able to write that rooftop scene. Another writer there, Heathcote Williams, will look after me. Heathcote is recovering from his affair with Jean Shrimpton and loves the place so much he won't leave.

Dr Woolfson is also putting me on a drug for manic depression – lithium – and warns me not to eat Marmite.

'Remember. Socialise,' he says as I leave.

29 December 1971

Springfields Mental Hospital is huge. Built eighty years ago, it looks like a prison. Heathcote tells me that half the two thousand inmates are kept under section, locked up day and night in their wards. I am given my own room.

I register with the consultant psychiatrist, and ask how long I'll be in for.

'Maybe six months – it depends on your progress.'

'But I've a movie to make.'

'All that depends on your progress.'

At ten o'clock a nurse comes round with a trolley and gives each patient a triple dose of tranquillisers. Springfields is out for the night.

30 December 1971

Breakfast is a bowl of watery porridge. Heathcote tells me all the patients are half-starved. Every day he goes on the 'chocolate run' to buy sweets for his friends under section.

'Shopping time!' he says, inviting me along. We walk out of the hospital and round to Tooting Bec market. He buys several boxes of chocolates, a lucky tie for me and a Mozart record.

Heathcote has keys to all the wards, but is only interested in visiting the women's. We distribute chocolate bars to all the starving girls under section and present the Mozart record to two old ladies who have been locked up for ten years, and will never be free again. They spend their days breaking up their furniture.

31 December 1971

It's the New Year's Dance tonight. The staff make a big effort, decking out the meal hall with masses of balloons and Christmas presents. I have a bath and wear my lucky tie.

I decide to obey orders and socialise. I choose for my partner a girl who turns out to be a brilliant dancer. We win all the competitions. She is also friendly and sympathetic, listening patiently as I tell her all about Gay and Bertie, remembering only the good times.

'You obviously love her very much,' she says.

The thought had never occurred to me, but it seems true. Wisdom from a simple heart.

1 January 1972

I walk out of the hospital and catch the Tube home.

1 March 1972

Gay and Bertie return.

19 March 1972

The day before shooting I'm at Lindsay's flat, still trying to rewrite the rooftop scene for the third time. Malcolm rings Lindsay: 'I've got to see you immediately. I don't understand a word of this script.'

Malcolm arrives. He thinks the character is a sheep, too passive. I tell him all the best actors are passive. They react. Look at Robert Mitchum. This is a reacting part.

'But he needs a bit more go, don't you think?'

'Well, you rewrite it, then. By tomorrow,' says Lindsay. 'Listen, you've got to pretend to be naive,' he says, 'it's how you were ten years ago. Go on now. You've just got to do it.'

So Malcolm goes away, content.

23 March 1972

The third day of shooting. I go to the set – the location is a coffee factory in south London. It is a sunny, suddenly hot day. Outside the factory stand generating lorries for our lights. Inside the skylights have been covered with tarpaulin to keep out the unexpected sun. Blocks of lamps hanging in the ceiling behind translucent paper provide exactly the same effect as the sunlight. The camera dominates everything. It is mounted high on a wooden scaffold at the far end of the factory floor.

I make myself inconspicuous next to a coffee-packing machine and read through, for the nth time, the rewrite of the rewrite of the rooftop scene. The detached ruthless attitude of the girl, Patricia, is still not there. I look at the coffee-packing lines away from the shooting area. They are working normally, but all the packers wear red badges on their uniforms, reading 'Imperial Coffee' instead of their own brand.

Lindsay, Malcolm and Arthur Lowe stand under the blaze of light, surrounded by boxes of coffee. Mirek lines up the shot on the scaffold. Lindsay suddenly puts his hand on Arthur Lowe's shoulder to draw his attention. Lindsay points an accusing finger straight at me.

'Him – the author – he's to blame.'

2 May 1972

Lindsay's mother is spending a fortnight in a hospital in Hendon, north London. Gay and I fly to Tunisia for a second honeymoon.

16 May 1972

We return to Platt's Lane to find the phone ringing. It's my agent, Judy Scott-Fox. She's in a panic. Lindsay needs me for vital script changes. I'm to stay in and wait for his call. Lindsay doesn't ring until 2 in the morning.

Without a word of greeting he gets straight to the point. His voice is clipped and brusque. 'The second half of the script, where Mick meets the poor – it's totally wrong and mini. I've got sixty old age pensioners in Shelter waiting to be shot tomorrow and a script that doesn't work. I'll have to stop the film unless you're on the set at 9 a.m. with a solution. And don't you ever dare again go off on holiday in the middle of filming. You've got seven hours.'

17 May 1972

9 a.m. I walk across the set to the production office, pushing my way through a crowd of pensioners waiting to do their scene.

'Well?' asks Lindsay, his face a mask.

'Cut it. Cut the whole thing.'

To my surprise, Lindsay agrees. 'Now, you'll just have to find a brand-new invention to put in its place. Got your typewriter?'

5 July 1972

I take Lindsay's mother to yet another hospital. A nurse and I tuck her into bed, and arrange her fruit. I show her how to work the magnificent hi-fi radio Lindsay has brought her. Suddenly she says, 'Gay is pregnant.'

I'm thunderstruck. Gay never told me.

'How do you know?'

'She came round to the flat with one of Bertie's puppies, wanting me to have it. I just knew. A woman can tell these things.'

'Well, you must have that puppy. He's lovely and he's for you.'

'Lindsay wants me to, but I can't.'

'You'll soon be better . . .'

'No – you'll never see me alive again.'

26 March 1973

Gay and I drive down to Malcolm's famous mill-house. A huge eighteenth-century millwheel spins swiftly as thousands of gallons of water churn through it. Margot has decorated the whole interior in white. I live in terror of dropping burnt pipe tobacco on her pure white sofas.

We take Malcolm and Margot out to dinner at the local pub. All through the meal they scream at each other like homicidal maniacs about the right time of year to plant apple trees.

Back at the mill we give Malcolm the script we've written for him and say goodnight. Our bedroom is freezing cold. Margot is so mean she won't use the central heating and provides only one blanket for our bed. We pull the Persian carpet over our bed and snuggle close like Eskimos.

27 March 1973

We get up early, looking forward to Malcolm's praise of our master-piece. *Assassin of the Children* is pretty sensational. It's about an ace marksman who shoots children at random. He demands a king's ransom to stop, and soon every playground in the country is empty and every child hidden away behind shuttered windows. Malcolm is to play the cop who catches the assassin. Lindsay has long said that Malcolm should play a cop.

Malcolm descends his spiral staircase, script in hand. He looks worried. He's not sure about our masterpiece. He'll have to show it to his friend, the director Mike Hodges, who lives ten miles down-stream. We'll go there tonight for supper.

It's pitch-dark when we leave. Malcolm gets his car out of the garage while I explore his orchard by starlight. I follow the dim shape of Malcolm's dog, Alex, and fall headlong into the mill-race. All I'm conscious of is the colossal force of the water. It's like being flogged. I'm drowning. I make a mighty lunge and just manage to grab a plant root. Malcolm hauls me out, appalled and laughing.

Mike Hodges made the cult film *Get Carter* with Michael Caine. He loves the script, but Malcolm sounds less and less interested. In any case he has other fish to fry. Tomorrow the snooker champion Alex 'Hurricane' Higgins is coming down. Malcolm says he'd rather play a snooker player than a cop. 'Cops are boring, *for God's sake*, David!'

28 March 1973

We spend the day with Alex 'Hurricane' Higgins. He looks pasty-faced from years of all-night snooker, and we take him to the seaside for some fresh air.

In the evening Gay and I drive back to Platt's Lane. I'm woken at midnight by Gay pacing the floor in agony.

'I've got a terrible urinary infection,' she sobs.

'No you haven't – the baby's on its way.'

'But he's not due for three weeks.'

'He's decided otherwise.' We call him 'him' because we want a boy, although we can't decide on a name.

29 March 1973

I drive Gay at speed to the hospital. All the time she sobs, 'Please, darling, make them give me an epidural. I can't stand the pain.'

Eighteen hours later the midwife calls, 'The head's coming! Huge pushes, Mrs Sherwin . . .'

'Push, darling, push!'

And the baby shoots out.

'It's a boy!' says the midwife.

In seconds he's giving his first cry in this world and being shown to his exhausted and very beautiful mother.

I christen him Luke after St Luke's Church in Platt's Lane and then I'm on the phone to the world on cloud nine.

Cannes again

18 May 1973

O, Lucky Man! is the official British entry for the Cannes Festival. I fly out and this time stay with the stars at the Colombe d'Or. There are no hotel staff in sight, so I explore. I hear peals of manic laughter. I open a door to see Malcolm, Margot and James Coburn lying on cushions beneath the Picassos smoking pot and out of their minds.

It is Warner Bros' fiftieth anniversary and every other poster on the Promenade is of Malcolm smiling his smile. With all this overkill I know we'll lose. Warners have also just finished building a five-star hotel in the hills, where the only guest is a very lost Rachel Roberts.

19 May 1973

The Warners limo picks me up from the Colombe d'Or and Rachel from the hotel. We are running late for the press conference. As we have no identification, gendarmes prevent us from entering the hall.

'Come on, they won't shoot,' I say to Rachel, and we barge past, to face a barrage of reporters. 'Mick is Candide' is all I can think of to say to their questions.

Afterwards there's a huge lunch on the beach. It turns to farce as Alan Price is asked to play songs from the film without a microphone and TV crews film us all drunk and stumbling in circles in the sand. Lindsay keeps well out of this foolery.

O, Lucky Man! *doesn't win a thing, but gets rave reviews and becomes a hit. Judith Christ, in* New York Magazine: *'A unique creation . . . This triumphant film is almost beyond full appreciation at a first viewing; it becomes funnier and sadder at a second. And I am resisting giving it instant-classic status as I anticipate seeing it again and again. Suffice it that it is one of the finest films of the post-*Strangelove *decade.' And in the* Sunday Telegraph, *Margaret Hinxman writes: 'Entertainment on a prodigious scale. What an amazingly fresh, scathing, exuberant movie it is. Malcolm McDowell increases in stature with every film. Alan Price's score is sheer pleasure, tough, witty, melodic and a perfect complement to the most explosive British film since* If . . . *except this one is incomparably better. Exhilarating!'*

If only they knew how close it was . . .

23 September 1973
The Falls

Alberto Grimaldi, the producer of *Last Tango in Paris*, asks me to rewrite a script by Hugh Wheeler and Franco Zeffirelli for a remake of *Camille*. The Garbo role as the doomed courtesan Marguerite, who loves camellias, is to be played by the jolie-laide Liza Minnelli. It's an odd brew and Grimaldi sends me a sheaf of notes tactfully pointing out how awful the Wheeler/Zeffirelli script is.

I like the original book by Dumas, and am mad keen to write a film about La Belle Epoque and Parisian life in the second half of the nineteenth century. One of my favourite books of corrupt nineteenth-century society is the Journal of those two bitter fly-on-the-wall diarists, Edmond and Jules Goncourt.

1 October 1973

Gay, baby Luke and I fly to Rome. We are greeted by Grimaldi's assistant, the gentle giant Chris Mankiewicz, son of the famous Joe. Chris tells us that Alberto, an ex-lawyer and producer of spaghetti Westerns, still can't believe the huge success of *Last Tango*, with Marlon Brando, which made him rich. He still works in his tiny office lit by a naked light bulb, and drives an old Mini.

I have a brief meeting with Grimaldi under the naked light bulb. I tell him I agree: the script is atrocious. The plan is to drive to Franco Zeffirelli's villa in the morning, and be diplomatic.

2 October 1973

The simple Grimaldi and I await the great Zeffirelli in the arched ante-chamber of his villa. Through an open door I see throngs of young girls and boys jumping into a swimming pool, but no Zeffirelli. I look up at the ceiling. It's badly cracked. The roses in the vase are dead. I look at the only picture on the wall. It is a signed photograph of our Queen Mother, with her robust signature: 'All my love Franco – Elizabeth R.'

At last Zeffirelli enters. He takes one look at me and whistles. 'You did not tell me he was so young and freaky, Alberto.' He sits down, and a fat old labrador sprawls before his feet.

Zeffirelli is a disappointment. I had expected a monstrous, glamorous queen, but he is really quite ordinary. Even his young boys look like scruffs from Gloucester swimming pool.

Before we have a chance to mention the script, Zeffirelli shows us a collection of huge blow-ups of Renoir paintings. He wants his Camille to be a soft and beautiful Renoir painting. Nothing like Liza Minnelli, and completely at odds with my acid Goncourt view of Paris. Not for nothing is Zeffirelli known as the 'Neapolitan window-dresser'.

I say Renoir is decorative rubbish and that ends the conference.

That night Chris Mankiewicz takes Gay and me out on a tour of Rome. It is the happiest night of my marriage. We start off with a midnight feast on the Via Veneto. Over a water ice Chris pronounces that *O, Lucky Man!* is 'a lump of shit'. He is so sweet and also so huge that I don't knock his block off, just grin and guzzle. We watch the beautiful modern Marguerites walking up and down their pitches, then visit the empty, silent and floodlit Forum and amphitheatre. They seem alive with ancient Romans. The streets of Rome, vile by day, have become spiritual.

9 October 1973
The Falls

I've bought a caravan especially for *Camille*. It will be my study. I've always had a fascination with, and dread of, prostitution, just like my Goncourt brothers, who saw it as a symbol of all that was wrong with their age. I'm in love with the subject and, lighting my pipe, settle down to write what I hope will be one of the best scripts of my life.

SCENE ONE. INTERIOR. NINETEENTH CENTURY. THE OPERA HOUSE
The scene rises on a childlike Marguerite as the Goddess Venus. A tense hush descends on the audience as she starts to sing of love, expressing all her power of sex. . .

6 December 1973
The Falls

Camille is completed in time for the afternoon post and tea. It's my fastest script yet. I think it's good and very commercial. I express-mail it to Grimaldi as his Christmas present.

My script shows Marguerite working all day to doll herself up for the night's work. It's not a question of a few hat-boxes from the milliners in her ante-room as in the other script. I've also given it a new ending, inspired by my life here at The Falls. In between work I've been playing with baby Luke, taking him to our coalmine and telling him fairy stories. Watching his face light up, I've never felt so happy in my life. So now Armand, Marguerite's true love, persuades her to give up the life of a courtesan and buy an idyllic cottage in the country, just like our Falls, where they can have their child. But away from Paris and her rich benefactors, she quickly becomes bankrupt. She is rescued from poverty by Armand's father, for the usual consideration. When the father boasts of his conquest, Armand cracks and abandons Marguerite.

Marguerite observes through her grief: 'Be it for a year or a day, only money's real, Armand.'

There is a bitter-sweet ending. Marguerite is reconciled with Armand on her death-bed and, as she dies of TB, gives birth to their child, whom Armand christens Jean-Luc.

10 December 1973

Grimaldi rings up. He has just read the script and adores it. He is going to take it round to Zeffirelli himself in his Mini.

11 December 1973

Grimaldi rings. The Neapolitan window-dresser hates the script. I try to get hold of him myself but he refuses to take the call.

The Killing of Koven

25 February 1974

I fly to Shannon, Ireland, to talk to a Mr Halmi about writing a script of *Rites of Passage*, a novella by Joanne Greenberg.

It is an eerie story about a wretchedly poor white farmer in America, Greelish, who has a paranoid hatred of his neighbour, Koven. He blames him for the failure of his farm, although Koven is as poor as he. Greelish hires an adolescent boy called Hobart, who is desperate to escape his protective grandmother. Hobart rebuilds the farm and makes it flourish but he is brainwashed by Greelish's hatred of Koven. One day he carries out Greelish's secret wish and murders Koven. But with his bitterest enemy dead, Greelish loses all reason for living. He destroys his farm and summons the police to arrest Hobart, crying out madly, 'He killed my neighbour. In the old days people loved their neighbours!'

It will be difficult to dramatise, but I find the story overpowering and identify completely with Hobart and Greelish. Their old farm reminds me of my patch at The Falls, a jungle of bog, giant fern and bramble which grows as fast as I can scythe it down.

Shannon airport is in the middle of empty grass fields. Ours is the only aeroplane I can see. I enter the tiny terminal building, where I am summoned by a voice on the loudspeaker, lilting and soft, the consonants almost indistinguishable: 'Will Mistar Sherwin please chontack the Aer Lingus representative in the Customs Hall.' I look around, but can see no one who looks like an Aer Lingus representative. So I open my briefcase and take out a copy of the published script of *O, Lucky Man!* with Malcolm's face on it and hold it above my head. A girl in a green uniform comes up to me. 'Mr Sherwin?'

'Yes.'

'Mr Halmi said you'd be carrying a copy of *O, Lucky Man!* but I didn't believe him. This way, please.'

She hurries me past Customs and we walk together out of the airport and across the tarmac.

Ahead of me is a tiny yellow helicopter. A short, grizzled man of about 45 with a jutting jaw opens the door of the helicopter and motions me in. He wears a well-cut cashmere suit and looks every inch the distinguished producer. He says nothing in the way of pleasantries as he climbs in after me. I squash my suitcase behind the helicopter shaft. Mr Halmi sits with the pilot in the front.

What have I let myself in for, I wonder, as the pilot starts the motor with a violent clatter. Mr Halmi hands me a map. Still no smiles.

Then as we lift off at last he speaks, staccato, with a mid-European accent: 'We are going to fly south over the whole of Ireland. I want you to see all the locations, all the possibilities for yourself. There is no other way. That is why we go by chopper. We shoot the picture in Southern Ireland. Make Greelish Irish – George C. Scott is dying to play the part. I show you all the goddam locations. My movie will be as beautiful as David Lean's *Ryan's Daughter*, but I shoot it in six weeks instead of a goddam year, rain or shine!'

We climb to a thousand feet and sweep over green fields. Mr Halmi peers left and right. When we pass a ruined monastery, he makes the pilot swoop down and fly between the cloisters. The sheep scatter in terror. He leans out of the helicopter taking photographs. He seems unaware of the danger as he clicks away. He turns and taps me. Ahead a ruined castle, overgrown with ivy and surrounded by ancient ramparts. We fly on.

'Look!'

Two weird horns appear floating on mist over the Atlantic.

'The Holy Schellig Islands. Once there were five hundred monks here, now nothing but goddam gannets. Ten million goddam gannets.'

'This is where Hobart can make his oath to kill Koven!' I shout.

Five hours pass. The pilot says he has fuel for about another twenty minutes. Halmi spots a cascade of water pouring down a rocky mountain.

'Down low. Last picture.'

Ahead of us on the seashore is a two-storeyed mansion. As the helicopter descends, I notice four police cars speeding along below us.

We land on a lush lawn where racehorses graze. The police cars surround the helicopter. Eight uniformed men train their rifles on us. They want to know who we are. They have been chasing us the length of Ireland, thinking we're the IRA. The pilot apologises for not having logged his flight.

Mr Halmi takes a group photograph of the Garda officers posing in front of their cars with their guns. Everyone is smiling.

As we walk towards the mansion, Mr Halmi tells me that it belongs to his friend Kevin, who is the richest man in Ireland. Kevin owns two hotels, a golf course, a building firm in Cork, and a short-haul airline. He is crucial to the whole film: he knows the Minister in Dublin, who it is hoped will grant finance and facilities for shooting.

Mr Halmi pushes open the doors to an airy room with a view of the setting sun and a bar full of booze. He pours a couple of Scotches and tells me that he wants the script by the beginning of May. Impossible, I say. That's only six weeks away and the minimum a professional contract stipulates is twelve.

He groans, 'All you goddam writers are the same. You take so goddam long.' But he agrees that writing the film will be difficult.

The whisky and the setting sun give me a sudden flash of inspiration. Our farmer Greelish should have a young daughter.

'We'll call her Finola. She was born dumb and Greelish blames Koven for making her mute. She and Hobart fall in love. And there's a happy ending. As Hobart is taken away by the police for murder, she finds her voice and calls out, "Hobart come home." '

'Good,' says Mr Halmi.

'And that should be the title: "Hobart Come Home".'

'No. It will be "The Killing of Koven". Have another Scotch and call me Bob.'

As Bob and I watch the sun dip over the western Atlantic, he tells me his life story. He was in the Hungarian resistance during the war. The Nazis captured him and sentenced him to death. He was going to be shot at dawn, but he made a hole in his cell with his bare hands and escaped with an hour to spare. Then he fought the Russians. They captured him and sentenced him to death too, but again he escaped.

After the war he became a *Life* magazine photographer. He worked a lot with Bob Capa. They both loved gambling. On their way to cover the Arab–Israeli conflict in 1948, they stopped off in Paris for a long gambling game, lost their cameras, stayed to win them back, and arrived in Israel just after the ceasefire. So Capa got out of his trench and, going up to the enemy lines, threw stones at the soldiers until they started firing again. 'Capa and I started the whole goddam war up again . . . But we got our pictures!'

Now he is an American citizen. America is the greatest country in the world, American TV and movies the best in the world. He loves America. He has just made a cartoon called *Hugo the Hippo* for his friend David Picker, head of United Artists. It will be the biggest grosser of the year.

At supper I meet Kevin. I ask if we can see some Irish pubs. He says that Waterville, which is the nearest town, has been shut all day because of a wedding between the butcher's daughter and a Kerryman now living in Birmingham, but we can try another place.

The three of us set off in Kevin's chauffeur-driven Mercedes on our pub crawl.

To our surprise the wedding feast is taking place in the first pub we enter. Kevin is greeted as the squire by one and all, but there is no class consciousness. It's 'Kevin, how's the golf course?' or 'Kevin, have a chaser'. When they hear I am a writer, they all want to buy me a drink. I've never known such respect. In England, if you say you're a writer, it's assumed you're a bum who can't hold down a real job, pushes drugs and lives off Social Security. Kevin tells me that Ireland is the only country in the world which encourages foreign writers to settle TAX FREE.

Bob tries to seduce a girl. 'I'm going to see the Minister in Dublin tomorrow. Can't you spend the evening with me? Four hours? What is a quarter of a day?'

To me, he says in his Hungarian accent, now very strong, 'Oh, David, she is so beautiful . . .' Then, turning back to the girl: 'You remind me of Hedy Lamarr. No, not Hedy Lamarr . . . Who is it? I know! Ava Gardner. You are like the young Ava Gardner!'

I talk about Ireland with the publican. 'Peace will only come through love,' he tells me. 'It will never come through the gun.'

The next day I return to The Falls.

12 March 1974

Gay is furious. 'One of your home-made beer bottles has exploded right next to Luke's feet. You're going to have to stop bottling beer in the kitchen.'

3 May 1974

I fly to America for a script conference on *The Killing of Koven*. I stay with Bob Halmi in his home in Greenwich, Connecticut. Halmi wants a love scene between Hobart and Finola, Greelish's mute daughter. 'I want it sexy but not dirty . . . They lie together in a field. The rain washes over them and we can see the outline of their bodies through the rain.'

4 May 1974

Bob's house is next to the Greenwich Country Club and golf course. Stockbrokers in purple and green trousers dash round the golf course in their electric buggies. Nobody walks anywhere. In the afternoon we go there with Halmi's eldest son, Robert Junior.

'I'm hungry,' he says. He orders a sandwich, only it's more like six – cheese on the bottom, meat in the middle, pâté and tomato on top. He opens his mouth wide and sinks his teeth through all three decks. These Americans have jaws like Afghan hounds.

'I'm still hungry,' he complains, and he orders more food: a steak and a pudding of peaches, pastry and cream. He stops halfway through the steak to begin on the pudding, then finishes off the steak.

'I'm still hungry.'

When we go home, we settle down to TV in front of a huge set in the trophy room. Bob stabs the remote control every few seconds, as he shifts through twelve different channels, looking for a sports programme.

When he chances upon a silent Cecil B. DeMille religious epic, he watches for fifteen seconds, says, 'Godammit, they don't make movies like that any more', and bang, bang, switches channels again in his hunt for sport.

Halmi the Huntsman. Wild animal heads adorn the walls, among them a sweet ocelot kitten that looks alive enough to jump off its branch and curl up on your lap.

7 May 1974
The Falls

I return to find Gay very unhappy here in the country. She feels she is vegetating. She wants to joke and be with her friends in London. She can't joke with me. She has to make an effort and be a different person with me. For two years she has tried . . . She has tried to make friends down here but there is no one she can communicate with . . .

'And little Gay always has to be the centre of attention,' she says.

14 June 1974

Desperate to be with Gay and Luke, I drive to Platt's Lane. I'm determined to live with her in London and give up The Falls. Gay throws a party for me. The minute Luke has fallen asleep and Gay's mother, who was looking after him, has left, she tears off her bra and dances in her transparent dress like my Marguerite in *Camille*. Her barrister friend John Haines falls into a glazed clinch with her, his eyes closed in bliss.

I drag him off her. 'How dare you dance with my wife like that!'
He looks astonished by my odd behaviour.

2 July 1974

I finish the first draft of *The Killing of Koven* and airmail it to Halmi in America.

But writing a script is a lot easier than making my marriage work. Gay repeats that she hates the country. She wants a career of her own in London. She has been spending more and more time away, and in her absence I have been turning to the barley wine, eight bottles a day. She returns from her trips to London in a worse mood than when she left.

'God, you stink like a drunken tramp. Out of my way, sot!'

Passing each other in the narrow cottage corridor is like the manoeuvring of enemy armies. The slightest touch and she screams how much she hates me.

10 July 1974

Halmi phones. He likes the script and wants me to come to Connecticut again to work on a second draft. Gay and Luke can come too.

Gay says she'll come with me to America only if I promise not to make a fuss if she decides to leave in six months' time.

11 July 1974

A bad day with Gay. I phone Lindsay to ask his advice.

'All women are mad,' he tells me. 'Come and see my new David Storey play, *Life Class*. I'll take you both out to supper afterwards and we can moan about Malcolm, who's off to do *Caligula* for *Penthouse* for half a million dollars.'

15 July 1974

Gay says she definitely wants a divorce once we get back from America. I can think of nothing to say and my silence infuriates her. She snatches off my spectacles and hurls them to the floor. When still I say nothing, she leaves the room and reappears with a carving knife . . .

My life is saved by the telephone. Jon Voight, star of *Midnight Cowboy* and *Deliverance*, phones from Hollywood. He's been talking with his friend Lindsay Anderson, who's said a lot of nice things about me. He's heard I have a beautiful wife and child. He too has a beautiful wife and child. He wants us to come to Hollywood where we'll all live as a happy family. He wants me to write with him a modern version of *Robin Hood*. Playing Robin Hood has been his lifelong dream.

I say, 'Great!'

Jon says he'll be in London at the Dorchester on 28 July. Can we meet?

Of course . . .

25 July 1974
London

Lindsay's *Life Class* is brilliant and quite shattering. It's set in a northern art school and ends with the students gang-raping the nude model. It introduces a new actor, Frank Grimes, who is astonishing as a stupid, recessive student, spending most of the time in a state of inner comatose stillness. After supper, Lindsay gives me Howard Pyle's book of Robin Hood stories as preparation for my meeting with Jon Voight.

26 July 1974

Gay gets an American visa and puts Luke's name on her passport. Why not on mine? I ask. 'Because I'm the mother. Because I'll always be the mother. Children always go on the mother's passport.'

28 July 1974

I catch a number 2A bus to Park Lane, and skim through the rest of the Robin Hood book. It seems a little simple, to say the least. I haven't managed to form any opinion about Robin Hood. And I have even less idea when I come face to face with the star in the Dorchester lounge. All I am conscious of is Jon's height, and his amazing lips. They are like a woman's. Soft pink rosebuds.

At least he's chatty: 'We both have beautiful wives and children. We can all live together as a big happy family, just like in Robin's day, and write the script. It'll be just wonderful!'

He writes his name and Hollywood address in my address book. He adds the names of his wife and child. 'Marceline and Jamie.'

'Gay and Luke,' I reply.

'We'll all get together when you've finished with Halmi. We'll live like Robin and Marian round the camp-fire . . .' He smiles dreamily.

Maybe life round the camp-fire with the Voights will help to mend my troubled marriage, I think to myself.

O Lucky Man!

1 August 1974

I place our three suitcases on the weighing machine at the Pan-Am check-in. Suddenly Gay darts forward and snatches back two of them. What the devil?

'You'll only need one case. I repacked everything last night. All your things are in that one.' She points to the case now bobbling along the conveyor belt towards the shute. 'I won't be coming with you, and I won't be here when you get back.' For the first time in ages she speaks in a normal and sincere voice.

I'm too tired to feel angry – just worn out with the war. 'OK,' I say.

She embraces me, suddenly sobbing. I hug her, then turn to my son: 'See you soon, Luke. Look after each other.'

He stares back at me uncomprehendingly with his big soft eyes.

So I never made it with Gay to Robin's camp-fire. As I look through the aeroplane window at Ireland slipping away below, I think with relief how five years of mutual torment are over.

Halmi meets me at Kennedy Airport. He twists his car keys nervously and gives me a wretched look. 'I know all about it,' he says. 'Gay phoned me.'

'Don't worry. I feel ten years younger.'

I grin and, as we climb into his Porsche, he grins back.

'You know, I haven't been so scared since I thought the Nazis were going to shoot me. I thought you'd be all in pieces!'

'Well, it was quite a strain.'

'But you're in great shape now for *The Killing of Koven*. You've got back your goddam sanity!'

We arrive at Halmi's house in Connecticut. As we draw up in the drive, his wife, Eleanor, hurries out to meet us. 'Oh, my God, you're so brave!' She is close to tears. 'I was so looking forward to looking after your little boy.' She embraces me warmly and her two elderly poodles look on with watery eyes.

President Nixon is having a difficult time too. After dinner we settle down in front of Halmi's televisions and watch the Watergate finale. Pat and Dick walk across the White House lawn and are whisked away in a helicopter. Gerald Ford is sworn in, and America goes on . . .

Bed, at last. One thing is sure: there'll be no more women in my life.

2 *August* 1974

We walk across the golf course to the country club, pausing every now and then to let someone play a shot.

'What a crazy game!' I say, as we duck to avoid a killer golf ball.

Halmi agrees. He prefers real big game. He's just come back from safari with David Picker of United Artists. They're going to make a film together, set in Africa. He wants me to write it – after *Koven*.

We reach the clubhouse and Halmi signs me in. I wait for him to start talking about *The Killing of Koven*, but we just sit on the patio of the country club and relax in the sun. 'Isn't this the best country on earth?' he says several times.

Finally I ask him if he has any comments on the script for me.

'Just two things. It's gotta be shorter. And remember, we want a sweet love scene between the girl and boy. Sexy but not dirty. It's the first time for both of them, you know. And when the rain soaks her dress, we see she has the most gorgeous body and all that goddam kinda stuff.'

That's the end of the script conference I've crossed the Atlantic for. Halmi orders another spritzer and says I can stay in this paradise for as long as I like.

But I miss Luke terribly. It's a new kind of hell. In the afternoon I ring my agent, Judy Scott-Fox, to discover that no one knows where Gay and Luke now live. They have vanished from the face of the earth. I decide I must return at once to find Luke.

4 August 1974

A farewell supper of monster steaks. Gay has packed my Elvis Presley zoot suit. When Halmi hears I have a zoot suit, he insists I wear it, although it was intended for Hollywood parties with Gay and Jon Voight. Like Elvis I'm too fat for it. As I descend their staircase, tottering on six-inch-high fancy boots, the Halmis applaud. But I throw the damn zoot suit in their bin. It's unlucky.

' "How I never wore my zoot suit",' says Halmi. 'You should write a story about it.'

5 August 1974
Platt's Lane

The first thing I see as I enter the flat is a note on the hall table in Gay's handwriting. 'If you try to find me, you'll never see Luke again.' I ring David and Debbie Owen, who refuse to divulge her address. Next I try mutual friends Sandra and Terry, publishers of the *If . . .* and *O, Lucky Man!* screenplays. Sandra says she's promised Gay not to let me know where she is, but I can see Luke tomorrow at the Snow White nursery in Hampstead.

6 *August 1974*

Luke runs up to me. He throws his arms round my knees and holds me tightly for several minutes. He knows everything of course. We spend an hour in silent grief.

10 *August 1974*

I have more work than I know how to deal with – *Robin Hood, The Killing of Koven*, and the script Halmi wants me to write for David Picker. With my life in such a mess, I need help. Sandra and Terry suggest an amanuensis. They know just the right person . . .

15 *August 1974*

Sandra and Terry introduce me to Ginny. She wears extraordinarily tight jeans and not much else: a tiny lace camisole top reveals huge breasts, extremely slim midriff and slimmer back. She has a mass of curly blond hair, which at the time I think is dyed. She gives Terry a big hug and kiss and shakes my hand. I explain the three scripts.

'Oh, I'll manage, I'm polyvolante, I'm good at everything,' she says in a little girl voice.

The work disposed of, she discusses living arrangements. Ginny (Virginia) doesn't have a flat of her own.

'I don't believe in possessions, they're too much responsibility. When I need a place I use someone else's.'

I tell her that Platt's Lane has two huge rooms. She can have the bedroom. 'It's got a water bed and a colour television.'

'You make it sound like being a fucking au-pair,' she says. 'I must have an equal credit, half your salary and we'll share the house-keeping.'

3 *September 1974*

Ginny moves in. She is a sex-bomb, but all girls leave me cold. She's reading *The Killing of Koven* and delivers a non-stop lecture on its faults. It needs to be more gentle, and I have got everything about Ireland wrong. She sounds so convincing with her bossy 10-year-old voice that I agree to all the changes.

21 September 1974

Halmi is in London. We meet him for supper at the Dorchester. Halmi says to me, obviously impressed by Ginny, 'How can anyone be so lucky?'

He tells us about his film with Picker. It is called *Dangerfield Safari*. Dangerfield, the hero, has built up a wonderful safari park in Africa. Then one day a government minister tells him the land is needed by the people for farming. Rather than destroy his beloved animals, Dangerfield takes them on an epic drive to a sanctuary hundreds of miles away.

'I have all the animals in Africa,' says Halmi, and a film crew out there waiting, but I don't have a script. I want a script in two weeks. Drop *Koven* and write *Dangerfield Safari*.'

'Three weeks,' I say.

'OK. One in London, and then you both come to my house in Connecticut. It's going to be a goddam great movie. David Picker is with me all the way. He said that Gay leaving you at the check-in counter was the most amazing story he'd ever heard. But now I'll tell him you're fine . . .'

'Halmi thinks we're having an affair,' I say to Ginny when we get back to Platt's Lane.

'Well, we're not! Ring him up and tell him we're not.'

'That's one way of convincing him we are.'

'I don't want him thinking that.'

'Ginny, it's not important.'

She clutches her open nightdress tight around her neck.

'Do you find me strange?'

'You're a damn sight more normal than people who claim to be normal.'

'Well, you're completely wrong. I *am* strange. I'm a Peter Pan. I've never had a real life. I've never been married or had a proper affair like you. My whole life has been surreal. I can't explain . . . I think I ought to be a nun. Sometimes I think I'm a lesbian. You see, people think that just because I have an hourglass figure and can't hide it, that if I talk to them I want to fuck them, when all I want is just to be friends.'

'You can be just friends with me. That's all I want us to be. I don't want to make love ever again.' I say goodnight. She doesn't seem to have heard me. At any rate, she doesn't reply, so I go next door and get into my narrow bed with a book Halmi has written himself called *In the Wilds of Africa*. He has given it to us for research. 'The author earnestly hopes this book will add to the reader's knowledge and appreciation of our fellow creatures.' There are vivid descriptions of the wild animals, written in a simple, touching way. He refers to 'mama gorillas' and 'mama and baby hippos'. He clearly loves wild animals and makes the point over and over again that they cannot be tamed and are the victims of modern civilisation. But then how can he bear to kill them and hang their heads in his trophy hall in Connecticut? Why, if *Dangerfield Safari* means so much to him, has he set everything up, but forgotten the script? Perhaps he still hasn't grown out of his days with Capa – restarting the Arab–Israeli war for the sake of a good picture . . .

6 October 1974
The Country Club, Greenwich, Connecticut

Halmi says he wants some love interest in *Dangerfield Safari*. As Ginny and I drink our spritzers by the golf course, he tells us his idea: 'Dangerfield has built up his safari park with the help of his devoted girl-friend. They have been through everything together. But then just as Dangerfield is planning the exodus, a plane lands and a beautiful girl photographer arrives. She insists on coming on the exodus. She thinks she knows everything, but she knows nothing about Africa. She just fucks up the whole goddam thing . . .'

Ginny disagrees. 'It's not her who fucks things up. It's Dangerfield, because he's a very simple man, and hasn't realised you can't move antelope with lions . . .'

Halmi proceeds to explain with barely concealed irritation exactly how you do move antelope with lions, and suddenly I realise who his sketch of the ignorant girl photographer reminds me of – polyvolante Virginia. I sense a huge mutual antipathy.

In the evening Ginny tells me Halmi is the worst chauvinist she's ever met and she can't work in his home with its hunting trophies and TV screens everywhere you turn.

I go to Bob. 'It's not a writer's house,' I say.

'OK. I'll put you up in a hotel in Manhattan. I need that script in two weeks.'

11 *October 1974*

Halmi has booked us into the Pierre, one of the best hotels in New York – a suite for me and a large bedroom further down the corridor for Ginny.

Ginny accepts that Halmi knows more than she does about wildlife, but fights every idea we have for dealing with Dangerfield and his two women. Although I point out that by her own admission she's never had an affair or been married, she insists she knows how men and women behave. I fight her every inch of the way.

Every evening after we've finished work, we order room service – lobster salad, a bottle of white wine and three beers, all with ice. Even Ginny has to admit that Halmi is generous.

17 *October 1974*

The phone rings. It's Jon Voight. He's in the lobby and he'd like to come up for a chat. I haven't a clue how he found us, but Ginny is delighted when I tell her we're meeting the great star. As is her custom, she has taken off her clothes and has been typing up our day's work in her 40s Jane Russell bra and knickers. She pulls on a denim skirt and lights a cheroot. Voight knocks on the door and I welcome him in. He stands in silence for a few moments staring at Ginny. At last he recalls himself and says: 'I hope you guys will do *Robin*. It's been my dream ever since I first heard the story at my father's knee.'

Ginny says she loves fairy stories too, and to my relief they take a shine to each other.

The plans have changed. Voight is doing a film with Maximilian Schell in Switzerland after Christmas and wants us to work with him in the evenings after shooting, and at weekends. We will meet for a proper discussion in London on 6 January, when Jon is stopping over at the Dorchester on his way to Switzerland.

'She seems very bright,' says Voight as I escort him to the elevator.

23 *October 1974*

The script of *Dangerfield Safari* is finished with a day to spare. We can go home.

29 October 1974

Ginny is terrified of flying and holds my hand tightly as we take off. Once we are safely aloft, she brings out her pocket Scrabble set. As always she beats me by about 200 points. I remember playing with Lindsay and Alan Price when we were working on *O, Lucky Man!* Alan always beat both of us by hundreds of points. I tell Ginny she should play Alan Price. She stops the game and goes into a silent sulk. I haven't a clue why. The sulk lasts the seven-hour flight to Heathrow. Then she grips my hand and rests her head on my shoulder. Poor terrified girl, I think.

10 December 1974

The Killing of Koven is completed. It is time for a holiday. Ginny says she needs a holiday too. 'But I can't afford it.'

'I'll pay.'

'I'll pay you back after *Robin Hood*.'

I go to Wings travel agents on the Finchley Road. The only winter sun holiday available is a two-bedroom apartment in Lanzarote. It sounds perfect.

December 1974

The first week really seems perfect. We swim, race each other along the beach and go for walks in the mountains. But at the beginning of the second week Ginny says: 'I've something very important to ask. If Gay said she wanted to come back, you'd have her back for Luke's sake?' I deny it firmly, but she insists I will and sulks for three days.

I start to read a brilliant book as research for *Robin Hood – The Pursuit of the Millennium* by Norman Cohn. It's set in A.D. 1000, just before Robin's time, when the whole world confidently expected the Second Coming. It is full of peasant heroes hailed as Christ, the Warriors of the Last Days, and heretical sects who believed in anarchy and free love. Mass uprisings take place in the name of the Common Man. It's a fascinating and modern story. I suggest to Virginia that she read it. Oh no – she doesn't believe in reading books. She can do it all from her amazing brain. She's 'polyvolante'. I return to my book and she doesn't say another word all week.

On Christmas Eve at last she speaks. 'You could write *Robin Hood* on your own now, couldn't you?' It's true, and I dread the thought of taking her to Hollywood.

'I suppose so . . .'

'You don't need me any more. I've done my job. I've made you better and that's it. Wham, bam, thank you, Sam.'

'Cheer up, Ginny – it's Christmas. Tomorrow we go home.'

'Home and goodbye.'

'Oh, don't be silly. Just read the book.'

She turns away without a word and goes into her room. She emerges in her nightdress, holding out a small package. 'Your Christmas present.'

I open the package. It contains a plain silver ring.

'Put it on.'

'It fits.'

Before I can thank her, she returns to her room without a word and switches off the light.

More silence – until we're on the plane home. Thousands of feet in the air, as the tropical blue turns into winter-grey cloud, she starts to weep uncontrollably. 'Is your wife ill?' the stewardess asks me.

'Oh, it's just leaving,' says Ginny through her tears.

I put an arm round her, trying to comfort her. 'Ginny – I do want us to go on working together. Just read that book.'

'You'll have to tell me every day you want me.'

27 December 1974
Clanfield Cottage

Ma and Pa have made a big effort for Luke's access stay. There are paper chains in every room. A Christmas tree fills the hall, decorated with their collection of fragile Edwardian glass ornaments. There is a huge sack of presents for him, which he rips open in a minute.

And then the visit is over.

28 December 1974

I return Luke to Gay. We meet on neutral territory – the flat of Brian Keith, a friend of John Haines. Gay opens the door and smiles at Luke with a brittle beam.

'Hello, little fellow.'

She seems not to see me.

'Come in, David, and have a drink,' says a friendly voice. It is Brian, glass in hand. 'You look very well, David,' he says.

'He looks a damn sight too well. He's having an affair,' Gay says with an insinuating leer.

'No, Gay. I'm not. Never again.'

'Pwuff!' Gay exclaims. 'I'll have your guts for garters if you are.'

'Have a whisky,' Brian says.

'No thanks. I'm off the stuff.'

'Oh, bollocks!' Gay sneers. 'How's Jon Voight?'

'Meeting him next week.'

'God, the talent you had, and how you've wasted it!' Suddenly Gay's face screws up in rage and she screams, 'Don't do that!' Luke, who has been playing with his toy car on the glass drinks table, has knocked Brian's glass, spilling Scotch.

'Get a cloth!' Gay bellows.

'Do you always shout at him like that?'

'Of course,' Gay says serenely, 'I've got to teach him. You don't.'

'Gay, it was so lovely having Luke at Ma's. Just like old times. When can I take him there again?'

'NEVER!' she screams. She gets up suddenly, taut with fury.

'I'll never let you have him again! I should never have allowed you! I knew you'd take advantage!'

'Well, when can I see him next?'

'Never!'

Her face looms in front of me. I have to get away from her screaming.

'Happy New Year,' says Brian as I run.

Back at Platt's Lane, Ginny is at last reading *The Pursuit of the Millennium*, lying on the waterbed with Bertie on her lap.

'I've got the flu,' she smiles sweetly. 'It's so nice to see you. You're right. Jon Voight will love this.'

I tell her about Gay.

'You can have a drink if you like.' She smiles a beautiful smile. 'I've bought us a bottle of sherry. It's on the shelf in your room. I'll have one too.'

I fetch the bottle and pour us each a glass.

'Cheers!'

'Cheers!'

I say goodnight. She smiles back. 'Goodnight.'

An hour later I'm just about nodding off when Ginny enters. She stands by my head. 'Wake up, David. Everything's changed. I don't feel platonically about you any more.'

'Ginny! I'm dead from the waist down.'

'Rubbish. Sometimes I've come into your room at night and seen you.'

'I respect you too much.'

'And I respect you.'

Suddenly she lies down on the floor. 'Please come and kiss me.'

To refuse would be plain bad manners.

Minutes later Ginny gasps: 'God, this is the first orgasm of my life. It's so wonderful . . . again.'

Three hours later she finally falls asleep in my arms on the waterbed. As for me, now I'd die for her . . .

A vision of Robin

7 January 1975

We enter Jon Voight's suite at the Dorchester. Even Jon's bulk seems dwarfed by the vast room and his six-piece set of luggage, which he hasn't even opened as he's commuting between Hollywood and Munich for *The Odessa File* with Maximilian Schell.

'Max would be great for King Richard,' says Jon, kissing Virginia on the cheek.

I tell Jon about our research – the Warriors of the Last Days, the cult of the free spirit.

'That's just how I think myself. We're all on the same wavelength. That's just terrific.'

Jon says he has been thinking a lot about Robin's character. Robin is primarily a lover of women like himself. He has this beautiful girl in the camp, but all the time he wants Maid Marian. She's always at the end of dreams. But there's no hope for him. They are two different worlds.

Jon goes on for hours about sacred and profane love and Robin being primarily a dreamer and lover. I can't make head or tail of it, but Virginia keeps gasping agreement so I assume he's very clever.

'Robin wants to follow every road,' Jon says. 'That's what I feel. He's got this vitality for life! When someone asks me "Are you happy?" I say I'm the happiest person I know. I'm not looking for happiness by going out shopping. Or putting my picture in magazines. I'm happy working it out! Looking for the experiences. And there's a practical side to this too . . .' Here Jon's voice becomes low and intense as he tells us the kernel of the film. 'What's true of me is true of Robin: he always wants everything to be peaceful, everything to be wonderful, everybody to be everybody!' Virginia sighs agreement: 'Everybody to be happy!'

'Everybody to be totally free and totally happy. And when it comes down to someone saying, "Let's do this and this", he says, "No, you can't do it." Know what I mean, guys?'

'Yes,' says Virginia.

'No,' say I.

'Freedom ends here,' Jon explains to me at length. 'Without somebody to bring harmony, everybody kills everybody. And eats everybody else. And he's got this girl and he can't show open affection. I think Marian symbolises an unreal yearning.'

Jon continues to discourse on his views of love until after midnight without a break for food or drink. Finally we leave him at 3 a.m., starving and bewildered, Virginia clutching a biography of Bob Dylan, whom Jon wants to play Alan A'Dale. Film stars have stamina if nothing else.

25 January 1975

Get a long and rambling letter from Jon written in a scrawled hand on a yellow legal pad. It seems he is planning to play Hamlet, and thinks Robin Hood should be like Hamlet, always agonising over any course of action. He is to be a tortured man forced into violence. Jon has spoken to Bob Dylan, who is eager to play Alan A'Dale. He has also been in touch with Muhammad Ali, another close friend, for whom we must write a part.

10 February 1975

The script is a mess. I phone Jon in LA to suggest we come over to collaborate with him round the camp-fire in Hollywood as he'd originally suggested. He is oddly ill-tempered, perhaps because I called collect.

'What you're really trying to say, David, is the script is bad because you're having trouble with your wife. I know all about that. You've done nothing so far but provide a load of research about the pursuit of the millennium that any university lecturer could have done.'

'But your ideas about making Robin like Hamlet just don't work.'

Then we're cut off, or he hangs up. I tell Virginia what Jon said about Gay.

She is livid. 'How dare he bring up your private life! Your wife! He thinks just because he's paying us, he owns us.'

I call Jon again, but not collect. A good move.

'Hi David!' He sounds pleasant.

I'm determined not to let him start a bullshit soliloquy. I speak fast and authoritatively. 'Jon, we've got to start using our imaginations and construct real scenes. You can't impose your fantasies about Bob Dylan, Hamlet and Muhammad Ali on a totally different story.'

'So my ideas are all bullshit. That's OK by me. You'd better come over with Virginia. I'll fix it with William Morris.'

The phone rings again. It's Lindsay. 'What's the matter?' he asks.

'Just had a big set-to with Voight in Hollywood.'

'I'm very glad to hear it. Come round in an hour.'

I go round to Greencroft Gardens. I take the book he's given me to read, *Diary of a Scoundrel*, and my notes on Robin Hood. I know he'll immediately ask me what I thought of *Diary of a Scoundrel*, which I didn't much like. So I try to forestall him.

'What do you think of it?' I ask quickly.

'You're evading as usual. What do *you* think of it?'

'I think it's good TV situation comedy.'

'Well, that's not bad.'

'But what's the point of us doing it?'

'To do a play.'

'But it's nothing brilliant.'

'Well, that's the end of that. Now about Jon Voight?'

I explain the mess we're in and how we have to go to Hollywood to work with Jon.

Lindsay groans: 'Why do you always fantasise?'

'Because I'm a fantasist.'

'You are. So's he. Show me what you've done. I suppose it's bits and pieces glued together. But in ten minutes I'll help you more than ten weeks spent wasting your time in Hollywood.'

Lindsay is as good as his word. He's actually off to America himself – a lucrative college lecture tour – and then returning to direct three plays in the West End. Joe Orton's *What the Butler Saw*, Chekhov's *The Seagull*, and an amazing new play by the Twenties farceur, Ben Travers, now ninety, a sex comedy called *The Bed Before Yesterday*. And on top of this he wanted to do *Diary of a Scoundrel*. Where does he get his energy from?

William Morris is in turmoil – no one can finalise the contract or organise the trip. My agent, Judy Scott-Fox, has left the London office to become head of the agency in Hollywood. Her place here has been filled by a Hollywood agent, Steve Kennis. Both Kennis and Judy seem to have lost their way in the switch. And Jon Voight, being a star used to having every door opened for him, can't be expected to organise himself, let alone book air tickets.

5 March 1975

Steve Kennis phones. 'Get packing, pals! You're leaving for Hollywood tomorrow. I had a long talk with Judy in Los Angeles last night. We talked about a lotta details, David, at great length, but the baseline is you're staying in a hotel. You do your own cooking and get thirty dollars a day. You'll need a car – that's eight dollars a day and it's eight cents a mile. See, David, the hotel you're staying at in Hollywood, you don't have them in England – you buy your own food and cook yourself. No restaurants.'

When I explain the arrangements to Virginia, she explodes: 'So I've got to do half the fucking work, and cook!'

I go to say goodbye to Lindsay. He greets me at his entrance wearing pyjamas, shaving foam all over his face. He's just got back from his lecture tour of America.

'Very weird, but I liked it. You know that part of me that likes telling people what they ought to think. There's a spark there that there isn't here.' We enter his living room. 'Listen to this record,' he says. It's a 1940s Hollywood collection of stars singing numbers from MGM musicals. Humphrey Bogart to Anne Sheridan. 'Do you know it?'

'Yes.'

'Liar.'

'It's Anne Sheridan,' I say, reading the label.

'Well, anyway, listen to it while I get dressed.'

Lindsay returns and we both listen in silence to Anne Sheridan singing of love. He lifts the dust-coated plastic cover of his hi-fi and turns off the music.

'Well, how much a day is Voight paying you for expenses?'

'Thirty dollars.'

'Thirty dollars! Thirty dollars a day for the two of you and you have to pay for a car! And you agreed?'

I nod.

'Well, it's just an example of how you let them treat you. It's just an example that Voight doesn't take it seriously. No professional writer gets fifteen dollars a day. No! I can't let you go on fifteen dollars a day! You won't have enough to buy a postage stamp. Ring up Steve Kennis and say you want sixty dollars a day, and a car as and when you need it. Now!'

'But it's lunchtime. He'll be out.'

'NOW! Leave a message with his secretary. If you don't ring and demand sixty dollars a day I'll never respect you again. Ring. Demand it. Voight will cave in. He's a very rich man. If you demand something, they give it to you. If you don't, they don't. That's Hollywood.'

I ring Steve Kennis's office. He is out at a meeting. I speak to his secretary: 'Please tell Mr Kennis that my expenses must be sixty dollars a day.' I add, 'It's pointless to be spending eight dollars a day on a car when we won't need it every day.'

I put the phone down.

Lindsay groans. 'You're so wet – all that blather explaining about a car. You should have said you want a car provided as and when you need it.'

'Look, Lindsay, it's all very well for you to be a prima donna – you've got a fantastic reputation and can get away with it.'

'So've you.'

'I haven't.'

'You've got a unique reputation. You just don't use it.'

We discuss making another film with our old friend Malcolm McDowell, when we've finished all our commitments. A sensible creative talk unlike the meanderings with crazy Jon Voight.

I return home convinced of my unique reputation, only to be sadly disillusioned. Kennis rings to say he daren't ask for sixty dollars. It's no way possible. Thirty dollars a day is ample. Basics are cheap out there.

6 March 1975
Los Angeles, 3 p.m.

Jon Voight meets us at the baggage checkout, wearing an old green parka, jeans and scuffed shoes. A kiss for Virginia, an unnaturally natural brotherly arm round the shoulder for me. A swarthy young man called Jim Gonzales loads our luggage into a Cadillac.

We drive to the Century Wilshire Hotel, our new home. The freeway to Hollywood is different from those in other big American cities. There are palm trees on high banks, and huge coloured posters advertising the latest movies. It is sleeting. Jon and Virginia are silent, both in some weird sulk. I make small talk with Jim Gonzales. His car is the quietest I've ever been in – you literally can't hear the engine.

'That's why I keep it. Best model Cadillac ever produced.'

I comment on the sleet.

'Coldest spring ever recorded in Hollywood. A freak.'

Silence.

It's hardly Robin Hood round the camp-fire.

At the Century Wilshire Hotel we inspect our quarters. A tiny bedroom filled with a double bed, a small living room with a kitchenette off. Virginia looks appalled.

Jon sees her look. 'Judy made the booking,' he mutters, embarrassed.

The hotel's president and owner, Mr Shulman, who has escorted us to our suite, tries to make the best of it.

'Look at the wallpaper, look at the carpeting. Isn't it beautiful? Isn't this a beautiful room?' He loves all his rooms like children.

It's not only poky but it's on the ground floor, next to Wilshire Boulevard outside.

'It's a bit noisy,' I whisper to Jon. 'The Boulevard . . .'

'It's a bit noisy for writers. The Boulevard . . .' Jon says to the President.

'I'd like a separate bedroom of my own,' Virginia says, in command.

'We have an absolutely beautiful executive suite on the third floor. It's wonderful,' says the President.

We take the tiny lift to the third floor and enter a vast, vast suite.

'Isn't this beautiful? Isn't this really something? Brand new carpeting! New linoleum in the kitchen!' enthuses the President.

He opens a second bedroom door off the large living room to reveal a huge bed. 'The King's bed!' he says.

'Or the Queen's!' says Virginia.

I say we'll take it and the President leaves us alone. God knows what it will cost Jon, but serve him right. He's a rich Hollywood star. He takes his revenge. Without any offer of a respite, food or drink, he sits down in the living room and starts to hector us about *Robin*.

'I want the story to be about truth, right and wrong, faith, life and death. I'm going to direct it like Ingmar Bergman. And I'll do all the stunts that Errol Flynn did in his *Robin Hood*' – suddenly he grins and shouts – 'but I'll do them a hundred times better! I want everything to be in this movie – Jesus Christ, love, little children – know what I mean?'

Virginia gives an almighty yawn that not even Jon can misconstrue.

'She's tired,' says Jim Gonzales.

'Well, I have been on the go for twenty-one hours.'

Jim gives us each one hundred and fifteen dollars – our week's expenses.

I query it. 'Will it be enough to live on – to eat out?'

'I don't want you eating out,' Jon says. 'It's very expensive eating out in Beverly Hills and Hollywood. I don't want you getting out of the hotel too much. You can eat here. Save time.' And with our allowance settled, he leaves. No sisterly kiss or brotherly hug. He'll be around on Monday to continue the script conference. We can have Sunday off.

Hungry and thirsty, we explore our beautiful suite's kitchen. Nothing. Not even coffee or salt. All the cupboards are bare.

President Shulman is at the reception desk in the empty lobby, acting as telephonist and clerk. There's a wonderful supermarket four blocks away, he tells us. Sells everything. Open till midnight. It's opposite Alice's Restaurant, a beautiful place. We'll love Alice's Restaurant. Everyone goes there. He speaks with the innocent enthusiasm for everything that only Americans have.

As Virginia and I walk back through the sleet, laden with big soggy brown paper bags containing bread, butter, milk, coffee, tea, oranges, apples, cheese, cold ham, mineral water, sauces, eggs, cooking oil, sugar, Virginia mutters, 'That Jon Voight could at least have driven us to the supermarket in that Cadillac. Twenty-one hours of travelling, and now a damned shopping expedition on top of three hours of him. If this is real life in Hollywood . . .' She cooks scrambled eggs, then flops asleep on the King's bed without taking off her clothes.

8 March 1975
Sunday

I wake up in my room at 6 a.m. Sun is streaming through the

window. A blue dawn. I'll use my unique reputation in Hollywood. I'll tame Jon. *Robin Hood* will be a masterpiece.

9 March 1975
Monday morning

Jon arrives on the dot of nine. Virginia and I take notes as he imparts his wisdom.

'The really terrific thing about Robin is his use of violence! It's always right. Never wrong. I was talking to Muhammad Ali about it – great guy – and he says he's so pent up before a fight it's like an orgasm. He just has to fight. It's just natural. In the same way everything I do is natural. I'm like Muhammad – we're always both instinctively right.'

Jon continues to lecture us until lunchtime, when Virginia asks him if he'd like something to eat.

'Terrific. What have you got?'

'I can make you a sandwich. Ham? Cheese?'

'Ham, please.'

Presented with food, Jon stops talking and eats with equal concentration. When he's gulped down his first round, Virginia asks him if he'd like another. Yes, please. In half an hour he goes through our entire stock of bread, cheese and ham. Full up, he resumes his monologue. Robin meets King Richard on the way to the Crusades. He loves the King and regards him as another Jesus. But also realises that his own duty lies not in the Holy Land, but saving his people in his own forest.

'Great,' I say, seeing the first possible scene. I should have kept my mouth shut because I inspire him to yet another soliloquy.

'Think of the other side of Robin – the Robin who loves everybody. I'll tell you a story . . .' He grins boyishly, intimately. 'I once asked my father what do you really want out of life? My father answered' – Jon's voice booms – ' "A million dollars, boy!" My father always told me, "You've got to earn a million dollars." He grew up in the Depression. Was poor most of his life. He wanted a million dollars. A million bucks were just words to him.'

Jon is the jovial patriarch. ' "Get the money, boy! Get the loot. Take any kind of goddam movie – make a million bucks!" A nice man. A very romantic and beautiful person. He always used to say, "Look at the flowers! Look at the trees! Look at the birds!" So I said to my father, "If I gave you a million bucks, what would you do with it?" "I'd go down to the Rolls Royce dealer at White Plains and buy a Rolls for you and Barry" – Barry's my brother – "and a chauffeur and send it wherever you were!" It was so goddam stupid – I don't even want a Rolls and certainly not a chauffeur – but it was so *lovely.*'

Jon the actor lowers his voice to a whisper, commanding we listen good. His eyes shine. He grips Virginia's hand. 'All he wanted to do was make me happy. All he was saying was "I love you." And that's all Robin's saying: "I love you." He loves everybody.'

And so on till supper time when he says he must be getting back to his family for supper. Jon has eaten us out of house and home. We go to the supermarket to replenish our stock of bread, cheese, ham and apples. One thing the supermarket doesn't stock is Virginia's favourite food, Marmite. They've never heard of it. 'What a place,' says Virginia. To ease her Hollywood-inspired tension I suggest a glass of wine at Alice's Restaurant. To my surprise she concurs.

This Alice's Restaurant isn't in the least like the folk-singer's den in the movie *Alice's Restaurant.* They've just borrowed the name. It's Ivy League, spotless, with a bow-tied young barman serving at the extra-long bar. I order red wine and beer. Virginia discusses Jon and our predicament.

'I really don't know what we're here for. He doesn't want original writers – only secretaries. Still if that's what he wants – but he always seems to be humiliating me.'

'That's just being a star. He can't help it.'

The barman has overheard our conversation. He tells us he wrote a script once. But nothing happened, and now he's just a Hollywood barman.

I puff on my briar. Virginia puffs on her gypsy clay pipe. A young light-skinned black man, dressed in Harvard grey, leans across Virginia to poke a biscuit into the cheese dip. He exclaims: 'Man, this is hot stuff! This really is hot stuff. What stuff are you smoking?'

'Just tobacco,' says Virginia.

'Tonight I'm going home to have some more cheese and fries. I'll dream some dreams tonight, huh?'

He giggles: 'I'll sure have some wild dreams of you tonight, ma'am.' He leans across to Virginia: 'Excuse me for intruding – are you New Zealanders?'

'English,' smiles Virginia, pleased at the flattery.

'Man, that's terrific! England. Chelsea. Liverpool. Windsor Castle. Those old places! I'm an anglophile. I always buy English.

Had five English cars. Got a '65 Triumph Herald right now. 1965! And does she just go! Soon as I can raise $500 I'm going to England to let it all hang out. I'm going to walk through Windsor Castle – me and a big glass of brandy! I'm half-English. My mother's from Yorkshire. I know I look like a goddam Egyptian but I'm half-English. An orphan. Got my papers five years ago. This little Triumph Herald of mine – can she go! Think I'll take her to England. That'd be something – an English Herald with Californian number plates. Man, I can't wait till I land at Heathrow in the fog with it all hanging out. Maybe I'll go to Japan first.'

We wish him well. He's insane, but no more so than anyone else here.

13 March 1975

Jon comes round to give us yet another dose of his philosophy of love and violence. And to eat. As he swallows his fourth round of ham, plus beer and apples, Virginia suddenly asks him, 'What do you mean by Robin loves everybody?'

Jon needs no encouragement. 'Robin loves all the children in the camp, and all the women!'

'How can he love all the women if he also loves Marian?'

'Don't be puritanical about this, Virginia. I love all women. You too, Virginia.'

This is too much even for me, who has been writing down every pearl of madness for the past six days. I get to my feet. 'Jon, all we've heard from you for days has been theory! Your theory. Do you realise we haven't written one single scene, not even discussed structure? Not had a concrete idea. It's all been waffle!' Lindsay would have been proud of me just then.

Virginia echoes my words.

Jon puts down his sandwich, aghast. 'Christ, you guys are scary!'

He leaves us, saying we can work on the scenes and concrete ideas by ourselves for a week. He's got this goddam stupid job – presenting an Oscar.

After he's left, Virginia gives vent to her hatred for Jon. He talks about loving everybody, but is chauvinist and insensitive, she says. I try to explain to her that to survive in Hollywood you have to be ruthless. Jon is a survivor.

15 March 1975

We complete a concrete plot of *Robin Hood*, but don't include any of Jon's ideas. There will be trouble if ever he turns up again. I phone Judy Scott-Fox to tell her we can't afford to eat, let alone feed the hungry bear, on thirty dollars a day. Typically she is out of town. I leave a message.

6 April 1975

Jon rings to say he's coming over, but can only stay for two minutes. He arrives, genuinely suffering. He has a chauffeur-driven Rolls waiting outside. Shit, this isn't him! he confides. Why did he agree to present an Oscar?

'I hate the ceremony. I'll have to wear a dinner jacket and bow-tie. Shit! Why did I say I'd do it?' Should he pull out now?

'Yes,' I say.

Then he witters on about his responsibilities to the Hollywood community, until Virginia interrupts him.

'Jon, I hate to say this, but you've been here for an hour. Your Rolls and chauffeur are waiting. And the others.'

'Shit – me in a bow-tie!'

He goes.

7 April 1975

Watching the Oscars on TV really cheers us up. As the famous guests arrive, I point out my old friend, Michael Medwin, escorting Lauren Bacall. Then, after a lot of song and dance, Bob Hope announces: 'To present the Oscar for best art direction – Raquel Welch and Jon Voight.'

Jon looks astonishingly small and neat in his bow-tie and DJ. Raquel Welch is beautiful, sophisticated and for once not décolletée.

Finally Bob Hope introduces Ingrid Bergman, who announces a special Oscar for Jean Renoir. 'Jean Renoir!' she says with unusual passion, 'A god in the cinema, the founder and father of modern cinema, a force for life in everything he touches! A god and a poet!' The dying, frail Renoir receives his final triumph. When young I saw his films over and over. How many people today have seen *La Grande Illusion* or *La Règle du Jeu*? Truly I was fortunate.

8 April 1975

Jon has recovered his height since last night's ceremony. He turns up in a scruffy anorak with a book about Jean Renoir poking out of his pocket. He shares with us his latest thoughts on Robin Hood.

'Robin is a force for life. I don't see him so much as violent. There are lots of children in the camp, and Robin's a founding father to them. My wife's having another baby – and maybe Robin has this girl in the camp who's having his child. I'll call her Delphina. Delphina knows lots of weird magic potions that cure everybody, all the outlaws, but after she's had Robin's child she falls ill, and her potions that cure everybody else – she saves Robin – won't cure her. She dies. And Robin gives it all such simple poetry. And Robin, being a founding father to them all, he's like a god and a poet . . .' And so he continues until lunch. He chews like a hog, without talking, then leaves us to digest his wisdom.

Virginia bursts into tears. She hates Jon Voight, and she can't stand another trip to the supermarket to stock up. I phone Judy Scott-Fox to demand more expenses. Her assistant says she's just slipped out of the office. Michael Medwin calls out of the blue. Would Virginia and I like to have drinks with him at the Beverly Hills Polo Lounge? Would we not? Virginia cheers up. At last the fabled Hollywood of legend.

9 April 1975

Entry to the Polo Lounge isn't easy, even for invited guests. Virginia and I are made to wait outside the polished wood and bronze doors while our credentials are checked. Luckily the weather has turned warm and balmy. The portals open at last, and Michael Medwin escorts us to a small round table. Next to us sit a starlet in a tiny black cocktail dress, Michael Parkinson in his habitual suit, and Terence Stamp, looking spaced out. No one makes any conversation. No one seems happy. I look round. The place is oddly small. Then it occurs to me that this isn't the real Polo Lounge – only the poor Brits' annexe. No sign of any real stars – Warren Beatty, Lauren Bacall, Robert de Niro or Robert Redford. Perhaps real stars don't come to the Polo Lounge – only out-of-work actors like poor old Terence Stamp.

The starlet next to me starts to make advances. She has a boy-friend back in England, a rich Rolls Royce dealer, but she's left him standing at Land's End waiting for her, while she makes out in Hollywood. She drops a hand to my thigh. Where do I hang out?

Virginia amuses the poor Brits with a shaggy dog story about a health farm she once went to. An old lady brought her sick parrot to the farm to try to cure it. The old lady died there of a heart attack and the parrot flourished. It took over the farm, disciplining the patients with the loud voice of command it learnt from the nurses. Virginia imitates the parrot giving diet and exercise instructions. Under this parrot's leadership the health farm flourished and is now the most successful in Europe. Everyone laughs. At least the Polo Lounge has one star that evening.

10 April 1975

Summer has arrived! A hot warm dawn. Virginia jumps into the swimming pool, in a joyous mood after her success last night at the Polo Lounge. I dive in after her. We're both good swimmers and race each other, length after length, enjoying the exercise and the quiet togetherness. Suddenly Virginia squeals. I look up: Jon Voight, dressed in an old flak jacket, has climbed the outside fire escape to the third floor and is peering down at us enigmatically. He has obviously been watching us together in the pool for some time. Virginia vanishes back into the hotel. I call Jon down and sit him by the water. I could happily drown him for spying on us in that sneaky way, destroying a brief moment of happiness. I decide it's time to give him some of his own medicine.

'I don't agree with your idea, Jon, that Robin loves two women, the witch Delphina and the princess, Marian.'

He starts to shout. 'Hell, I've got a wife, but I want to fuck a hundred women!'

I say, quietly, but with authority, 'I don't want to write a film about your marital problems.'

Jon yells, 'Shit! I didn't say that! I don't have a marital problem!'

'Well, I understand that you want Robin to be like a god. But I disagree with you. It's not my view.'

A long silence.

Then Jon says very quietly, 'Do you want to quit?'

At that very second Virginia appears and before I can say 'Yes!' she replies in my stead: 'No! It's not a question of quitting! We are professionals. Three people can't have identical dreams and fantasies. But we can act as a catalyst for you – by listening to you talking and responding to your beautiful ideas.'

I think, What incredible timing. That girl is gold. Later, when we are alone, I say to her, 'You must have been listening.'

'No,' she replies. 'I heard him say, "Do you want to quit?" and I remembered your story about Seth Holt. How de Laurentiis tried to get him to resign when he was directing *Diabolik*, and Seth kept saying: "Never resign. Always get fired. That way you get paid your money." Did I do the right thing?'

'You were brilliant.'

Later that evening Jon phones: 'I think I could write the whole thing by myself. You guys stick around to help me on the history.'

17 April 1975

An agent phones from ICM. A Harry Uffland. Could we meet? I suggest Alice's Restaurant. ICM are William Morris's chief rivals in Hollywood.

Harry Uffland, young and dressed in a pale-grey Ivy League suit, enters Alice's Restaurant, where I'm already seated. 'What a nice place, and I never knew it existed,' he says as we sit at a quiet table which features a built-in video war game. Harry Uffland shows me a copy of *Film Quarterly*. Robert de Niro is on the cover. He won an Oscar for Coppola's *The Godfather*. Harry manages him, and also represents Martin Scorsese. He'd like to manage me. Fed up with not hearing from Judy Scott-Fox and for the dirty one-room booking last month, I say fine.

Martin Scorsese wants me to write a musical about Shelley and Byron. I say, fine, so long as I can work with my co-writer Virginia. Fine. Scorsese will be at the Edinburgh Film Festival in August. ICM has an agent in London who'll arrange everything – Otis Skinner Blodgett. Again I say, fine. Martin Scorsese is a great fan of *O, Lucky Man!* He's seen it five times. At present he's shooting with Robert de Niro in New York, but he wants to go from his very streetwise modern films to something classical, romantic. De Niro will play Byron. Great casting, eh?

Harry tells me that, in homage to *If . . .* and *O, Lucky Man!*, Scorsese has named his hero in *Taxi Driver* 'Travis' – Malcolm McDowell's name in both films. I tell Harry there's something magical in that name. Malcolm will be called Mick Travis again in my next film with Lindsay Anderson. The name is a real one – the hero at my prep school who could pee the furthest and was always getting flogged. And so I join ICM and quit William Morris.

When I tell Virginia about changing my agent and doing the new movie with Scorsese, she just bursts into tears. She wants to go home. She's going mad here in Hollywood. She hasn't had her period. She is terrified that she's pregnant.

Then she cheers up. *Carry on Doctor* is on TV. These corny *Carry On* films, which we so despise in England, are regarded as sophisticated high comedy here in America. Virginia laughs and smiles at those wonderful British faces – Kenneth Williams, Barbara Windsor, Sid James . . . Home still exists.

Virginia keeps her good humour even when Jon Voight rings to confide ingenuously, 'Writing's damn difficult. I can't write the script. I really need you guys.'

He's arranged for us to see the original Errol Flynn version of *Robin Hood* tomorrow at Warners' studio. Seeing this, he thinks, will put us all on the same wavelength. We must make a new start. He's got special permission to view the only copy of the film in existence – it's an old inflammable nitrate print and kept in a guarded vault. Isn't that great?! He'll pick us up tomorrow at ten.

18 April 1975

Jon drives us to his home where we are to meet the family and all go on to Burbank. 'Nice car, Jon,' I say to fill the silence as he drives us in a Mercedes 250 sports car.

'Oh, it's not mine. It's my wife's. Marceline's. I bought it for her birthday.'

Jon's home in South Roxbury Drive, Hollywood, is not at all like a star's home. It's in a grey granite apartment block with a pot-holed drive. Jon's wife, Marceline, is 'getting herself ready', so Jon sits us down in the living room. The room is overflowing with dolls – stuffed dolls, Victorian dolls, Edwardian dolls, Dutch dolls, animal dolls, giant dolls, dwarf dolls, dolls of every age and race – all I suppose for his 2-year-old son Jamie, who is nowhere to be seen. Jon sits among the dolls, looking his dreamy winsome self: 'I do appreciate what you guys have done on *Robin* – we'll be a great team after seeing this picture! You know, I've never seen it before.'

As we reach Warners' Burbank studios, we see a mile-long queue of boys, all wearing Jewish caps. Barbra Streisand is directing her first movie here. She's put out a casting call for a Jewish boy who wants to be a star. Every boy in LA has turned up, hoping. There are black boys with Jewish caps, Chinese boys with Jewish caps, blond American boys with Jewish caps, Mexican boys with Jewish caps, even a few Jewish-looking boys with Jewish caps. They all want to be movie stars. If only they knew the horrible truth. Perhaps they are already learning the number one torment. Waiting. Endless waiting.

We sit in a row in the old viewing theatre. Jon is like a kid at a baseball game. He cheers and roars and hoots at Errol Flynn's every swashbuckling leap and adventure. Sipping margaritas in the studio bar afterwards, he says, 'That's exactly how I want it. I want everything of that movie in mine. I want glamour!'

We've had enough, we want to go home. But if we break our contract, we won't get paid, Virginia points out. I tell her to leave everything to me. Tomorrow when he turns up, I'll get us out of this mess.

19 April 1975
Century Wilshire

'Sit quiet at the far end of the table. Trust me,' I tell Virginia.

I pull out the sleeves to the mahogany table and make three coffees. When Jon arrives, smiling his dreamy smile, I sit him down and stand at the head of the table with my legal pad, as if chairing the board. I announce that we've got to have our first professional script conference.

'Can't wait,' breathes Jon uncertainly.

I don't give him time to think. 'Jon, we don't understand the story. Can you give us a recap?'

'Sure. It's about truth, love, poetry, belief, faith, love, magic and dreams – and above all heroes! What does a hero mean? Life and death – he has all the power. Got it, guys?'

'No,' I say, very matter of fact, 'we still don't understand it. It's all theoretical. Can you be specific, Jon?' (Being specific is a dictum of Lindsay Anderson's, the master.)

'Well, Robin's a dreamer! I'll tell you what I mean. He's got a quality that gives death meaning to the dying. I have it too! It sounds crazy, but I can cure people! When someone's dying of cancer, I tell them life's stopped being all defused and messy, life's being refined down to their fingertips!' Jon raises his large right hand and bends his little finger, gazing intently at it, like a pussy cat.

'When I talk to them they see life being refined into their little fingertip – like no one else can see it. I tell them death is a privilege.

And Jesus – It's crazy! It's bullshit! – but I really believe it when I tell them!'

He looks at us both like a saint. 'I don't know how I do it. Where I get it from. But it's an amazing quality. I have it and Robin has it . . .' Jon drops his voice to a dramatic whisper. 'He and I give meaning to the dying. He's holy.'

Jon smiles broadly and gulps his coffee, pleased with his specifics.

'He sounds more like a priest to me,' I say, my hook baited. 'I prefer the simple, swashbuckling Errol Flynn.'

'But I'm more than that!' Jon shouts. 'I *am* like a priest! I believe we're all like priests if we want to be! I believe I know everything about you, David, Virginia, and you know everything about me. We're all fucking priests! And like me, Robin lets everyone share his priesthood, his dreams!'

'So you want him to be primarily a priest and a dreamer?' I ask, casting the rod.

'He's primarily that because that's the greatest quality he can give. I'm the happiest person I know because I'm a priest and a dreamer. And Robin lives his dreams: he loves the girl in the camp, the beautiful witch Delphina, and he loves Maid Marian. He's always looking for dreams, experience.'

Firmly I tell Jon that if Robin loves two women at the same time this will ruin the purity of the legend. 'I respect that you want Robin to be a dreamer and a priest' – I pause, sip my coffee as if I am completely in charge, while Virginia just stares at her legal pad – 'but I fundamentally disagree with you about the nature of Robin Hood, and so does Virginia. I think you're going to ruin the original true hero.'

There is a desperately long silence. No one moves. Finally Jon says: 'I guess I should find myself some other writers.'

'Yes . . .'

15 May 1975
Platt's Lane

Virginia has her period at last. It was a phantom pregnancy brought on by the stress of Jon Voight. Like the phantom Robin Hood the baby never existed. She's ecstatic. I'm stricken. I would have loved her child.

17 May 1975
The Spaniards Inn, Hampstead

I meet my new agent at ICM, Otis Skinner Blodgett, an American. He looks more like a nineteenth-century clergyman than an agent. He has a flaming red beard, pince-nez and an old-fashioned, perfectly tailored three-piece suit with a gold watch-chain. He is an anglophile refugee from Hollywood. He grew up there but hates it.

'I tell you, David, there are monsters in Hollywood not even you could invent.'

I explain to him I'm going to take six months off just to be together with Virginia at the Falls.

'That's fine, but you're to meet what's his name – Martin Scorsese – about his Shelley musical, after – what's it called – *Taxi Driver* – has premiered at the Edinburgh Festival.'

I like Otis and his gold watch-chain, and in the evening phone my ex-agent, Judy Scott-Fox, to tell her I'm leaving. She's upset and immediately offers me $50,000 for five weeks' work rewriting the script of *Voyage of the Damned*.

'And your friend Jon Voight is starring,' she chirrups. Fifty thousand dollars for five weeks' work is big money, more than any English writer has ever been offered. Tempting. Damned tempting . . .

3 June 1978

I read *Voyage of the Damned*. It's a true story about a shipload of German Jews whom Goebbels and Hitler release before the war as a propaganda gesture. Only the Jews don't make it. I'd hate to make big money out of the world's greatest horror, and turn the film down.

The rewrite is rubbish and Voight doesn't star. Malcolm McDowell isn't so fussy and plays a steward.

Summer 1975
The Falls

Virginia and I are cut off from the real world. We make love all day. Our life is an idyll. When we're not making love, Virginia paints rainbows all over the cottage and I learn to slope-soar my model glider, the Cormorano, on the Malvern Hills.

From the highest point on the Malvern Hills you look over land which is flat all the way to the Urals two thousand miles away. People come from all over England to soar their models thousands of feet in the rising air currents. I meet a fighter pilot who tells me how much he hates being in his jet. The magic of flying is completely lost. But here his dreams of flight come true. Another model glider friend works in the Government's nuclear bunker 5,000 feet under Malvern. Every evening he sends his glider as high as he can into the skies.

25 August 1975
The Malvern Hills

I'm alone, lying on my back, watching the Cormorano circle up and up into the sun. Everything becomes hushed. The birds and grass-hoppers are silent. Then I hear my name being called from the sky. The sun turns black. Shrieking, discordant sounds batter my ears. Something dreadful has happened to Ginny. The glider can fly away. I race home, petrified.

But there she is, completely safe, finishing off a rainbow on the terrace. She's especially happy because her two old friends Lorna and Angelo are coming. They saved her when she was living a sad life in Florence. They're bringing with them their little baby.

'I never knew I'd find what I've always been looking for here,' Virginia says. 'We'll get married and have a baby too.'

Our guests arrive at midnight. They greet Virginia like a long-lost child with endless fondling and kissing. They talk Italian into the small hours and ignore me completely. When Virginia and I finally get to bed, for the first time we don't make love or sleep in each other's arms.

26 August 1975

Lorna and Angelo go horse-riding with Virginia. I look after the baby. She plays with me, clutching my fingers just like Luke used to. A longing overcomes me. I want Luke now, here, with Virginia.

I call Gay and congratulate her on her wedding to John Haines. Then I make my request.

'Let him stay with an unknown woman! In a house he doesn't even know! Never!'

'But he was brought up here. And I've known Virginia for a year. Please, Gay – you haven't let me see him for months . . .'

'I'll never let you have him, David. Not for a single night! Never! You don't care about him. All you want to do is irritate me. You're not fit to be a father! And I'm starting new proceedings. John is going to adopt Luke. He's got such a generous heart and Luke loves him, calls him "Daddy".'

'Gay – I've father's rights!'

'Father's rights? Pffuf! Luke doesn't even know who you are!'

'Please, for the love of God!'

'My lawyers will be in touch about the adoption.'

She hangs up. I redial, but the phone is off the hook. The iron goes out of me. I wander into the garden weeping. And there in front of me are Virginia and her friends. I can't stop crying and through my tears tell them about Luke. But they don't want to listen. They wander off with their horses. Virginia too. She has turned to ice.

I wait long hours with the baby. When at last they return, they talk excitedly in Italian while I make dinner and wait on them like a servant. Angelo explains he's had the most wonderful day in his life. He was photographing the planes at the nearby aerodrome when a rebuilt Spitfire crashed. 'Pilot nearly killed!' But he got some wonderful pictures of Lorna posing sexily on the wreckage. 'Not so often a crashed Spitfire and a beautiful girl. *Il Tempo* will buy them.' But when he tries to rewind the film, he discovers he forgot to put one in. He starts to cry. Virginia whispers consolingly into Angelo's ear, like a lover. After dinner she tells me it's over. She says she feels dead inside. She's leaving with her friends in the morning and I must sleep in the caravan tonight.

It's not happening, of course. Tomorrow I'll wake up to real life. Virginia and I are meeting Martin Scorsese in three weeks. We're going to write a film . . .

27 August 1975

I awake in the caravan. Outside I see a silent procession make its way to Angelo's car. They seem to be in a trance like the figures in *The Seventh Seal* possessed by the devil.

Absurdly I shout, 'Cheerio. Drive safely.' Virginia doesn't look back.

The thermometer in the kitchen reads 100 degrees. As I tip Virginia's pots of rainbow paint into the bin, hundreds of bluebottles swarm around me. I lift the lid again: dead fish and baby shit. They must have been chucking it in the whole time. I feel so ill. I want to be dead. I drive like an automaton to the Radcliffe Hospital in Oxford. I explain to a doctor in Casualty that I'm researching a film.

'My young hero is dying of a strange disease. What's the most tragic disease you can die from?'

'What are your hero's symptoms?'

'He can't eat, he's wasting away. Yet he doesn't feel hungry.'

'Oh, that's a classic. Misthena Gravis. Young people only. It's beautiful. It takes two years.'

I return to Platt's Lane, close all the curtains and prepare to spend the next two years dying from Misthena Gravis. I've got it, all right. I don't feel hungry at all.

25 September 1975

A violent banging on the front door. I try to ignore it, but it goes on and on until I answer. And there stands an old friend, Nigel Mallinson, whom I haven't seen for years.

'Christ! What's happened to you? You're a skeleton!'

I explain about Virginia and Luke and Misthena Gravis.

'I'm taking over,' he says, hugging me close. 'First I'll buy you some Guinness. There's nothing more nourishing. Then you're going to ring Scorsese in Edinburgh and fix up a meeting. And then you're coming to live with me and my wife.'

Scorsese sounds incoherent. I make out that he's very ill, but he'll see me in three days at the Dorchester.

28 September 1975
The Dorchester Hotel

I arrive at Scorsese's suite to find two tough young New York Italians and a scrawny, half-naked blonde. Martin's still sleeping, the blonde tells me. Shooting *Taxi Driver* has drained him. It turns out that the idea for the Shelley musical is hers. I tell her what I know about Shelley. I explain the theory of evil which dominated his life.

'He believed evil is contagious. If you have evil done to you, you pass it on to someone else. You have to commit evil in turn. There is no escape. Shelley's first game as a child was to pretend to be living in hell.'

The blonde thinks Martin will love this. A long wait while she dances up and down the room. Eventually a little man, bare-footed, with a week's growth of beard, appears and slumps in a chair. This is the great Martin Scorsese. I repeat what I said about Shelley and evil, but he doesn't seem to be listening. I realise he's comatose and take my leave.

29 September 1975
Platt's Lane

The two tough Italians turn up and say Martin wants all my notes on Shelley and Byron. I give them everything, even essays I wrote as a schoolboy. They are gone before I can get them to ask Martin to call me. Then all the strength goes out of me . . .

. . . the next thing I know Nigel is carrying me into a large, plush room. Scorsese's suite? A thin man tells me to take off my clothes and sit on a bench. He taps my knees. My only reflex is to look at Nigel and weep.

The thin man tells me I'm suffering from the eighteenth-century illness of melancholia and must pull myself together.

'What's melancholia?'

'Feeling too much. Very unhealthy. But I'll cure you. I must point out my fees are £30 a session. It's vital to be clear about money.'

And he commits me to the Greenways clinic in Hampstead. He arrives for his first session shrieking and melancholic himself. His car's been stolen and in it his address book with all his clients' names. He can't work without it and he's terrified that he might be blackmailed. He knows so many important people's secrets. As he's got more important things to do, he tells me to write down my dreams and give him a cheque for £30. I refuse and call him the Whore of Harley Street. He bangs his walking stick violently, says I'll stay in this clinic till I pay, and rushes out in a rage.

His rage and greed cure me. I haven't lost my address book and in it is a very special name. Monika Escott. I don't know who she is, but that doesn't matter. I remember her sweet smile. She kept smiling through all the disastrous publicity parties for *O, Lucky Man!* She was the chief publicist's slave: Fred Hift sat in his cardigan smoking a cigar while she scurried everywhere at a thousand miles an hour and fixed up everything from finding Alan Price's missing amplifiers to booking tables at the Escargot, where Warners couldn't get a meal because a different Mr Warner had block-booked the restaurant.

She might have moved, I think, and of course someone as nice as her is bound to be married or have a nice boy-friend. Still, I ring and she answers immediately. Yes, she'd love to come out to supper. Any time.

I don't explain that I'm committed to a loony bin and can barely walk. I've got the flu, I tell her, and invite her to the premiere of Lindsay's production of *The Seagull* in five weeks' time.

'That would be lovely!' she says.

30 September 1975

A nice egg for breakfast and then a visitor. Nigel with a briefcase full of Guinness. Nigel and I have a lot of catching up to do. In the old days, he was Seth Holt's partner and helped finance *Crusaders* until the dreadful day when they both went bankrupt. Now he packs my case and hauls me out of the clinic, telling the duty nurse he is prescribing a dose of fresh air. At Nigel's beautiful Highgate flat I am reunited with Bertie and meet Nigel's wife, Penny. Poor Nigel and Penny are dead broke and are £700 in arrears on the rent. I have £1,100 in my account. I pay off the arrears and move in.

11 October 1975

Nigel and I take our customary stroll around Highgate Square. We order Scotches at the pub to celebrate the package of films we are planning for our comeback. The first will be a sequel to *O, Lucky Man!* called *Tough Luck*, about the continuing adventures of Mick Travis with his boss Sir James; the second and third will be *Hangover Square* and *Slaves of Solitude* by our favourite writer Patrick Hamilton.

2 November 1975

Nigel and I return late from our big-shot talk in the pub to find the flat smashed to pieces, and Penny lying in a pool of blood. Murder. But then Nigel realises she's slashed her wrists. He tears off his tie and binds her arms tight above the elbows. I call an ambulance.

Life really is a turkey shoot, and most of us are the turkeys. You think everything is fine, you're rushing along in this discordant, infernal machine, flapping your wings, almost flying, yes, nearly off the ground, when bang . . .

4 November 1975

Back in Platt's Lane a missive arrives from Gay informing me that I'm not fit to look after Luke and that John Haines is going to adopt him. I immediately phone Roger Alexander, the only lawyer I know. This time somebody else is going to be the turkey . . .

9 November 1975
The Seagull

I had forgotten Monika was so beautiful. I meet her in the theatre foyer, and we exchange warm smiles. She watches wryly as Mia Farrow entwines Lindsay in a snakelike embrace. After he has extricated himself he gives Monika a courteous handshake and nods to me. Then he is bear-hugged by Peter O'Toole.

In the middle of the play tears start to trickle down my face. Nina, the would-be actress, is so like Virginia. Monika is crying too. She whispers to me it's exactly like the rotten, hopeless relationship she's just getting over. The beauty and poetry of the play are too much. We leave, crying, in the second act, and walk tearfully arm in arm back to her tiny flat, not far from Lindsay's.

'Do you mind my Jesus?' she asks.

A huge expressionist painting of a red and green Christ nailed to the cross takes up most of the room.

'He's wonderful,' I say.

'Most people hate him.'

'May I make love to you?' I ask politely.

'Of course,' she says gently.

It all happens as simply as that.

9 January 1976

Monika and I win weekend staying access for Luke. 'Now make up and be friends with Gay,' says my QC.

10 January 1976

We take Luke to see my parents. All too soon our visit is over. 'It's dreadful having to split him up like this,' says my father as he kisses sad Luke goodbye.

16 March 1976

Harold Wilson resigns as Prime Minister. James Callaghan takes over and makes Gay's ex-boss the youngest Foreign Secretary since Anthony Eden. So the premiership is in Dr Owen's pocket. I just don't understand why Wilson has given up. I liked him so much. I'll never forget how he helped the British cinema.

Spring 1976
The Falls

Monika loves the cottage. She paints all over Virginia's rainbows and makes the place her own. We sit on the back of a tractor and, bumping up and down, plant a ton of seed potatoes, two thousand baby cabbages and a quarter of an acre of tobacco.

23 June 1976
The Hill Street Gaming Club, Mayfair

Bob Halmi and his business partner take us out to supper to discuss a new film, *To See America*, about an English librarian who becomes a stripper in America. Halmi, I can tell, is getting heartily sick of me bouncing back with striking women. His partner, a huge cadaver of a man from Texas who insists on wearing a full-length fur coat throughout supper, keeps saying, 'Christ, you can tell they love each other!'

Halmi, thoroughly irritated, tells us to go gambling, shoves £100 at me, then disappears into the darkness.

30 October 1976
The Falls

There has been a drought all summer, and our boggy land is the only field in the Forest to produce potatoes. We harvest fifty tons of them by hand. Lovely work.

Nureyev and the nightmare

9 November 1976

Frank Dunlop, manager and director of the Young Vic, rings. He asks me to write a movie called *The Dream* for Rudolph Nureyev. 'It is about Mum and Dad,' he lisps mysteriously. I imagine a comic nightmare about high-class parents like *The Discreet Charm of the Bourgeoisie*. I am excited, doubly so at the chance to work with the greatest ballet dancer of our age. When Monika collects a copy of the treatment from the theatre, Dunlop warns her not to read a word: it is so pornographic that it will shock her to the core.

Monika of course reads the treatment on the bus home, and returns in a fit of giggles. It's a silly gay fantasy based on *A Midsummer Night's Dream*. The only pornography I can find is when a gang of old men centaurs mount a gang of boy centaurs. Quite why, I have no idea. As *The Dream* must obviously be short-hand theatricalese for the play, I assume 'Dad' and 'Mum' are Oberon and Titania, King and Queen of the Fairies. I remember my own daringly décolleté performance as Mum at the Dragon School in Oxford when I was 12. Ever since I have loved the play, but this treatment will have to be dumped.

11 November 1976

I climb the rickety stairs to Frank Dunlop's office atop the Young Vic Theatre. He tells me a Colombian multi-millionaire is behind the project. He wants to shoot the whole picture in an exquisite seventeenth-century Mexican town where he produced *Macbeth*. Dunlop explains the nub of the play. Both Oberon and Titania want to have sex with a lovely boy whom Titania has stolen from an Indian king. Oberon, wild with jealousy, is driving mortal men insane and upsetting nature – 'the mazed world can't cope with the progeny of evils.'

'We start,' lisps Dunlop, 'under water with the little boy naked on a giant water-lily leaf.'

I suggest we set the film in the nineteenth century. I have a book of weird nineteenth-century inventions which would be perfect for the comic Bottom and the townsfolk.

'Nice,' lisps Dunlop.

'I've also got a book of wonderful Hieronymus Bosch monsters. They are full of holes and ladders and warrens, where the ill-starred mortal lovers can chase each other, hide and be bewitched.'

'Nice,' says Dunlop, white and round like an insect under a stone.

And so I get to work. With the text of the greatest writer in the world, it should be plain sailing.

3 January 1977
The Falls

I awake, very highly sexed, and say to Monika, 'Darling, you're pregnant!'

'Yes,' she whispers, 'and our baby is going to be a girl because you want a girl and I'm calling her Skye and she will be born on September 23rd, which is a Thursday.'

So Skye is all fixed up.

On with *The Dream* . . .

17 March 1977
New York

Dunlop is directing a big Broadway play here in New York. I have come with him to work on *The Dream*. After a week it seems more like a Buñuel nightmare, and as usual I'm in the wrong film. While Dunlop is staying with the Colombian magnate in his luxury apartment on South Central Park, I'm at the Mayflower just round the corner on Westside. The place has no double-glazing, and the noise of the traffic has rendered all thought impossible. On top of this, meals are served only to guests wearing ties, which on principle I refuse to do. I am starving, and, as I have given up alcohol so that Skye will have a sober father, I make do on half a gallon of pure grapefruit juice a day.

My routine is simple. Every morning I am awoken at six by the roar of traffic and sirens. I drink my grapefruit juice and then dial Monika and Lindsay, dangling the receiver over the balcony for a while so that they can savour the full hell of Central Park. Then I have a long wait. I gaze down at the traffic and across to the magnate's apartment. When Frank Dunlop draws back his art nouveau bedroom curtains, I know it is time to set off for our daily conference. But no work is done. Frank spends the entire time on the phone to 'Jessica' and 'Anne', the stars in his Broadway play. After an hour I return to the hotel for another day of not being able to think for the roaring traffic.

17 March 1977

A brief respite. Bob Halmi and his wife Eleanor take me out for a meal. We go to a better-class hotel where ties are not required. Real food is good!

Bob wants to develop his *To See America* story. When I've finished *The Dream* I'm to travel America with Eleanor and research the kind of American men our British librarian-cum-stripper could meet in her travels.

In the Men's, Bob explains that the trip is really therapy for Eleanor, who recently nearly died and has to have open heart surgery. But at the same time it will make 'a goddam great movie'.

Sunday 21 March 1977

Absolute silence. The park is closed to traffic. I do two weeks' work in a day and show it to Dunlop, who says my typing is so atrocious he can't read it. The Colombian magnate hires me a secretary.

22 March 1977

Gwen, my beautiful black secretary, takes a shine to me and rescues me from the hotel. We work in her home, where she cooks me delicious filling meals while I type. My health is restored but, as Gwen gives me loving looks from the kitchen, I'm aware that I'm treading on dangerous ground. Very Buñuel. I expect a bomb to go off any minute.

27 March 1977

Nureyev is celebrating his birthday tonight. For his present he has demanded the severed head of Baryshnikov, his chief rival. Gwen and I are walking to the party with Dunlop and his young friend when suddenly the boy bursts into tears and begs to be allowed to go home to England. Dunlop tries to cheer him up and decides not to go to the party. He gives us directions and stays behind with his boy. Gwen and I walk on and on through midnight Manhattan, get utterly lost, and end up back at her house. Her son has had a terrible nightmare, in which Gwen and I have had our heads chopped off and are being eaten by Nureyev. More Buñuel.

28 *March* 1977

I phone Bob Halmi. I'm seeing so many extraordinary and crazy things that I'd like to borrow an old camera to record them. When I turn up at his studio I find not an old camera, but a large box containing the latest Nikon. Bob's eyes shine with pleasure as I thank him.

As usual, he's surrounded by his Magyar Mafia. He tells me he has just read my version of *Camille* and thinks it's the raunchiest script ever written. He's trying to buy it from Grimaldi.

'This boy writes a dirty script!' exclaims a Magyar.

'And *If . . .* and *O, Lucky Man!*'

'He looks too simple.'

'Well, he is and he isn't,' says Bob.

Frank Dunlop rings. Nureyev has read my script and wisely decided he doesn't want to be in a pornographic film. And that is the end of *The Dream*.

5 *May* 1977
The Falls

'Stop in your tracks, Farmer Jones, or I'll kill you!' I aim my air-gun in the moonlit night and fire at a fleeing figure. Too late. Farmer Jones escapes with all his sheep that I'd impounded for eating yet another crop of Monika's cabbages. We've reported the matter to the local policeman. All he said was, 'Sell them tonight, or they'll be gone in the morning. There's no stopping Farmer Jones and his dog.'

6 *May* 1977

Monika believes in reason, not murder. She goes to visit Farmer Jones and her sweet smile melts his poacher's heart. He gives her £200, and a promise never to hurt her crops again.

7 May 1977

I'm building the Graupner Mosquito, the world's first electric-powered model glider. It spans a hundred inches and weighs a mere twelve ounces. It's the most delicate model I've ever built.

8 June 1977
Connecticut

'Hi, Angie 109. I can't make the party but the road is free.'

'Hi, Bobby 106. I can't make the party, either. The road is wide and clear, but I'm short on gas . . .'

Robert Halmi Jr is driving me through the wilds of Connecticut, showing off America's latest toy – Citizens' Band Radio. Halmi Senior wants me to research it for *To See America*. He thinks this new craze will change the whole story. I'm not so sure. It may be a miracle that everyone in America can radio everyone else, but no one seems to have anything sensible to say. And what makes it even more silly is that Bob has had a script of *To See America* already written. I read it and tell him it's very good.

'It hasn't got an ending,' says Bob.

'Well, get the poor guy to write a different ending.'

'No. I want you to take that trip with Eleanor next May. I want the English view. I want you and Eleanor making a journey together in 1978.

I don't understand why this trip is so important.

Venom

3 July 1977

A book arrives from my New York agent, Marty Bauer, a thriller called *Venom*. Would I be interested in adapting it for the screen. It's a very easy read – about an international gangster, Jacmel, who kidnaps a millionaire's delicate son, Philip. The kidnapping goes wrong and Jacmel holes up in the boy's Chelsea home. They are besieged outside by the police, and terrorised inside by a deadly black mamba. I need the work, and it should be a simple job. So I say yes, of course. I agree to go to New York to write a treatment with the film's producer, Martin Bregman, on condition that I can bring Monika. She's pregnant and I can't leave her behind. No problem, says Marty Bauer. Bregman is a real producer. He's known as the high flier – flies his own jet – and produced the hit of the year – *Dog Day Afternoon* with Al Pacino. He won't mind paying Monika's air fare. He looks after his artists.

16 July 1977

The contract is settled – $5,000 for the treatment, $15,000 if Bregman goes ahead with a first draft. With Monika, unborn baby and typewriter, I land in New York.

Marty Bregman is a charmer. A young 40, he is athletic and quick in his walk, although he has only one leg. He takes us to a private screening of *Wait Until Dark*, in which Audrey Hepburn plays a blind woman trapped in a house with a maniac. He thinks it will give us some ideas for *Venom*. After the screening he invites us to dinner with his girl-friend, who looks daggers at Monika, thinking she's another actress. Her jealousy vanishes when Monika murmurs she's just a housewife. We talk about the Audrey Hepburn film. I remark on what a dreadful actress she is: she wandered round her house as if she had perfect sight, although she was supposed to be blind.

'Who are you to judge a superstar?' says Marty's girlfriend.

'David's quite right,' says Marty. 'Audrey Hepburn drives me up the wall.' He whispers to me, 'I think we'd better cut dinner.'

We meet a snake expert at the Bronx Zoo, and actually see a black mamba. It's twelve feet long, thin, jet-black. One bite can kill a gazelle – certainly a man. The death is agonising. Our civilised script conferences take place in Bregman's oak-panelled office decorated with beautiful models of old clippers. He carefully explains that *Venom* must be like *Dog Day Afternoon*. It's an inside and outside movie, all the time switching between Jacmel, the boy, the mamba inside the house, and the police outside. Like *Dog Day*: the bank inside, the cops outside.

At two of the conferences, Bregman's friend Sean Connery is present. He is to play the boy's neurotic uncle who saves them time and again from the mamba, finally overpowering Jacmel and becoming a new man. I've met Sean Connery a couple of times at Michael Medwin's. He's a quiet, sober man, quite unlike his dazzling image as James Bond. He best likes talking about money – the orphans' homes he's founded, his golf courses, how much it all costs him.

When I congratulate him on his brilliant performance in John Huston's *The Man Who Would be King*, he says with a dour smile, 'But it didn't make a cent.'

My first attempt at a treatment runs to fifteen pages. Bregman wants it longer and much more detailed, virtually a first draft. Another week goes by. One night there is thunder and lightning. The lights flicker, then go off. The great New York blackout has begun. It's quite cosy, being stuck in the hotel room, writing in the dark. The management provide mineral water and candles, but everyone is scared – as though they are living through a war. There is a vile stench from the lavatory. The cisterns are electrically operated and don't flush.

I go out on to the streets of Manhattan alone, thinking it too dangerous for Monika. But New York is transformed. The traffic lights don't work, there's not a car in sight and crowds stroll, happy and friendly, down the avenues. Manhattan has become a paradise.

Four days later, New York gets its electricity back. At a huge cinema on 42nd Street we see *Star Wars* with a black audience all smoking pot. I'm high on the audience's marijuana fumes, and *Star Wars* seems to me an even more fantastic dream than it is. We also see *The Deep*, starring Jacqueline Bisset. Dreadful. Maybe that needed pot too. Twelve years ago, when I was a photographer in London, Jacqueline Bisset came to my studio. I thought: what a drab au pair. I didn't even take test shots of her, and now she is the Queen of Hollywood. Well, anything is possible in the movies.

After six weeks' work Bregman is satisfied with the treatment and commissions the first draft. Monika and I fly back home.

25 August 1977

Monika insists I marry her so that Skye won't be a bastard. The registrar tells us our solemn oaths don't matter. He himself has seen too much. He doesn't believe in marriage. The only one overcome by the brief ceremony is faithful little Bertie, who suddenly starts to cry.

23 September 1977

Exactly as she predicted, Monika gives birth to our daughter, Skye. She is a happy, smiling baby, and never cries at night. Surrounded by happiness, I finish the first draft of *Venom*, and post it to Martin

Bregman. From whom I hear not a word.

1 *January 1978*

My New Year's resolutions. To be a good father and husband, and above all to write something worthwhile again.

15 *January 1978*

To write something worthwhile again . . . I phone Lindsay. He is of the same mind. We decide to revive the story of Malcolm McDowell's mill and all our friends who go down to it. It is to be about 'the family'. 'Let's meet,' he says. Malcolm is back in London after making *Caligula*.

25 *January 1978*

I arrive at Lindsay's London flat to be greeted by Malcolm. Lindsay is on the phone in the living room. In the kitchen Malcolm pours a glass of Lindsay's white wine for himself, and a glass of his whisky for me.

'You know,' Malcolm says, 'Lindsay can't really write this sort of thing. It's up to you. You should write your own experience. All those traumas with Gay. Not some tomfoolery about my mill-house.'

'I agree.'

'Tell Lins that – I'll back you up.'

While we're waiting for Lindsay to get off the phone, Malcolm tells me about his experiences on *Caligula*.

'It took willpower. It's only willpower that makes a star. Helen Mirren and I had to learn this special sexual dance that we do together. We practised for weeks with the dance instructor. You know – sideways and forwards – incredibly phallic. It took total concentration for weeks – one of the reasons we are stars and earned millions. Of course I also asked that much because I hate *Penthouse*. I hate those kinds of pictures. On the set there were all those doped-up *Penthouse* girls lying around.'

Suddenly Malcolm shouts, 'Lins! We're agreed!'

Lindsay, looking quizzical, has silently entered his kitchen. 'I suppose, Malcolm, you've been poking around as usual, reading my private mail.'

'No – just discussing *The Great Advertisement for Marriage*.'

'Oh – is that what it's called?'

'You invented it,' says Malcolm, winking at me.

'Seen Gay?' Lindsay asks me.

'Not in six months. Monika does the pick-ups. To avoid rows.'

'I keep bumping into this enormously fat woman in Waitrose who shrieks, 'Hullo, Lindsay!' Then I realise it's Gay with this grinning loon in tow. I suppose that's her husband. What's he called?'

'John Haines. His family owns half of Kentish Town. Gay still hates me. I still get phone calls.'

'Somehow women have created the myth that all men are mad and irresponsible, when in fact all women are ruthless monsters,' Lindsay pronounces.

23 April 1978
The Falls

I am working peacefully on *The Great Advertisement* in my caravan at the bottom of the garden when Monika hurls open the door. Her face is stricken. She has just had a call from our clever, friendly lawyer, Roger Alexander.

'Gay's served a warrant on you under the Married Woman's Property Act demanding you immediately sell our home and give her half the value. She also demands £5,000 for the furniture. My God, the work I've put into our home! The bitch is making Skye homeless.'

24 April 1978

The very first couple to see The Falls immediately make an offer and pay a deposit of £1,000. I see an ad for a cottage on the other side of the forest. I rush round and, although it is a roofless, tumbledown ruin, make an offer on the spot to old Mr Evans of 24,000 imaginary pounds. It's love at first sight. The view is magnificent – thirty miles across the Severn Estuary to the Cotswolds on the other side. I offer Mr Evans a bottle of Gold Label, which is his favourite tipple.

'Mr Sherwin,' he says, 'You're a forester like me. My house will be yours.'

25 April 1978

Monika sits like a mad woman, cradling her child, on the front terrace, staring with utter misery at the sun rising over her crops. After Gay has taken her share of the money for The Falls, how will we be able to buy Cherry Tree. The situation is desperate, but then Otis Blodgett calls with a life-saver. More than a life-saver: 'Marty Bregman wants you to go to California to write the second draft of *Venom*. It's for real this time – with Paramount. Paramount are giving you a first-class fare, and I've asked for expenses of $750 a week.'

I explain to Otis about my family being homeless. Monika and Skye will have to come too.

Blodgett checks with Marty and calls back ten minutes later: 'That's fine. Marty will change the first-class ticket for two economy fares. I have suggested – now it's only a suggestion – that Monika packs up the cottage, does whatever is necessary here, while you go the day after tomorrow to New York to meet Marty, and then travel on to Hollywood. Marty understands and will take good care of you all, but the word is "action at once!" '

'Fine by me, thank you.'

'This is a big Hollywood picture – just work hard, David.'

I tell Monika of our sudden amazing turn in fortune. We'll be successful in Hollywood and set up a new home there. We'll start a new life.

'Maybe,' she says, happier.

The phone rings. 'Lindsay!' shouts Monika from next door. I go to the phone.

'How are you?' he asks.

'Off to America to write *Venom*.'

'You bloody fool. That rubbish.'

'I'm not a fool and it isn't rubbish. You're doing that play, *The Kingfisher*, with Rex Harrison on Broadway, I'm doing *Venom* with Sean Connery in Hollywood.'

'You shouldn't be writing this crap! What's wrong with your personality? You're a bloody fool! What have you done on *The Great Advertisement*?'

'Just writing it and living it.'

'Liar.'

'Well, I'm going to California on Wednesday.'

'How long for?'

H-O-T in New York, 1969

John Howlett, seeking inspiration, 1965

Generous Gilda: my first picture of her with the Nikon she gave me

Val, who added her own poetry to 'Crusaders'

*Very tough child model on Hovis
commercial shoot, 1966*

Gay, before it all went wrong

Seth Holt, our lion-hearted first producer

*My favourite picture of Lindsay,
with the bishop in If . . .*

*Mick Travis (Malcolm McDowell)
dreams of changing the world*

*If . . .: a knight
awaits his fate*

'Look into my eyes, I have eyes like a tiger': the café scene in If . . .

If . . .: Mick Travis being flogged for having the wrong attitude to life

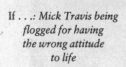

Lindsay enjoying himself on If . . .

Lindsay, framed by myself and Bo Widerberg,
after being thrown out of the
Palais du Festival at Cannes, 1969

'Polyvolante' Virginia, meditating on her mantra

Jon Voight

Brooke Shields, who starred in Wet Gold

*Venom,
the 'Jaws on dry land':
was this what it was
all for?*

*Bob Halmi, Nikons at the
ready. He is set to produce
58 films in 1996*

*Jo Janni, the best British
producer I worked for*

'I don't know.'

'You don't know. You're your own person – or were.'

I get pompous: 'I don't put a time limit on our scripts – I can't on this.' Lindsay slams the phone down. I'm free of everything now, aren't I? Free to conquer Hollywood!

1 May 1978
Manhattan

I enter Marty Bregman's gleaming aluminium skyscraper on Lexington Avenue and announce myself at reception. I'm told to go straight through. Seated in the chair where Sean Connery had sat nine months ago is an odd figure – a huge, round-shouldered man of about 60 with cropped hair, a beaked nose and a cross-eyed stare. He doesn't acknowledge me, he just stares fixedly at the ceiling. Then Marty swings into the room in his jaunty, athletic style and introduces the stranger as Frank Rosenberg. I will be working with Frank in Hollywood.

'Won't you be coming?' I ask, aghast.

'No.'

'Oh. I thought that was the whole point.'

'No, you'll be working with Frank.'

Marty sits down behind his enormous desk.

Rosenberg gets up and gives me a ten-page document. 'Paramount's comments about *Venom*,' he says humourlessly. 'Brave of them actually to commit themselves to paper.' He reads the notes out to us slowly. The upshot is that the studio sees *Venom* as a *Jaws* on land. The memo is signed Jeff Katzenberg and Don Simpson, Vice Presidents in charge of production. After he has finished reading, Rosenberg goes to the men's room.

'Isn't Frank dreadful!' Marty says. 'Any problems out there, just lift the phone. I'm always here – and I'm the bottom line.'

I don't understand. Why is Frank Rosenberg dreadful? Why am I to work with him instead of with Marty? What's Rosenberg got to do with *Venom*? What hold has he over Marty and why? Rosenberg comes back into the room doing up his flies. I say goodbye to Marty. He repeats he's the bottom line. The secretary in the front office gives me an envelope. It contains $750. I sign for it and forget my worries.

It's a fine afternoon, and Rosenberg, very friendly now, asks me to walk with him to his hotel, the Sherry Netherland. We're to meet there tomorrow morning to take a Paramount limo to Kennedy for the flight to Los Angeles. He hesitates for a moment in the hotel foyer, then invites me up to his room for a drink. He's got a huge suite, with real oak furniture and an emerald wool carpet. He asks me about Lindsay Anderson, and I start to tell him my life story. I notice he's staring at me in a strange, fixed way.

'Am I boring you?'

'No. It's good to communicate. I like you.'

I tell him how Monika saved my life.

'Oh, women! I don't give a shit!' he says with a strange violence.

He gives me a sheet of paper headed 'Cutlass Productions'. It states that Suite 107 at the Sunset Marquis, Hollywood, has been booked for Mr and Mrs Sherwin at $55 a day. I haven't heard of the Sunset Marquis, but at nearly $400 a week it must be wonderful. I ask Rosenberg if I can make a quick call to Monika about our new luxury home in Hollywood. All our worldly possessions are in the warehouse, the cottage is gone for ever, but she sounds happy.

'Kiss!'

'Kiss!'

Rosenberg looks out at the view of Manhattan. I ask him if he's married.

'Thirty-five years. But I don't let home life intrude on my movies.'

'Any children?'

'No – just an Airedale dog, but the local ferrets keep biting him. He may have to go.'

Back in my tiny room in the Mayflower Hotel I ring ICM. I want to ask Marty Bauer who the hell is Rosenberg, but he has left ICM and they don't have a number for him. Damn.

2 May 1978

We board the 747 together, and I make to follow Rosenberg up to First Class.

'No,' he says, 'you're travelling Economy.'

Odd. If we're supposed to be working together, why aren't we sitting together? I sit above the wings in Economy, and the exhaustion of being on the go for thirty-six hours sweeps over me. I fall asleep for the first time on an aircraft.

A finger prods me awake. Rosenberg is sitting beside me. He looks very pleased with himself. 'Up in First Class I sat next to David Begelman. He says the word in Hollywood is that *Venom* is going to be bigger than *Jaws*.' Even I have heard of Begelman. He is the most successful studio head in Hollywood. [*A year later he goes to jail for absurdly forging a cheque for $5,000.*] I tell Rosenberg I'd like to talk to Begelman myself, but he insists I stay in Economy. Begelman wouldn't like it. I don't understand, but the news that *Venom* will be bigger than *Jaws* sends a flood of adrenalin through me. I'm obviously going to be the most important writer in town. I'm filled with a sense of my importance.

At Los Angeles, I'm brought down to earth. Rosenberg disappears into another Paramount limo, while his secretary, chubby Sue from Michigan, drives me in her tiny Ford Pinto to the Sunset Marquis, just off Sunset Boulevard. Suite 107 is horrible. There's a cramped living room the size of my writer's caravan, a tiny double bedroom, a shower off left and a tiny kitchenette off right. The carpet is green and plastic. Monika will go berserk.

3 May 1978

Rosenberg's supposed to pick me up at the Sunset Marquis at 10 a.m. for our first day's work at the Sam Goldwyn Studios, where he has an office. I sit in the tiny living room wondering how Monika will react to the dump. It's 10.20 and still no sign of Rosenberg. I look out of the window and there he is, sitting in a Chevvy, parked outside the hotel in the intense heat. Why didn't he come in? I pick up my briefcase containing *Venom* and my whisky, and go down.

Rosenberg taps his watch disapprovingly and drives off. Deciding against making enemies, I weakly excuse myself for being late. He says not a word. We pass the armed guard at Goldwyn Studios – a lot of wooden sheds painted bright brown. We park outside one of them, and Rosenberg silently motions me to follow him up a wrought-iron staircase to his office. On the door is a sign which says 'Cutlass Productions'.

The office is a long windowless room divided by a partition into two separate enclaves. Sue, his secretary, sits at a typewriter in one. Rosenberg has a narrow desk with four phones in the other. No pictures on the walls, no wife, no clippers, no movie posters. Is this the heart of Hollywood. Is this a bigger picture than *Jaws*? Who is this lunatic? I break the sulky silence by suggesting we work like I did with Jo Janni when we rewrote *Sunday Bloody Sunday* for John Schlesinger. We will discuss each scene, and then Rosenberg will dictate an outline, or 'scalata'. His broody face lights up. He thinks this is a wonderful idea, and we set to work.

At mid-morning, he lifts his phone and dictates his scalata to Sue, hidden on the other side of the partition. He says we'll wait for her to type it out. Monika and Skye are arriving in the afternoon. I ask Rosenberg if he could give me a lift to the airport. No, he couldn't. Instead he phones Paramount and asks for a chauffeur and limo to drive me there. Paramount agree, and for the first time he smiles. This is a wonderful achievement, which proves our power with Paramount. They don't just provide a limo like that. 'Even Jeff Katzenberg and Don Simpson have to take taxis.'

At 1 p.m. Rosenberg declares that it is lunchtime. He sends Sue out to fetch hamburgers and chips. After she's gone, he suddenly relaxes and grins widely. 'Guess what? Six weeks ago she was a typist in Michigan. One of a million. Now she's a secretary in Hollywood!' The Hollywood myth – from a nobody to Rosenberg's secretary.

The three of us munch our hamburgers in the same enclave in silence. Then Sue clears up the remnants and disappears behind the partition to finish her typing. Rosenberg stares morosely at the blank wall. I don't understand. Why am I here in this divided room with this cross-eyed egomaniac, instead of with the intelligent Marty Bregman? Otis Blodgett never explained, and I can't find Marty Bauer. What am I to do? Should I call Bregman? It's a bit early – I'll give it a week. A phone rings. It is Miss Michigan: she has finished her type-up. Rosenberg tells her to bring two copies through.

'Fine,' I say, glancing through my copy.

'It is not,' says Rosenberg. 'It's a mass of spelling and punctuation errors. I want it perfect.' He lifts up a phone and dials through the partition to Miss Michigan. Slowly he starts to dictate his perfect scalata, spelling every single word and correctly placing the punctuation. It's the opening scene – the discovery of the mamba. It takes an hour. We could have been discussing the next scene – the arrival of the gangster Jacmel. We could have been doing something useful, instead of Rosenberg giving his grammar course through the partition. Perhaps he's just trying to make the innocent girl from Michigan pay for her luck at being a secretary in Hollywood. He's still dictating full stops and apostrophes when another phone rings: my limo has arrived from Paramount.

Bob the chauffeur is in full uniform. His Cadillac is equipped with air conditioning. Just as well – the temperature outside is in the hundreds.

The airport is packed, everyone sweating in the dreadful heat.

'Christ, this is worse than Calcutta,' says Bob. The flight is delayed. We've got three hours to wait.

A woman in a neat pink blouse and skirt comes up to me. 'Would you like to know World Consciousness for $15?'

'I know it already. I meditate.'

'I'm psychic – I thought you were. Here . . .' And she places a pink plastic flower in my jacket lapel. Psychic – that's the second time I've heard that word. When my young doctor back in England had come to say goodbye, I asked how he knew we were going since no one had told him. He said he was psychic. Is there some psychic freemasonry around me, keeping an eye on me?

Bob waits dutifully, muttering, 'Christ, this is worse than Calcutta!'

At last the flight lands.

In the cool of the limo, Monika relaxes and tells me about the journey. Skye smiled the whole time at the man opposite, who said she should be called 'Happy'. Monika's mood changes to livid fury when she sees the tiny suite at the Sunset Marquis. 'They expect me to live and look after Skye in this hutch. Jesus Christ – is this Hollywood?'

4 May 1978

I wake to discover that Monika and Skye have vanished. I go into the living room, where I find Monika asleep on the couch and Skye smiling in her cot. Monika wakes with a start. Do I realise I tried to murder her in the night? I tried to strangle her, yelling, 'Gay, I'll kill you!' She's not risking her life again. From now on I must sleep on the couch. I was like a madman.

But I'm not mad, am I? Surely just under strain at losing our home.

10 a.m. Rosenberg waits outside, broiling in his un-air-conditioned cheap Chevvy. I go down and ask him if he'd like to come in and meet the family. No – he'd rather go straight to the studio. At the studio he spends another two hours dictating our scalata through the partition to his secretary. The script will take a year at this rate.

5 May 1978

Rosenberg's English lesson through the partition continues. When he comes to a point of disagreement with me, he stares at me, cross-eyed, and says there must be an easier way of earning a living. He quarrels over the slightest things. He refuses to believe that an Uzi machine-gun is spelt the way it is. He insists on spelling it his way through the partition. He is adamant that Easter is held on the same day every year. I suggest that it is held on a different day because no one knows the exact date of Christ's crucifixion. He swings his chair round, and stares cross-eyed at his blank wall. I'm not quite sure how we got into this argument. It has nothing to do with the script. Anyway, *Venom* is held up for half an hour while he sulks about Easter.

Monika hates Hollywood. She has nothing to do all day. No sights to see. Only the intolerable heat and the relentless roar of traffic down Sunset Boulevard. Los Angeles is the most soulless city in the world. Further, the smog has caused Skye to get an eye infection. It's the first time she's ever been ill. Monika rings Rosenberg's doctor, who says that Skye must see a child specialist. The child specialist gives her a tube of cream and charges $80. 'At least in England we had clean air and free medicine. This is a land of crooks,' says Monika.

6 May 1978

It's the weekend. We are desperate to escape the Sunset Marquis, and hope that Rosenberg will invite us out as Marty Bregman did. He doesn't, so we ring Miss Michigan instead, and offer to treat her to lunch on Sunday. She is absolutely delighted. She's heard of a famous fish restaurant some way up the Pacific coast. She'll pick us up at 11 a.m. and drive us there.

8 May 1978

Sunday. Unfortunately, everyone in LA has the same idea. The road to the Pacific is jammed. We move at five miles an hour. Miss Michigan's little Ford Pinto doesn't have air conditioning, so we keep all the windows open and edge forward enthusiastically. I ask Miss Michigan about Rosenberg. She doesn't know who he is, or why he's working on *Venom*, or what his relationship is with Marty

Bregman. She's never been to his home or met his wife.

At last we pull on to the shores of the Pacific. The restaurant is large, marble-floored and cool. The sea breaks just beyond the window. Perfect. We all order seafood salad and wine. Skye, propped up in her baby buggy, smiles happily. Then I notice the fish tank. It is full of large tropical fish, swimming in the water. Faint rock music pounds. I get up and dance in rhythm with the fish. My whole body vibrates. I feel like a fish. Why don't the others join me? It's the natural thing to do. But they just sit silently at the table. Odd. I break off and rejoin them.

'Well,' says Monika sourly, 'have you finished showing off?' Why is she so cross? Aren't I a star in Hollywood? Don't stars behave just as they like? To lighten the atmosphere I tell my Victor Mature story. Once that great old ham was refused entrance to an exclusive nightclub which didn't permit actors. 'I'm not an actor,' he said, 'and I've reviews to prove it.' Monika, who has heard the story before, just continues to feed Skye morsels of fish. I am the only one to laugh. Everyone in the restaurant looks at me strangely.

9 May 1978

Another day with Rosenberg. He insists that when we first see the boy's mother, the audience should know she's very rich.

'How do we do that?' I ask.

'By the scarf she's wearing.'

'What scarf?'

'She's wearing a Gucci scarf.'

'But,' I protest, 'everyone's got Gucci scarves. How do we know it's a Gucci scarf?'

'By the stitching. By the label, for Chrissake!'

'You mean we have a big close-up of the label?'

'Oh, Christ – do you think I haven't made movies before?' And he swivels his chair to stare sulkily at the blank wall.

Eventually I suggest a crummy idea. The mother comes out of Harrods with a load of parcels and is met by her chauffeur, who opens the door to her Rolls. Rosenberg likes the idea and comes out of his sulk. He stares at me, cross-eyed: 'What I really hate about Hollywood is the young guns. The young guns have taken over this town and they know nothing. Steven Spielberg, George Lucas – they know nothing . . .'

After our day's work is finished, I return to the Sunset Marquis.

Monika is worried. Paramount still haven't sent our expenses and the hotel bill is due. When I phone their accounts department, a woman tells me that they only pay expenses at the end of the week, and then only what we've spent.

'So if we sleep on the beach and spend nothing, we get nothing. Very apposite, I think.'

'We only pay what you spend. And we require dockets.'

'That wasn't my contract,' I reply, angry at how they treat their star writer. 'It was a guaranteed $750.'

'I haven't seen the contract. We have our standard practice.'

'If you don't send the cash round by tomorrow morning, I'll sue you.'

'I'll have to find out about this,' says the woman hesitantly.

'Do, or I'll sue the whole of Paramount.' Pleased with myself, I put the phone down.

Monika is less impressed: 'You should never make enemies of accountants – they run the world.'

'They don't run me.'

'Your trouble is you think you're important. You're not at all important.'

I'm speechless. Doesn't my wife understand anything? Has she taken leave of her senses out here? At that moment, the room starts to shake with a colossal rock beat from the suite above. A group of musicians are jamming on their balcony. I run outside and yell at them to stop. I'm David Sherwin and I'll have them thrown out. But the music is so loud they can't hear, and they play on. Skye starts to cry for the first time in Hollywood. 'I'm taking her out,' says Monika helplessly. 'I can't even get her nappies washed here. We're going to the launderette.'

The launderette is on the other side of Sunset Boulevard, across eight lanes of traffic. Scared and a little exhilarated, we manage somehow to manoeuvre Skye's pushchair past the cars and into the launderette. We pace fretfully up and down while we wait for our laundry. The heat from the drying machines is unbearable. Then Monika notices a sign above a door at the back: TO THE MARKET. She pushes the door open to discover a cool courtyard shaded with orange trees. There are stalls under a marquee, and a table with wine. We wheel Skye into this refuge.

A bearded man offers us some wine.

'You're English. I can tell,' he says.

'Yes.'

'I'm Simon. Welcome to the English community in Hollywood.'

Simon used to be props manager for Warners, and is selling off the props he has acquired during thirty years making movies. He wants to return to England and run a country pub. Skye is fascinated by a rocking horse which is the size of a pony. It even has real pony skin.

'Climb on,' says Simon. Monika gets on and I hand Skye up. 'Elizabeth Taylor rode him in *National Velvet*. He's electrically powered. Pull the reins once and he trots, twice and he canters. Three times – he gallops.' Monika does so, and Skye's face is pure delight.

'Yours,' says Simon, 'for $350 plus shipping costs. It's unique – but I've got to get rid of it.'

I've never seen anything like this electrical horse. It's better than any funfair. 'We'll buy it when Paramount pay our expenses,' I say. 'I'm writing the new *Jaws* for them.'

'Are you mad?' cries Monika. 'We haven't a home to put it in.' She is implacable, and so Simon tries to interest us in something else. He shows us a leather-bound volume.

'This is an album of film premiere invitations at Grauman's Chinese Theatre,' he explains. 'It contains every film premiered there, each invitation autographed by the stars – John Wayne, Jean Harlow, Rita Hayworth . . . It's a symbol of Hollywood. I would be honoured for a very special price to present it to the writer who wrote *O, Lucky Man!*'

How wonderful, I think. I could give it to Lindsay as a reconciliation present. He'd love it.

'And I've one other unrepeatable bargain,' Simon confides in a hushed voice. 'Marilyn Monroe as the world has never seen her.' He hands me another leather-bound volume, explaining that there are only five copies of these prints in the world. The Kennedys had the CIA destroy the negative.

'David – I'm going,' says Monika.

'But this is a party,' I say.

'Well, you stay as long as you like – I'll look after the laundry.' And she leaves without a smile.

I drink some more wine with Simon and tell him my life story – all about Gay, John Haines and David Owen, and the secret script I'm writing about them for Lindsay. It will be bigger than *The Godfather*. The hours race by without our realising, and now it's dark and the marquee is empty. Simon gets to his feet, interrupting my flow. 'Got to go, David,' he says, giving me an actor's farewell hug, 'and you ought to get some sleep.'

Back at the Sunset Marquis I fix myself a whisky from the fridge, ready for the couch. Suddenly the bedroom lights come on.

'David, is that you?' Monika screeches. 'I thought you'd been killed. I thought you'd died crossing Sunset Boulevard. And the worst part was – I didn't care!'

'What do you mean?'

'It makes me sick the way you let yourself be conned.'

'You're mad!' I retort. 'Simon's the first nice person we've met.'

'I know his sort. He's a crook. They're all crooks out here.'

15 May 1978

Jeff Berg, my Hollywood agent, is taking me out to lunch today. Berg isn't just my agent – he's chairman of ICM. At 32, he's the youngest chairman of a major agency ever. A phenomenon. Monika tidies the suite and dresses Skye in her pretty pink gingham frock. Berg arrives dressed in frayed blue-jean shorts and a red sweatshirt. Not at all what I had expected.

'A present,' he says, handing me an envelope. Inside is a membership card of the Writers' Guild of America, West, Inc. Now I really belong here . . .

Berg shakes Monika by the hand, briefly picks up Skye, and ushers me outside to his car: a red Porsche 911. Unlike other swish cars in Hollywood, which look as though they haven't left the showroom, it is filthy. We drive 300 yards to a vegetarian restaurant. As he tucks into his foot-high salad, he asks me how much I'm getting for *Venom*.

'$15,000.'

'Jesus – out here you're worth $125,000, and 5 per cent of the gross!'

'We plan to settle here.'

'You must. Bob Altman wants to meet you. Just think: the director of *M.A.S.H* and the writer of *If . . .* and *O, Lucky Man!*'

In spite of his athletic build, Berg's voice is a thin screech. 'Have you anything for Bob?'

'A true story about Kalinda, the most wicked woman in the world. She got all her eight lovers to kill each other.'

'Just the sort of thing Bob loves!'

'And a story about marriage – a comedy with Lindsay Anderson.'

'You two are a winning team. Could be a great picture.'

'And something with Robert Halmi – he's flying in to discuss it –

To See America.'

'Bob Halmi's a terrific guy,' says Jeff.

Fantastic, I think. Three pictures at $125,000 each. 'By the way,' I ask, 'Who is Frank Rosenberg? He's very strange to work with.'

'Oh, he used to work for Howard Hughes – he's known as the Howard Hughes Slave.'

'But why am I working with him rather than Marty Bregman?'

'I'll check it out and call you back tomorrow.'

Berg switches his total attention to his salad. He munches his lettuce and carrot like a rabbit. I feel much too excited to eat. I look at the restaurant. It's built in steps like a tiny Greek amphitheatre. At a table on the level below us, a Franciscan monk talks to two women disciples. They could be in their twenties or fifties – it's impossible to tell in Hollywood. The monk explains how he has made contact with all the great dead jazz musicians and is recording them in the afterlife. 'Paul Robeson's got his voice back. He's singing as well as ever.'

'Why isn't he in an asylum?' I ask Jeff Berg.

'Everything is permitted in California. That's what makes it the only place to live!'

He rises from his feast, pays the bill, and drives me the 300 yards back to the Sunset Marquis.

The news that Jeff Berg is at last going to get Paramount to pay our expenses puts Monika into a good mood. The dollar signs in my eyes become contagious. 'We need to hire a car and get a nanny for Skye. So when Jeff Berg rings you can say we can't possibly survive on $750 a week. If you're so important, damn well prove it.'

Doesn't she realise that Jeff Berg is the top agent in Hollywood, and I'm the top writer? 'Stop being such an English working-class peasant,' I tell her. 'Tomorrow we'll be rich and famous!'

'So you keep saying. But I *am* a peasant, and I've had my home taken away from me. I worry all the time about Skye, and what's going to happen to her. We can't go on like this.'

Suddenly the door to our suite is pushed open. A small black man in a uniform enters, holding a cocked gun. 'Security. I'm checking the rooms. Your door was unlocked. You must *never* leave your door unlocked in this town. Especially with a baby. It's a dangerous place.'

Monika takes to the security guard, and offers him a cup of tea. He declines, explaining that he is on duty.

I ask him his name.

'Webster Popper.'

A thought occurs to me: maybe Webster Popper is the answer to all our problems. 'Can we meet?' I ask him.

'I'll be in the underground garage at 11 p.m. tonight.'

'Thanks.'

'And keep that door locked at all times.'

I am sitting on the fender of a Rolls Royce when Webster Popper shines his torch on me at precisely 11 p.m. I tell him how Monika and I hate the Sunset Marquis – how we have to put up with the pop musicians, and don't even know why we're staying in this dump. We need special guarding, I tell him. Not just my family, but there's a script in the suite – *The Great Advertisement for Marriage* – all about my ex-wife, David Owen and President Carter. 'If it fell into the wrong hands . . .'

Webster advises me always to be in the suite when the maids are cleaning, and to leave nothing on view. He gives me his home number in case of emergency. In return I promise to arrange a viewing of *If . . .*, which he has heard of but never seen. We are great friends, united against the dangers of our lives.

He grips my hand: 'Remember – always be in the room when the maids come in, keep the script under cover, and look after your passport.'

My passport? I haven't seen it since I arrived in Hollywood. Webster looks serious: British passports with American visas are worth a small fortune to terrorists. He will come up with me and do a room search.

'Don't wake my wife,' I ask.

'I'm trained – don't worry.'

We enter the tiny suite. Webster gives a professional glance around, but the passport is nowhere to be seen. He fingers the curtains, looks under the couch and behind the television. The passport has vanished. He goes into the kitchen and opens the fridge.

A scream echoes from the bedroom. I explain to a distraught Monika that our friend, Webster Popper, the security guard, is looking for our missing passports, invaluable to terrorists.

'Are you mad?' Monika groans. 'They're in the suitcase. Do you think I'd leave them lying around for terrorists? God, my first night's sleep and now this!' She slams back into the bedroom.

I thank Webster and apologise.

'You have a lot more problems than I have,' he says, clasping my hand in farewell. 'Take it easy.'

19 May 1978

More torture with Rosenberg in his bleak office on the Goldwyn lot. I disagree with everything he says. He disagrees with everything I say. He keeps groaning, 'There must be an easier way to earn a living.' To try to cheer things up, I mention I've read a very good book: *Travels with a Son*, about an English journalist who tried to get to know an estranged teenage son by taking him on a journey through the wilds of savage Africa. It could provide some ideas for the relationship between the boy in *Venom* and his uncle, Sean Connery. Would he like to order it?

'Order it yourself,' Rosenberg snaps. 'You're the writer – I've done enough for you.' He tells me to go away and write anything I like, but if he doesn't like it, he'll cut it out. Oh, for the creative, collaborative days with Lindsay Anderson!

Jeff Berg still hasn't called back. Monika orders me to phone him and insist that $1,000 a week is the minimum we can survive on. Berg's secretary tells me he's in recess, and will phone back in half an hour. The intolerable sound of rock drums pounds from the musicians above us. Half an hour later, I phone ICM again, and am told that Berg is still in recess.

'What does that mean?' I ask.

'Oh – it means he's with his girl-friend.' Jeff off duty with his girl-friend! And his nickname in Hollywood is the Iceberg.

Fuming, I decide to go right to the top. I phone Paramount, and ask for Don Simpson. The girl at the end of the line has never heard of him.

'He's Vice President.'

'Oh, we have so many Vice Presidents.'

'Don Simpson's in charge of production. You are a movie company, aren't you?'

'We have a John Simpson in charge of packaging.'

'Is Jeff Katzenberg there? He's also Vice President in charge of production.'

'Yes. He's on vacation until next week.'

I put down the phone in despair, and it rings again immediately. Skye's prospective nanny is downstairs in the lobby. I tell her to come up and meet our daughter.

'My name is Dorothea. I'm 73. I've got my health, my driving licence, and I'm going to love Skye.'

She has shorn dyed blond hair and wears a pink jumpsuit.

'I'll try my little love-test,' she says, lifting Skye up. She emits a buzz from her mouth, kissing Skye.

'Buzz – Buzz – Buzz – Beautiful!'

Skye roars with laughter.

'We're going to get on fine,' says Dorothea.

The phone rings. Dorothea looks panic-stricken. 'If it's for me, say I'm not here!'

'Right.'

I lift the phone. It's Marty Bregman.

He's direct and sympathetic: 'I know what you're going through with Frank Rosenberg. He's *dreadful*. I'm sorry. If you want to, why don't you come back East and write the picture here?'

I look across at Dorothea buzz-buzzing and Skye's happy laughter. 'No, Marty. Thank you. We're just about settled here. I'm in fine shape.' I put the phone down, realising I've made the most stupid decision of my life. But then the Iceberg did say I was a star, and, as Malcolm McDowell said, what makes a star is willpower. I've got that. I can keep going for ever on a bottle of whisky and a couple of hours' sleep on the couch.

Dorothea, who is relieved that the call wasn't for her, says, 'If anyone rings me from the Eleanor Roosevelt Nursing Association, you've never seen me! OK? You don't employ me!'

'Why's that?' I can't understand her obvious terror.

'The Eleanor Roosevelt Nursing Association sounds a good name. Eleanor Roosevelt, wife of our greatest president – a great name in good works. But it's just a front. You phone in, you get a baby-sitting job, and then the bitch that runs it takes 50 per cent of your wages. I was in the office when your wife came in and said she needed a nanny. I noted her number but I didn't tell the agency I was interested in the job. I phoned your wife later – well, I'm 73, and making seventy-five bucks a week, but I have to give thirty-seven bucks to that bitch. So I don't make a cent. I have to work to survive. So I came here on my own. Please don't ever tell them that I work here.'

'We won't.'

'My husband was like you – he was a showman.'

'Oh?'

'But he committed suicide.'

'Oh.'

'I'll be round on Monday. I'll look after Skye as if she was my own. I'll wheel her round the hotel – it's not safe outside.'

Dorothea buzzes Skye goodbye. 'Oh, look – she buzzes back!'

Now I have not only Monika and Skye to protect, but Nanny too. I tell the front desk that I will accept calls from only ICM and Paramount. But then I think again and add Marty Bregman, my mum and Lindsay. I pray that Lindsay will be in touch. I've sent him several postcards – Wild West scenes with the message: 'I know now why they hang you without a blindfold!' I know he'll understand.

Monika begs me not to make any more mad phone calls.

'Mad phone calls? Remember what Malcolm said: unless you behave like a star, they don't treat you like one.'

'But Malcolm *is* a star.'

20 May 1978

Rosenberg fixes me with his cross-eyed gaze. 'I hear Marty Bregman rang you.'

'That's right.' How does he know?

'What did he say about me?'

'Oh – well, I said we were doing fine.'

'Ring him now and say everything's wonderful.'

'But he'll think it's strange.'

'Just do it.'

I do so, and then Monika rings with some good news. She's picked up the expenses from Paramount, and, what's more, they paid $1,000, not $750. Now we can hire a car and pay Dorothea.

Rosenberg is astonished. 'No one in Hollywood ever gets their expenses upped! It's unheard of.'

'Well, I did it.'

'You're a tougher man than I thought.'

The phone rings again. Paramount offering us a double suite of offices, but Rosenberg tells them it won't be necessary.

I could have had my own office! What is going on? Why is Rosenberg so all-powerful? How did he know Marty had rung me? Did he bug my phone? After all, he worked for Howard Hughes. Rosenberg presses home his advantage by declaring that he is absolutely right about the beginning of *Venom*. He understands the thriller – he's been making them for thirty years. He suggests I go away with my big expense account and write a new treatment from scratch. This one's terrible.

I lose my temper. 'I wrote that treatment a year ago. Both Marty and Paramount like it. They also like the first draft. We're supposed to be doing the second draft, but after three weeks we haven't even settled Scene One.'

'Do whatever you want, but if I don't like it, I'll cut it.'

'So you keep saying, but whoever directs this picture will want to make changes – the director's changes.'

'That's why I hate these young guns.'

21 May 1978

It's amazing what $1,000 will do. We are a happy family at last. We go off to the sea in our new air-conditioned saloon to celebrate. Before we can ascend the steps of Santa Monica Pier, a figure hails us. He is stocky, with a handsome aquiline face and a shock of pure white hair. He pushes a supermarket trolley full of empty returnable bottles.

'Can you spare a dollar?'

'Sure.'

'I've just got out of jail. Busted for sleeping on the beach.'

'Have ten.'

'No, I only need a dollar for a beer and a sandwich.' I give the noble hobo a dollar. He smiles at baby Skye, and then at us.

'Have a happy day on the beach,' he says, going off in search of more returnables.

His entire presence exudes common sense, tranquillity and health. The first sane person we've met in LA is a beach bum.

Monika is very impressed: 'I've never seen anyone so happy and handsome.'

For a few hours on the beach we are a happy family too.

22 May 1978

I deliver my ultimatum to Rosenberg in a calm voice: 'Frank, we've spent three weeks writing outlines. You keep saying I'm the writer. Well, I really am going to write the movie by myself now.'

He gazes at me in amazement: 'I've warned you . . .'

I pull my old Nikon out of my battered briefcase and snap his crazed look before he can blink. I am keeping records.

23 May 1978

Paramount ring: Jeff Katzenberg and Don Simpson, the Vice Presidents in charge of production, are on the line for a conference call.

Jeff, who sounds friendly and young, apologises for having been away. 'From now on I'm going to chain myself to my desk,' he says.

Don Simpson, who sounds cold, asks if there has been any 'creative input' into the script.

'None by Rosenberg. I'm going to do it by myself. I'll need three more weeks.'

'That's fine,' says Jeff, 'Three weeks, but no longer. We're very keen to get into production.'

'And we'll keep *you* chained to your desk,' adds Don Simpson, without a hint of humour.

I try to make some sense of Rosenberg's fifty pages of notes, almost all about the opening scene. The musicians above are practising the same chord over and over again. Suddenly I've had enough. I could kill them. I go down to the lobby and demand to see the hotel president.

'The President's out,' says the bored receptionist behind the front desk. I notice a door marked 'President' and go towards it.

'You can't go in there!' the receptionist shrieks as I throw open the door. The President is eating lunch. Beside him sits a young girl. I explode. This hotel is a whorehouse crawling with drugged musicians. I'm a great writer. I demand he throw the musicians out.

But the President is not impressed: 'You come in here – stinking of alcohol – complaining about musicians. Well, those musicians are millionaires!'

3 June 1978

We have changed hotels. Back to the Century Wilshire where I lived with Virginia on *Robin Hood*. I am pleased to have escaped Suite 107 and the drugged rock musicians, but nervous about *The Great Advertisement for Marriage*, my script for Lindsay. There is so much secret stuff about David Owen, the Foreign Secretary, and he would do almost anything to get his hands on it. In our new hotel room I don't trust the telephones, which could easily be bugged. I wish Webster Popper was here to advise me.

5 June 1978

Last night Monika heard me whispering messages to Harold Wilson into my dictaphone. It is strange behaviour, she says, even if he was the saviour of the British film industry. I am imagining things and must stop worrying about *The Great Advertisement*. Our hotel room is *not* bugged. MI5 and the CIA are *not* following us. Some fresh air will do me the world of good, and she insists that I take the day off. On the way to the beach I try to explain my fears: our lives are in danger, Skye could easily be kidnapped and constant vigilance must be our motto . . .

Monika refuses to listen. 'Any more nonsense and I'm going straight back to the hotel!'

We park in the multi-storey car park by the Santa Monica pier. As we walk to the exit, Monika notices a woman in white overalls touching the cars' tyres with a long stick.

'What's she doing it for?' she asks.

'The whole country is riddled with spies,' I explain. 'She's a spy . . .'

Monika turns on her heel and pushes Skye back the way we have come. A few moments later the car screeches past me and out of the car park. It is a 10-mile walk back to the Century Wilshire.

As I pass Frank Sinatra's house on Santa Monica a girl in her twenties runs into my path. She has long, greasy hair and wears bright crimson trousers and a baggy white blouse. She is distraught and clutches at me.

'Excuse me, there's a snake in my house!'

'What kind of snake?' I ask.

'A green snake.'

'Oh, I'm sure it's harmless,' I reassure her.

'It keeps coming out of holes and looking at me.'

'Well, I only know about black mambas. I'm not a snake specialist.'

'Aren't you? Couldn't you come into my house and look?'

Suddenly it occurs to me. It is a trap. They are even trying to trap me with *Venom*. I push the girl aside and run all the way back to the hotel.

6 June 1978

Brood till dawn on the couch. Monika taps me on the shoulder. 'I'm taking *Venom* down to read by the pool.' I give her Rosenberg's notes, although I think it a waste of time. What is *Venom* compared to the new battles I'm fighting? Five minutes later Monika comes storming back from the pool. 'If this is all you've done, you'll need all the help you can get to finish the script in two weeks.' She insists I get a typist. I don't understand why she is so concerned, but to placate her I ring Paramount. They have hundreds of typists and will send one around. Dolores Jones, a woman in her forties, arrives half an hour later. Only she does not call herself a typist: she is a Production Co-ordinator, co-ordinating *Venom*. She orders an IBM Electronic on the telephone and says she'll be back tomorrow.

Soon after she leaves, two men wheel in a giant electric typewriter on a trolley.

'Tomorrow you'd better do some real work with that woman,' Monika warns me. 'You've only thirteen days left. I'll take Skye out, so you'll be able to concentrate.'

7 June 1978

Dolores arrives promptly at nine. I sit beside her on the couch. 'Fact is so much stranger than fiction,' I say, thinking of the last few days. 'Don't you agree?'

'It sure is.'

'You must have a story to tell.'

'I sure do. No one would believe me.'

I nod sympathetically. 'Tell me . . .' And as Dolores tells me her amazing life story, I write it down on the back of Rosenberg's *Venom* scalata.

Then it is my turn. I tell her my life story, making notes for her on the back of the scalata. I tell her what Malcolm said about willpower and being a star, I tell her about the spies. She laughs and agrees that mine is an amazing story too.

At four she gets up and says her day's work is done. I tell her I look forward to continuing our work on life tomorrow.

Pleased with such a good day's work, I treat myself to a drink in the bar. When I get back to our suite, I find a note attached to my 'Life of Dolores' in Monika's handwriting: 'If this is your day's work on *Venom* with Dolores, consult me.'

Before I have time to ponder the significance of this note, Monika enters the room.

'Well?' she demands aggressively.

'What's the matter?' I ask.

'That!' She points to my brilliant notes on Dolores's life. 'You've been here six weeks doing fuck all. I'm going home with Skye on the next flight. You can stay here with Dolores or come and finish *Venom* at your mum's. I've already spoken to her. She says we can stay with her until we've found a home. If you stay here, you'll never see me or Skye again – it's your choice.'

I've heard such words before. In an instant every dream I had of Hollywood turns to dust. 'I'm coming home . . .'

8 June 1978

Dolores arrives early for work on life. I tell her we're returning to England.

'Well, in life nothing is certain – except death and taxes,' Dolores says sadly. 'Some jobs in this business don't last long.'

I sit on the couch and ponder. Will they let us leave Hollywood alive? Surely I know too much. And what if they find *The Great Advertisement* in our luggage?

'You're ill, David,' Monika tells me. 'You're not well.'

Could she be right? Have they finally got control of my mind?

I listen in on the extension as she talks to Otis Blodgett in London.

'If I can get him to England . . . He can't do it here. You know, he's going to have a mental breakdown.'

'Well, we're taking a risk.'

'What risk?'

A spy comes on the line. Someone from Paramount for Dolores . . .

'Otis – are you still there?' asks Monika.

'Yes. The reason you can't hear me is because you have the extension open. It cuts the decibel rate by HALF! Which is why I'm having to scream!'

'I see,' says Monika.

'Now the point is this. If David walks off – just goes to the airport and takes a plane—'

'We're not going to do that.'

'No. I understand that. Monika, please will you both listen to me. You're both so upset, you're not listening to what I'm saying. The important thing is that David should officially deliver a letter to his employers—'

'But who are they? I still don't know,' I say.

'Monika – he can tell anybody whatever he wants to tell them – that he's going back to England for business – not for food! But he must make it clear that he is ready, willing and able to complete the script on time. It's very important that the letter be delivered if that's what you want to do. David's contract says he'll obey the direction of his employer and the employer has said he'll render his services in California. He's breaking his contract! He won't be paid!'

'Yes, I know that,' replies Monika. 'But three weeks ago Marty Bregman said David could come back East to work if he liked. I think he might consider letting us go back to England.'

'Well, I think I had better get on to Marty. I'll ring you back,' says Otis.

'Thank you for all your help,' says Monika tearfully, and she puts the phone down.

'After all that, there's still one thing we don't know,' I point out. 'Who are my employers? Is it Marty? Or Rosenberg? Or Paramount?'

'Otis will sort it out. Leave it to him.'

Then I remember the Iceberg. He must be told what is happening. As usual he is in recess, but when I tell his secretary that I am leaving Hollywood, he quickly rings back. To my surprise he is all for us going back to England. He'll explain it to Jeff Katzenberg, who is a great guy. I give him my sister's number in Oxford, where I can be contacted. She's a Classics don there. Jeff sounds so fascinated when I explain that my parents are Oxford Classics dons too, that I take him through the Sherwin family tree, right back to my earliest known relative – the Blessed Saint Ralph Sherwin, a Catholic hung, drawn and quartered by Elizabeth I for refusing to renounce his faith. Americans have a deep respect for family trees.

Marty Bregman rings. He has every confidence in me, he says, and invites us to stop over a few days in New York on the way back. I explain that we have to catch a direct flight, and assure him that in England I'll finish the script in no time.

'Both Marty and Jeff have every confidence in me,' I tell Monika.

'They all think you're mad,' she replies. 'They're just hoping you're a mad genius.'

9 *June* 1978

We are airborne. A hatchet-faced man in a green suit sits next to me. Monika sleeps with Skye in the opposite aisle.

'Goodbye, Hollywood,' I say.

'The filthiest city in the world,' says the hatchet-faced man. 'You're David, aren't you?'

'Yes.'

'You live in the Forest of Dean?'

'Yes.'

'Guessed so. I'm Ron.'

Panic floods through me. I rise in my seat and shout, 'Help! I'm being escorted by a CIA agent!'

The other passengers burst out laughing. Then I notice how small the plane is. Not a Jumbo but an old 707. A spy plane of course!

A stewardess comes up to me. 'Don't worry. You are in safe hands, Mr Sherwin.' Yes – in the hands of the CIA and the KGB.

As we come in to land at Heathrow, Monika talks to me for the first time on the flight. 'Don't say a word when we're going through Customs.'

My father collects us and drives us home, where to my astonishment I find my parents' doctor waiting for me. I take him into the sitting room and tell him the whole story, from working with Frank Rosenberg to coming home on the spy plane. 'Now go and tell them I'm not mad,' I say.

'All right,' he says, but in the kitchen, where everyone is waiting, the doctor simply shakes his head and says goodbye.

'You lied!' I scream, and chase after him as he climbs into his car. I hurl abuse at him, scratching his gleaming sports car with my keys. He calmly turns the ignition and drives off.

'David, why don't you lie down,' my father says. 'You must be very tired.'

Night. THEY are going to kill me. I have to communicate the truth to Monika. But there are bugs all over the cottage. I grab the telephone notebook to write the facts to her, so THEY won't know, ordering her not to speak but to communicate likewise in absolute silence. It's our only chance.

Seeing spies all round, I scribble in silence.

EVERYBODY
KNOWS –

THIS IS THE BIGGEST
SECURITY JOB EVER
I AM
TERRIFIED.
BUT I DID AT
LEAST WARN THEM
(TWAS ME WHO
TOLD COPS) ROGER
CERT & DEBBIE
DID 'USE' ME

10 June 1978

Monika wants me to see my own doctor, Colin Bell. Nonsense, I say.
I'm as fit as a fiddle. She bursts into tears. Do I realise that last night
my parents ordered an ambulance from the Warneford – the lunatic
asylum – with a straitjacket to carry me off? She prevented them. She
refused to sign the committal orders for me to be put away under
section. She'd phoned Colin Bell, who'd told her that would really
drive me mad. So I must see him – for her sake, and Skye's, and the
marriage's.

We drive to the Forest of Dean. Colin allows me to smoke my pipe
in his office and shyly asks, 'How are the spies?'

'Oh, everywhere!'

'Do you think they mean to harm you?'

'I did the first night back in England. Not now.'

'Well, if you don't think they mean to harm you, you're not paranoic.'

'What am I?'

'Manic depressive. What you've always been. I'm going to give you a new drug to bring you down a bit. Haloperidol.'

'What's Haloperidol?'

'It was invented by the Russians. Administered in large quantities to political dissenters in Soviet psychiatric hospitals, it makes them gaga. But in small quantities it keeps people like you sane. You'll be on it for life.' I must also finish *Venom*, Colin says. I must work for five hours a day – no more. The rest of the day must be free time.

In the car on the way home Monika says, 'I'm behind you – just give us some peace and write *Venom*. I'll help you all I can. I grip her hand. She returns the grip.

22 July 1978

Venom is finished on time! I post two copies to Marty Bregman and one to Otis Blodgett. I am pleased it is over, but an important question remains to be answered. 'Darling,' I ask Monika, 'when everyone said I was bonkers . . .'

'Mmm. Don't talk about it now.'

'Well, I wasn't. I couldn't have invented an American girl in the road saying a snake was looking at her—'

'Shut up!'

'No. It's important to me that I was sane!'

'You were nuts, and you nearly drove me nuts.'

'But that girl. She stopped me in the road . . .'

'Dreams. You were dreaming.'

'But I remember it all so clearly.'

'You're crazy. Shut up!'

24 July 1978

Monika leaves for a week's well-earned rest with her parents in Tiptree, Essex. I phone Lindsay. He is working on his John Ford book. He invites me for a meal after his driving lesson the following Saturday. When he opens the door of his new flat in Stirling Mansions, I embrace him and start to tell him the whole story from the beginning.

'Not that fisherman's tale. I can't bear it. Come and do the sprouts.'

It took three years for Venom *finally to go into production. The screenplay was rewritten by another writer and reverted literalistically to the original novel. All my inventions and subtleties were cut out bar one original line of dialogue. The first director, Tobe Hooper, who made* The Texas Chainsaw Massacre, *had a nervous breakdown trying to make a film out of this scenario. He was replaced by Piers Haggard, a young theatre director from the Royal Court. It is sad; it could have been a great movie.*

Life with Elliott Kastner

28 July 1978
Clanfield Cottage

A call from Otis. The director George Cosmatos loves *Venom* and wants to meet me tomorrow at Elstree Studios, where he is dubbing his film for Elliott Kastner.

A couple of years ago George wanted me to write a film of Kazantzakis's lengthy tome *Freedom and Death*. I'd produced a hundred-page treatment. George, smoking like a maniac in ICM's Georgian office, said, 'Make it two and I'll read it.' He'd been assistant director on *Zorba the Greek*, and I thought he was a nice bull-shitter.

As for Elliott Kastner, I'm already involved in some hugely complicated way in a plan he has to make a film about Nijinsky with Rudolph Nureyev.

29 July 1978
Elstree Studios

George tells me of yet another idea he has which Elliott Kastner is crazy for. *Second Sight* is the story of two identical brothers. One of them is blind, but can communicate telepathically with his twin. Suddenly he realises his brother is the target of a terrifying murder plot . . .

'Take it from there, David,' says George.

15 August 1978

My lawyer and friend Roger Alexander rings. He's at last persuaded
Gay to agree to the terms of the sale of The Falls. Cherry Tree House
is ours.

18 August 1978
Cherry Tree House, the Forest of Dean

Monika, Skye and I move into the shell that is our new home.
Monika will have to sell all her jewellery to pay for the building
work. One godsend is that we don't have a phone. And, according
to the Post Office, we won't be getting one for a year, such is the
shortage of phones and lines. All communication will have to be
made from the public phone box across the green. Back to basics.

2 September 1978

A telegraph motorcyclist comes all the way from Gloucester with a
telegram. I'm to ring Otis about the Nureyev/Nijinsky film. I trudge
across the green to find a fat woman in the kiosk, idly flipping
through the Yellow Pages. After about ten minutes of this she comes
out without making a call.

'Sorry, were you waiting?' she says as she gets into a silver Saab.
The kiosk reeks of BO. I make a reverse-charge call to ICM and
stand half out of the kiosk, trying to breathe fresh air. Otis comes on
the line.

'Hi, David. How are you?'

'Fine. I've had a telegram to ring Maureen Fawcett about meeting
Nigel Gosling.'

'Who is Nigel Gosling?'

'The *Observer* ballet critic. Nureyev lives with him and his wife
when he's in London. There may be new developments on *Nijinsky*.'

'I'll call Maureen. I know her well. Now, George Cosmatos has
asked me to ring . . . er . . . er . . . er what's his name . . . er . , . er—'

'Elliott Kastner,' I interject helpfully.

'Yes. Kastner. The word is Kastner's in trouble. Not real trouble,
but he may not have the finance for er . . . er . . . er . . .'

'*Second Sight.*'

'Yes. So I'm calling him right now. Can you ring me again in an
hour – and invest in those homing pigeons or I will.'

Back in my mouldering room I brew some coffee on the stove and an hour later return to the call box.

'Jesus, David, I've only had two minutes, Kastner is engaged.'

'Have you rung Maureen Fawcett?'

'No. Do you want me to?'

'Well, you said you would.'

'I'll find out just what the hell everyone is playing at. You go back and do something therapeutic. Ring me at home on Sunday.'

Lucky Dostoevsky, who could write glibly for money and from his soul for God. I decide to accept *Nijinsky* on any terms and phone Tessa Kennedy, Elliott Kastner's girlfriend. A deep male voice answers. 'Tessa's gone down to Runnymede for the weekend.' He gives me another number, but when I dial it, I get the out-of-order tone.

'Could you put me through to Runnymede,' I ask the operator.

'Where's that?'

'It's where the Magna Carta was signed and also there's a memorial to John Kennedy there.'

'There is no Runnymede listed. Sorry.'

10 September 1978
London, Soho

A meeting with Tessa Kennedy, Frank Dunlop and Robert Dorn Helm. Robert is the Austro-Romanian who will direct the film. Dunlop will produce.

'I see it as a symphony,' Robert Dorn Helm says. 'Movement, then halt. It will be in eight languages. The original Nijinsky costumes are in the Paris Conservatoire. I will use them. Also I will use narration.'

'But Robert,' says Tessa, 'this is supposed to be a feature film. Where's the story?'

'Well, Elliott said he wanted an action story, but I think I have heard this from many producers – they all want action. But this is maybe an art film.'

Afterwards, outside the restaurant, Frank Dunlop says, 'Christ, what a charmer that Robert is. A real gigolo. I'll have to ring Rudi tonight and ask if he's screwed him.'

25 October 1978
London, Notting Hill Gate

Visit George Cosmatos to discuss *Second Sight*. He lives in a Georgian mansion set in its own grounds behind Gothic iron gates. George waits on the front porch, puffing a cigarette. We climb the stairs. The rooms are huge and full of eighteenth-century furniture. The place is an idealised version of a British embassy.

'What would you like to drink,' George asks as he leads me into an empty room.

'What have you got?'

'Wines, whiskies, anything. I don't drink.'

'Whisky, please, George.'

'Ah, we have an alcoholic writer.'

I show him my notes on *Second Sight*.

'Ah, the brother and the girl have a Madame de Staël and Voltaire relationship – I like that. But that there is a gold mine, I don't like – it's been done before.'

I tell George that we have a beginning but no middle or end. There's no plot. Only a hero, a blind man getting his murdered brother's eyes. In short, a title, *Second Sight*. What we need is Hitchcock's Macguffin, a peg – it can be anything – to hang the action on.

By this time, George, the non-drinker, has smoked a pack of Dunhills. He opens another pack. As he talks, he sticks each cigarette violently into his mouth, like a suicide with a revolver. He expires each cigarette with five or six enormous puffs and then immediately lights another one. 'Yes, the Macguffin. I agree. What I like is poison. Do you know, one man with a tiny bottle can exterminate the world? What about milk? They're poisoning milk.'

'Milk isn't very visual. What about hamburgers?'

'Hamburgers? What do they look like?'

'They're round. Americans eat two hundred million of them every day.'

'Ah, yes. And in our story everyone in America has to become vegetarian. My wife is vegetarian. She will approve. Or Coca-Cola – the Macguffin could be Coca-Cola. You see, the film must have a message. It is stupid to say if you want a message, call Western Union. I want a message. Also fantastic locations – if Kastner will pay for us to go to Spain, Portugal, South America, Japan, Indonesia, then I know he is serious. You must buy *National Geographic*. Charge it to me.'

To stop myself from laughing I light my pipe and drop the match in the ashtray, which is overflowing with George's butts. The match bounces out and onto the antique mahogany table. It is still alight and causes irreparable damage. I swipe at it, but like a swatted wasp it refuses to die.

'Don't worry. The man who owns this place is a rat,' says George.

'We have two things going for us,' George continues. 'What any film needs if it's not going to be another script on the shelf. First me, the director. Second, a great part for a star. Every star gets offered to play a cop. A star wants two things: money and not to play a cop. With this film he can walk into the Beverly Hills Polo Lounge and say, "Guess what? In my next movie I play two parts – a blind man and his brother." Elliott Kastner says I think like a producer. I don't want to be a producer, but maybe I should.'

In the evening when I tell Monika about meeting George and what he said about stars in the Polo Lounge, she says, 'I feel ill.'

28 October 1978

Luke comes for a visit. He seems sad.

3 November 1978

I drop Luke off at his mother's on my way to Lindsay's for a good bash on *The Great Advertisement for Marriage*. Luke has been depressed all week. When Gay opens the front door he runs straight past her up to his room.

Gay tells me she has to go into hospital in February and has to stay there till her baby is born in April. Her last child had lung and brain damage and the machine was switched off after ten days.

'Well, I must be going,' I say earnestly. 'Take care of yourself, Gay.'

'I don't give a damn what happens. Nature will have to take its course.'

Then she advances. 'What's all this propaganda you're telling my son? He's been saying that Daddy and Monika had to sell their house because Mummy took all their money.'

'I suppose it's the truth.'

She grimaces, and I make for the car.

Is Luke sad because he is worried that the new child may die or is it because he knows that he comes from a split home? When his baby brother died he said, 'He's lucky. He's in heaven.'

I stand outside Lindsay's new apartment block and press the bell to his flat. Moments pass and I put my ear to the intercom. Nothing. I step back and a voice shouts, 'Hello, at last!' I look round. The street is empty. Then I look up. Lindsay leans out of a third-floor window. 'Just checking. You can come up.'

He opens the door, giving his silent raised eyebrow appraisal and then proffers a regal hand.

'You're late.'

'I got held up returning Luke.'

'Liar. You were in the pub.'

'Smell my breath!'

'OK. Well, Frank's coming in a minute.'

'Frank Grimes?'

'Yes. Frank. You know about Frank and Cheryl – they're thinking of splitting up and he's got lots of experiences to tell which will help you. You need a catalyst.'

The bell goes.

'Answer it – it'll be Frank.'

Frank gives me the actor's one-armed hug, twirling me around. It is the new fashion. Malcolm does the same.

'How are things, Frank?' asks Lindsay.

'Cheryl is throwing me out. I may not have a home tonight.'

'Oh, Lord. And how's the wig?'

'The producer's insisting I wear it as it cost £800.'

'Tell David about the wig.'

The wig is for Frank's TV series *My Son, My Son*. It's been designed by the best wig-maker in London to make him look like Bernard Shaw, but it is half an inch too short. Frank wanted to adjust it himself, but the BBC make-up department said if he touched it with a finger they would go on strike and halt the production.

'Now, what would you like for lunch?' Lindsay asks. 'Chops or cheese?'

'Chops.'

'Chops.'

'Well I'm having cheese salad,' says Lindsay, starting to prepare the meal.

'Forget about your wig, Frank, what about our story? What about *The Great Advertisement for Marriage*?' Lindsay asks.

Dead silence except for the chops sizzling under the grill.

'Well . . .' begins Lindsay, 'I thought it ought to start with a young actor auditioning. He's on stage giving his best when suddenly he realises no one is listening, no one is out there, they have all left the theatre. So he goes home. His wife tells him she's pregnant and they'll have to find a new home. He's out of work, but they've heard of a wonderful basement apartment . . . Frank, do you remember when you were living with Michelle and Miriam Clore said she had a marvellous flat in her very Belgravia house, which you could have if you did a bit of hoovering and answered the phone? And you remember, Frank, how we all went round and Miriam went on and on about how marvellous the flat was, but wouldn't let us in. So finally I said, "Look Miriam, we've come all this way to see the flat. Shut up and show it to us," and we went in and it was repulsive. Miriam kept saying, "Look at it, isn't it marvellous?" And then I punched her and she fell on the bed.' Lindsay hoots with mirth, continuing to hoot to himself as he serves the chops.

'Anyway, the actor and his wife move into the basement and work as servants until one day the actor meets one of the Holland Park druggies, played by Jill Bennett. Do you know what Holland Park druggies are, David?'

'No.'

'Well, if you do have to bury yourself in the country. You'd better do some research – find out about life. Anyway, the actor is seduced by the Jill Bennett character and goes off with her and then they – you know – have . . .

At this point Lindsay drops a clipping from *Playboy* onto the kitchen table. Frank reads it out with dramatic gusto:

YUMMY! I have been experimenting with various foods and flavours during love-making and the results have been utterly delicious. My first attempt involved spreading a soft chocolate marshmallow cookie over my lover's cock and balls. I intended to lick it off immediately, but since the feeling of that sweet, sticky goo was driving him wild, I took my time and spread it all around his crotch and up to his navel. And then I started licking slowly working my way to his quivering dick. It was such a trip to literally eat while going down on him, that I almost came myself while he exploded in my mouth.

After that first luscious episode, we've tried other tastes, textures and even temperatures. My man has licked warm oatmeal off my breasts and gone down on me after drinking hot soup. We've played with everything from peeled cucumbers to Jell-o . . . I might dab a few drops of almond extract onto my shoulders and thighs and ask my lover to explore my body with his tongue and find the tasty spots. It feels like he's searching for some new erogenous area that only I know about.

My current fantasy is making love in a bath tub full of chocolate pudding but the prospect of making and cleaning up all that pudding has kept this venture in the idea stage.

Name withheld by request. Chicago, Illinois.

Frank suddenly changes his theatrical tone. 'Christ, I'm not doing all this with Jill!'

'I didn't say exactly that. It's just *like* that – sex.'

'But Jill's not attractive. She's old. She's fucking ugly! I can't get off with her!'

'It oughtn't to come as news to you that many consider Jill extraordinarily beautiful.'

'Why can't it be someone like Cheryl?' asks Frank.

'Because that's boring,' says Lindsay.

'I agree,' I say. 'The real Gay and the *Great Advertisement*–'

'Oh, shut up, you idiot,' snaps Lindsay. 'She's an old wives' tale.'

Frank roars stagily, 'Jill Bennett, for God's sake, Lindsay, is disgusting!'

'Are the chops OK?' Lindsay asks.

'Tasty,' says Frank.

'Tasty? Do you know how they're made?'

'I've never cooked in my life. It's my working-class background.'

'Well, at least one thing a public school teaches you is how to fend for yourself. You can't even cook a chop?'

'NO!' Frank roars.

'It's easy. You sprinkle it with Worcester Sauce and garlic salt.'

'Worcester Sauce – what's that?'

'Here. And you let it sit for thirty minutes and then grill it. Can you boil an egg?'

'No. My mother wouldn't let us touch the stove.'

'Well, your mother's not here.'

'I wish she was.'

'The sooner you stop wanting mummy the sooner you'll grow up.'

'Jill Bennett!' Frank roars again. 'It's disgusting!'

'Can't you see how it adds a whole new dimension to the piece?

It gives it style. It makes it comic. Anyway, you explain, David. I'm going next door. If I get involved too early I'll be destructive. Get on now and watch the Gold Label. Oh, by the way, you realise what the theme is?'

'Marriage,' says Frank with a strange smile. Then he breaks into a peal of actorly laughter and thumps the table: 'Marriage for fuck's sake! *The Great Advertisement for Marriage.*'

'That's the title. I'm talking about the theme.'

'The attempts of a man to find his soul.'

'No. The struggle, the eternal struggle, in all its forms. If you want any cheese you'll have to help yourself. Leave the washing up.'

Lindsay leaves the room and Frank helps himself to brandy.

'Cheers.'

'Cheers.'

Frank's eyes are desperately tired and when he laughs he looks like a middle-aged female impersonator. His teeth are packed closely together, each tooth perfectly square. It is as if he has a mouthful of sugar lumps. I ask him how come they're so perfect.

'Zeffirelli wanted me to play Jesus in his film and had me go to this dentist. The teeth cost Zeffirelli £1,000, but then he wanted to seduce me. I was staggered. I was so innocent then. Of course I said no and didn't get the part. So I was on the next plane out of Rome.'

I switch on the tape recorder. 'Maybe this story of ours is another version of the Hans Christian Andersen story: the Snow Queen stole the little boy and tried to keep him from the little girl who loved him by blinding him with a chip of ice.'

'Yes! The Snow Queen and the Angel. That's the wife. My wife. When she found out I was being unfaithful, I said, "Look, I love you, but we were married too young. I need this for my acting, I need to sow a few wild oats. Let me spread my wings. If you love me you'll let me go and then I'll come back to you a better person." And she said "All right, I love you. Go!"'

'She really said that?'

' "I love you. Go. I'll always be here." '

'That's an amazing story.'

'Do you think so?'

'Brilliant. Go on.'

'Hey. Do you think we'll get paid?'

'Well, at some point we'll have to be. I've got to live.'

'What did you get for your last script?'

'$35,000.'

'Christ – it's great being an author.'

After only a few more minutes Frank says he's got to go and gets up to say goodbye to Lindsay. 'You know Lindsay is like a father to me.'

I say nothing. I'm tired of joining in the Lord God Almighty stakes. As I wash up the plates I can hear Frank talking to Lindsay in his bedroom. 'I love her, but I'm not *in* love with her any more. I could leave tonight.'

'Then why don't you? Instead of waiting for her to throw you out so you can blame her.'

I enter the bedroom. Lindsay lies full-length on the bed. Frank sits on the end of it.

'Well,' says Lindsay. 'Can you work together? Are you a partnership?'

After a long pause I say, 'I think we could be.'

4 November 1978

Lindsay leaves before I am up. He is directing Alan Bennett's *The Old Crowd* for London Weekend. For the first time I have a good look at his new flat. I'd helped him find it a year ago when he left Greencroft Gardens. It's immense. Everywhere there are posters, prizes and plaques marking his successes in cinema and theatre. In the living room there is a vast collection of film history books, cuttings books, tapes and LPs. It is a museum. A lifetime in drama put carefully on display. In the corridor I peer at framed photographs of Cheltenham College boys posing with their sports trophies. I recognise Lindsay's brother, Murray, in the Cheltenham College athletics team of 1939. I examine a picture of the young Lindsay. Even as a child, his worldly-wise eyes deliver a mocking stare.

I go into the kitchen, which is the friendliest room in the flat, and pour myself a Scotch. I wipe down the vast kitchen surfaces and think about the Snow Queen. It is of course absolute rubbish, this idea of the actor being seduced by a druggie. And where does it all end? Back with the brave little wife. Pathetic.

The phone rings. Donald Howarth asks if he's expected for supper. I tell him he is, but Lindsay is not back yet. He says he won't set off until Lindsay rings to confirm – he might be tired and not want to see him. 'I can always eat supper at home.'

I think this is a bit peculiar and take another swig of Scotch. I look at the pile of scripts on the kitchen table. Mostly rubbish that people send Lindsay. He has lost the Royal Court, his mother, his wonderful old flat in Greencroft Gardens. Now he just dictates lugubrious pontifical letters to the world, brings Frank and me together for mutual therapy, and writes notes in the margins of appalling scripts. I wipe down the kitchen surfaces again. Everything in his flat must be spotless.

The phone rings. Lindsay is at the Tube station, but has left his spectacles at the TV studio. He will be an hour late.

'What an idiot,' he says when I tell him about Donald Howarth, 'I'd better ring him.'

By the time Lindsay finally arrives, my unfocused anger against him and his too perfect flat has evaporated. Donald Howarth turns up soon afterwards. A tall, thin, elderly man in a grey suit, carrying a bicycle pump. He has cycled all the way from Notting Hill. He takes off his jacket to reveal a clinging, see-through woollen sweater.

Lindsay shows him the flat. Over dinner Donald tells us about the new play he has written. Michael White said he liked it. Then, another producer, Helen Montague, who put on those brilliant hits *The Bed Before Yesterday* and *The Seagull*, also expressed an interest. Because of Michael White, Donald said that the play wasn't free.

'You are an absolute fucking idiot, the biggest idiot I've ever seen. Of course the play is free. God, what a fool!' sneers Lindsay.

Donald's smile vanishes. He looks as though he is about to cry.

'You are a fool,' Lindsay repeats brutally.

After a silence Donald mumbles, 'Yes, I probably am, but I don't like to mess people about.'

'You mean, wetly, you don't mind if they mess you about. You make me puke.'

If I were Donald, I would have left. There is a naked violence in Lindsay – this man is not a guest. Were they once lovers?

I ask Donald about his cycle.

'Three-speed, you know. Upright handlebars, but as soon as I get on it I know I'm on my way – you know, moving. Last Sunday I rode it down to the "Coleherne" pub – you know the "Coleherne"?'

Lindsay says he doesn't. Donald explains. 'Well, it's the only real gay pub in London. On Sunday it was packed. We were all enjoying ourselves and then at closing time they rang this big heavy bell . . .'

'Yes, well, have some pudding – treacle tart,' says Lindsay.

'I'll get fat.'

'You need feeding up. I'm going to feed you up. Here – cream?'

'Yes, please,' says Donald and he eats up his portion.

'More?' asks Lindsay.

'I shouldn't.'

Lindsay becomes flirtatiously bullying. 'Go on. More, Donald. Nice treacle tart, Donald.'

'I shouldn't, I really shouldn't.'

'It'll make you big and strong.'

'Ooh, er, yes, well, please then.'

Donald forks another triangle of treacle tart into his giggling mouth.

'Can you tell the difference from home-made? Can you? Tell me the truth?'

'No, I can't,' squeaks Donald. 'More, please.'

'Good boy.'

5 November 1978

I sit at the kitchen table and light my pipe. I am waiting for my old friend Ian Rakoff, the assistant editor on *O, Lucky Man!*, to come and brief me on Holland Park druggies.

'What are you doing?' demands Lindsay, who is preparing lunch for an American director, Curtis Harrington.

'Smoking.'

'God, you irritate me.'

'Why?'

'You ought to be preparing questions to ask Ian, going through that tape you did with Frank, not sitting around like a loon.'

Ian arrives. We go into the sitting room, where he tells me all about snorting cocaine, Dr Dudu who sells the stuff, and high society.

'Shall we split?' he says, when the American director turns up and we are pointedly not invited to lunch.

We go to my old escape hole, the 'North Star' pub.

'How's Lindsay?' Ian asks.

'Still pretty vicious.'

'Well, if he wasn't, you wouldn't know you were alive. How's Frank Grimes?'

'I really don't know him.'

'I met Frank at the retrospective I helped put on for Lindsay at the National Film Theatre last year. Frank was behaving like God, so I walked out. Lindsay loves these innocent actors, because he thinks he can transform them.'

I think it goes much deeper, but still . . .

As Ian jumps aboard a no. 31 bus back to Notting Hill Gate, suddenly he says: 'Lindsay is brilliant at getting the minimum efficiency from the maximum people.'

Back at the flat, Lindsay and Curtis Harrington are listening to music. Lindsay puts on records and asks, 'Who's singing is this?' It is one of his favourite games. Curtis Harrington gets all the songs wrong. I go into the kitchen and wipe down the surfaces until Frank turns up for another session on *The Great Advertisement*. But once again he soon gets bored and goes off to talk to Lindsay, who has just seen off Curtis Harrington. Another session on Frank's relationship with Cheryl. My therapy is washing up the dirty lunch plates.

The doorbell rings. It is David Storey.

'He's coming to supper,' says Lindsay.

'Come on, Frank, let's get back to work,' I say.

'No, I've got to go and see David Storey.'

'We ought to do some work.'

'No, I must speak to him.'

Typical actor, fawning on the famous. I give up. I put away my tape recorder and wipe down the surfaces again.

Lindsay's eyes look up to heaven as Frank tells David about his experiences of EST. David listens politely, clasping a glass of wine with both hands. His face is still young and boyish, although deep lines are etched around his huge, glistening eyes.

'They ask what's your greatest ambition,' says Frank.

'So you said you wanted to win an Oscar,' says David Storey.

'I said I wanted to be myself and be successful. They said, "That's fucking vague. When you come here you are nothing. When you leave here we'll have taught you what you want and how to get it." They talk to you fifteen hours a day, and if you ask a question, it's "Shut up! Idiot." Only they are allowed to talk. You're reduced to a quivering pulp and then you're reborn.'

David Storey turns to me and asks what I'm doing.

'Trying to write something original.'

'It'll be good if you can get writing again,' he says softly.

'There's one question I've always wanted to ask you,' I say. 'How many hours do you write a day?'

'Twelve.'

'Every day?'

'Oh yes.'

'How long does it take you to write a play?'

'Two days.'

'Two days – really?'

'Well, they say you should put more into a play than that. I suppose they're right,' he says modestly.

Somehow this modesty seems arrogance. If what he says is true, he writes 180 plays a year.

'You're looking very well, very slim,' Frank says to him. 'Do you do any training?'

'No, I just stay the way I am.'

'And you don't do anything? Not even jogging?' I ask.

'Nothing.'

'Good Lord, that's marvellous. How old are you?'

'Forty-seven,' says David Storey. 'And you?' he asks.

'Thirty-six.'

'Thirty-six and burnt out,' says Lindsay loudly from his prone position on the couch.

It's time to go, I decide. 'Bye, everybody!' I say, jumping to my feet. 'Bye,' they echo, and I leave.

The night streets are like empty caverns, free spiritual places. I kick the autumn leaves, released from Lindsay's Royal Court. Back to Cherry Tree House and Guy Fawkes night, sparklers with Skye and Monika.

6 November 1978

I phone Lindsay, needing a Scotch to do so.

'The Snow Queen stinks. I'm not going to work with Frank any more. *The Great Advertisement for Marriage* is going to be my own work. I'm going to write it as a novel. By myself.'

'I'm absolutely delighted,' Lindsay says. 'Onwards!'

The crash of Hollywood

10 November 1978

Otis Blodgett has sent me a novel from a Hollywood producer called Chuck Fries. The best thing about *The Crash of '79* is its cover: THE NUMBER ONE INTERNATIONAL SUPERSELLER. The blurb is promising: 'With a keen eye for big money and magnificent women, financial wizard Bill Hitchcock manipulates international futures and astronomical fortunes from the most powerful spots of the world – New York, Washington, Saudi Arabia, and finally the Shah of Iran's fabulous chalet at St Moritz – as events draw him and the world he has helped to shape toward a stunning and utterly mesmerising climax.'

'It could be a blockbuster,' Monika says.

3 December 1978

I arrive in Los Angeles to work on *The Crash of '79*. The warm sunny evening makes me feel overdressed in my English winter woollies. I stand in line, half hoping that Immigration will act on the information of my good old spies and label me an undesirable alien – then I can go home. When it comes to my turn, the Immigration officer is surprisingly pleasant. 'Welcome to the States! Have a good trip!' But the Customs officer is suspicious.

'What is the purpose of your visit? Business or pleasure?'

'Business.'

'What kind of business?'

'I'm here for a script conference.'

'You mean you're here to try and sell a script?'

'No. I'm a writer. I'm here to discuss the script I've been hired to write.'

'Do you have any scripts on you to prove it?'

I open my bag and show him Monika's handwritten ninety-page breakdown of the book. He studies it closely, flipping the pages. I feel I'm already in a script conference. The Customs officer likes it. 'OK,' he says, initialling my declaration form.

I take a taxi to the Howard Johnson's motel where I'm staying. Howard Johnson's – how are the mighty fallen. But it is a good lesson: this trip I'll do what I'm told and on no account open my mouth.

I go to bed and watch TV. As it's still Sunday, there's a programme about a faith healer. He's a grotesquely fat young man who can only cure bad ears. Deaf old folk who have tried everything without success come to him as their last hope. He makes them bow their heads. Then he sticks a podgy finger in each sufferer's earhole and incants: 'In the name of the Lord – Hear! Suddenly he jerks out his finger and shouts, 'Pop!'

'In the name of the Lord – Hear! – Pop!'

4 December 1978

Go down to breakfast. The waitress has huge fat legs, but still wears the orange Howard Johnson micro-mini. She spills the whole coffee tray over my one and only suit. She makes no apology, but says, 'If you bill the motel, they'll pay for that to be cleaned. More coffee?'

'What a start to the day,' says a friendly looking man opposite me. 'I've just moved to LA. Start work in a month. I'm from the East. It's a whole new beginning for me.'

I go back to my room. At 9.15 a.m. the phone rings. Malcolm Stewart, who is producing *The Crash of '79* with Charles Fries, welcomes me to LA. He's sending a car round to take me to Studio City. I wait in the lobby, where there is a huge real Christmas tree and an artificial fire with metal imitation logs. A boy of about 18 comes up to me. 'Mr Sherwin?'

'Yes.'

'Charles Fries Productions – the car's outside.'

He leads me to a silver Porsche. It is gleaming, but the inside is filthy. I remove several empty Perrier bottles from the passenger seat and climb in. The boy revs the engine and we shoot off.

'Is this the studio car?' I ask.

'No. Mine. I usually use my Ford but it's off the road having new carbs.'

'Have you been with Charles Fries long?'

'Six weeks, but I'm moving on – they use too much of my lunch break.'

Studio City at first sight seems unlike any other studio I've been in. It is brand new. The carpets are thick and clean. One wall is sheet glass from ceiling to floor, and offers a view of the distant mountains. Charles Fries Productions is an open-plan area, off which are a cluster of offices. A small, slender man in a tight sweater comes up to me, extending a hand. He is Malcolm Stewart. He leads me into his office, which is piled high with hundreds of books. There is only one picture, a beautiful photograph of a gannet gliding over the sea. Malcolm Stewart is obviously 'the taste' in Charles Fries Productions. He lights a cigarette and sits down, not behind his desk, but beside me. He talks about *The Crash of '79*. He speaks very, very slowly, and his voice is oddly husky, as though he had taught himself to talk deep to make up for his smallness.

He tells me his theory of drama. The ideal stage play is one in which the curtain goes up on an ordinary living room. A man comes in and hides a bomb under a chair. He leaves the room and the audience never sees him again. The play's characters enter and start talking. No matter what they say, the audience is hooked. I light my pipe and listen intently as he goes on to tell me his theory about Bill Hitchcock, the central character in *Crash*. He must be an ordinary jock, with whom the movie fan in Arkansas can identify. I want to point out that our hero must be an extraordinary jock to be the financial genius the Saudi Arabians have picked to run their country, but remember my new resolution to keep my mouth shut.

Chuck Fries joins us. He has jet-black hair and is enormously fat. He talks very fast. There's no way the film can follow the book, he says, as its successful villain, the Shah of Iran, is in real life about to be toppled by the Ayatollah Khomeini. We will have to have a 'what if' plot. He also thinks the Shah's atomic bomb should not go off. Remembering Malcolm Stewart's theory of bombs I break my silence and insist it must. Instantly I realise that I've been a fool.

'Could you write some kind of treatment today,' Fries asks.

'Now?'

'We can get you a secretary.'

Trapped! I try to stall. 'She'll have to be a good secretary.'

'We'll get you the best in Hollywood. You can work here in the office next door. I'll be very quiet, and you can stay all night if necessary.'

'Fine.' After *Venom* I'd sworn never to work in a studio office again, but there is no way out. And I am determined to cooperate.

Half an hour later Iris, the best secretary in Hollywood, arrives. She is in her fifties, smiling and eager. We settle down to work. I dictate and she types directly onto the page. When she can't understand something she asks, 'What was that, dear?' Progress is rapid, except that every time I say 'Riyadh', she stops, laughs and says, 'Riyadh – where is the Y, dear?'

After an hour or two there's a knock on the door. It is the chief secretary from reception. 'Do you want anything?' she asks.

'I'd love some coffee. Can you get me a cup?'

My secretary frowns with disapproval. 'No, dear,' she says. 'I have to get your cup.' A faux pas. Everyone here, even a runner who has had too much of his lunchtime used up, has a rating . . . Nowhere is the class system more rigidly enforced than in Hollywood.

5 December 1978

I invite Mike Legge, one of my old photography partners, round to lunch. I've kept in touch with him ever since he fled England for the magic and the girls of the Far East. He hasn't eaten for two days, and has two rounds of the Howard Johnson's junk meal.

'Nothing worries me any more,' he says. 'It's like this: you go on holiday for two weeks and you feel a bit better. Well, I went to the East for five years and had my brain scrubbed clean.'

He tells me about the jungle. 'You hack your way in and then in a minute it grows behind you. You're trapped in the darkness of the rainforest with the screams of wild animals. There's nothing like it in the world.'

Once, in the deepest depths, he came across a tribe watching *Kojak* on an old television. They worshipped Telly Savalas like a god.

I am astounded to learn that Mike the photographer did not take a single picture in the jungle. Its magic cannot be captured, he says. He prefers the memory. Now he has come to Hollywood determined to succeed as a movie photographer.

I tell him that one day we will write the movie of his exotic adventures in the East.

He replies, 'Here, when you say you come from the East, they say, "Oh, how's New York . . ." They don't know about the East and don't care. We can't write a film about that.'

We part.

6 December 1978

I wake very early and jog round the bedroom. The hours pass. No phone call from Studio City to say what they think of my treatment. I phone Jeff Berg to warn him I may be fired, and soon afterwards I finally get a call summoning me to a meeting in the afternoon.

I have lunch with my old friend Chris Mankiewicz. He turns his nose up at the Howard Johnson's and drives me twenty miles to a restaurant where, as the meal is on Chuck Fries, he has two helpings of each course. His huge frame will be stocked up for the next week. Chris is one of the few unconceited people in films. I have known him since he was Grimaldi's assistant on the Zeffirelli fiasco, *Camille*. He admits that he is the only Mankiewicz without talent. His uncle wrote *Citizen Kane*; his father, Joe, directed *All About Eve* and his brother Tom is now writing James Bond films. But Chris has a big plan: he wants to come to England and make a film with the comedian John Cleese. He is convinced that John Cleese could be a film star and he wants me to write the script. He will be in touch as soon as he raises the money to get to England.

At Studio City Malcolm Stewart introduces me to the third producer, Tony – 'the conscience behind this outfit'. Tony, who is even smaller than Malcolm, has long, flowing, ash-blond hair and a tired, bony face. He says he finds the treatment incomprehensible, but is going to 'scrape a few ideas off the side of the wall'. I switch on my tape recorder. He speaks brilliantly for about four hours. I'm suffering from jet-lag and just mumble, 'Great . . . I agree . . .'

10 December 1978
Cherry Tree House

I play the tape back to hear nothing but Tony endlessly repeating 'We must make something like Hitchcock's *North by Northwest* without being too James Bondish.' That's all the advice I have for travelling all the way to Hollywood.

14 December 1978

It's freezing cold and snowing heavily. The forest is pure white. I write the first scene of *Crash*, set in the hot desert.

5 January 1979

We go for a walk and see a new-born foal in the snow. I put *Crash* to one side and write a sad chapter of *The Great Advertisement for Marriage* – all about Gay kidnapping Luke. I remember every detail and every word. I post it to Lindsay.

10 January 1979

A postcard from Lindsay. 'The chapter is brilliant. Perhaps *The Great Advertisement* will be a masterpiece. No shrimshanking, mind. Love, Lindsay.'

I write a happy chapter – Luke's birth – then shrimshank and return to *Crash* to earn my daily bread.

28 May 1979
Cherry Tree House

A hot calm day. Good model-flying weather. I finish *Crash* and post it to Chuck Fries in Hollywood.

6 June 1979

A telegram arrives from Otis: 'Phone Malcolm Stewart for script conference. Reverse the charges.'

I set out for the phone box with the script and a fresh notepad. The conference goes well. Malcolm likes what I've done and is going to discuss it with Chuck Fries. We're to have another conference tomorrow.

7 June 1979

Disaster. They've totally changed their minds overnight. Now they do want it James Bondish. They want me over there to do the rewrite. I refuse. I care no more for James Bond than I do for Margaret Thatcher. I'm fired in my phone box.

9 June 1979

Otis Blodgett sends me a very thin book called *9½ Weeks*, which Frank Konigsberg wants to adapt as a screenplay. Am I interested? 'Frank Konigsberg is extremely well known to me,' Otis writes, 'and is a man I think you may get along with very well. He is intelligent, honest (relatively) and with extremely good taste; a cut above the average Hollywood producer.'

9½ Weeks is a bourgeois, apparently true study of sado-masochism. The best bit, as always, is the blurb on the back:

By day she was a high-paid young executive in a Manhattan office. By night she was the willing slave of a man who bathed her, fed her, dressed her . . . and choreographed her every move in an ecstatic and terrifying ritual of total sexual surrender. This is not fantasy. It is the actual night-by-night diary of a woman who gave herself unconditionally to a man she hardly knew. It is perhaps the most powerful erotic book ever written by a woman.

I go to the phone box and reverse the charges to ICM. 'Otis, it's a bit boring and a bit pornographic.'

Otis explodes like a raging bull. 'If it's pornographic don't touch it with a barge-pole! If you write something pornographic, you'll be dead in Hollywood.' So I turn it down.

Today in 1995 9½ Weeks is number 67 in the list of top-grossing movies of all time. Skye teases me about my folly. Ah well . . .

Britannia Hospital:
The Unofficial Diary

5 December 1979
Cherry Tree House

It comes as a bolt from the blue.

It is too cold to work in the caravan, my refuge from the family and the phone. So I'm in the upstairs junk room trying to write an awkward chapter in my novel. Monika calls from the stairs. 'Telephone!'

I unlock the door, which I've bolted against the exuberant Skye. 'You answer it. If it's for me, I'm not in.'

'I'm not answering it, it will only be another wrong number.'

We only get wrong numbers on our new phone. It goes on ringing and ringing. I can't think to type my next line. I go downstairs, cursing the wrong number, but to my amazement find it is Lindsay calling from America.

'How's the novel?' he asks.

'Stuck.'

'Then it's just as well I've got you your next job. *Memorial Hospital* – you're writing it. I've done a two-picture deal with Fox.'

I am dumbstruck, overjoyed – the opportunity to make another film with Lindsay after so many fruitless attempts. *Memorial Hospital* . . . I remember back two years ago to a stay at Lindsay's cottage in Rustington. We were walking along the old shingle shore, discussing *The Great Advertisement for Marriage*. 'Of course,' he'd said, walking through low tidal pools of water towards the sea, 'what you also have to write is *Memorial Hospital*.' Standing like Canute before the oncoming sea, he told me some of his ideas. Two years earlier Charing Cross Hospital had been besieged by people demonstrating against fee-paying private patients. A union official known as Battling Granny Brookstone led the protests. Turning ambulances away from a hospital in the name of humanity struck Lindsay as absurd. The film would be about the utter madness and selfishness of society.

'Do you remember the "Winter of Discontent" last year?' Lindsay asks.

'Yes. The whole country on strike. Cancer patients being refused treatment and begging the pickets for mercy. Ambulance-men refusing to pick up dying patients.'

'Bombs going off. It's what happens every day in the newspapers. You don't have to be clever or write your usual "funny" lines. It's all in the subject, but you'll have to experience it for yourself. Get out of your caravan. Go to a hospital and research. Talk to those bloody-minded union leaders.'

'I'll do it.'

'You can write anything you like. Everything must be in this film.'

'What's the poetic key?'

'Dramatic extremism. I've also negotiated a brilliant contract for you.'

'Oh – how much?'

'You'd better be grateful. It's a better deal than your agent could ever negotiate.'

'Really? But how much?'

'$25,000 for the first draft, $50,000 on the first day of principal photography, and $2^{1}/_{2}$ per cent of profits.'

'Jesus! How much are you getting?'

'Mind your own bloody business.'

'What about the other deal?'

'Oh, that's going to be Ian Rakoff's *Report from the Sex Factory*.' Ian has been writing a novel based on his experiences as a porn movie maker. Lindsay tells me it is brilliant stuff.

'Sounds very commercial.'

'So's *Memorial Hospital*. Not bad – two development deals in one day. Almost as good as Milos Forman.'

'How is Milos?'

'As he's a millionaire on his farm in Connecticut, I can't talk to him any more. Just get your agent to phone Fox. Get it settled. Get on with your research now – and don't spend all the money at once. And don't forget – keep a diary.'

'I do.'

I put down the phone, shaken. 'Write anything you like. Everything must be in this film.' It's the challenge of my life – and one apparently with a pot of gold. Fifty thousand dollars on the first day of shooting.

Monika at first doesn't believe me. Then she is transformed. We won't have to sell our home. We can pay off all our debts. All this, thanks to Lindsay.

Ideas race – a hospital boss who loves his hospital and is prepared to sacrifice his life for it; Professor Millar reappearing from *O, Lucky Man!* to conduct even more extreme experiments with human life; a Royal visit to inspect his penis transplants; an Odessa Steps sequence in which the army mows down the strikers.

6 December 1979

I ring my agent, Otis Blodgett. Excitedly I tell him the news.

'David, I'm sorry to tell you I have other news. Lindsay made that deal with Sandy whatever his name is, who only a month ago was appointed as President of Fox. Today, he's resigned. The other Vice-President's resigned too. There's no one I can deal with until a new leadership is appointed, and then they may turn down Lindsay's development deal. I'm sorry, David, but it's a different language in Hollywood. The monsters out there make *Jaws* look like a film about a goldfish pond. Now, listen to me – do no research, put not your bluntest pencil to paper until things become less hazy on the horizon.'

In spite of Otis Blodgett's advice, I go ahead with the research anyway. I ring my GP and friend Colin Bell and find out that a Mr Winston Taylor is in charge of the Gloucester Royal, the biggest hospital in the county. He finances all the local health centres, the cottage hospitals, every penny that is spent on health, every piece of equipment a doctor or surgeon needs. Obviously Winston Taylor is the hero of our film.

I ring the Gloucester Royal. After cackles of girlish laughter, I am eventually put through to 'Admin'. I explain that I am researching for a film, and would like to talk to Winston Taylor.

'Winston's up on the wards. But I'll get him to call you back, David.'

First names already. A good sign.

Winston rings back at 4 p.m., full of apologies. I lay on jam. The hero of the film is to be a sector administrator just like himself – trying to cope with everything. Winston sounds flattered. However, it is the Christmas period. He is very tied up and won't be able to see me until the New Year.

Otis rings. He has spoken to a lawyer friend at Fox. All hell has been let loose. Sandy what's his name certainly did make a deal with Lindsay Anderson, but now he's gone, no one knows if it will be honoured. Don't do a thing, he warns me. 'I'm reading you the eleventh commandment: do nothing.' I return to my novel.

12 December 1979

A call from Otis. Apparently, part of the confusion has been that the Fox lawyer couldn't reach Lindsay's agent to clarify his side of the contract. He's just done so and the deal is on. I phone Lindsay, who has briefly returned from America. 'This amazing lack of communication,' he comments. 'It's all quite simple really. They are all so fucking lazy.'

14 December 1979

A letter from Lindsay.

> My dear David,
> I'm dictating this before I set out for New York. It suddenly occurred to me that you might like to see the treatment that had originally been prepared by Martin Turner, that strange assistant I had on *The Old Crowd*. There are two versions. You'll see from my comments that I didn't think a great deal of it. When I tried to sit down and work with him, he revealed himself as being just too paranoid, though sympathetic and humorous, but unable to get that mixture of reality and outrageous invention on which I think I may say our style is based. I started myself to rough out an outline – the one in red Tempo writing – but didn't get very far. However, it may give you some ideas.
>
> It needs an enormous amount of work and invention and something really ingenious at the climax (not only ingenious but horrifying. Perhaps Millar unveils a succession of monsters, hybrids, spine-chilling possibilities).
>
> I do hope you make good time with *The Great Advertisement*. The writing really is excellent. You're certainly going to get a

book out of it, anyway, and then you'll be able to sell the rights in that before you start writing the script. I will give you a call when I get back, which will be at the end of next week.

Love, Lindsay.

Lindsay has enclosed three documents: his Tempoed outline for Millar's arrival at his research centre and the two treatments. I find them both unreadable – a verbose mixture of farce and silliness. Lindsay has drawn his red Tempo across most of the pages. But there are two good ideas. The BBC cameraman who with dog-like devotion films the great Professor Millar. And Cheerful Bernie, the hospital disc jockey who is supposed to express the quintessence of vulgarity.

2 January 1980

I arrive at the Gloucester Royal Hospital, early, for my research. A sign by the main entrance states that the doors are broken, and I enter through a side door. I go into a chapel. I see a priest hurrying across the concourse to the chapel, cycle clips around his ankles. Prayers for patients and staff are every Thursday, and can be heard on the hospital radio. I notice off-duty cleaning ladies smoking and eating their breakfast sandwiches. Nurses and doctors pass by. They are smoking too. Everyone in the hospital is smoking. When I finally get to Admin, Winston's personal assistant, Ms Beard, is smoking. Details for the picture.

Winston, the sector administrator, is in his early thirties. At first he is nervous, but I apply the jam about the hero being a sector administrator like himself. Does he often have to deal with strikes, I ask him. No – the only time was when the sewers flooded in the kitchens and the kitchen staff came out as a protest against the health hazard. He invites me to look around, and to speak to whoever I like.

Ms Beard takes me on a tour of the hospital. The wards are new, each with only six beds. Quite an improvement on the Nightingale wards which used to house thirty or forty neglected patients. She shows me the 'Cass Call' system – a console of 680 lights each representing a patient in bed. It reminds me of Houston Mission Control. When a light flashes, the operator radios the nearest nurse. The system is Ms Beard's pride. She raised the funds to install it.

We see Bulova House, a one-storey modern block on the other side of the road from the towering hospital. It houses young terminal patients suffering from muscular dystrophy and multiple sclerosis.

Ms Beard introduces me to Jonathan. Only 27, he looks like a spider and lives in a mobile chair which he operates by sucking and blowing. A suck-blow chair. 'He does like to be independent,' says Ms Beard. 'They're all as cheerful as anything. It's a happy unit.'

Indeed the whole hospital seems happy. The nurses and patients smile and chat while I hover waiting for something dramatic to happen. Nothing does. I meet the chief engineer, who shows me the boiler house, the most modern in England. It is fully automatic and supplies the whole hospital with independent electricity and hot water. The police also use it to burn confiscated pornography. I ask if they suffered from the oil tankers' strike last winter which threatened to close many hospitals.

'No one strikes around here,' he tells me cheerfully, 'Anyway we've six months' supply.'

A 16-year-old unmarried mother watching her baby in Intensive Care tells me it's the best hospital in the world. Over real ale and cigarettes in the Social Club, Ms Beard sums it all up: 'We've got our faults, but ours is the best system. I've travelled. In America, they can't look after their poor. In Africa, women sell babies on the streets. In Germany it's all clinics for the rich. Medicine for profit. This is medicine for caring. I wouldn't change it for any other system in the world.'

21 January 1980

Lindsay rings to find out how I have been getting on. I tell him that the National Health Service is marvellous. I can't see much material in it for *Memorial Hospital*.

'So your research has been a complete waste of time. I'm not interested in making a documentary about a nice hospital. This is about the world.'

I tell him we have another problem: we don't have a plot. Only ideas.

'Then why didn't you ring me earlier? Come up.'

23 January 1980
Stirling Mansions

I drive to Lindsay's flat in London. I mumble my way through the arrival of the sector administrator's assistant at the bomb-struck, strike-ridden hospital and I stop. We agree that the sector administrator, Potter, should be played by Arthur Lowe, and his assistant, Biles, by Brian Pettifer from *If . . .* and *O, Lucky Man!* With the help of adrenalin and whisky, our ideas begin to flow. I have learnt that plying Lindsay with Scotch frees his acutely critical barrister's mind.

22 March 1980
Cherry Tree House

I post my forty-page treatment to Lindsay asking for his immediate reaction. I have filled it full of blood, humour and dramatic extremism. I have tried to patch up the holes in the plot.

23 March 1980

Lindsay rings. 'It's incoherent and dreadful. Mini Alan Bennett. Funny-ha-ha. I told you not to be clever. I'm sorry but you asked for my immediate reaction and that's it. Mini English.'
    I want to cry. I can't go on, I tell Lindsay. I'll have to resign.
    'Fair enough.'
    I put down the phone. I tell Monika *Memorial Hospital* is off. She doesn't speak to me for the rest of the evening. All the Fox money has gone on the overdraft and we are broke.

25 March 1980

A postcard from Lindsay:

> Dear David,
> It is much better to be professionally honest about these things – as you are being – than trying to make a fantasy work. In other words if you can't make anything of *Memorial Hospital*, don't try to force yourself, or to fantasise about writing a DIFFERENT script about a hospital. You had better get on with your own work, i.e. 'The Great Advertisement' which shows every sign of being excellent and successful. I will speak to Blodgett today. Meanwhile, don't feel badly. You have acted both honestly and professionally, and there is nothing unusual about such an impasse. I battle on through rehearsals. *Old Crowd* is on!
>
> Love, Lindsay.

29 March 1980

Financially, things are a mess. Otis Blodgett persuades me to continue with *Memorial Hospital*. During the next few weeks I rework the treatment. I reread Büchner's *Wozzeck*. I invent a new character – Sir Geoffrey Brockenhurst, a surgeon in the hospital, a sworn enemy of Professor Millar and his mysterious experiments. 'You're not a doctor, you're a vampire. To you the patients aren't suffering beings to be cured, they are raw material for your monstrous ego!' shouts Sir Geoffrey.

12 May 1980

A call from Lindsay. He's just about to open *Early Days*, David Storey's new play with Sir Ralph Richardson. He sounds very cheerful. 'An idea occurred to me. When I've seen *Early Days* through its first couple of weeks, we might go down for one of those weekends at Rustington. I have an idea we could write the whole script in three days. Doing it straight into the tape recorder. At least it will be something for Sherry Lansing and we'll all get our money.'

'Who's Sherry Lansing?'

'The new head of Fox. I'm hopeful.'

25 May 1980
Stirling Mansions

I arrive at Lindsay's flat. He has lost his spectacles and has spent an hour searching for them. This happens at least once a day. I find his spectacles and Lindsay shows me a *Vogue* photograph of a beautiful girl with long, wet hair. It is Sherry Lansing, the new President of 20th Century-Fox. She looks about 18.

'How did she get the job?'

'Don't ask naive questions. By the way, how does the title *Britannia Hospital* grab you?

'Epic.'

'This has got to be epic. I don't know why you've lost your epic feel. You were the one who invented the term. All those years ago on *If . . .*, quoting Büchner and Kleist at me.'

'Writing *The Great Advertisement*, I've become a subjective writer.'

'Well, you'd better bloody well remember what epic means.'

'Define "epic".'

Lindsay takes off his spectacles, sits back and thinks for a moment. He puts his spectacles down on the kitchen table. I make a note of where they are.

'The epic is concerned with narrative structure, not decoration. Decoration is bourgeois.'

I write this wisdom down on a sheet of A4 and, when we get down to Rustington, fix it to the wall of my room. Fuchsia Cottage is the perfect place to work. There is absolute quiet and no TV. I set up my typewriter beneath the A4 sheet on the wall. We decide to write out the plot while it's fresh in our minds. It will serve as a guideline tomorrow when we start our marathon. Lindsay pours two Scotches and I start to type. We talk and type until two in the morning.

Before I go to bed, Lindsay tells me that his 19-year-old nephew, Sandy, is visiting tomorrow. Sandy has absconded from his Polytechnic in Oxford and is hiding in London. He wants to discuss his woes with Lindsay. We'll just have to cope.

26 May 1980
Rustington

I wake up early, elated after the previous night's good work. I run a bath. The water is freezing cold.

Lindsay emerges from his room still in pyjamas. 'God, you're keen. It's only eight o'clock.'

'The boiler is on the blink. It's not heating up the water.'

'But it's running.'

The boiler is indeed pounding away in the corner of the kitchen. It is brand new. Lindsay finds the instructions but can't make head or tail of them.

'Perhaps it's the main fuse,' he says.

We go to the fuse box, high in the outhouse. Lindsay produces a chair.

'You look. You're not so valuable.'

I climb up and pull out the fuses. The wires are all intact. The mystery is insoluble and we'll never get an engineer out on Saturday in Rustington. Lindsay goes upstairs to shave in cold water.

At 9.15 we settle down in the living room. Lindsay inserts one of my two-hour cassettes into his tape recorder and sits in the only armchair. I sit at the mahogany table to avoid facing him, with the ten-page plot structure open at page one. We commence.

For a couple of hours we are on a roller coaster. Lindsay keeps saying, 'Yes – what next?' Then after a few minutes' discussion he presses the record button and dictates into the machine, indicating commas, stops, paragraphs, characters underlined and descriptive brackets. Professor Millar's speech at the end of the film is chilling.

'As they shrank, the seas cast millions of unadapted aquatic creatures on to newly created beaches . . . Those who couldn't adapt perished. So today: those who cannot adapt will perish, washed up on the shores of the future. It's the scientist's job to change mankind. We have two weapons, man himself and his brain . . .'

Such high-speed collaborative writing is exhausting, and at three o'clock we come to a grinding halt. There is a massive hole in the plot: Andy Crisp, the militant left-wing union leader who refuses to serve the patients breakfast, is also the leader of the engineers when they come out on strike some twenty-five scenes later. He is in both the kitchen and the boiler room at the same time.

'Propose a solution,' asks Lindsay.

I pace, thinking.

'How long does it take you to answer a question?'

'I don't know. It's your eyes, staring at me.'

'I won't look at you, but give me an answer. I'll time you.'

Lindsay puts on his spectacles and stares at his watch. I go into the kitchen to get out of his presence. I ask him if he would like a Scotch.

'A Scotch and an answer. Two minutes fifteen seconds.'

As I add water to his whisky, the obvious solution comes to me. There has to be an additional union leader: Andy Crisp runs the kitchens, Bill Sharkey runs the engineers. Both walk out at the crucial moment to join the revolutionaries.

'Three and a half minutes,' Lindsay pronounces as I give him his glass. 'And how is this Bill Sharkey introduced to the audience?'

'He's at the presentation to the Queen Mother. Another engineer in the boiler room switches the power off, all the hospital lights go out, and Bill Sharkey joins his lads outside.'

'It's very weak, David.'

But neither of us can think of anything better, Scotch or no Scotch, and that's how it remains.

Lindsay takes a break to baste the chicken, while I look after the Brussels sprouts. Brussels sprouts are Lindsay's favourite food and must be prepared in a special way. Each one has to be peeled, notched four ways top and bottom, soaked in a mixture of lemon juice and pepper, boiled for precisely five minutes and then given a dab of butter. Pleasant work compared to writing, but he keeps firing questions at me. There is another hole in the plot. How is the arrival of the Queen Mother and the Royal party communicated to the outside rioters, so enraging them that they storm the hospital? I come up with the idea that the journalist Jeff is spying on Professor Millar with a tiny video camera. He is caught during Professor Millar's operation and killed. While his body is being stored for future use, a doctor finds the spy camera and nonchalantly pockets it. At the Royal luncheon he idly turns it on and the revolutionaries pick up the transmission in the commandeered recording van.

'Very weak,' says Lindsay, as usual.

As there is no sign of Sandy we go back to work. It is eight o'clock and we are halfway through the screenplay. It's like being a minstrel telling a ballad . . . An hour later and there is still no sign of Sandy. Darkness is drawing in. We decide to have our delayed supper.

'Perhaps he's just vanished into the maw,' Lindsay says. 'He may never be heard of again.'

But two hours later, as we settle down to work through the night, there is a knock on the front door. A tall moustachioed figure stands in the doorway. Sandy. He has come by train from London with a tenner Lindsay posted to him a week ago. All his worldly possessions are in a small haversack. The last time I saw him was fifteen years ago – a plaintive little boy asking, 'Uncle Lindsay, can I watch *Thunderbirds*?' Lindsay: 'No. We're working.'

'Hungry?' Lindsay asks Sandy.

'Quite.'

'Chicken?'

'I don't eat meat. I've brought some rice.'

He eats his rice, starving.

After dinner Lindsay wants to have his confidential chat with Sandy. Sandy is a lost soul. Many lost souls come to Lindsay to pour out their worries. He has a huge amount of love to give.

'Writing is the most horrible business on earth,' Lindsay once said to me, 'but I'm quite good at making constructive comments. I hate all the bullshit of film-making. What I'd really like to do is set up a hotel and give food and lodging and good advice. Why don't I do that? I'd be very good at it.'

27 May 1980

I wake up early and have a bath. Oddly the water is now boiling hot. I make two coffees and show Lindsay the draft of Professor Millar's speech.

'Mmm – not bad.'

The three of us go to the resort of Littlehampton near by. It has an old harbour with sailing boats, sea-front cafés and a funfair. Lindsay explores the cafés. They all look exactly the same, but one sells egg and chips for 65p, another for 75p. Lindsay can't understand why everyone doesn't eat in the cheapest place. A further proof of man's stupidity. We go to the funfair. Lindsay insists I drive a dodgem car with Sandy. He wants to take a photograph of us both. I hate dodgem cars. Lindsay threatens to abandon *Britannia Hospital* if I refuse. He means it, so I get in a car with Sandy. Lindsay aims his camera from the side. There is an enormous collision and everything goes blurry, but *Britannia Hospital* survives . . .

Back in Fuchsia Cottage, Sandy laughs from the kitchen as he overhears our lines, and adds one of his own for Professor Millar: 'We can foresee cabbages on the moon, supermarkets on the stars.' Lindsay likes the line but I find it 'mini English-ha-ha' and delete it.

Finished. The first draft of *Britannia Hospital* fits two 120-minute tapes. I drive Lindsay back to London, Sandy to Oxford, and home to Gloucester where Monika is to transcribe the tapes.

30 May 1980

Monika dispatches Skye to a baby-sitter and sits down at her typewriter. Lindsay's dictation, with commas, punctuation and spelling, make her job easy. She types twenty-five pages the first day, thirty-three the next. She is close to the end of the second tape and I am afraid the script will be too short. It has to be at least ninety pages to look like a feature film. So I tell Monika to type only four words of dialogue to a line and to start the page lower down. The trick works. Just before lunch on the third day she types the ninety-second and last page of *Britannia Hospital*. On the cover sheet I type 'First Polished Draft'. This is because I am only to get the rest of my money when I've produced a first draft plus a 'polish'.

10 June 1980

We go to London to see *Early Days*. The play is good, but not a David Storey masterpiece. It is naturalistic and pared to the bone. Ralph Richardson gets an ovation. When I congratulate Lindsay, he groans, 'Why is it that I can do things naturalistically in the theatre, but am forced into surrealism in the cinema? It ought to be the other way round. The trouble is I don't believe in naturalistic cinema. People being boring in front of the camera.'

3 July 1980

Fox turn down *Britannia Hospital*, and, further, refuse to accept that it is a revised or polished first draft. So no final payment. That's that. The end of six months' work. Another one for the shelf. Back to the caravan and *The Great Advertisement for Marriage*.

15 July 1980

Lindsay's secretary, Kathy, rings from London. She is retyping the script, and can't read the last two lines of page 78. When I ask her why she is retyping the script, she tells me the amazing news. Virtually the only producer making films in Britain is Clive Parsons. He made *Scum*, *Breaking Glass* and *Gregory's Girl*. He rang Lindsay out of the blue and asked him if he had a film he wanted to make. Yes, said Lindsay, *Britannia Hospital*. Clive has read the script and wants to make the film. He is showing a copy of the script to the National Film Finance Corporation, who will meet in a week to give their collective decision.

21 June 1980

Lindsay rings. Good, bad and sad news. The good news is that the NFFC like *Britannia Hospital* and will put up $1 million providing another company put up the remaining $2 million. The bad news is that the only major production company left in Britain, EMI, don't like it. The sad news is that Rachel Roberts is suffering from acute manic depression. Rachel has been a friend of Lindsay's ever since she starred in *This Sporting Life* as the tormented Mrs Hammond. She has again tried to commit suicide. She has nowhere to live as she has sublet her homes in New York and Hollywood. So Lindsay is putting her up in his Finchley Road flat. He daren't leave her alone in the place with all that booze. She needs proper medical attention. He doesn't trust any of the quack psychiatrists in London or America and asks if he can have the number of my friend Dr Bell. He was impressed by how Dr Bell cured me of manic depression after *Venom*.

A couple of hours later, Rachel rings. She speaks in a hoarse dramatic whisper: 'Lindsay told me not to phone you.'

'Oh?'

'I've got to talk to you. I'm seeing your doctor next Saturday. Will he save me?'

'I don't know. He's a common-sense ordinary doctor.'

'He won't make me talk, will he?'

'Not unless you want to.'

'I'm so sick of talking to psychiatrists. Blathering on and on and not getting anywhere. I want to commit suicide and be done.'

'At least see Colin Bell.'

'Is he any good? I'm desperate. I used to think I was the fun person in Hollywood. Now I can't wake up in the mornings. The little Welsh butterfly has turned into a faded grey moth. I tell you, I'm laying my last on this trip. You see I hate my work. I detest acting. I will never act again.'

'If you take Colin Bell's medication and stop this Hollywood rubbish you'll feel healthy again.'

'See you, love.' She puts down the phone.

Colin rings. There are no private or public psychiatric homes in Gloucestershire. If he is to treat Rachel properly, she will have to stay in a hotel. It's going to be a difficult job.

'She's desperate,' I tell him.

'I know. I don't know what to do.'

23 July 1980

Lunchtime. Lindsay calls from a phone box. Rachel and he are stranded just outside Ross-on-Wye, where their hire-car has broken down. They were on their way to see Dr Bell. Can I let him know that they are going to be late.

At five o'clock Lindsay calls me from Dr Bell's. Rachel wants to visit us.

'Do you?' I ask Lindsay.

'No I fucking don't.'

'Then don't bother.'

'Well, Rachel wants it. How do we get to you?'

6.30 p.m. Skye is having her bath. The front door opens and in walks Rachel, wearing tailored jeans, high-heeled boots and a seemingly calm face. Skye, hearing her, runs naked out of her bath and into Rachel's embrace.

'My God. You have a beautiful child.'

Monika offers her some fresh raspberries and cream. She declines but when Lindsay accepts a bowl, she asks for some of his.

'Oh, God, Rachel! That's typical. You never eat anything of your own – that's your trouble.'

'Did you know you were mad?' Rachel asks me, taking great spoonfuls of Lindsay's raspberries.

'Not at the time. I just thought I was the only sane person in the world.'

'But I *am* mad. All those times I had when I thought I was the happiest person in the world. I was mad! I am mad! Oh, God.'

'What did the doctor say?'

'I should take some pills and see him again. But how can I travel 350 miles a day?'

A hiatus.

Lindsay is eating his second bowl of raspberries. Monika is putting Skye to bed. Rachel is close to collapse. I can think of nothing to calm her down. Then Lindsay says, 'I'd like to see this caravan, where you work.'

I lead the way. Monika instinctively knows I need a private chat with Lindsay and takes Rachel to inspect the new addition to our family, Pinkie, a small white Welsh Mountain pony that nobody wanted, now living in our orchard.

Lindsay tells me *Britannia Hospital* is unlikely to come to early fruition, but we must meet at Rustington in a fortnight's time to rewrite the first draft. This will give Clive Parsons a proper chance to sell the script.

Rachel, bored with Welsh Mountain ponies, climbs into the caravan, which she finds equally dull. The charm of rural life is beyond her.

As they leave, Lindsay tells me to keep on with *The Great Advertisement for Marriage*.

26 July 1980

A letter from Stirling Mansions.

Dear David,
Thank you so much for the intro to Dr Bell. Rachel really is in a bad way. I suppose this is about the last hope. Certainly all these shrinks she's been seeing, intelligent or otherwise, fraudulent or not, have done NO GOOD. Frightening, eh? I think there is real vitality there that may pull her through. But I am a bit scared at the prospect of being transformed into a male nurse. It was very nice to see your little grey house in the West at last. It is charming, and I do understand the advantage of removal from metropolitan distraction. I am sure *The Great Advertisement* can be a success and so can *Going Mad in Hollywood*.

Early Days can't really survive. The National Theatre is a pernicious, bureaucratic organisation and has quite fucked up the transfer possibilities.

Don't be depressed at the rejection of *Hospital*. Inevitable. Also – you'll see – SEX FACTORY. Skye was/is charming and so QUIET! Love to you and Monika. Thank you. Those raspberries were delicious – Lindsay.

Two weeks pass. Rachel does not respond to Dr Bell's pills and is unable to visit him or he to get her into a suitable hospital.

3 August 1980
Rustington

Lindsay and I rework the script. We want to make it richer, madder, funnier and more dense.

In our new version Professor Millar no longer murders his own creature in disappointment ('Pity, it's not what I wanted'). Indeed, his creature, on gaining consciousness, viciously bites its maker's hand and holds it in a vicelike grip. In the ensuing tug of war the creature's head is ripped from its composite body. The creature perishes, but Millar is untroubled. 'No long faces – the time for "Brutus" has come.' 'Brutus', Millar's ultimate achievement, will be revealed to the Queen Mother. I also think up a new way of letting the demonstrators and revolutionaries outside know about the Royal party within. It is journalist Jeff's girlfriend, Nurse Persil, who finds the video camera after he has been killed. To avenge his death she videos the Royal luncheon, transmitting it to the revolutionaries outside.

At 1.30 Lindsay asks me to drive him to the station to pick up Rachel Roberts. She wants to spend the weekend away from London in the country. She has stopped drinking and wants to see the seaside.

'Won't she get in the way – like Sandy?'

'No. She promises to be very good.'

That night, while I'm working in my room, Rachel comes in, wearing a long pink nightie. She leans over my shoulder as I type. She obviously wants to talk.

'You ought to get out of Hollywood,' I tell her.

'It's the only place I've got. I'm going back to kill myself there.'

'Couldn't you go somewhere else? Travel? See places you've never seen?'

'It's different for a man. A woman can't travel on her own.'

'Couldn't you go back to acting? Lindsay wants you to play the Queen in *Hamlet* and Matron in *Britannia Hospital*.'

Her voice rises. 'I detest acting. I'll never act again. This is the last time you'll ever see me.'

I desperately cast around for a reason why Rachel shouldn't kill herself. All I can think of is a glib statement I'd once heard on *Woman's Hour*, that suicide was an act of violence against others.

'If you kill yourself it will be an act of violence against Lindsay.'

'Balls!' she says with great vehemence. 'It will only be an act of violence against myself.'

I give up. 'How are you going to do it?'

'I know all the ways. They say carbon monoxide is quite pleasant.'

'It isn't. You suffocate to death. Pills are much easier.'

'Oh, I've thousands of pills. No one cares. Perhaps Lindsay a little. My sister hates me. She wouldn't even travel down to see your doctor with me. I have no family. No children. Nothing. I used to think that when I laughed at parties and made myself the centre of attention, I was amusing, but all the time it was madness. There is nothing wrong in not wanting to go on living. Psychiatrists, psychotherapists, pills, lithium – it's all fucking rubbish!'

I can't help her and I can't work. I ask her if she would like to read the script. Yes, she would. I go to Lindsay's bedroom, where he is writing a chapter for his book about John Ford. I tell him about Rachel's suicidal mood.

He pushes his spectacles on to his forehead and sucks his red Tempo. 'She actually drives me to a point where I can't listen any more. There's only one hope . . .'

'What?'

'That Rex will ring. That's what keeps her going.' Lindsay means her husband, Rex Harrison, but they've been separated for seven years. I am amazed.

'She still loves Rex?'

'I don't know what the word "love" means, but now her only hope is that he'll ring and take her back.'

Rex never rings.

5 August 1980

We are all downstairs. Rachel sits in Lindsay's chair, reading the script and sipping tonic water. Lindsay is in the kitchen next door carving the remains of a chicken.

Rachel closes the script. 'It lacks a third act, Lindsay. Lins – are you listening to me? It lacks a third act.'

'What do you mean by that?'

'It seems to end very suddenly.'

'Rachel, I'm surprised at you. You're another person who has no sense of the epic.'

Rachel speaks in a low, little-girl voice. 'I was stating a simple person's opinion, Lins – I'm terribly sorry.'

'Well, stop talking rubbish and eat for once.'

The atmosphere is tense. Lindsay eats, Rachel nibbles and I sip Guinness.

'The trouble is,' Lindsay says, after Rachel has gone to bed, 'no one can read scripts. The ending is the most powerful part of the script. They don't actually visualise what's happening on the screen. Of course, Rachel has no sense of humour. That's another of her problems.'

6 August 1980

Rachel spends most of the day in her room writing her diary. She comes down for lunch, very bright and cheery, and cooks the remains of the chicken into a stew. After lunch, she and Lindsay go off for a walk by the sea. She returns apparently happy and there is no more talk today of suicide. In the evening, while Lindsay and I work on, she sits quietly in the living room, completely absorbed in her diary. She goes for a pee, leaving the diary open on the table. I get up and glance at her last sentence. It's a sad sentence: 'Went to Ned Sherrin's party and I felt so pretty. I am still pretty!'

7 August 1980

Drive Lindsay and Rachel back to London. Rachel says it's a bit stuffy in the car and asks if we can have a bit of fresh air. We wind down the windows.

'They do say carbon monoxide is the best way.'

'Either do it or stop talking about it,' says Lindsay.

'Yes,' says Rachel in her punished little-girl voice.

I drop Rachel off in Baker Street. She has to see some doctor in Harley Street. Lindsay tells her it's only 200 yards away, but as soon as she is out of the car she hails a taxi.

'Two hundred yards, the sun is shining and she has to take a taxi. That's what Hollywood does for you. Anyway, there's nothing I can say. She's going back to Hollywood. She's convinced Rex will take her back.'

'And if he doesn't?'

'Look – stop it. It's catching. At least I've a few minutes free of her presence. I don't enjoy being a male nurse thanks to these useless doctors.'

We discuss Rachel, madness and Hollywood all the way back to Lindsay's flat, where I bid him farewell and good luck.

3 November 1980

I hear on the radio that Rachel Roberts has had a fatal heart attack in her garden in Hollywood. Lindsay tells me the truth. She swallowed a bottle of lye, a kind of sulphuric acid. The worst way to go. You burn alive inside.

Lindsay says, 'Let it be a lesson to you. The horrible way alcoholics end. Still, if I could call her back, I wouldn't.'

9 November 1980

Monika finishes typing the first draft of *The Great Advertisement for Marriage*. I have four copies xeroxed and send one to Lindsay.

15 November 1980

Lindsay rings. He loves *The Great Advertisement*. 'It was a pleasure to read. A perfect mixture of sentiment and irony – a near-masterpiece. Just improve the ending and it will be a masterpiece.'

'How's *Britannia*?'

'I've given Clive Parsons until 28 March to find finance. Or then I'll commit to *Dress Grey*.'

'What's grey dress?'

'*Dress Grey*, you idiot.'

Dress Grey is the story of a homosexual murder at America's military academy, West Point. Gore Vidal is writing the screenplay and Lindsay is to go to Hollywood to work with him – a real Hollywood project. Before that he is to direct a video production of Malcolm McDowell in *Look Back in Anger* on Broadway. This is Malcolm's first stage play in America and a big success. There is not much hope for *Britannia*.

22 December 1980

A Christmas card from Lindsay. A couple with shopping bags by Duane Hanson.

> This is treadmill work (*Look Back in Anger*). Rehearsing every day since I arrived. We tape the show next week. I only hope the technicians know how to do it, because I don't . . . Malcolm is in good habitual form. I try to think of myself as a PROFES-SIONAL, like everyone else, but without success. I have given Malc *Britannia* but of course he hasn't got round to reading it . . . I grow more sceptical of the chance of finance – retirement looms enticingly ahead. Love Lindsay. P.S. Monday – Started taping. I am not a good hack alas. P.P.S. Happy Christmas to you, Monika and Skye.

March 1981

Monika, a teenage champion horse-rider, teaches Skye how to ride Pinkie and we go for gentle walks and rides in the forest. Then Monika discovers Pony Club shows and a new art form, as she creates intricate fancy dress for Pinkie and Skye – the Owl and the Pussy Cat, Little Miss Muffett, and a Christmas tree. But competition is vicious, and the judge always chooses the Potato – a friend's fat child wearing a sack over his head. We get to hate the Potato. I return to my other love, finishing a model glider I'd begun to build after I'd gone mad in Hollywood.

28 March 1981

I'm doping the wings of the glider when the phone rings.

'Congratulations on your next screenplay credit.' It is Lindsay calling from the States, but what the hell is he talking about?

'What screenplay credit?'

'*Britannia Hospital*. It's being made by EMI.'

'Who's EMI?'

'EMI . . . Are you cracked? Listen, this is an international call. It's costing money. We start shooting on 10 August. Budget 3 million dollars. Eight-week schedule.'

'What about *Gay West*?'

'*Dress Grey*! God, this is a good beginning . . .'

Lindsay is out of *Dress Grey*. Clive Parsons just made it at the eleventh hour. 'I'm off to have breakfast with Barry Spikings at his Malibu residence to sign the deal.'

'Don't say anything to fuck it up.'

'Now start thinking. You'll have to improve the "Rachel" draft. I'll be home in three weeks.'

I rush out to find Monika, who is mucking out Pinkie. Neither of us can believe it. Was I hallucinating? I ring Lindsay's hotel in Los Angeles and catch him just as he's leaving. No, it's all true. I get the Fox contract out of the files. $50,000 on the first day of shooting. I can be free of hack work forever.

21 April 1981

Lindsay rings. 'That name of yours for Millar's brain – Brutus – it won't do.'

'But Brutus was the noblest Roman of them all,' I say.

'Piffle! I want a new name for the brain. Phone me back in two and a half minutes.'

'What about Manhattan, like the code name of the first atom bomb?' I suggest to Monika.

'Not well enough known.'

'Adam?'

'No. Genesis – the beginning of life.' Perfect! Monika can be brilliant when she wants to be.

I phone back. 'Genesis!'

'Good Lord, you can be brilliant when you want to be.'

28 April 1981

After a week spent rewriting the script I join Lindsay in Rustington for another session. The third act is expanded. EMI, like Rachel, think it is thin. Some good news: Malcolm, our choice for Jeff, the journalist investigating Millar's crimes, agrees to play the part, providing he can have a flight on Concorde. So Jeff becomes Mick Travis, our hero in *If* . . . and *O, Lucky Man!* This gets the adrenalin flowing.

30 April 1981

On the way back to London, Lindsay talks about his *Hamlet* with Frank Grimes. 'I think it's going to be a very intelligent production of the text. Very unlike Jonathan Miller. Straight. I don't expect the critics will like it, but ordinary people might, if they get the chance.'

I think he is mad trying to produce *Hamlet* by 28 May, when we have the whole of the film to prepare. But Frank Grimes has been demanding to play *Hamlet* for two years, and Frank Grimes always gets his way. Lindsay and I will meet again at the end of June, when *Hamlet* is hopefully sailing under its own steam.

5 May 1981

I install the radio control into my new glider. Monika, Skye and I drive to the Malvern Hills for its test flight. We watch as it rises high on the air currents, turning and hovering, the sun glinting through its silk wings until it is far above us, a sculpture in the sky.

27 May 1981

Monika and I go to see Lindsay's *Hamlet*. Not very good. But luckily Lindsay is in bed with exhaustion and we don't have to make phoney noises about another Anderson masterpiece.

28 June 1981
Stirling Mansions

Lindsay greets me with his weary handshake and leads me into his kitchen where he introduces me to our art director, Norris Spencer. Norris is black and very young, with a friendly smile and a wiry, energetic body. He has only worked in commercials before. Norris, who wants the picture to be as extreme as possible, is on the right wavelength. He invites me down to the studio. I didn't know we had a studio yet, but we do. Lee International at Wembley Park. Lindsay is delighted because it's only one stop on the Tube from Finchley Road. On the way down to Rustington, he tells me he wants *Britannia* to look like a commercial. He will leave everything to his first assistant and a brilliant cameraman called Mike Fash, who has only worked on commercials before. Lindsay will stay in his caravan on the set and direct the whole film on a video monitor connected to the camera, like Buñuel. It's his last picture, he says. He's going to retire and open the boarding house he dreams of. I don't believe a word.

3 July 1981

The start date, 10 August, has concentrated our minds wonderfully. But the time at Rustington was too short. Lindsay agrees that I should come to London for the shooting. I book myself into a cheap hotel, the Avoca, near Lindsay's flat. The Avoca has special terms for long-stay residents: £45 a week. Malcolm will be staying at Blake's Hotel – £150 a night. I ring Clive Parsons and ask him if he will pay the bill. He refuses point-blank. 'I could afford a couple of extras for that' – an example of the writer's true worth.

11 July 1981

Lindsay is travelling up and down Britain in search of a venerable Victorian building for the exterior riot scenes. He inspects old universities, disused hospitals, crumbling mansions. The recent riots in London and Liverpool do not help. The news pictures of riot police and brick-throwing mobs are so like our scenes in *Britannia* that Salford University, the most feasible location, do not give permission. They are afraid that the events of the film will become all too real. Lindsay has just visited an abandoned military hospital in

Woolwich with Clive, but turned it down.

'It's this or Sheffield,' Clive Parsons tells him.

'That's like asking me which ball I'd rather have cut off.'

Another disaster. We can't get Arthur Lowe to play Potter. He's in a TV show as a Catholic priest.

'What do you think about Leonard Rossiter?' asks Lindsay.

'Brilliant,' I say, thinking of *Rising Damp*.

'You fool. It's an absolutely dreadful idea.'

But Leonard Rossiter it is.

17 July 1981

A phone call from Ted Craig, Lindsay's personal assistant on *Britannia Hospital*. There's a rehearsal next Monday afternoon. I am to attend. Lindsay knows more work needs to be done on the script and wants me to be in London. 'Clive Parsons will pay you £45 a week for your hotel,' Ted tells me. 'Could you be at Lee International Studios at 1 p.m.? I'll meet you in the foyer.'

20 July 1981

At Lee Studios, Ted Craig tells me that the big rehearsal has been cancelled and we are to do rewrites immediately. I follow him along featureless corridors until we come to a door marked 'Private'. Ted knocks and enters. Lindsay, in unusually smart cavalry twills and a beige woollen sweater, is sitting with his feet up on a desk. When he sees me he throws himself back and hurls his arms over his head. 'Oh my God, David Sherwin!' A theatrical performance for the benefit of the occupants of the tiny office, which irritates the hell out of me. He introduces me to his other assistant, who is also the second unit director. 'Richard Tombleson.'

'Oh – hullo.'

'Don't just say "Oh – hullo." Don't you recognise him?'

'Sorry, no.'

'The fat boy from *If* . . . For God's sake, David.'

Richard shakes my hand, grinning. He has just found the perfect location for our hospital. Friern Barnet, in North London. A huge neo-classical pile, it is England's largest mental hospital, with 900 patients. Richard found it by sheer chance. He'd taken a wrong turning while looking for another possible location, got lost and soon found himself driving past the huge Victorian building.

Lindsay introduces me to the other people in the room. Patsy Pollock, the casting director, and Norman Hull, a strange, twitchy character in a purple punk suit, who will shoot a documentary on the making of the film.

'And now you must meet Clive Parsons.'

'Why do I have to meet Clive Parsons?' I ask testily.

'Because he's the producer.'

Clive Parsons is a nervous, thin schoolboy with giant spectacles. One look at him and I am convinced that the picture will be a disaster, running hopelessly over its eight-week schedule and $3 million budget. A monster is being created. The making of this film will resemble its subject – an example of folly, almighty ambition and petty-mindedness and a strange passion that makes intelligent people like Lindsay, Ted Craig, Richard Tombleson and myself think this madness so important.

The phone rings. Friern Barnet Hospital grant us permission to shoot. Their inmates will have to be locked up in padded cells for the duration. Lindsay suggests we should send the hospital administrator a bottle of Moët et Chandon.

'Couldn't we make it half a bottle?' asks Clive.

'No, we certainly could not, old boy. They get little enough in their lives.'

In the evening I check into the Avoca Hotel. My room, Room 66, is narrower than a houseboat, with a single bed at either end. The painful green wallpaper is peeling from the walls. The carpet is stained purple flock. A lone electric socket dangles dangerously out of the wall. But at least it is quiet. There is no phone, and messages are taken for me by the receptionist in the foyer. Outside calls can be made from a kiosk near the TV lounge, but when I try to ring Monika I find it is out of order.

I am awoken at midnight by a siren. In accordance with fire instructions I race downstairs and out of the front entrance. On the way I overtake the hotel manager, Mr Maguire, who is carrying a girl upside down. 'Just a drunk, setting off the alarm,' he says, hurling the girl in a heap on the pavement. 'It happens all the time – go back to bed.'

'Is she all right?'

'She's very happy.'

27 July 1981
Lindsay's flat

A good day filling in the holes in the script.

'A very passable piece of work,' says the Almighty.

Alan Bates rings. He realises we have no money, and offers to act in the film for free. Lindsay suggests the part of Macready, the dying man in intensive care whom Millar decapitates for his first experiment. The severed head is placed in the deep freeze, but rots when the union cuts off the power. So Mick Travis's head is used as a substitute.

'Alternatively, Alan, you could be a private patient and push Sir John Gielgud in a bathchair when the private patients are kicked out of the hospital.'

Alan accepts.

'Once one's in it, they'll all want to be in it. We'll get Larry Olivier being pushed out by Ralph Richardson. It will be a very funny sequence,' says Lindsay, pleased.

28 July 1981
Lindsay's flat

More solid work on the script, but we get stuck when we reach the scene in which Mr Potter and the Palace officials look for patients suitable enough to be presented to the Queen Mother.

'I'm sorry, David, all this stuff about double mastectomies is just jokesy and in bad taste. Now I can see you're panicking. Don't panic. We'll take a walk.'

We walk up and down the Finchley Road, Lindsay inspecting every restaurant menu we pass.

'They're all terribly expensive.'

He peers into shop windows, noting prices, asking, 'Would you buy that?' He spots some water beds. 'Are they any good?'

'They're very good for making love.'

'But is it really like floating on water? Do you believe it? Where is your water bed now? How much did it cost?'

'£100.'

'That's very cheap. Now what's the answer to this problem? Come on! I'm counting on you!'

'The patient's in a coma . . .'

'Great – so you don't have to invent any dialogue. Rubbish!'

'No, her family is around her, recalling memories, and she says something.'

'Says what?'

My mind goes blank.

'And what about Arthur Lowe?' asks Lindsay. Arthur can spare a couple of days to be a patient in intensive care.

'He says something Shakespearean before he dies. This other Eden, demi-paradise . . . This precious stone set in a silver sea . . . This England . . . This England!'

'Not bad.'

29 July 1981
Lindsay's office, Lee Studios

Casting problems. Lindsay and Patsy Pollock cannot agree on who should play Mrs Grimshaw, the senior trade union official. Patsy says we should offer the part right away to Joan Sims.

'Joan is a sweetheart, a real girl.'

'Hmmm,' says Lindsay.

Patsy adds that Joan Plowright, Lindsay's favourite choice, is lost somewhere in France, although her agent says she may ring.

Another problem is the midget who is to play Sir Anthony Mount, senior adviser to the Palace. Lindsay met a very upper-class midget who would have been ideal, but he is also president of the Small Peoples' Society and is off to Canada for the World Conference of Small People. Midgets, I learn, are extremely rare, and quite different from dwarfs, who have overlarge heads; midgets, although tiny, are perfectly in proportion. There is one midget who might do – Dr William Shakespeare. But he is a full-time doctor and has real patients to care for. So we may have to scrap the whole idea. 'Patsy, do you think we'll ever get this shot?' asks Lindsay, sipping a Perrier.

Richard, Ted and I, who have been putting in more work on the script, go off to the studio canteen. There is a choice of steak and bacon, salad and ham, or sausage, chips and four fried eggs, all for 90p. We are surrounded by chisel-faced men and women in Edwardian evening dress, all bronzed in phoney pancake make-up. They are extras from Lord Brabourne's latest film, the Agatha Christie mystery *Murder on the Nile*. These Lords, Ladies and Gents, in their antique finery – here is the paralysis of class which our film blows up.

Back in Lindsay's office Norris, the art director, is explaining how he's just been told at a production conference that he has only £15,000 to finish the picture, although he has yet to build the base of The Millar Centre (a 50-foot erection in the grounds of Friern Barnet) and dress every set.

'I thought it was a Clive Parsons joke. But he was serious.'

'Norris, what we must do is push on into the first two weeks and have a great row with them then,' says Lindsay. 'If Clive thinks there's a problem now, he may panic and go to EMI and they'll fold the picture.'

At 5.30 p.m. Clive Parsons rings. As no one's heard from Joan Plowright, the script is being sent in a radio cab to Joan Sims. Lindsay puts down the phone and shrugs at our watching faces.

'Patsy will be pleased,' says Ted.

But seconds later the phone rings again. It is Joan Plowright's agent. Joan has committed to playing Mrs Grimshaw. We now have two stars playing the same part. Once more the phone rings. Clive is very worried. How can we get the script back from Joan Sims before she reads it?

'Send a motorcycle messenger,' Richard suggests.

'What if we're too late?' asks Clive. 'How can we take the part back without paying her?'

'I think we should do it as painlessly as possible,' says Lindsay. 'I'm not talking in legal terms. I'm talking in human terms. Joan Sims?! Of course I'm not going to pay her money. Clive, grit your teeth.'

Clive rings back two minutes later. Patsy, who thinks Joan Sims would make a marvellous Mrs Grimshaw, is given the task of telling her she's sacked. Clive is worried that she may sue. 'Let her sue,' says Lindsay.

30 July 1981
Lee Studios

A wooden crate arrives from Los Angeles. It contains a mould of Malcolm's head, which Special Effects will use to create a head that Professor Millar can hack to pieces with his cleaver. We assemble in Clive's office for a ceremonial opening of the crate. Drinks are poured and the lid comes off to reveal a mass of blue plastic chips.

'This ought to be the opening shot of Norman Hull's documentary,' says Lindsay. 'We'll have to restage this. Keep the packing.'

Clive fetches some waste-paper bins and with his hands sweeps the chips out of the crate. 'I can feel the nose,' he says.

Malcolm's head emerges. A distorted Malcolm. The cast was made for his most recent film, *Cat People*, and his eyes are slanted.

Back in Lindsay's office, the first assistant director, the boss of the floor, complains to Lindsay about the new script pages.

'Excuse me, sir, but you can't number your pages like this. You're wrecking the schedule. You can't go Scene 74, Scene 75, Scene 76, Scene 74 continued.'

'Why not?' asks Lindsay.

'Because once they've read Scene 74 and gone on to Scene 75, Scene 74 is finished.'

'You mean they can't read the script? They can't read forwards?'

'That's right. You have to go 74, 74A, 74B, 74C, 74D and so on . . .'

At this point Norris enters with sketches of Malcolm McDowell's spy camera – it will cost £1,500 to machine, although the budget stipulates £40.

'Couldn't you make it of balsa wood?' asks Lindsay. 'It only has to look – it doesn't have to function.'

'If we were making an on-the-run picture, I could fix it.'

'We *are* making an on-the-run picture.'

I travel home with Lindsay on the Metropolitan Line. The train is fast and sends sparks flying as it rattles over the points.

'I like this train. It's like a ride in a funfair,' says Lindsay. 'Only the funfair ride would cost 20p not 60p.'

Suddenly, enigmatically, he says, 'Mike Fash . . . I like the way he says "No problem" to everything. Someone who can shoot it like a commercial, that's part of the whole thing. Don't you realise? He is amazingly positive. Very un-English.'

I have yet to meet this paragon who will save our skins.

Back in Room 66, I dream super-real dreams of production meetings. I wake up trying to claw my way out of the wardrobe.

3 August 1981

The first rehearsal.

The actors assemble in a large banqueting hall in a nearby hotel. They sit giggling and anxious. Lindsay introduces the movie.

'There is a gratifyingly large turnout of talented people this morning, but – believe it or not – you are not the entire cast. The idea of this get-together is that I just feel the need to start with us all here.

David Sherwin

There may be people, amazingly enough, who are all part of this enterprise, who will, sad to say, never see each other again. It's so awful, I think. There must be one time in the course of the picture when we've all been together, and then you can say, "Yes, I was in *Britannia Hospital*." It's a bit of a hangover from the theatre really. It's the ordeal of going through the script. Now because it's a film script, it's not as easy to read as a play. Also it is this rather interesting genre – i.e. Epic Picture. I don't need to tell any of you that I mean epic in the Brechtian sense as opposed to the Hollywood sense, because we haven't got enough money to make an epic film in the Hollywood sense . . .

'I'm not going to introduce all the actors to each other because I will immediately get nervous and forget everybody's name although I've known them for half my life. I'm going to ask Ted Craig – sorry Ted, but it will be your responsibility – to read the script, to go through the parts of those who aren't here, so we'll stumble through the entire thing somehow. Then we'll feel we have accomplished something and started on the right foot.

'I have also got to tell you, by the way, that whatever this film turns out to be like it will be well documented. Mr Sherwin there, who wrote the screenplay, is also writing a book about the making of the film. So that's why he'll be around making notes, and if nobody will publish the script let us hope they will publish his account of how the film is made. Also we've got a film being made about the film being made by Norman Hull.

'It is a film that is really dedicated to the exposure of human folly. In other words it is not a film that attempts to present a balanced view. In this respect it is completely unlike what we are obliged to do all the time by institutions like the BBC – all television, which is dedicated to balance, and therefore to compromise. This film is a cautionary word to the human species. Now, none of us can be arrogant enough as artists to think that we can do anything really to change history, but at least we can be seen later to have been on the right side.

'There's a book by Marlon Brando's ex-wife called *Brando for Breakfast*, which is actually quite good. At the beginning she quotes a phrase from some oriental scriptures: "There is nothing that is real or nothing that is true except God, human folly and laughter." I'm not quite sure about the presence of God in the script but we must try and put Him there, but the other aspect of it – of human laughter – I hope will be in the film. In other words, it is a comedy. It is truthful, I hope, to certain aspects of experience and I think the only way that we can possibly say anything that is actually helpful in the present situation is really through laughter or through satire. The, so to speak, serious attempts at comments on the human condition are of no avail, because people don't want to listen. To this extent, what we are doing is a serious venture, an extravaganza. It's a comedy, but it's also serious and it does mean that every character has to have total conviction. You all know what I'm talking about really. I'm not boring you, am I?

'Well, I've said enough and we also know that on these occasions none of us is expected or required to give performances. We're just going through a rite of Bunting. At various times during this week I hope we'll get an opportunity to look at scenes so that we don't come to shoot them entirely unprepared, which is so frightening in the cinema if you have been used to working in the theatre. OK, so here we go. Well, we start with a shot of the Houses of Parliament and a title, pinched of course from Dickens. "It was the best of times, it was the worst of times, it was yesterday or this morning or perhaps tomorrow . . ." '

And so our first rehearsal gets under way.

5 August 1981
Lindsay's office, Lee Studios

Mike Fash, the unknown saviour, makes his first appearance. He is tanned and wears a white suit with white sports shirt. He is Australian and as cool as a cucumber. From the window I can see his silver Ferrari. To every problem – how to light and match, for example, the studio interiors of the journalists' van and the location exteriors – Mike Fash responds, 'No problem . . .' 'No problem – flare it all out.'

6 August 1981
Rehearsal room

The cast wait around while Lindsay talks to the Special Effects Department on the phone.

'So what you are saying is, we can't do the head coming off.' He announces the news to the cast: 'The Special Effects Department can't do Malcolm's head coming off because they have never been given Malcolm's head – it's been sitting in Clive Parsons's office for ten days and no one has done a fucking thing about it.'

'But that's terrible!' says Jill Bennett.

'It's not terrible – it's typical.'

'I'm being naive.'

'Did you get that?' Lindsay asks Norman Hull, who has been lurking in the background with his camera crew.

'No.'

'Everybody misses the best moments.'

Malcolm arrives amidst thunder, lightning and torrential rain. He wears a floppy white judo costume. He runs round the hall greeting everyone.

I ask him if he still has his house in Beverly Hills.

'No. We only go there to pick up the loot. No – New York is the place. Do you know, David, five and a half hours ago I was washing my son's nappies – three and a half hours on Concorde and I'm here!'

'I suppose, Malcolm, coming to England for you is a bit like us going to Poland. You know – poor but struggling,' comments Lindsay.

We practise pulling Malcolm's head off his body. Richard Tombleson stands in for one set of doctors and nurses pulling Malcolm, I stand in for the other set of doctors pulling Graham, his fingers trapped by Malcolm's teeth. This is fun.

11 August 1981
Lindsay's flat

Our midget, Marcus Powell, who is 72, can't play the fast-moving scene 90. So I rewrite the scene without the midget. I know Lindsay hates a perfectly typed script, so I show it to him full of crossings out and arrows.

'Good. Now for a drink.'

As we sip our whiskies I notice a small white box about the size of a biscuit tin on Lindsay's coffee table. Painted on its side in green is the name Rachel Roberts.

'Is that her?'

'Yes.'

I pick up the box and shake it. Its contents rattle like coffee beans.

'Is it yours?' I ask.

'She wanted me to cast it into the Welsh sea. For now I'm putting it on the shelf, next to the embryo in Millar's specimen room.'

19 August 1981

Officially a rest day according to the schedule. I try to write some
sparky lines for Frank Grimes and Mark Hamill, Malcolm's assis-
tants in his control van outside the hospital. Then I visit my ex-wife
Gay in Camden to see my son Luke, who is now 8. The visit is a disaster. The adults are all pissed. A drunken advertising producer
shouts, '*If* . . . was fucking parochial, *O, Lucky Man!* was shit and
Anderson can only direct two actors in a shoebox. As for you, don't
tell me you consider yourself a significant writer! Do you? Do you?'
   I leave, avoiding a fight.

21 August 1981
Room 66

I dream I am wandering through the studio, but there are no actors,
no crew, no Lindsay, and I have lost the only copy of my rewrites.
   Yesterday evening was terrible. I had wanted to discuss some
scenes with Lindsay. I saw his unmistakable profile through the
frosted glass of Clive Parsons's office, but when I knocked and
opened the door they both shrieked 'Get out!' I beat a retreat and
waited down the corridor. I could still hear them both yelling. Was
the picture being closed down? After waiting an hour, I decided the
adult thing would be to go back to Room 66. Later I rang Lindsay
from the kiosk in the foyer to ask him what the row was about.
   'Brian Pettifer's rail expenses. He has to come from Scotland and
Clive wouldn't pay.'

27 August 1981
Lee Studios

The sets are a revelation. Millar's operating theatre has been painted
matt black instead of the usual surgical white. This not only gives an
impression of limitless size, but is very sinister. The instruments
gleam dimly. It looks like a futuristic torture chamber. Norris's idea.
The 'donor' room, where Millar keeps his 'components', is in the
process of being painted matt black. Dim shapes of severed limbs,
lumps of flesh can be seen through frosted glass. Everything has a
demonic quality. This sense of the demonic is reinforced when I go
to the set where we are shooting the decapitation of Macready.
When Graham Crowden brings the electric surgical saw down on

Alan Bates's neck, the smoke of burning flesh engulfs him. The Professor can just be seen smiling, weird and fanatical, through the fumes.

In the editing room I look at the week's rushes. It looks superb, but Malcolm's performance lacks the 'total conviction' that Lindsay has so clearly impressed on the rest of the cast. He grins and waves cheekily at Millar. He seems to be in a different film. At lunch in the canteen Valerie Booth, the continuity girl, and Mike Fash both go into a dirge about him. When Malcolm was supposed to be hidden on a trolley in the Millar Centre corridor, he stood up on his trolley and waved his video gun around. Then he began clapping his hands and shouting, 'Linds! This is a boring scene! I hate scenes like this! For God's sake liven it up! I'm bored!'

'Say something to Lindsay,' asks Valerie. 'He'll listen to you.'

Back in Room 66 in the evening I get to thinking. Malcolm is far away from his wife and baby. He probably feels alone and lost like me. I phone him.

'David, I can't live on my own in a hotel room. I can't put up with this!' Mutual sympathy. He too hates his room. He feels an outsider, not part of the team.

I tell him the film looks great and Mike Fash is brilliant.

'Oh, really? And what about my performance?'

I had wanted to talk to Lindsay first. 'Well . . . I thought you were playing him like you played Flashman. You weren't serious enough. You've got to play the lines absolutely straight.'

'Don't you think it has to be played against the lines?'

'No, I don't. Everyone in the story is dead serious, that's what makes it funny.'

'So my whole performance has been wrong?'

'Wrong for this film.'

28 August 1981
Lee Studios

I am working on the nineteenth revision of Frank Grimes and Mark Hamill's scenes, when Ted enters the office.

'Lindsay wants to see you on the set.'

'What about?'

Ted, who is usually more forthcoming, gives an enigmatic grimace. 'Something's cropped up.'

I go down to B stage. The set for the Body Parts Donor Unit is thronged with technicians, nurses and surgeons. I spot Malcolm.

'I'm going to play it serious from now on!' he shouts.

Lindsay is peering at a side of thigh in a display unit, talking to Mike Fash. I advance.

'Get off the fucking set!'

I retreat behind a scenery flat, where Valerie Booth is typing continuity notes on a crate. 'Thank God he's shouting at you instead of me,' she says.

'Any idea what it's about?'

'Malcolm's worried . . .'

'David Sherwin!' Lindsay shouts.

I go back on to the tiny set. Lindsay beckons me close. He speaks quietly. 'If you have anything to say about the artists' performance, you say it to me, not to them.'

'I only rang Malc up for a chat. He asked me.'

'You said his performance was silly. Deny it.'

'I don't deny it. I apologise. It won't happen again.'

'All right. Anyway, you were correct, but artists get very neurotic.'

30 August 1981
Lee Studios

Today is going to be tough. According to the mythical schedule, we have to film Millar's creature attacking his maker, the head coming off, and the death of Jill. We have several different but seemingly identical versions of the creature whose headless torso is going to strangle Jill. Malcolm himself is being made up to look like a composite man. Glued to his neck is a piece of skin which will tear, releasing blood, and indicate the moment of decapitation. He also has a black penis and furry legs like an ape.

I visit him in his dressing room. He lies half-prone in his dentist's chair. Linda, the make-up girl, is adding pieces of latex skin and black stitches to his body. He has been lying motionless for thirteen hours and there's not a frame of film in the can. He compares the ordeal to being made up in his last film, *Cat People*, although that only took three and a half hours. Malcolm worries about the additions to his body. They are terribly fragile. He asks Lindsay if he can appear lying on a surgical bed. It will be much safer. Lindsay adds more grafts and scars with a marker. He orders more stitches to be added around the feet, toes and shoulders – the parts of the creature which will first jerk to life after the operation. Malcolm's oriental groin and black penis are magnificent. The crew agree to work late tonight.

7.10 p.m. 'B' Stage
The first two attempts at splitting the blood patch on Malcolm's neck fail. The patch splits – but no blood. We have only one neck patch left.

'Good luck, Malc!' shouts Lindsay. 'Good luck, everyone! Our last chance.'

'Here we go,' says Malcolm, 'our last possible chance!'

'Valerie,' Lindsay asks, 'when it bursts, will you scream, please?'

The neck splits. Valerie Booth screams. Malcolm whoops with delight: 'Well done, Linds!'

After the nightmare of Malcolm's head, the real Malc can now vanish back to Hollywood to pick up some real loot.

6 September 1981
Lee Studios

I sit on one side of the desk working on the revolutionaries' speeches while on the other side Richard Tombleson painstakingly drafts storyboards of the riot. We have 300 revolutionaries and 150 riot police – all extras.

Clive summons me to his office. He has a proposal. If I persuade Lindsay to cut the whole of the riot, which is costing over £300,000 we don't have, he'll give me £5,000. I refuse the bribe. The riot is the climax of the film.

7 September 1981

Last night I was caught sleepwalking by Mr Maguire. He tells me I have been walking naked into all the rooms in the hotel. In one room I spent an hour terrifying a woman and her daughter. I am asked to leave the hotel. I phone old friends of Monika, Hugh and Abbi, who have a house in Sumatra Road not far away. They would be only too happy to put me up, though they have the builders in.

1 October 1981
The generating rooms, University College, London

We are shooting the scene in which Potter orders the striking electrician to switch the power back on. The electrician refuses and Potter kills him with a coal shovel. In the finished film the coal-fired generators will be absolutely silent, but in reality they are deafeningly loud and the heat is unbearable. The crew work in their underpants and communicate by walkie-talkies. Lindsay wishes there were more Potters in Britain – people passionate but pragmatic, who will do deals one day but will kill a man if necessary.

At last the shot is ready. The electrician struggles with Potter, who picks up a props coal shovel and hits him. Our stuntman collapses, gushing real blood, and is rushed to University College Hospital. He'd foolishly made the prop shovel, for which he was responsible, with only one blunt edge. Leonard Rossiter smote him with the other, sharp side. Another day lost, while a new stuntman is found.

'Fucking idiot,' says Lindsay. 'I hope he dies.'

3 October 1981

I skive off from the generating room and go to see a friend, John Landers, who is now a fellow of University College. He has a set of quiet, cool rooms.

'God, you look like a Jewish refugee from the Warsaw ghetto,' he says, as I sip a lovely cup of coffee in tranquillity. It must be nice to be a University don and have a job for life.

4 October 1981

While sleepwalking at Hugh and Abbi's, I fall over a builder's ladder and crack a rib. I ask the studio doctor about my sleepwalking. He suggests I visit a Harley Street hypnotist he knows, and makes an appointment.

8 October 1981

I visit the hypnotist who tells me he can stop me sleepwalking, but I'll never write again. I tell him I very much want to go on writing for the rest of my life, and decline the treatment. He keeps my cheque. Some people earn £50 damn fast in this world.

12 October 1981

The unit at last moves to Friern Barnet Mental Hospital for the riot. The grim building is enveloped in Union Jacks and bunting. Generating lorries throb, cables snake along the roads, a high crane holds the camera and Mike Fash atop.

13 October 1981

There's nothing much to do except stand around. I am hovering in an empty corridor when Lindsay accosts me.

'David, what are you doing hanging around like this? You are supposed to be writing the diary of the film.'

'Lindsay, film-making is the most boring thing in the world. For 99 per cent of the time there's nothing for any of us to do, except for you and Mike Fash.'

'Bullshit! Look over there. A camera and all that cable being hauled by three men up a staircase. That's fascinating. A film camera going up a staircase in a lunatic asylum. It's poetic.'

'Bullshit, Lindsay. Maybe what I should do is live with the lunatics and get their reactions to the filming.'

'Brilliant. And it would do you good.'

But the patients, who are doped up to the eyeballs, only want to watch colour TV all day. They don't give a fart about the filming outside. They're only interested in old movies, sport and soap on TV.

17 October 1981
Friern Barnet

Mark Hamill has his birthday party with his wife and baby daughter in the canteen. Everyone is given a tiny piece of pink cake. As I am walking back to my table, I bump into Ginette, Frank Grimes's girl-friend.

'What are you doing here?' I ask her, surprised.

'I'm an extra in the riot.'

'Getting £20 a day. Great.'

'Don't be silly. I'm getting £80.'

'What? £80? The extras are getting £80 a day?'

'Well, I am.'

I think how much I've put into this picture for free, worked round the clock seven days a week. Six hours later I am back at Cherry Tree

House. Steaming with fury, I write a letter to Clive Parsons, detailing my contractual rights: £25 a day writer's attendance money, first-class accommodation, first-class travel. He owes me £2,500.

19 October 1981

Lindsay rings. He understands my fury, but the production is broke. He needs me. Clive will pay me £50 a week expenses from now on. And so I return.

21 October 1981
Lee Studios. 7.30 p.m.

The final production meeting. Lindsay asks me to attend with a tape recorder. The situation is that there are too many sets to build and dress in twelve weeks. We're already 100 per cent over budget and Lindsay is worried they might close the picture. It is finally agreed to go into a thirteenth week and to work with a reduced unit. All seems chaos.

22 October 1981

Lindsay asks me if I could rush down to Cherry Tree House and bring up some of my beautiful model aircraft to dress Biles's bedroom. He is unhappy with the planes already there.

22 October 1981

The set for Biles's bedroom is above a pub in north-east London. Four model aircraft, supplied by Henry J. Nicholls model shop at a cost to the production of £28 a day, hang from the ceiling. They have been there since shooting began and have earnt Henry J. Nicholls £1,000. They are hideous, plastic, radio-controlled toys, and not nearly as nice as my gliders. But before we get very far redressing the set, Norris rings: he's rebuilding Biles's bedroom at Lee Studios.

23 October 1981

Fulton Mackay, who is playing Superintendent Johns, summons me to Friern Barnet. He is a very distinguished but conceited actor. He is upset with a line that the hospital administrator Potter says to the superintendent: 'Hold the Royal party for five minutes.' He insists that the superintendent never takes orders from Potter. I say of course he would in this situation. He replies patronisingly, 'Well, I need something. You have fallen down a bit here.'

So I give him a line to make it clear that the superintendent is his own man: 'I'll hold her for 360 seconds.'

Fulton replies, 'No. "I'll hold her for five minutes." ' Fine, I say, and Fulton is happy. But then he adds: 'You know, David, I'm very worried about this film, it's in great danger of becoming Alice in Wonderland.'

That's exactly what the film is meant to be, but Fulton will never understand.

8 November 1981

It's nearly the end of the road, but the set for Biles's bedroom is appalling. Norris is at the end of his tether, and Lindsay appoints me to redesign it by tomorrow. Richard warns me, 'Put everything in writing, every detail down to the hair brushes, because if you don't and they get it wrong, you'll be in trouble.' So I draw up a list:

Biles's bedroom:
  Painted terracotta.
  Delicate model aircraft to hang at angles over the worktable.
  Next to worktable, a fishtank.
  To the left of bed, side table with telephone.
  On bed, small teddy.
  Biles's worktable: pots of model dope, tools and PVA glue, plus radio control set.

I add to the worktable an OS60 4-stroke 10cc engine. This is the latest Japanese invention, that knocks spots off the simple snarling 2-strokes. It's as quiet as a sewing machine and will revolutionise model aircraft. I would love to have one, but it costs £220. It would at least be nice to see it, and Norris says he might be able to hire one from Henry J. Nicholls.

9 November 1981
Lee Studios

Norris arrives with the items on my list. He has completely recovered and is determined to go out with a bang. He has spent £220 of EMI's money on the OS60 4-stroke 10cc engine. He gives me a brotherly smile and says it's mine after the shoot tomorrow.

11 November 1981

Lindsay says the Biles set looks very good, but he wants to make one change: no teddy bear. The cameramen, hardened hands, keep handling my OS60 4-stroke, amazed at the miniature tappets and rockers. It is a delicate piece of machinery. I have to tell them to be very careful.

14 November 1981

The last day of shooting. The mad Millar, now transformed into a force for good, gives his final speech and presents Genesis – a glowing pyramid – to the revolutionaries, the Queen Mother, the staff of Britannia Hospital and the police.

Friends, fellow members of the human race! Welcome! We are here for a purpose. Join us! Let us look together with Mankind. What do we see. We see Mastery. What wonders Mankind can perform. He can make deserts fertile and plant cabbages on the moon. He can have what he chooses and what does Mankind choose? Alone among the creatures of this world, the human race chooses to annihilate itself for principle. Since the last world conflict there has not been one day in which human beings have not been slaughtering each other in at least three hundred different wars. Man breeds as recklessly as he lays waste. Out of every hundred human beings now living, eighty will die without ever knowing what it feels like to be fully nourished, while the tiny minority indulge themselves in absurd and wasteful luxury.

We waste, we destroy, and we cling like savages to our superstitions. We give power to leaders as small-minded and prejudiced as ourselves – and why is this? It is because Mankind has denied intelligence. The unique glory of our species – the human brain.

A new era demands a new intelligence. A new human being. Only a new human being can save Mankind. Only a creature of pure brain . . .

At this point, the glowing Genesis bursts into unintended flames. The plastic is overheating. Luckily, Norris has made three Genesises.

Number One is scrapped and Millar continues.

> . . . I do not speak of dreams. Such a creature exists already. I have created it! It is here. Now! Prepare yourselves to meet the man of the future – a unique human being . . .

Genesis Two bursts into flames. One Genesis to go!

> . . . Human because it has been created by humans. 'Being' because it exists – neither man nor woman; greater than either. I have given it a name – Genesis. People of today – behold your future!

The pyramid opens – to reveal a large sulphurous brain controlled by Heath Robinson mechanics. Genesis speaks:

> What . . . a . . . piece of work is man . . .
> How noble in reason . . .
> How infinite in faculties.
> In form, in moving, how express and admirable.
> In action how like an angel –
> In apprehension how like a God . . .
> . . . How like a God . . . How like a God . . .
> How like a God . . . How like a God . . .

Genesis is stuck

THE END

7.00 p.m.
The farewell party.
Horrible.
No music.
No Auld Lang Syne.
I leave feeling sad, so sad.

1 January 1982
Cherry Tree House

I have so many faults it's hard to make a New Year's resolution, but I do all the same. I must cut out barley wine and be a better husband and father.

2 January 1982

Luke arrives for his Christmas visit. He has 'a present for Daddy', a plastic Spitfire he has made for me. I show him the model trains I have been collecting for him for eight years.

'I don't suppose I'll see them again for another year,' he comments sadly.

3 January 1982

Lindsay rings. He wants me to come up to London to write six minutes of additional dialogue. Neither the BBC nor ITV will release pictures of British bombings or riots and the new footage for the TV screens in Potter's and Biles's bedrooms doesn't correspond with what I wrote six months ago. Lindsay sounds desperate. 'I think the first three reels are rubbish. Come up and I'll show them to you.'

Luke and Skye type thank-you letters on my old Olivetti.

At bathtime we find we all have nits in our hair . . .

5 January 1982

In London I stay with Hugh and Abbi. It is snowing. I draw back hessian-blue curtains to see pure whiteness. My Citroën Dyane is stuck, so I walk through drifts of snow to Finchley Road Tube station and catch a Jubilee Line train to Wembley Park. Sparks of electricity flash like lightning across the snow.

In the studio foyer I see Barbra Streisand striding past in quilted snow-white coat and thigh-length boots. She looks fit to fell a polar bear.

Lindsay arrives. A rough cut of *Britannia Hospital* is going to be shown to the bosses of EMI this afternoon. They've flown over from LA and will spend five days in the Connaught just to see the film. It's all going to be appalling, Lindsay says.

3 p.m. EMI House, Wardour Street

The EMI bosses and the boss of bosses, Barry Spikings, sit cheerful and expectant in their luxurious viewing theatre. The lights dim. The opening shot of the Houses of Parliament appears on the screen – and then there are flames licking round Big Ben. And it's not a surreal part of the picture, it's really happening. The projector is on fire. The projectionists call an engineer, but he is stuck in a snowdrift in Bromley.

3.10 p.m. Clive Parsons amazingly takes charge and arranges for the bosses to see the film at Warners' viewing theatre across the road.

3.14 p.m. Warners phone. Their projectionists have gone home early because of the snow. Our EMI projectionists refuse to operate the different machines.

3.17 p.m. 'What about showing the film with gaps? Barry Spikings suggests. The surviving projector could be laced up and the film shown with ten-second gaps between the reels. Lindsay agrees. He doesn't mind gaps. Just show the film. Minutes pass. No picture on the screen.

3.27 p.m. Mike Ellis, our editor, goes into the booth to find that the projectionists are refusing to work. The change-overs, which would have to be done by hand, are dangerous, they say. A finger could easily be lost.

3.29 p.m. Barry Spikings suggests they use a pencil or ruler, instead of a finger. They maintain that that would be dangerous too.

3.30 p.m. Barry Spikings sacks them on the spot.

3.35 p.m. Clive Parsons's secretary reports that the Coronet is available, a tiny viewing theatre 200 yards down Wardour Street.

3.40 p.m. The bosses go up to their offices to fetch their cashmere coats while Lindsay, the *Britannia Hospital* editors and I carry the tins along the snow-covered pavement. The wind is cutting, the path icy. If one of us were to slip into this blizzard, I think to myself, that's the end of *Britannia Hospital*.

4.15 p.m. In the sleazy Coronet, one of the bosses, John Cohn, son of Harry, king of Columbia, sits next to me. I notice that his new suede shoes are untouched by snow. He travelled those few yards by limo.

4.20 p.m. The film starts. *Britannia Hospital* is viewed without a murmur. Not one laugh. A deadly silence. Afterwards no one says a word. For ninety seconds the bosses sit like stone. Then with one movement they get to their feet and leave.

6.25 p.m. We struggle back to EMI House with our unloved cans of film.

8 January 1982

I go over to Finchley Road. Lindsay is still in bed. He says he's exhausted and never wants to see *Britannia Hospital* again. He didn't get home last night until 1.30 a.m. He had dinner with Barry Spikings and his wife. Spikings didn't mention the film once, and didn't arrange for any transport to take Lindsay home, although the trains had stopped running. Lindsay had to wander around for an hour in the snow, until eventually an unlit taxi stopped for him.

9 January 1982

The snow has stopped. I dig my Citroën Dyane out of a roof-high drift. I drive through snow hills to Finchley Road, determined to write. I get going while Lindsay phones Clive Parsons. Clive is about to go to Texas for ten days to raise cash for his next film. Lindsay reminds him that he hasn't finished this one yet. There is still the dubbing, additional shooting, publicity, advertising and music to sort out. 'Listen, DARLING, are you the producer or aren't you? This is what producing means.'

By lunchtime all of Lindsay's guests have arrived except Sandy.

'Joe Cunt will have to do the cooking as usual,' says Lindsay sourly.

I show him some finished lines of dialogue. 'Fine,' he says, basting the chicken. Sandy turns up and goes to sleep on the couch. Eleanor Fazan, dancer and choreographer and a great friend of Lindsay, showers everyone with Christmas presents and kisses. Murray, Lindsay's brother, starts hammering like a madman in the spare room, putting up some bookshelves. I might as well go, I decide, but Lindsay catches me at the door.

'You fucking skiver.'

'I've finished.'

'Give it me.'

I give him the pile of script.

He explodes. 'What's this mess, you skiving bastard? I can't read a word of it.'

I try to calm him down. 'It's been written in total chaos, Lindsay. I'll copy it out neatly in the morning.'

'God speed you, and drive safely.'

6 April 1982

A letter from Lindsay.

Dear David,
Essential news on the picture is good. Tom Nicholas and Bob Webster (Distribution and Exhibition respectively) want to show the picture *soon* – opening in London at the end of May, and going round the country, with a heavy print order, two or three weeks later. Favre Le Bret, from Cannes, was impressed and delighted with the picture and unhesitatingly has invited it to Cannes. I had a drink with him the day after he saw it, and he spoke of it with intelligent respect and amusement – in complete contrast to anything that has been said about it here, except by understanding friends.

Myself, I'm quite exhausted by the effort to complete the picture, and really haven't the energy to carry the battle on against critics, journalists, publicists, advertising agencies etc., etc. Unfortunately the enthusiasm which the film is arousing means that everything has to be done in a rush. They will have to get on with it.

I told you, didn't I, that Clive was off in New York trying to help Davina set up that musical? He's also dismissed the secretary, Chrissie, because she asked for a rise. And Barry Spikings flew back from Beverly Hills last week.

Love, Lindsay

14 April 1982
London

I attend the British Association of Film Producers' showing of *Britannia Hospital*. When Arthur Lowe dies on the screen, the audience boos loudly, and there are shouts of 'Cut it out!' Arthur Lowe died on stage two months ago.

The establishment loathes the film. Gerry Lewis, the publicist, says to me, 'David, you've got to stop doing this sort of thing.'

19 May 1982
Cannes

Britannia Hospital's official showing. The black-tie British storm out of the cinema, screaming abuse at the screen. Success! We've achieved what we set out to do so blindly two years ago. An assault on Thatcher's Britain that hurts.

27 May 1982
Cannes

A rave in *Variety*. The Americans and Europeans love our film.

31 May 1982
London

The press show of *Britannia Hospital*. Otis leaves at the end without saying a word. My old flame Val accosts Lindsay, saying, 'Why can't you make nice warm films like Satyajit Ray?'

25 June 1982

Britannia Hospital is withdrawn by EMI less than a month after its opening.

26 June 1982
Coleford, the Forest of Dean

Monika and I have a Guinness in the Angel Hotel. I overhear a group at the table next to us say how much they want to see 'that film with the Queen Mother in it'.

27 June 1982
Stirling Mansions

I have dinner with Lindsay at our beloved Cosmo restaurant. As Lindsay climbs the stairs to his flat, he suddenly says,
    'You know, I'm a broken man.'
    'You're not!'
    'No, I am. Broken . . .' and he means it.
    Britannia Hospital's failure in England, which he loves passionately, and hates passionately, is a wound that will never heal.

Going back to madness

21 August 1982
Cherry Tree House

Otis rings in high excitement. It's about Frank Konigsberg, who he says is a fan of mine. I'm to ring him immediately at the Montcalm Hotel. I phone expecting another $9^1/2$ *Weeks*. To my astonishment, Konigsberg tells me he's succeeded in getting the rights to Saint-Exupery's masterpiece *The Little Prince*.

I tell Konigsberg how much I love the book. I have three copies in the house.

'Serendipity!' he exclaims.

19 November 1982

The Montcalm Hotel, just off Hyde Park, is so exclusive it never advertises. It's here that I am to meet Frank Konigsberg with my treatment of *The Little Prince*.

Frank Konigsberg is thin with a bald head and a large Adam's apple. We have our first conference standing up in his tiny room filled with suitcases bulging with scripts.

He makes no comment on the treatment except to say he has to show it to Jim. Jim, I learn, is a king, a pop promo composer for MTV. Jim sleeps all day and works at night. We wait until it gets dark and then go down to the king's suite. He emerges from a large sunken bedroom encased in black motorcycle racing leathers and colossal black leather gloves.

Jim doesn't say a word about *The Little Prince* but talks endlessly about musicals. He clearly knows every shot, every movement of every musical ever made. When it's nearly dawn, he asks to see the treatment and takes it in his giant muffs into the bedroom.

'He's a genius,' Frank comments. 'He'll do the music and dance numbers – if he likes the script.'

A few minutes later the king returns. 'Great,' he says. 'I'll get my friend Russell Mulcahy to direct.'

'Wonderful,' says Frank.

Jim tells me that Russell is the highest paid director in the world. He makes promos for top pop stars. Konigsberg seems delighted, but

I'm confused. *The Little Prince* isn't a pop promo. But these men seem to know what they're doing. Jim goes to bed and I catch the 9 a.m. train home.

22 November 1982

A postcard from Lindsay of an old wind-up gramophone with a record titled 'HIT of the week'. On the back he has written: 'Dear David, This seemed made for *you* . . . I am not liking NY so much. My awareness of the universal bullshit has become agonisingly acute. On "Good Morning America" the other morning guess what "wonderful actor" was saying with engaging charm, "I give a lot of sympathy. I'm a compulsive sympathy giver. I'm not just empathetic, but sympathetic . . ." *and* "There are lots of areas of compulsion in me which are less sympathetic." Yes. Jon Voight has TWO PICTURES READY FOR RELEASE! Love, L.

19 December 1982

I finish the first draft of *The Little Prince*.

7 January 1983

Konigsberg rings to say he's very happy with the script and is setting it up with CBS and Russell Mulcahy.

8 March 1983
London, Mayfair

I'm staying at the posh Montcalm Hotel writing a script for Bandra, a young Pakistani shipping magnate. Every day Bandra has me chauffeur-driven in a white Rolls Royce to his huge Mayfair office, but he won't pay my hotel bill, which is running up in tenners by the hour.

Bandra is going to direct an epic, Pakistan's answer to Sir Richard Attenborough's Indian *Gandhi*. It will tell the story of a young man, very like Bandra, who runs a shipping business, is a killer with women, and becomes Pakistan's saviour and President. Bandra is convinced that after the movie he will become President of Pakistan himself. His country needs him.

Our film will have, by my reckoning, 300 scenes, involve 200,000 extras, last 18 hours and cost 45 million dollars. But all I want to do is get out of this hotel, where I've been stuck penniless for a week.

Then a miracle. The leading American film critic, Vincent Canby of the *New York Times*, has devoted a double spread to *Britannia Hospital*, which has just opened in America. He's hailed it as the greatest British film ever made. A woman from the *New York Times* rings up, saying the review is unique in the paper's history. They're running another double spread next Sunday about Lindsay and myself. Can I give an interview?

This is all very well, but it doesn't pay the hotel bill. Then the phone rings again. It's Frank Konigsberg, with whom I had worked in this same hotel last year.

'What on earth are you doing in the Montcalm, David?'

'I don't know.'

'No news from CBS about *The Little Prince*, but in the meantime I'd like you to write another film. A modern version of *The Treasure of the Sierra Madre*, set underwater. The central character is a girl. I'm calling it *Wet Gold*.'

'All about greed and lust?'

'Yes, but underwater. Very existential.'

On the promise of dry gold Lindsay pays my hotel bill.

9 March 1983

Home. Our beloved little dog, Bertie, the great survivor, has a stroke. She can't see, hear or even walk. After we try in vain to hand-feed her, we take her on her last trip to the vet. It's the end of an era. Bertie has been part of the family since *If . . .* She had fun and soul in every fibre. We bury her in the garden with flowers and a cross made of sticks.

15 April 1983

No wonder Bandra wouldn't pay my hotel bill. The Six o'clock News on BBC1:

> The Massey-Brent merchant bank, one of the City's newest, collapsed today and filed for bankruptcy with outstanding debts of £350 million.
>
> The cause of the bank's collapse was its heavy involvement with

the film and shipping magnate Mamoud Bandra's merchant fleet and the falling price of wheat. Mr Bandra has also been declared bankrupt, but when we contacted him today we found him busily at work directing his latest film . . .

. . . and there, on the screen, is a shot of young Bandra in his living room, single-handedly working a movie camera, and directing a pretty girl having a cup of tea.

Bandra's greed and lust, surreally on screen, make my day. I work all night on my own epic of greed and lust, *Wet Gold*.

6 May 1983

Here I am back in Hollywood, at a nice old hotel, the Beverly Hillcrest. I am to meet someone called Larry for lunch to discuss *Wet Gold*. Larry turns out to be very young and is dressed in obligatory nautical blazer with gold buttons. He's Frank Konigsberg's co-producer. Frank is so busy right now that Larry hasn't seen him for a week, but we'll be meeting him tonight at nine in an Italian bistro to prepare for our network conference at ABC tomorrow.

The bistro is so dark that we can hardly see each other's faces. Konigsberg, who has arrived an hour late, reads by candlelight, eats, takes phone calls and rewrites the treatment simultaneously. He rattles off comments, smokes non-stop and stubs out his cigarettes in iced water.

I really don't understand him. What is he after? He seems different from the Hollywood types I've been used to. No obvious interest in either money or power, no obvious ego. He has a sun-blistered head from driving around in a beaten up old Alfa Romeo Spyder. He has a wife crippled with arthritis whom he sees for about half an hour a week, and he keeps four Hungarian sheepdogs to guard her. Now he is on a strange crest, producing at the same time two features, five specials and several mini-series. He rations himself to half-hour working lunches and these late conferences. The only way he shows anger is to throb his large Adam's apple and gulp. He reminds me of the Hurricane Higgins of old, playing the shots as fast as he can, the more games the better.

8 May 1983

I order coffee and eggs and bacon for breakfast. I spill the coffee over the treatment and throw up. I sip a little Gold Label to calm myself. Larry drives me to Century City. We meet Konigsberg in the ABC lobby.

'You'll have to do the talking,' I say nervously.

He assures me that Eileen Burg, the ABC producer, is 'a very nice lady' who will bring me out of myself.

While we're waiting, Konigsberg fills in the time by amending a draft of *The Little Prince*.

At last a secretary ushers us in. Eileen Burg, plump and young, kisses Konigsberg and shakes my hand.

'I loved Alan's music in *O, Lucky Man!* He's a genius.' She also adores The Animals, loves the other British bands and thinks what we did in the Falklands was terrific. I relax a little. An anglophile. I relax even more when her plump ankles swing onto the glass table, crashing into the coffee saucer I'm using as an ashtray.

'So what's the story, David? Is it lush? Joe has only sent us one memo – he wants it lush. I want it poor.'

Stumped, I look imploringly at Konigsberg.

'It is poor, but lush,' he says brilliantly.

'I like it! I love it!'

He begins to read from our treatment, and Eileen keeps on saying, 'I love it! I love it!'

But then his Adam's apple throbs.

'Um . . . we don't have an ending. Sorry, Eileen.'

'Oh, dear. The last writer we had from England we turned round in twenty-four hours. Will Friday be OK?'

'Not Friday. I'm viewing locations in Dallas and Vancouver.'

'Monday?'

'David, can you stay on till Monday?' His Adam's apple throbs again. There is only one answer.

'Fine.'

A final afternoon conference at Konigsberg's office at Fox Studios before he dashes off to Dallas and Vancouver and Statten Island. Projects and scripts sit in orange boxes. There's no protocol. Everyone works the coffee machine, and no one seems to mind when I splatter my filthy pipe tobacco or add whisky to the coffee.

9 May 1983

Frank has flown off to Dallas and Vancouver. I am to produce revisions of the treatment for Larry. But first we view *The Treasure of*

Monika, at The Falls, 1977

Pa and Luke, Christmas 1977:
'It's dreadful splitting him
up like this . . .'

Darling Monika and baby Skye

Lindsay directs Malcolm McDowell in
O, Lucky Man! *Mick wears his*
lucky gold suit

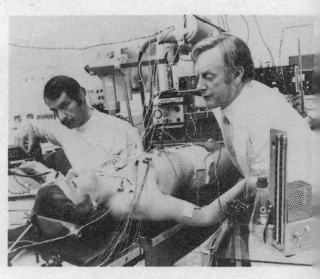

O, Lucky Man!: *Mick, having*
sold all rights in his body to
Professor Millar

Mrs Richards (Rachel Roberts) about to
commit suicide over the cost
of living, in O, Lucky Man!

O, Lucky Man!: *Mick, about*
to meet death and rebirth . . .

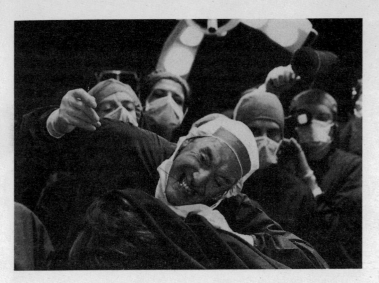

Britannia Hospital: *Professor Millar sews on
yet another head*

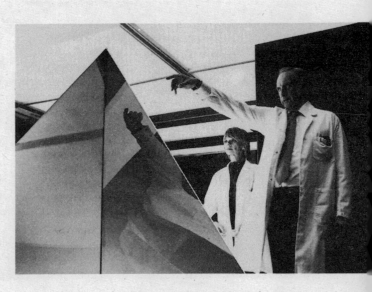

'Genesis' in Britannia Hospital
*Opposite: the rioters and
my slogans*

Lindsay by me at his beloved Fuchsia Cottage, 1991

Myself by Lindsay at my beloved Fuchsia Cottage, 1991

Mike Legge:
'There is no bullshit in
Hollywood'

Malcolm McDowell and his wife Kelley,
Ojai, California, 1994

Charles Drazin, my brilliant editor,
about to cut a hundred pages
from my diary

Lindsay, 1992: 'Is that all there is?'

the Sierra Madre. Afterwards I say, 'It was brilliant.'
   'Too linear,' says Larry.
   Apparently, as I am quickly learning, 'linear' and 'explanatory' are dirty words.

12 May 1983

We now have our ending. Eileen is happy. 'How long,' she asks. 'Four weeks?'
   'Six?' I venture.
   'Ten.' Says Frank.
   Free at last. I can go.

20 September 1983
Cherry Tree House

Larry rings. I'm to come immediately to LA to finish *Wet Gold.* I tell Larry that Friday is Skye's sixth birthday. I can't miss it. I'll come on Saturday.

Saturday 24 September
Hollywood

Oddly, Frank has given me a day's rest, but then I learn he wants me to do a rewrite of *The Little Prince* too.

25 September 1983

I phone Malcolm and we arrange to meet. I'm going to treat him to the hotel's speciality: their English Sunday lunch of roast beef and Yorkshire pudding is served every day except Sunday and attracts a crowd of nice Jewish ladies. He says he has a treat for me, too.

26 September 1983

A script conference with Marion Briggs, the head of special productions at CBS. 'We read *The Little Prince* last night . . .' They read it last night! They've had it for seven months! 'We like your script, or you wouldn't be sitting here, but we don't like the black satire. We want white satire. That's what Americans like. So change everything to white, happy satire.'

'Impossible!' I say, and that is the end of *The Little Prince*.

In the evening Frank and Larry come round to the hotel to work on *Wet Gold*. At 2 a.m. Frank rings his wife to say he'll be late. 'I'm doing good work with David and Larry.'

Frank is going to be away for three days. He is off to Vancouver to prepare a movie. He also has a TV show just about to go on air and three specials now in production. Then there's another movie called *Glitterdome*, which will begin shooting next week. He has little time for slackers.

'You're to stay in the hotel,' he tells me when he finally leaves. 'I want you writing every minute of the day.'

27–29 September 1983
The Beverly Hillcrest Hotel

I work happily away on the script. I live on a wonderful diet of shrimp cocktail and Bloody Marys filled with fruit, which I order four times a day. The room service waiter, Alfredo Gonzalez, is an elderly Mexican and a charming serf. He's in trouble. He has to serve the whole hotel single-handed, and some bitch, who's complaining he's slow, is going to get him the sack. Will I write him a good reference?

'With pleasure.'

30 September 1983

Larry rings. He is hooting with laughter. Frank's back from Vancouver and he didn't do any work at all. 'He spent the whole time fishing! Can you imagine Frank Konigsberg fishing for three days? I just can't believe it. Mind you, he didn't fish himself. He sat in the boat all day while his rod hung over the side with a little bell attached to it in case he should catch anything.'

'And did he catch anything?'

'No. But he's been fishing. This is history.'

I am summoned to Frank's office to work with him on the script, but every few minutes he is called away to attend to some urgent problem.

James Garner is refusing to appear in *Glitterdome* unless he has director approval.

'No one gets director approval. We fire them all the time. It would set a bad precedent. No!' Frank's Adam's apple throbs with anger.

The leading actress demands that she should be provided with a special $2,000 Hollywood wig. Larry thinks she ought to provide the wig herself. 'You expect an actress to come with her body parts.'

Amidst all these problems little work gets done and Frank decides that we should continue in the evening at the hotel. Another all-night session, in which Frank concentrates endlessly on petty detail. And there are endless weeks of this ahead.

3 October 1983

Malcolm rings. He's seeing his agent, so we change Sunday lunch to Wednesday.

'We've a lot of catching up to do, love,' he says.

In the office, Frank's Adam's apple oscillates rapidly as he loses his temper. In my script I have written, 'The yacht rounds a headland . . .' Frank refuses to believe there's such a word as headland. I insist that boats have been rounding them for centuries. But he summons an American dictionary – and he is correct. 'Headland' is not an American word.

After an hour of trying to think what boats do sail round in America, I come up with 'cape' and Frank checks it in the dictionary. 'Cape' is OK, it's American, so our heroes can sail a little further on their long voyage in quest of treasure.

That night in the hotel Frank is in a good mood. 'David, you're going to win us an Emmy.'

5 October 1983

Reception calls. 'Mr Sherwin, there's a very distinguished English gentleman to see you.'

Mystified, I go down to the lobby. It's Malcolm, his face wrinkled and ravaged almost out of recognition.

'You look good,' he tells me.

'You too.'

'Give us a big kiss,' he says. 'Now for the surprise.'

Outside is a gleaming black turbo-charged Porsche 911.

'God, it's beautiful,' I say.

He takes me for a ride at a hundred miles an hour round Beverly Hills.

'Wonderful, Malc. Just like mine in the old days.'

'We're both flash buggers at heart,' says Malcolm with that grin of his. The hotel valet parks it in the lot beside five other gleaming black Porsches.

In the restaurant Malcolm sits down and much to my surprise orders fish and mineral water. He's a reformed man, he tells me.

'I was drinking two bottles of wine a day, snorting $5,000 a week of cocaine and spending a fortune on my psychiatrist. Then one day I booked into the Betty Ford Clinic, had someone called a sponsor who said I was full of shit, and since then I haven't touched a drop. And I don't smoke . . . Thought I might as well give up cigarettes while I was about it.'

As I begin on my third Bloody Mary with fruit, Malcolm tells me about his family. He and Mary Steenbergen, who won an Oscar for *Melvin and Howard*, have two children.

'We are something of an institution here because we put family before work. We always travel together and we never make films at the same time. I love her. I don't want anyone else to make love to her, and I don't want to make love to anyone else. Mind you, I've got these topless housemaids and nanny. They're young. I love it, but Mary doesn't. They're getting the sack. God, David, you're not still smoking that disgusting pipe!'

We chat about the past.

'I didn't behave too well on *Britannia Hospital*, but I didn't feel part of it. I was just hauled in, and I hated that hotel, Blakes.'

'I'm trapped in this one,' I say. 'I'd like an apartment with a top-less maid.'

'Watch out, or they'll give you one! God, love, it's good to see you again. I suppose Lindsay is hurt because I haven't sent him a picture of Charlie and Lillie. I'll give you one to take back. God, David, that pipe – you'll have me smoking again.'

A hotel clerk gives me a message from Frank. He wants me at the office.

'Tell them to fuck off!' says Malcolm.

'I can't or I'll be here till Christmas. You don't know what it's like.'

Malcolm calls a waiter. 'Another Bloody Mary for my friend – and it's on me.'

When I do get to the office, Frank is nowhere to be seen. His new show has flopped and he's got to sack the actors.

In the evening Malcolm rings to thank me for the meal. I hear him telling his little daughter, Lillie, not to play with the light switch. I miss Skye like hell. I can't phone because of the eight-hour time difference, and feel like catching the next plane home.

From my tenth-floor balcony overlooking Century City I see an incredible sunset. It looks just like a scene from *Blade Runner*. I count eleven light planes and six helicopters as the sky over the city turns from orange to moonlight. It starts to rain. Strange circular wisps of cloud, formed by the heat of Century City, are pierced by a faint, moonlit rainbow. I feel sad and happy and drink English Bass beer.

8 October 1983

Once more I arrive at the office to find Frank and Larry off on their other movies. I decide to do something. I tell them they're wasting my time and their money. I'm leaving on Monday. That does the trick. Frank makes the effort to concentrate on one thing for a change.

11 October 1983

I fly home, after four days' non-stop work. Free again.

After further rewriting, Wet Gold *goes into production in the Bahamas with Brooke Shields as the leader of the treasure hunters, and Burgess Meredith as the hobo who becomes their guru. Brooke Shields has a lot of fun throwing Larry fully-clothed into their hotel swimming pool.*

Wet Gold *premieres and receives surprisingly good notices. It is shown over and over on American television. But my ex-agent, Otis, who came into some family money, was so quick to leave ICM that he forgot to put the vital clause in my contract that I get 5 per cent of the gross.*

Lindsay, who is in America directing David Storey's In Celebration, *sends me a copy of the US TV Guide.* Wet Gold *is on the cover.*

'Congratulations on making the big time! Hope you are writing me an inspired script of If 2. . . Onwards!'

Going mad in Brazil

21 September 1984

I set off in the Citroën Dyane for London to discuss *If 2 . . .* and to see Lindsay's new production, *Playboy of the Western World*. The plan is that I will take my sister Sue to the show, spend the night at her new London flat, and then return tomorrow for Skye's seventh birthday party.

I arrive at Stirling Mansions to find Lindsay still in his pyjamas. It is 3 p.m. He is having lunch in the kitchen with Kevin Brownlow, the film historian.

'Do you know David?' Lindsay asks.

'We met about a hundred years ago,' says Kevin.

They are discussing Lindsay's TV programme on British cinema. Lindsay's analysis is categorical: the Americans have energy but no depth – the recipe for a popular commercial cinema; the British have no energy and no depth – hence a disastrous cinema. The only place where you find both energy and depth is Poland.

'Don't you agree, David?'

Kevin asks Lindsay to guess which other director will be doing a programme on British cinema.

'Alexander Mackendrick?'

'No. You wouldn't mind him. It's Richard Attenborough.'

Frank Grimes, who is starring in Lindsay's new production of *Playboy of the Western World*, takes me out onto the balcony. They're talking crap, he says.

After Kevin has left, Lindsay and I sit down at the round kitchen table to discuss *If 2 . . .* Frank immediately questions the whole premise of the film.

'What's this thing you've got with Mick Travis? Mick Travis is dead. He dies in *Britannia Hospital*.'

'No, he didn't. He's over here making *Gulag*,' says Lindsay.

'He's *dead*,' insists Frank.

'Is it a presentation to Mick Travis?' Lindsay asks.

'Are certain old boys to be made governors?' I say.

'Do they get to sing the school song, which has been abolished in the name of progress along with everything else?'

But before we get any further, the phone rings.

Lindsay answers, his voice for once not humorous, mocking or dramatic, but deadly calm.

'Yes, his full name is Alexander Anderson. He is my nephew. Yes. Yes. This is home. Correct. No, his father is in Bombay. Correct . . .'

Lindsay puts the phone down and gives us the bad news. 'The Foreign Office have received a telex from the consul in Rio de Janeiro. Sandy's burnt his passport, his air ticket and all his clothes. Apparently he's in a mental hospital in Rio.'

Lindsay phones the travel agent Sandy used and discovers that the cost of Sandy's original excursion ticket was £500. The refund is £250. To fly out another excursion ticket would take three weeks. It can't be telexed. However, a normal, full-fare, one-way ticket can be telexed but will cost £900.

'I can't leave him in a mental hospital in Rio for three weeks,' says Lindsay, and he calmly begins to organise everything on a sheet of A4 paper before ringing back the Foreign Office.

'Ah, hello. I've rung the travel agency. He went on a reasonably priced excursion which cost £500 . . . No, it's quite a lot. £900 full fare. But how do I know, if the air ticket is telexed, it will reach him? And he'll need clothes . . . How can I pay for them? Lindsay sighs as he puts down the telephone. The Foreign Office won't accept a cheque. They want cash before they'll clothe Sandy. And the person dealing with Sandy's file has gone home and won't be back until tomorrow. Nothing can be done until then.

'They can't go home at 5 p.m. and leave all those Britons abroad,' I say. 'It's unbelievable.'

'Everybody keeps saying everything's unbelievable. It isn't . . . I'll phone the consulate in Rio.'

A recorded message tells him everyone's gone home for the weekend.

Next he phones the travel agency to buy the ticket. 'Can I do it on a credit card? . . . My maximum? I've no idea. I've American Express, Barclaycard, Diner's . . . Now do you assure me the full fare can be telexed tomorrow? . . . Can you give me the ticket number, airline, name of airport and – oh, yes – the computer codes?' Lindsay writes all this information on his A4 sheet, which is now full of names, telephone numbers, card numbers, ticket costs, and, despite the crisis, all written with Lindsay's absolute precision.

Frank comes in. 'Lindsay, the time. Are you coming to the theatre?'

It's 6.45 p.m. Lindsay is still in his pyjamas. I rush off to pick up Sue, who is coming to see *Playboy* with me. She teaches Greek history at London University and has swapped a lovely house and

David Sherwin

garden in Oxford for a tiny flat in King's Cross. We take the
Piccadilly Line to Hammersmith and only just get to the Riverside
Theatre in time.

I feel completely drained and let the poetic Irish of *Playboy* infuse
me.

In the interval the first person we meet is Lindsay, awaiting our
reaction.

'It's like music,' I say.

'Is it? I've no idea any more.'

We all deserve a drink, I decide, and offer to buy a round. I order
my first half of bitter of the year. I'm supposed to be off the booze
for life, so drink my beer straight off at the bar, hoping that Lindsay
and Sue won't notice. God, it's delicious! I'll never be able to live
without the taste of beer.

'What was that?' Lindsay asks.

'Shandy . . .'

Lindsay is amused, Sue disgusted.

Back at Sue's flat, I ask for a boring book to send me to sleep and
she gives me a history of the Phoenicians. I climb into the camp bed
with coffee, the Phoenicians and peanuts. Read about the
Phoenicians until 2.30 a.m. All they did was make money and sacrifice children, believing their deaths would make them more money.
Thousands of children's corpses have been discovered in pots at
Carthage. Feel wide awake and ready to write *If 2*. . . But what does
it all mean? The Phoenicians making so much money and sacrificing
children to do so, Sue leaving Oxford and living in a shoebox in
London, Sandy going off to Brazil for the trip of a lifetime and going
mad . . .

22 September 1984

At Stirling Mansions I find Lindsay ready, shaved and dressed. We
order a minicab to take us to Petty France. There we meet Mr
Maine, the duty officer looking after Sandy's file. He is tall, puffy,
athletic and pirouettes on his feet like a dancer.

He is on the phone, sorting out another case. 'That engineer who
was killed – how much would it cost to bring the body back from
Djibouti to Liverpool? They want to arrange it as quickly as possible
because of the decomposition . . . Yes, thank you.'

'Now, Mr Anderson, your nephew?'

'I've brought cash,' says Lindsay.

'Good. I'll just give you a receipt, then I'll send a telex.' Mr Maine counts the money carefully. '£60. Good. Now I'll make you a receipt.' He fills in a slip and hands it over.

'Is it all right?' Mr Maine asks.

'Yes. But how do I know he'll receive the money?'

'Are you sure the receipt is all right?' Mr Maine seems extraordinarily anxious to have his receipt acknowledged.

'It's fine,' says Lindsay. 'But when I rang the consulate in Rio yesterday, they'd all gone home for the weekend. So how do I know the money will actually get to him today?'

'The number I'm telexing is special. There is someone waiting by the machine all the time. It's the rule.'

Mr Maine starts to make out a telex, dated 22 September, timed at 10.30.

'But they're four hours behind us,' says Lindsay.

'We all work in Zulu,' explains Mr Maine. Zulu, I remember, is army code for GMT, unchanged since the Zulu wars in 1890.

Lindsay also gives the airline information and we wait for the telex to be sent.

At last Mr Maine looks up at us from the telex machine.

'Your nephew will arrive in London, Heathrow, on Sunday at Zulu 14.30,' he says proudly.

'Good,' says Lindsay. 'Now all I have to do is pay for the ticket. And he'll be working at Waitrose in the Finchley Road for the next two years.'

A lady duty officer escorts us out of the building – in case we steal secrets? In the lift she presses 'down' but nothing happens. We're stuck.

'This is always happening,' she says.

'I suppose you hear some quite amazing things,' says Lindsay.

'Oh yes. One day I'm going to write a book.'

Next stop the travel agent in Turnham Green, which has hardly changed since I was there twenty-four years ago interviewing the Thirties actor Henry Oscar in my first job for *TV Times*. There is a spacious High Street with trees in leaf, antique shops and a new addition – wine bars.

After we have found the travel agent and paid for the ticket we walk back along Turnham Green High Street. Lindsay stops at an estate agent's window. He points at a modern three-bedroom detached house.

'Don't look at the price. How much does it cost?'

'£120,000.'

'£338,000, including sauna.'

'Best stay where you are.'

'Yes. I think at my age I ought to simplify life – instead of which I complicate everything. I suppose now you'd like a pub?'

'I'd love a beer.'

'What was that you had last night?'

'Half of bitter.'

'You were lying. Well, you can have a ginger beer. With a dash of lime.'

Lindsay brings us our drinks and sits down. He closes his eyes. He looks like a lopped silver birch. Absolutely at the end of the road.

'How's the new play about Gay getting on?'

'I'm getting Monika to type it out.'

'Then what?'

'I'll send it to my agent.'

'It's all ridiculous . . . Everything . . .' he says.

We go home on the Metropolitan Line. Lindsay comes back to life when we pass a greengrocer's near Stirling Mansions. He spends fifteen minutes selecting raw corn cobs. They almost all have mouldy tops. Finally he finds three in good shape and buys them.

I get back to Cherry Tree House just in time for Skye's birthday party. I take photographs of her blowing out her seven candles. There are no guests. Skye is a peculiar loner. The highlight of her day is watching a video of *Some Like It Hot*, her favourite film.

I ask if I can watch it with her.

'No!'

'Why?'

'You wouldn't understand it.'

'Why not? You do.'

'It's like horse-riding. There's a thousand things you have to know.'

'I've got to start somewhere.'

'No. It's too difficult.'

'It would be good for my writing.'

'Oh, *Some Like It Hot*'s not like your films. You're not to watch.'

'But if I did, I might learn.'

'Yes, it would be a whole new experience for you.'

The phone rings and I leave Skye to watch the masterpiece on her own. The call is for Monika and I go upstairs to listen to the news on the radio. After the national news, a sad local item: a Cardiff man drugged his 6-year-old daughter with twenty sleeping pills, drove to the Severn Bridge, stopped, and in full view of other drivers threw her body into the estuary where she drowned. At his trial the father said, 'What future did she have? Drugs . . . Prostitution . . . Nuclear war . . .'

Skye and Monika's hysterical laughter resounds from below. I shut my door. And so to bed with the history of the Phoenicians, whose only purpose in life was to make money, and who left no other record of their civilisation than pots of murdered children.

The late 1980s were years of struggle, harder than I had ever known. There was a wonderful renewed friendship with Jo Janni, miraculously recovered from a near-fatal stroke on the last day of shooting Yanks. *A truly great and kind man. Good work was produced but came to nought. Further good work flourished briefly with the young director David Hutt, but that also came to nought.*

Mostly it was free-loaders wanting something for nothing. The mad fantasists movies attract like moths. The saddest is a burly, bearded transvestite director who wanted me to don a frock and go with him to the transvestites' annual ball at Bournemouth. We were, he said, having written our film about transvestites for nothing, to 'climb to the top of a very tall building, hold hands and jump'. I did a lot of jumping from tall buildings – but in January 1989, when the Secretary of State for Employment personally refused me my rightful dole money, I lost my temper and wrote an account of my frustration. The Guardian *published it, and here it is.*

Picking the bones of social security

It was only in 1985 that I first learned that self-employed writers had the right to the dole while unemployed. Work in Britain had dried up after the disastrous reception of the film I'd written, *Britannia Hospital*, a black comedy which had managed to offend critics, right and left. There had been one rave review in the *New York Times* and work in Hollywood – but I wished to remain a British writer. But how? I was broke.

'Go on the dole,' said a director friend, David Hutt, after we had just received a rejection letter from the National Film Finance Corporation for our story of life on the Severn Bridge, 'Better than the Golden Gate'. David Hutt was an emphatic believer in working the system. 'I always sign on the day I'm out of work. It's the only way I can survive. There's only one trick question. You must say you are available for any work. But of course there isn't any work round here.

The next day I go down to the Social Security office in Lydney – the nearest town to my Forest of Dean cottage. Simple. Straightforward. No shame. No guilt. A pleasant girl gave me a sheet of paper to fill in. I ticked the box that said I would accept any job. She gave me a white card with my National Insurance number on it, which I must bring in to the office every fortnight to sign on, and a form to fill in.

The form was surprisingly easy. It told you, like Monopoly, which questions were applicable, and which questions you could skip to reach Go. The form had won a prize as the best government document ever devised. Monika, my wife, posted it off and four weeks later we received a cheque for £324. It was enough for food, the mortgage, two tins of pipe tobacco a week and a daily paper. In between infrequent contracts I regularly signed on. In 1987 the dole money mysteriously dropped from £81 a week to £65. Monika took to buying 'second-hand' bread – yesterday's left-overs. Toilet paper was a luxury and my craving for pipe tobacco, now nearly £3 a tin, provoked hysterical family rows.

It wasn't much fun on the dole. In fact our marriage was breaking up. Only Skye, our 10-year-old daughter who was going through a socialist phase, was sanguine: 'It's better to be poor than rich,' she remarked, devouring a hunk of bread without butter. Her ambition was to become leader of the Labour Party or an astronaut – certainly not a writer. 'Writers don't get paid.'

February 1988
My colleague Lindsay Anderson finishes work on his film, *The Whales of August*, and we resume our collaboration on *If 2 . . .: Reunion*. There's even money, £2,000 from the Film Fund. I immediately sign off the dole. Although I'm delighted to be working again with Lindsay, the £2,000 makes only a small dent in the overdraft and the bank manager isn't as impressed as he should be when I tell him I'm working with Britain's greatest director: 'Lindsay, is that a boy or a girl?' (His wife is called Lindsay.) 'I want to see you earning really big money, my friend. Or the bank will have to take an interest in your home. You've got to be more businesslike.'

I ignore him and concentrate on the work. *If 2 . . .* is not the usual kind of sequel but a view of the original characters of *If . . .*, twenty-five years on, to be played by the same actors.

15 April 1988
The phone rings. Lindsay: 'I've bad news. I've got to go over there to work.'

'New York?'

'No. Over there means LA. It's a project that's come up with a lot of money. I can't turn it down. Come up till I have to leave and we'll get as much done as possible on *If 2 . . .*'

I drive up to Lindsay's flat in London. We work from 7 a.m. to lunchtime, finish our revised draft, and Lindsay departs for six months. As I say goodbye, I wonder if the work will kill him (he has to shoot seven minutes of film a day for thirty-five days), if I'll ever see him again, and if *If 2 . . .* will ever be made.

4 May 1988
I go down to Lydney to sign on the dole. I know something is up when I find the doors to the Unemployment Office locked and chained. A sign reads, 'For Unemployment Office go to Job Centre'. The Job Centre is in the same block. I'd once been there. The only jobs on the notice board were for bar staff in tourist hotels – at £1.80 an hour. I enter it today and it looks like a genteel clinic: wall-to-wall carpet, low wooden desks set with vases of flowers, computers and cordless telephones – quite unlike the lino and plywood cubicles of the old Unemployment Office.

I sink into an armchair beside a low table. Eventually a girl leaves her computer and sits in an armchair opposite. I explain I'm self-employed, out of work and want supplementary benefit.

'There's income support. You may be qualified for that.'

The girl gives me new forms and explains that Lydney has been chosen as part of a government target scheme to get people out to work as soon as possible. 'Sounds a very good idea,' I say, beginning to realise it may be bar staff at £1.80 an hour.

The new form is quite different. It runs to thirty-two pages and takes Monika and I all day to fill in. Seven weeks pass and no money arrives.

25 June 1988
A letter printed on grey paper arrives, saying we will be visited in the morning by a person from the DHSS to interview us about my

claim for income support. We must have bank statements, mortgage accounts, every financial detail of our lives for this person
who will identify himself/herself as belonging to the DHSS.

26 June 1988
9 a.m. A grey-haired lady carrying a briefcase taps briskly on the
door. I sit her down at the dining room table in a chair facing the
wonderful view of the Severn. I hope the vibes will be a good
influence. No, she doesn't want a coffee. Monika sits at the far
end of the table with a file of money matters.

The person pulls out the income support form Monika and I
filled in two months ago and starts to quote from it. 'You can
imagine the pickle old people get into with this form,' she says.
'You state that you get up and think about work from 7.30 a.m.
to 5 p.m.'

'Well, that's only approximate,' I reply. 'I think all day and have
dreams at night. Sometimes I write down my dreams.'

'So how long would you say you spent actually *working*?'

'I don't know. But I never switch off.'

'If you work more than twenty-four hours a week, that's over
the limit for income support. I'm not fully acquainted with all the
niceties of the new Act yet. In fact, I don't know where it all comes
from. I think it comes from up there!' She lifts a bony finger and
jabs at the heavens. 'Up there,' she repeats mysteriously. I don't
know whether she means God or Thatcher or both.

'Well, I don't know how long I work. I've never figured it out.'

The person looks at me: 'I'll figure it out somehow. Often after
I've left the office with a problem I think about it – and suddenly
the solution will come to me, and I know it's right!'

'So you're working out of office hours?' I ask.

'No.'

'I call that work.'

She continues to hammer home this one point. 'How long do
you spend working? . . . I had a case the other day of a self-
employed carpenter. He said he only spent eighteen hours working. But in fact he spent an extra ten hours a week preparing for
work – he didn't get income support.'

'But I thought you'd come about money – my overdraft. Aren't
you interested in that?

'No. You can never tell with this form when the relevant point
will emerge. How long do you work, Mr Sherwin?'

Very angry, I march up the stairs to my study and a quick pipe. I hear Monika below trying to explain to the person: 'Writers don't clock off like normal people.'

I run down the stairs, furious. 'I think all day – ninety-six hours a week. Put that down.'

'You mean you work ninety-six hours a week?'

Alert, I respond: 'Do you call our meeting work?'

'No – it's an interview.'

'To me this is work. I've been observing you. The way you point to heaven when you get to a tricky bit.' That blows it, of course.

'I'm writing down that you work in excess of twenty-four hours a week. Can you sign it?'

'No.'

'I'll be here all day if necessary.'

Monika senses my rising fury. Placatingly, she says: 'Just sign it, David.' I sign, the person places it in her briefcase and scurries to the door. 'I think I can confidently say you won't be getting income support' – and she is gone.

28 June 1988

A form arrives from the DHSS, confirming that I am not eligible for income support since I work in excess of twenty-four hours. I can appeal.

I go down to Lydney and sign off. I prepare my appeal, stating that the assessor bullied me into signing her form and that my wife is a witness to her bullying. Moreover, I was not working, but thinking.

22 July 1988

During the period I had been signing on I had also been doing a lot of job-hunting in London. The American writers' strike excluded work 'over there', but in Browns Hotel, Mayfair, I had had tea with a producing couple, John Hardy and Shelly Bancroft. Our meetings resulted in a contract to write a thriller, 'Saving Grace', which is signed on 22 July. I receive a cheque for £875 from my agent and start work.

15 August 1988

A letter from the DHSS. It states that the decision that I worked in excess of twenty-four hours a week was made in error. The correct decision is that I was not eligible for income support because I was not available for work. 'Buck passers,' comments Monika. I appeal.

3 November 1988
A thick A4 package arrives in the post from the DHSS. The first page tells that my appeal is to be heard in less than two weeks, on 15 November, before the Appeal Tribunal at Shire Hall, Gloucester. There are forty almost illegible photocopied pages of the evidence. The reasons for the DHSS refusal to grant me income support are full of simple errors – 'The Adjudication Officer does not consider the claimant would suffer hardship if income support were not paid as he has capital and should be able to secure a loan.' (Capital? The overdraft, perhaps, or the mortgage?) 'Paragraph 3 as inserted by regulation 6 of the Income Support (General) Amendment Regulations 1988 (SI 1988 No 633) deals with persons, other than those to whom regulation 10 (I) (h) applies, to whom none of the provisions of Schedule I applies.'

I don't understand any of this but am determined to fight my case as a matter of principle – it seems obscene that the state persecutes innocent, genuinely creative self-employed writers, artists, actors and actresses, and not only denies them a pittance to live on when they are out of work, but actually forbids them to do their own work, which is the only way they have any hope of surviving.

14 November 1988
The evening before the case, I feel I have no chance of winning but ring an old friend, the actor Frank Grimes, for advice. 'I'm going in all guns blazing,' I say.

'For God's sake, don't do that. They're bureaucrats. Be meek.'

15 November 1988
The morning is sunny, with a dense low fog. I was going to take Monika as a witness, but three months ago she was knocked down in a hit-and-run accident, suffered a serious head injury, was unconscious for three days in Gloucester Hospital, and now can't take any strain. So alone I mount the steps to Shire Hall, swallowing my nth Fisherman's Friend, the throat pills I'm addicted to, which I'm sure contain opium.

I'd imagined the tribunal would be delayed, like most court

cases, but everyone is expecting me. The clerk of the tribunal comes up and asks how much I wish to claim for expenses. 'It's a 36-mile round trip. I came by car.'

An extremely beautiful Eurasian girl introduces herself as Kalpna Vora. She's a journalist on the *Gloucester Citizen*. Do I mind if she sits in on the case. Of course not.

The clerk reappears and gives me a handful of pound coins for expenses. Kalpna Vora shows me a piece about the case in the *Western Daily Press*: 'Top scriptwriter David Sherwin is taking on the state over a wordsmith's prerogative to cerebrate . . .' All this seems much better than working in real movies – expenses money on the dot, a glamorous journalist.

The case is about to begin. The three members of the tribunal sit together. Mrs Dobbs of the DHSS, who is to present the case against me, takes a seat opposite the chairman. Kalpna Vora lounges on a side couch, shorthand pad at the ready. The chairman introduces himself as Mr Southworth. He has pale blond hair, a pale yellow shirt, and a yellow tie. A businessman? His two colleagues, who sit on either side of him, look like bucolic JPs. Mr Southworth asks me if I mind Mrs Dobbs giving her case first. It usually saves a lot of time. 'I quite agree,' I say. I'm going to be meek.

Unfortunately Mrs Dobbs has a bad cold. She can hardly speak. She chokes through the DHSS evidence, coughing. I offer her a Fisherman's Friend and tell her they cure everything, but she declines. She continues, referring to xeroxed pages of evidence against me, which none of the tribunal can find.

Mrs Dobbs sits down and the chairman asks me if I have any points. Yes. First, I don't have any capital to raise a loan. Only an overdraft. And I'd spent a lot of time while out of work seeking a job. I now have one.

If the Adjudication Officer's decision is upheld it will amount to me not being able to think creatively, as I would be denied income support on the grounds that I was not available for employment whilst thinking creatively.

One of the JPs has a practical question. 'How much do you earn for a contract?'

'Not much. On the present one, £9,000 – but that may be two years' work and it includes expenses, everything.'

'No, it isn't much,' he agrees. For every Jeffrey Archer there are hundreds of poets and writers who are very, very poor.

The chairman has one final question. 'What about this bullying business?' I answer frankly: 'It was horrible. Eventually my wife asked me to sign the form to end it.'

The chairman asks Mrs Dobbs, Kalpna Vora and myself to leave the room while they reach a decision. Tense moments outside – then the clerk asks us to re-enter. The chairman says their decision is unanimous. I am entitled to income support from 4 May 1988. 'You will be getting a letter confirming our decision and your money in a couple of weeks.'

When I arrive back at Cherry Tree House, Monika is chopping wood for the fire. I give her a grin. 'We won!'

'I thought I'd be getting a phone call saying you'd punched two policemen in the face.'

'And we're getting a cheque for £600 or £700.'

'Perhaps we can have central heating at last. I'm dreading this winter, with my head.'

'We will, I promise.'

2 December 1988

A phone call from the DHSS. The official says he is just making out my cheque following the tribunal's decision. But apparently the DHSS overpaid me £151 in 1986. It will be easiest if they just deduct the money from the present cheque. I have no way of proving them right or wrong, so say, 'Fine.'

'You'll be getting a cheque for £486 in a day or two.'

20 December 1988

The bottom falls out of our rusty 13-year-old car. It is a write-off. We are carless. Now we desperately need that £500.

23 December 1988

Still no DHSS cheque. I ring the office in Gloucester. The tribunal section is engaged. They'll ring back. Three minutes later the phone rings. Terrific – it'll be to say the cheque's in the post. Probably a Christmas oversight. I pick up the phone, pleased.

'Mr Sherwin? The General Manager, DHSS, speaking. We're not sending that cheque.'

'Why not?'

'You made a statement to the press.'

'I've never made a statement to the press in my life.'

'Well, I read it in the newspapers, and so did headquarters.

They've picked it up and asked to see all the documents.'

'Who are headquarters?'

'Headquarters are headquarters!'

'Well, *where* are headquarters?'

'London.'

'Who precisely wants to see the documents?'

'The Secretary of State.'

'What's his name?'

'I don't know his name. There are so many Secretaries of State.'

'There must be someone in charge at headquarters.'

'Oh, that's John Moore. He's the chief Secretary of State.'

'And who is the one who's demanded to see the documents?'

'I've told you. I don't know. But we're stopping the payment.'

I'm out of my depth in the shadowy world of Authority.

'But the chairman of the tribunal shook my hand and said I'd be receiving my money soon.'

'His words didn't mean that.'

I rush upstairs and fetch the appeal tribunal's verdict. 'Full text of unanimous decision on the appeal. Appeal allowed. Mr Sherwin is entitled to income support from 4 May 1988.'

'It doesn't say anything. It doesn't count.'

'It doesn't count? Christ, this will make good material.'

'Are you threatening me?' he says threateningly.

'No. But it's good material. What's more, an officer from your department rang me three weeks ago and said he was just posting the cheque.'

'And I stopped it. I had an idea. We hadn't looked at all the possibilities.'

'I won my case in black and white.'

'Oh no, you didn't. You might have been earning £500 a week before you signed on.'

'I earned £2,000 in February – and I was on the dole for a year before that. I'm càrless, I've had to take out a second mortgage. How dare you or the Minister of State stop the cheque!' I'm shaking with rage.

'I'll send someone round tomorrow to look at your books.'

'Tomorrow! That's Christmas Eve.'

'Well, after Christmas,' says the man, whose name, I found out, is Mr Gladhill.

27 December 1988

Monika rings the DHSS to find out what is really going on. If the Secretary of State or Mr Gladhill is denying income support, why didn't they tell us four weeks ago? Mr Gladhill is on holiday until 3 January.

3 January 1989

Monika speaks to Mr Gladhill. He insists on seeing the year's profit and loss account before he will decide what we are entitled to. Monika tells him again we are in loss – and adds that she had all the accounts ready for the assessor in June.

Mr Gladhill insists on new accounts. He will send another assessor. Distraught, Monika agrees, but says it will take a couple of weeks.

I won my appeal before an 'independent' tribunal – or did I? Now we are being means-tested and harassed by the state. Nothing surprising in today's Britain. There are still more than two million people on the dole. But from now on it won't just be the out-of-work working classes who will be jumping through the hoops of Thatcher's New Order – it will be the middle and professional classes as well. I read in the *Daily Telegraph* that 'People who lose highly paid professional or academic jobs will be required to take lower-paid employment' – bar staff at £1.80 an hour? – 'or risk having their benefit withdrawn. A new Social Security Bill seeks to close a loophole highlighted by the case of Dr Julius Tomin, the Czech dissident philosopher, who lost an appeal against the withdrawal of his £67 a week benefit.'

The DHSS withdrew it because he was deemed to have made himself unavailable for work by spending his days in the Bodleian Library, Oxford, studying Socrates while waiting to secure an academic post. He told an appeal tribunal he was willing to sweep streets, but would not take any job that would distract him from philosophy. He later secured a part-time job as a philosopher at a public house in Swindon. The right to think?

My battle with the state continues . . .

17 March 1989

A week after the article is published, I get my dole money.

The power of the press.

18 March 1989

A call from the *Mail on Sunday*. Will I meet Stewart Steven, their editor, next week? It will be greatly to my advantage.

19 March 1989

A call from Mark Shivas, who let me sleep on his floor back in the Sixties. He is now Head of Films at the BBC. Will I meet him for lunch next week?

22 March 1989
Fleet Street

I meet Stewart Steven in his vast editor's room at Northcliffe House.
   'I read your article and loved it. I wish I could write like you. *Britannia Hospital* is my favourite film. We've had a discussion and we've decided we can't let this happen to you. We've got to do something. So I'm offering you a retainer of £100 a week for two years, and should you write anything for us, we'll pay a pound a word. Mind you, remember one thing – there are two sorts of journalists: those who write long and those who write short. We like short articles.
   I phone Monika. 'Darling, it's a licence to print money!'

23 March 1989
High Street Kensington

Lunch with Mark. He hasn't changed at all – the same svelte, boyish good looks he had thirty years ago. He tells me that he'd like me to write a film based on the *Guardian* article.
   I already have a title, *When the Garden Gnomes Began to Bleed*. It's been quite a week.

When the Garden Gnomes
Began to Bleed

1 January 1990

My God, what a start to the New Year.

My whole family, except, oddly myself, is hysterical.

Monika is hysterical because the bank owns half the house.

Skye is hysterical because she hates Monmouth, the public school to which she won an assisted place two years ago. What proud, yuppy parents we were then: our daughter was going to enjoy the privileges of an education at a top private school. But now she yells that Monmouth's buildings are evil, the teachers are lazy and the other girls are all snobs who only talk about their Laura Ashley bedrooms. She says she wants to go to school with normal children and begs us to send her to a comprehensive. She's desperate for a real friend, and watches Rob Reiner's film of young friendship, *Stand by Me*, over and over again.

Only Skye's puppy, a black lurcher called Coco, is happy. He regards the cottage's carpet as his Christmas present and is ripping it to shreds.

I sit in my room and try to keep calm. I am finishing off *When the Garden Gnomes Began to Bleed*. I sip Drambuie and suck Fisherman's Friends. I notice the price – 39p for a 23 gram packet. That's nearly eight old shillings. The world has gone mad.

2 January 1990

Garden Gnomes is finished. I've poured all our family's unhappiness into it. 'It's strong stuff,' I tell Skye. 'The BBC will love it.' Sweetly she offers to print it out on the word processor.

The next thing I know Monika is storming up the stairs and slamming the script down on the table. 'It's terrible. Lies! You are telling lies about us! I hate your writing! Skye and I are going down to the lawyers to get a divorce!'

I post the script to Lindsay and wait to be divorced.

Monika and Skye return two hours later. Instead of divorcing me, they've bought themselves baggy T-shirts, jeans and a bottle of wine on the credit card.

3 January 1990

Monika goes to see Skye's headmistress, Miss Guischard. She explains that Skye twice won the Eisteddfod Poetry prize for the school, but is now so unhappy that she refuses to write poetry. She is thinking of moving her to a comprehensive. Miss Guischard shows not the slightest concern at losing a bright child: 'At Monmouth square pegs have to fit into round holes.'

5 January 1990

Lindsay phones. He thinks the script is 'a brilliant mess'. He suggests we spend a weekend together working on it in Fuchsia Cottage away from the bedlam of his flat and my family. I go sleepwalking as I always do when excited and step on Coco. He howls through the night.

11 January 1990
Fuchsia Cottage, Rustington

One week's work on the script becomes three. Lindsay is committed. He sees my battle against the state as a contemporary epic struggle. But he insists I make myself and my family less mad than in real life.

'No one is interested in mad writers,' he says. 'Only successful Woody Allens.'

One thing that has changed about our work together is supper. In the old days Lindsay would oversee the preparations for the evening feast as if he were directing the climax of a movie. But now he is a member of Weight Watchers and as keen on starving himself as he once was on guzzling. We eat once a day: six ounces of liver each, half an onion, a baked potato with slimline marge and a spray of broccoli. Also, as we are not receiving much to be thankful for, we no longer have to say grace before the meal.

1 February 1990

Monika rings in a state. Skye is suicidal. She has stopped working, her eyes are vacant, and she just watches *If . . .* over and over again. 'I can't bear to see her Public School turn her into a nutcase like it did you. I'm seeing the headmaster of Monmouth Comprehensive tomorrow.'

'A big day for the Sherwins tomorrow. Trust Skye's instincts,' says Lindsay.

2 February 1990

Monika rings. She's happy. The headmaster of the comprehensive is fantastic. He treats all his children as individuals, not square pegs who must fit into round holes. He showed Monika the school. The facilities are ten times better and Skye can start tomorrow. He's also putting her up a year, so she'll be in the top stream doing her GCSEs a year early.

3 February 1990

Skye has a wonderful day at school. All the boys in her class ask her out, but she modestly says they'll have to wait until she knows them better. Her classmates are friendly and praise her when she does well. The teachers answer her questions instead of ignoring her, and she receives not a single nagging word. May the miracle last.

'I don't know why all our girls don't go to the Comp – it's a much better school,' said Skye's old headmistress, Miss Guischard, when she heard Skye was leaving.

23 February 1990

Lindsay and I finish off our draft of *When the Garden Gnomes Began to Bleed*. It now has a happy, magical ending: I sell a script for a fortune and the fictitious Skye's horrible garden gnomes slowly, gracefully come alive and begin to dance.

I drive home, to be greeted with hugs and birthday presents a day early. Monika gives me a half bottle of whisky, Skye gives me a bottle of deodorant, and Coco throws me to the floor with an enthusiastic kiss.

I ring Mark Shivas to tell him the script is on its way and Lindsay is ready to start shooting.

He replies: 'Unfortunately, I have to go to LA tomorrow. Then Australia and New Zealand. I'll be doing a lot of reading, so I won't be able to give you a go-ahead till the end of next month.'

Lindsay thinks it is a bad blow. 'Mark Shivas may not like the script and I can't live in limbo. There are other things I could commit to. I've got to earn a living too.'

That night I dream about Mark Shivas. He agrees to make *Garden Gnomes* on one condition – that I take off his shoes. I do so. Then he summons Lindsay: he will accept him as a director, on condition that he put the shoes back on. Lindsay does so, and filming starts.

24 February 1990

My birthday. Lindsay's present is a book of Woody Allen's screen-plays. It is inscribed: 'For David – the Woody Allen of British Cinema. Love and Bravo – Lindsay (And of course remembering Garden Gnomes).' Monika gives me a card of Miss Piggy bugging Kermit the Frog, with the words: 'Ours is a strange and wonderful relationship. You're strange and I'm wonderful! Skye has made her own card for me: it shows Coco eating up the house. Inside it says: 'To the nicest Daddy in the world'.

The biggest surprise of all is a phone call from Luke. It is the first time he has ever rung on my birthday.

'Happy Birthday, Dad,' he says and I start to chatter, delighted to hear from him.

He cuts me short: 'Sorry Dad, I've only got two minutes.'

I invite him out for supper at the Cosmo, my favourite restaurant. 'The best Hungarian food in London, Luke.'

'Sorry, Dad, I'm a bit picky about what I eat. I don't like Hungarian food.'

'Well, what would you like?'

'The Pizza Hut.'

'The Pizza Hut, for God's sake! No, the Cosmo. You'll love it. It's our one night out.'

'Sorry, Dad. The Pizza Hut or nothing.'

5 March 1990

Skye comes home from school in a good mood. She scored 84 per cent in her first science test. She chews Coco's dog biscuit and calls out, 'Mum, do you remember when I was little, I used to eat dog biscuit?'

'Yes, I do.'

'Well, it's delicious. I still love it.'

'No wonder you're a bit odd.'

'I'm not odd. Being a vegetarian and liking dog biscuit is better than eating little piglets like you do.'

'At least we don't insist on vegetarian Cheddar cheese. Our sausages cost 66p. Your vegetarian Cheddar is £1.90.'

'At least I'm not causing suffering.'

'But Daddy has to pay. He suffers and I worry.'

15 March 1990

We win the Football Pools! In the post, among all the bills and free prize draws, I find an envelope from Littlewoods. It contains a pink cheque. Yelling excitedly, I run into the living room, where Monika is trying to hoover the remnants of carpet left by Coco.

'Don't open it – I will,' she says soberly. She takes out the cheque and hands it to me. We have won £1.04.

20 March 1990

Mike Legge arrives. We are writing a script together, 'Love and Madness on the Richter Scale', based on Mike's true experiences in Los Angeles.

We tackle our favourite scene: Miles, our hero, is invited to dinner by Imelda, the mad Filipino. She explains how she has been buying up all the worthless desert land to the east of the San Andreas fault, and her AMERICAN DREAM is about to come true:

> When the big one comes, all the land to the west of the fault will slide into the ocean. DISAPPEAR. Gone for ever! And what will be left, my clever ones? Why – PRIME WATERFRONT PROPERTY, that's what! To build the new Los Angeles on, and I will own it all! I will be worth millions, BILLIONS, TRILLIONS ...

Mike is as broke as we are. But he never gives up. He is a tonic. Like me he also has to see his bank manager. He owes over £90,000.

'I'm not in the least bit worried. Something always turns up. Why, Jeff Berg may like our script.'

26 March 1990

Go up to Lindsay's with some revisions and new scenes for *Garden Gnomes*. I talk to Malcolm. He is a star again, having made five pictures over the past year. In the last one he played Albert Schweitzer, quite a change from Caligula and Alex in *A Clockwork Orange*.

Malcolm loves *Garden Gnomes* and wants to play me. 'Mark Shivas should go down on his bended knee and thank you for this script,' he says. Malcolm is about the only sane person I know, in spite of his wonderful marriage to Mary Steenbergen having crashed.

In the evening I take Luke out to the Pizza Hut. I admire his new motorbike.

'Did Mum buy it for you?'

'No. Mum's company. Sometimes in the holidays I work there as a messenger.'

Bored, he leans back in his chair and crashes into the girl behind him. He apologises like a gentleman.

'Is that how you pick up your girl-friends?'

'Oh, shut up, Dad.'

His ambition now is to learn Japanese. 'If you know Japanese, you can earn big money.'

Strange how Luke has life sorted out already while I never will.

5 April 1990

As we drink our morning coffee, Monika and I look out at our wonderful view of the Severn Estuary.

'It's so lovely here,' says Monika. 'Too lovely for us. Your bank manager's bound to take it away, like Gay took your first home. I wish we could run away to a desert island.'

The phone rings. It's dear Jo Janni.

'David, would you like to write a black comedy about Stalin?'

Stalin and Hitler are my passions. I accept instantly.

'Good. I have an Italian partner. A very intelligent producer, who made *Investigation into a Citizen Above Suspicion*. I'd like you to meet him next week. He will drive down in his Ferrari.'

I doubt if anything will come of it. I love Jo, but he is as broke as we are, and paralysed too.

12 April 1990

I meet Jo's partner, Daniele Senatori, at the genteel Bay Tree Hotel in the Cotswolds. He has come not by Ferrari, but British Rail, 2nd class. His grey slacks have holes in them through which I can see wads of money. We sit in a cosy, stone-flagged snug and exchange our views on Stalin. I say he mustn't be the static monolith we know from the newsreels, but a comic figure who can seem sane one minute and a paranoid monster the next. I suggest Kevin Kline for the part. I mention his brilliant performance in *A Fish Called Wanda*.

'Ah, you think like a producer,' says Daniele, pulling out a wad of money which he puts on the table. 'A thousand pounds for you. It's for good faith. It's how we do business in Italy before the contract is signed.'

I am astounded. Not even a cheque. Real cash . . .

'Do you want me to sign for it?' I ask.

'No, no, I trust you. We do good work together.'

I'm not quite sure where to put the thousand pounds, so I just stuff the notes into my top pocket, where they bulge out like a handkerchief.

16 April 1990

A letter from BBC television. Mark Shivas hates *Garden Gnomes* and everything it stands for. He doesn't think it's a film. It's 'unreal'. I am dumbfounded. Lindsay and I were so enthusiastic and positive. Surely we can't be mistaken. But then we had exactly the same reaction in the early days of *If* . . .

Lindsay is not dismayed when I tell him the news. 'We all know what the BBC and Mark Shivas really stand for. They've never in my life employed me.' He suggests that we meet our agents in the morning and find another backer.

17 April 1990

I've been sleepwalking again. Skye tells me I came into her room, told her Uncle Esmond was coming to lunch and looked for the meal under her bed.

'I kept telling you Uncle Esmond was dead, but you insisted we had to find his lunch.'

'Poor Daddy,' says Monika. 'He loved Uncle Esmond.'

Indeed I did. Uncle Esmond was a retired High Church clergyman who would visit us once a month. He would have lunch and then watch old movies afterwards. His favourite was *Casablanca*, of course, but he liked *Britannia Hospital* too and thought the mad professor's speech the best sermon he'd ever heard. He died of a heart attack in his sleep three years ago. He had a twinkly, naughty smile and was one of the few members of my family with a sense of humour.

18 April 1990

Lindsay and I arrive together at Paramount House, where my agent, Ian Amos, has an office. Lindsay's agent, Maggie Parker, is waiting for us in the gleaming aluminium foyer. Aged about 70, she is a Forties beauty who is still beautiful in spite of her hunchback and little girl laugh. She treats her clients, chiefly Lindsay and Helen Mirren, like children. 'Lindsay, little one, you coughed. Have you a cold? Are you keeping warm?' She brings them round soup when they are ill. But behind the granny is a steely business mind, which is why she still lives and works in Park Lane.

Ian's shabby office is a bit of a comedown and the two rivals obviously hate having to meet. There isn't really much to say. Just the usual story I've heard all my life about the British film industry being bankrupt. They swap lists of possible producers and agree to press on. I could have done the same staying at home. But the trip is not completely wasted. On the way out, while Lindsay is examining a pile of Arnold Wesker's old plays, Ian motions me over to his desk and hands me a cheque for £12,000 from Daniele Senatori. Like me, he is amazed. Daniele isn't a fantasy – Stalin is on!

19 April 1990

I ask for books on Stalin at our small local library. They don't have them, of course, but they will do a search in every library in the land. Daniele especially wants me to find *I was Stalin's Cook*.

1 May 1990

The library tracks down *The Secret History of Stalin's Crimes*, written in 1950 by an NKVD defector named Orlov. I learn that Stalin financed the revolution by robbing banks and running vice rings. It is an astonishing story – how this mealy-mouthed pimp came to control a whole continent. And today the Russians jeer Gorbachev off the Kremlin stand in the May Day procession. Are they still mad? Poor old Gorby. I tremble for *glasnost* and Russia.

13 May 1990

Lindsay rings. He is going to send *Garden Gnomes* to Channel 4 himself. Further, he's figured out where we're going wrong on *If 2*. We must get rid of the old narrative plot and make it like a dream.

Jo Janni phones. He thinks the Stalin film should be like *The Great Dictator*, and he wants to show a treatment to Stanley Jaffe, head of Paramount, in ten days' time. I tell him I want to write the film with Lindsay and he must pay Lindsay $25,000. Jo is happy to since it is Daniele's money.

26 May 1990

Mike and I post *Love and Madness* to Jeff Berg in LA. We've made friends with his assistant, Annie, who has promised to place it alone in the very middle of his desk.

3 June 1990

'Oh – someone called Jeff Berg rang last night,' says Skye, eating honey.

'What did he say?'

'He's calling again tonight.'

I'm amazed. 'Do you realise that Jeff Berg is the most powerful man in Hollywood?'

'COME AND HAVE YOUR HAIR BRUSHED FOR SCHOOL!' screams Monika. Soon they are both shrieking over the morning torture. This happens every day and takes an hour to recover from.

Jeff Berg rings at 9 p.m. 'I read the script and love it. All the guys in the office love it too. I'm faxing you a list of ten directors for your choice.' I wait all day for the fax of directors. Nothing.

22 July 1990

Maggie Parker, the protective mother hen, has been behaving as if Jo and Daniele were gangsters, but now at last she agrees to Lindsay's Stalin contract.

30 July 1990

We finish our thirty-page treatment, which we've called *The Private Death of Joe Stalin*, and give it to Jo and Daniele. Daniele is euphoric. 'It's a hundred carat diamond,' he says.

August Bank Holiday 1990

I drive Lindsay and the contents of his fridge down to Rustington for a final session on *The Private Death of Joe Stalin*. As we unpack the groceries, Lindsay's nice neighbour, Don Chapman, calls over the garden hedge: 'David! Lindsay! I've just heard the news. Gorbachev's resigned. Communism is over. Russia is a democracy!'
   So much for Joe Stalin.

10 September 1990

Stanley Jaffe, head of Paramount, rejects our script.

August 1991

A year passes. I work on *If 2 . . .*, then start to type out thousands of pages of diary. It's over thirty years since that May day in Oxford which began everything. Little did we know where Wordsworth's words, 'Poetry is experience recollected in tranquillity', would lead us. I give my diary a title: 'Going Mad in Hollywood'.

23 September 1991

Lindsay collapses at the Prague Film Festival. He is rushed to hospital, where he is visited by the Czech President, Vaclav Havel, who promises him the best care in the world.

28 September 1991

Mike Legge, full of dreams of success in Hollywood, leaves England for good to set up in Los Angeles.

3 October 1991

A postcard from Mike Legge in Hollywood. 'David! Well, here we are in cloud cuckoo land again! I think this town is ready for us and *Love and Madness*. I called Jeff Berg, who was AWFUL!'

8 October 1991

A letter from Mike Legge:

> Dear David,
> Ooops! Here I am – the dastardly deed is completed and I have hurled myself into the abyss! What have I done . . .? I keep telling myself everything's going to be just fine. Everything HAS to be just fine . . .!
> I picked up my Computer/Word Processor – an Apple Macintosh Classic – and have been tearing my hair out over the past two days ploughing through its 280-page manual! I finally figured it all out now and I have to say it is an absolute joy to use and the quality, as you can see, is absolutely superb. It is also so FAST to work with, I just love using it. All I have to do now is WRITE something of the same quality . . .! But I figured I deserved it if I'm going to be chained to it for the foreseeable future! Anyway, I'll communicate frequently as I get more settled.
> Hope all is well with you and do give my love to everyone. I'll send you the re-done 'Forests' in about two weeks . . .
>
> > Very best wishes
> > Michael

14 October 1991

I start another attempt at *The Monster Butler*. This is the extra-ordinary true story of Roy Fontaine, a brilliant con-man, who becomes butler to the rich, lunches with the Queen Mother and commits five murders. He is now locked up in Broadmoor. Malcolm will star and Lindsay direct. The book, by Norman Lucas, is an incredibly complicated read. I break it down into a thirty-page action plot.

The first intimation of mortality

3 December 1991

Lindsay's secretary Kathy rings. 'Have you a chair to sit on? . . . Lindsay's had a heart attack. I wanted you to be the first to know.' I'm to ring the hospital in the morning.

4 December 1991

I ring the Royal Free, Hampstead, and ask for Mr Anderson's ward. Sister tells me that he is undergoing ECG but will be all right. The next day I hear what happened from Lindsay himself. He felt ill and walked all the way to the Casualty department of the Royal Free, where he started to fibrillate. Hospital is rather fun, he says. He loves being looked after and having cornflakes every morning. He thinks he'll be ready to get cracking on *The Monster Butler* in the New Year.

I promise him a fragment of my diary *Going Mad in Hollywood*, as a Christmas present.

'Onwards!' he says.

5 December 1991
Cherry Tree House

Death is in the air. Major Edney, our neighbour, is killed in a car crash on the A48 that runs past Viney Hill. No one knows how the accident happened. His wife is reported 'comfortable' in hospital. The Major went jogging for two hours every day. He looked 50 when in fact he was nearly 70. To be so fit and then to die for nothing on the A48. When Monika was nearly killed in the hit-and-run accident, he and his wife brought us cooked meals.

8 December 1991

A local farmhand fell into an agricultural machine and was mashed to pieces in two minutes. A train crashed in the Severn Tunnel. Signal failure. The driver was killed and a hundred people seriously injured. Outside Viney Hill church I saw a car catch fire. The elderly occupants just sat inside it. I ran over and opened the door. 'You'd better get out – quick!'

They were frozen in fear. A fire engine arrived and I stepped back as they put out the flames. In the evening I help Skye with her homework. An essay on *Romeo and Juliet* with the idiotic title 'Were Romeo and Juliet immature?' No, but they died all the same. Yes, death is in the air – including mine if I don't stop drinking.

2 January 1992

I get to Stirling Mansions to find Lindsay too pale and exhausted even to cook. We go out to lunch at a wine bar. He has to take pills from six different bottles at every meal. He loses count of them and I feel helpless and worried. Nonetheless, we set off for Rustington to work on *The Monster Butler* as planned. Lindsay for the first time ever lets me carry his heavy suitcase.

16 January 1992

An encouraging sign that Lindsay is getting better: he insists on being driven all the way to Worthing in search of his favourite Scotch biscuits, which he has been unable to find in Waitrose on the Finchley Road. After asking in about six shops, at last we find them in Marks and Sparks. We drive home triumphant to Fuchsia Cottage on the first sunny day of the year.

21 January 1992

The Monster Butler, our last chance, is finished. As I cross the threshold of Cherry Tree House for the first time in three weeks, Skye greets me cheerfully: 'Christ, Dad, your body language is shit!'

I post the script to Lindsay's new agent, David Watson.

28 January 1992

I meet David Watson. He's convinced Working Title will back *The Monster Butler*. It's a certainty, he promises me. Malcolm loves the script and his friend Gary Oldman wants to play Kitto, Roy Fontaine's accomplice and lover. Nothing can go wrong.

I ask him for a little money for my work on the script, and for Monika's perfect typing.

'Typing, yes. Script, no,' he says as he carefully adjusts the black tulips he has flown into his office every day from Holland.

24 February 1992

My fiftieth birthday and all there is to celebrate is bad news. Working Title won't commit to *The Monster Butler* in spite of Malcolm and Gary Oldman.

Jo Janni rings. 'Listen, Da-veed, not even the richest man in England, not even the Duke of Westminster, is rich enough to finance *Sta-leen*. How are the horses? They eat better than you, eh?' It's Jo's nice way of saying Lindsay isn't commercial.

Among my birthday cards I find a letter from Stewart Stevens, who promised to try to find a publisher for *The Great Advertisement*. But no luck. He's shown the novel to a score of editors, and none shares his enthusiasm for its black humour. That book is true to life, but not true to art.

I phone Lindsay in despair. Is there any hope for *Garden Gnomes*? I know he has sent it to over twenty producers, and that Elliott Kastner was keen.

'Poor old Kastner,' says Lindsay. 'He's worse off than you. He's been declared bankrupt. The judge even took his watch, left him with only five dollars to live on.' Lindsay's voice changes. 'Actually, it's tragic. He made over forty films. Many of them good. Now our only hope is *Going Mad*. It's what this bullshit is all about. It will make us all fashionable again. And then all our films will be made. We're counting on you, David. Get down to it – shape the material that exists. Don't fantasise and don't drink.'

Sta-leen off. *The Monster Butler* off. *The Garden Gnomes* off. *The Great Advertisement* off. And we're £6,000 overdrawn.

'Keep your chinnywig up, Daddy,' says Monika. 'You can do it.' But one little can of Extra Strong Export Ale to celebrate my birthday won't hurt . . .

Twelve cans later Monika is yelling at me, her face swollen with tears, 'I've totally lost respect for you! You're a completely useless person. If I didn't have Skye and the horses, I'd go. I can't wait for you to be dead.'

25 February 1992

Skye is in her room getting ready for her party at the rugby club tonight, a process that takes all day. I do some good work on *Going Mad* until she starts playing her rap music. There's no sound more infuriating than rap thudding through a wall.

'Can I shut your door?' I ask her.

'No – it's my door.'

'But these are my ears, and the reason I live in the country is because I have to have quiet to work,' and I shut her door.

She bursts it open again, yelling, 'You're manic! You ought to leave my home! Why can't you go away?'

After half an hour of screaming abuse she shows me her hairstyle and changes her tone.

'Dad, am I beautiful?'

'Absolutely gorgeous, darling.'

'Dad, listen – this sums up Christianity: "When the missionaries first came to Africa, they had the Bible and we had the land. They said, 'Close your eyes and let us pray.' So we closed our eyes. When we opened them, we had the Bible and they had the land." '

'Did you make that up? It's brilliant.'

'No. Bishop Desmond Tutu. I'm going to quote him to our RE teacher. She's so holy. Dad, do you mind if I have a tattoo and a gold nose-stud?'

'Yes – you'll look like a square old hippy.'

'I'm an Alternative, not a hippy.'

'What's an Alternative?'

'We believe in being at one with everything. Peace.'

'You, peace! You're Armageddon.'

And she storms off into her room slamming her door. God, I've got a TEENAGE DAUGHTER! Still it's good material for the modern teenagers in our other sleeper – *If 2 . . .*

3 March 1992

Skye has her nose pierced with a golden stud, and her new headmaster suspends her from school.

Skye says, quite rightly, 'It's my body, I can do what I like with it.'

I phone the headmaster and say we've got to find a compromise. Suspending girls from school is the sort of thing that makes them run away from home. But he won't be budged.

5 March 1992

A postcard from Lindsay: 'Golden nose-studs are only the beginning, I'm afraid.'

Skye tearfully agrees not to wear her nose-stud in the school grounds. Disaster averted.

29 March 1992

We've no money and Monika has been working herself into the ground teaching children on Pinkie. We've had endless family rows, but today she manages to look on the bright side. 'At least you don't go out to the pub at night and have affairs. You're not all bad. Those spoilt brats – Charles, Fergie: they have everything, yet they whore around. At least we don't do that. We've been through seventeen years of struggle together. We're fighters. We've something . . .'

3 April 1992

Mike Legge calls from Hollywood, hugely excited. An ICM director, Alan Arkush, adores *Love and Madness on the Richter Scale*. 'Come out as soon as possible and work on the script with him,' says Mike.

'Will ICM pay?'

'No, but the flight is nothing. And living is cheap out here. I'll put you up.'

I book my ticket – on a credit card, naturally.

16 April 1992

Mike picks me up at the airport in a friend's Mercedes. I discover he has only six dollars and seventy cents to his name. It looks like I'll be paying for everything, including the rent. But Mike's not worried. Soon he'll be photographing models for a rich Filipino make-up artiste and auditioning girls for a pornographic lesbian shoot. He'll be rich.

'Just stay in your room when I'm photographing.'

I thought I'd come here to work hard with Alan Arkush.

19 April 1992

Alan Arkush comes to tea with his two young children. He has only two contributions to make. One: the big dinner scene in which Imelda reveals her plans for making trillions out of the LA earthquake, and also tries to murder her husband, should be split between two different locations. Two: he thinks our heroine, Stephanie, is boring. There are thousands of girls like her in Hollywood.

2 May 1992

Mike is doing his big shoot for the Filipino make-up artiste today. I'm to vanish. He suggests I visit the Mall on Wilshire Boulevard and see the hit of the season, *Basic Instinct*. That will teach me what Hollywood wants. I take a taxi. The driver is so overwhelmed when I tell him I wrote his favourite film, *O, Lucky Man!*, that he doesn't charge me. He's writing a script too.

When Michael Douglas yells his famous line to Sharon Stone, 'YOU'RE THE FUCK OF THE CENTURY!', the audience titter with mocking laughter. I'm half-asleep and miss the shot that has made Sharon Stone a star, when she uncrosses her legs, pantie-less. An exhausting bore, this blockbuster.

3 May 1992

We finish our changes to *Love and Madness* and send the script round to Alan Arkush. In the evening we watch his new TV serial. It's so awful it's impossible to tell the difference between the endless commercials and the short stabs of drama. American TV at its worst. What have we landed ourselves with?

4 May 1992

Alan Arkush and his children come to tea. He thinks the script is 'fine, just fine'. He asks us if we'd seen his serial on TV. I have to say, 'We couldn't tell the difference between the commercials and the movie.'

5 May 1992

On TV the notorious video film of the LA police beating Rodney King is shown over and over again. King is a black petty thief and the officers who arrested him are on trial for brutality. The jury is giving its verdict today. Guilty, of course, everyone thinks. But at 3.20 p.m. there's a news flash. The unanimous verdict: NOT GUILTY.

After an hour of shocked silence, the blacks go mad. They torch white-owned stores, and as the Chief of Police, Daryl Gates, is busy promoting his autobiography, no one can give orders to quell the rioters. Television takes over. The camera crews are everywhere, fanning the flames, encouraging the rioters.

6 *May 1992*

Forty-four slain. Two thousand seriously injured. ICM and the studios raise the barricades and hire security gangs. Hollywood's whites jam the freeways, making for the safety of the mountains. The smoke is so thick that planes can't land at the airport.

The Catholic Archbishop is interviewed on TV.

'What are you doing about this catastrophe, Monsignor?'

'I've faxed the Pope.'

'And what has the Pope done?'

'He's faxed me a prayer.'

7 *May 1992*

The city is being systematically sacked. Poor whites join in the torching and looting. It's a class war against the haves. Mike and I are glued to the TV. Normal programmes have been long ago suspended as Los Angeles is ripped apart, and TV reporters, like mad Pied Pipers, identify the districts that have not yet been burnt and are clean of police, leading the rioters to fresh spoils.

The burning mayhem has reached Hollywood. Sammy's, the great Hollywood camera shop, goes up in flames.

I say to Mike, 'We'll be next. They'll be closing our supermarket. We're out of food. Hurry!'

We make it just in time. The bars are going up. The place is packed solid and the shelves are almost empty. For the first time I realise I'm in a war.

Sleep is impossible. Too many helicopters throb overhead.

8 May 1992

The class war becomes a race war. The blacks turn on the Koreans, the most successful immigrants in Los Angeles. Korea Town is burnt to the ground.

9 May 1992

Sanity returns. There is a sense of overwhelming sorrow. Everyone mucks in to clean up the mess. People are neighbours again.

11 May 1992

Lindsay rings. He has good news. When I come back to England, I will be writing *The Monster Butler*. David Watson is confident that Working Title will go ahead. Gary Oldman has committed.

Poor Mike is in the doldrums. He doesn't have a well-paid job to go home to, and the rich Filipino is refusing to pay him for his pictures. He hasn't a cent. He will be evicted from his apartment.

I promise him that when I get home I'll send him $2,000.

The curfew is lifted. There is peace in Los Angeles.

12 May 1992

We drive round Los Angeles taking in the horrible destruction. Many of the buildings and homes are uninsured. They'll never be rebuilt. Korea Town is a blackened empty shell.

13 May 1992

At lunchtime Mike drives me to the airport. On the way we see tanks in 'Desert Storm' camouflage coming into Los Angeles on huge tank transporters. Once again I've been living in a far more important movie than the one I'm writing.

On the plane I sit next to a broken Korean businessman. He's leaving America for good. He doesn't understand America, he says.

'Nor do I,' I reply.

30 May 1992
Stirling Mansions

Another session on *The Monster Butler*. Lindsay has another film
to make – all about himself. It's part of a series for BBC Scotland
called 'The Director's Place'. He will be paid £20,000 and he's going
to call it 'Is That All There Is?' He hasn't been able to produce a
script, but he wants me to do something in it. We haven't a clue
what.

We also do some work on *The Garden Gnomes*, which Lindsay
wants to make more than any other project. I tell him about an idea
I'd like to add. 'Monika has done the most amazing thing. She's
taught a little blind girl to ride and jump, and when she goes into the
forest she pretends she can see: "I can see a hundred trees, Monika,
are there a hundred trees in the forest?" – "Thousands." – "I can see
thousands – what colour are they?" '

'Be careful of sentimentality,' says Lindsay.

'It's not sentimentality. It's real life.'

'Of which there's far too much.'

Lindsay tells me about Sandy, who has moved back into the flat.
Yesterday he took all his clothes off and went outside at 1.30 a.m.
He got into a fight with some Indians, and Lindsay had to save him
from being killed by a brick.

31 May 1992

A fax from Mike Legge:

Dear David,

Nice to talk to you on the phone just now. I'm glad you got my
letter but hope you didn't feel it to be too critical! After your
'high' in LA I felt you might not be able to keep it up back in
Great Britain! Now that I know you are inspired I'll stop criticis-
ing (you've got Lindsay for that!) and start encouraging.

I don't see why we shouldn't be a successful, mega-rich writing
team. I mean, our first joint project was given the 'go' by one of
the most powerful agents in Hollywood in a matter of days. It's
taken its time since then – but I think that's the way it is here. It
did go to six directors in fairly quick succession – it's just that they
held on to it for about six weeks each before passing it on, which
is over seven months waiting time.

Chasing Dragons should go too – we both think it's got

everything . . . (*This was the script about Mike's adventures in the Orient.*)

Otherwise, although things couldn't be much worse, I'm still very happy living here, in this apartment, around pool with the sun shining every day.

Michael

15 *June* 1992

Working Title pull out of *The Monster Butler*. I don't tell Monika.

17 *June* 1992

A fax from Mike Legge:

Dear David,
Please find enclosed the next selection of pages of *Chasing Dragons*.

I see from your comments on the script that we may be running into a snag. Max is now in Singapore with Steve, writing and night-clubbing, Robert is with Yasmin in Kuala Lumpur engaged in their love affair – both are having good times and these are going to be the most difficult scenes to write. You are writing across everything 'Too much boring night clubs, restaurants, pool sides' or 'corny Cinzano commercial' – which is fine until I see the word 'boring' and realise you are doing to me *exactly* what Anderson does to you! When you put in 'pretty girl' in your script he crosses out 'girl' and puts in 'boy'. You are letting your hangups and inhibitions get in the way!

I realise you don't like enjoying yourself in the same ways as most others and, most importantly, like *our audience*! I mean by actually going out and having a Good Time. If you got £1 million today how would you *enjoy* it? I remember my time in the Orient as a *blur* of eating and drinking in great restaurants, wonderful food, gorgeous Asian girls, fun evenings, poolsides, beaches – it was fantasy time. The sort of stuff that, yes – movies are made of! Try and remember that when you get the blue pencil out!

Also, please try and be aware of the movies that are currently successful – it's very important. It's what we have to aim for – at least at first. Rule 1: get some big bucks in! So get some videos in and go see some movies. Currently the most successful movie, world-wide, is *Basic Instinct*. The writer got $3 million. Why? What's he doing right that you are doing wrong? Even if you didn't enjoy it I really would have thought, at the very least, that you would have been intrigued in trying to analyse it, making mental notes. Instead you walked out.

Michael

18 *June* 1992

A fax from Mike Legge:

Dear David,
Good to talk to you again yesterday, and I look forward to our chat on Sunday. Hope you had a good – and profitable – time away! It's desperately depressing here without money – or any hope of getting any by the looks of things, by any ways or means! I'm pushing the photography – the book is out every day – I'm soliciting for work, script reading, proof reading, anything!
    Things have to get better!

Michael

23 *September* 1992

I go up to Stirling Mansions to appear as myself in *Is That All There Is?* The flat is full of film equipment. A movie at last! There is no script. We will improvise a scene of Lindsay reading out to me all *Garden Gnomes*' patronising reject letters.

Filming can't start because the assistant cameraman has lost the clapperboard. We all search the flat high and low. It turns up behind Sandy's huge chest of clothes.

When I say my first lines, the sound recordist yells in agony. Apparently, I've a nervous cough which sounds like a bomb going off in his earphones.

I'm just about to go home after shooting my scene when Lindsay has an inspiration: he will film me making a typical arrival at Stirling Mansions, climbing the stairs laden with my typewriter and heavy bags of scripts and beer. Eighteen takes later the shot is perfect – and I've climbed 600 stairs. We actors get very fit.

9 October 1992

Tomorrow we are going on a boat trip up the Thames. The ashes of Rachel Roberts and Jill Bennett, who died of an overdose two years ago, will be cast into the river. All Lindsay's friends will be on the boat to pay their last respects. It is to be the finale of the film.

Lindsay and I buy flowers from the stall by the Finchley Road station to cast on the waters. It wasn't so long ago we were crossing the Finchley Road with Jill Bennett, all holding armfuls of Lindsay's empties for the bottle bank. Lindsay had dropped his bottles in the middle of the road and Jill had risked her life picking up the smashed glass. That evening was the last time I saw her. I thought she had an unquenchable spirit. But I was wrong.

10 October 1992

The cameraman drives us to the South Bank quayside from where the boat will depart. On the way he buys a rope. He is convinced Lindsay will fall into the river and drown while directing unless he is bound tightly. At 2 p.m. we go on board. A spread of unlimited champagne awaits us in the cabin. I hate champagne and don't drink. I talk a lot to Lindsay's secretary Kathy's husband, Jim. He shows me some of the Thames's most beautiful sights. He loves the river. The stars form their little cliques at the tables on the upper deck.

When the boat is directly opposite the House of Commons we are all ordered on deck. Lindsay makes a speech of farewell to his dead friends, then tosses two boxes containing their ashes into the water. He shouts directions for us all to cast our flowers. A kilted Scottish piper plays the 'Last Post'. Alan Price at his piano starts to sing a song he has written for the farewell – 'Is That All There Is?' – and Big Ben chimes three o'clock. Then, three hours of retakes.

But the day isn't over. There's still one dreadful task ahead. Lindsay told me that Jill, when very young and poor, made a joke will leaving everything to the Battersea Dogs' Home, and forgot all about it. Now the home have all her money – £750,000 – but don't want her possessions, which are stored in her secretary's house. We have to go there and clear the place of Jill.

'Take everything – that's what Jill would have wanted,' says the secretary.

The drunken mourners throw books hither and thither across the rooms, and stuff her belongings into carrier bags. One of her ex-lovers, her plumber, falls over drunk and bursts into tears . . . Yes, this is Jill's funeral. I take her marked-up copy of *Britannia Hospital* and a photograph. I feel like a thief.

'Is that all there is . . . ?'

14 *October 1992*

A fax from Mike Legge:

> Dear David,
> Thank you very much for the $100 – it was much appreciated and every little bit helps! I'm afraid I had to sell all my photographic equipment last week . . .
> I have been looking carefully at ads in the papers recently – especially the free press, which is full of small ads . . . One said, 'Screenwriter wanted to work on story set in Germany 1850–1940'. Turns out it was from some kind of a well-off guy who has a 'great story' he wants turned into a treatment or script, I went to see him. He was impressed by me because he didn't know any better. I said it would cost him 'a lot' to turn it into something that could be submitted to a studio . . . I'm really on my toes these days.
>
> Michael

24 *October 1992*

A fax from Mike Legge:

> Dear David,
> Thanks for your phone call earlier today, and the follow-up message. Depending on your point of view, a healthy and honest exchange of views is a *good thing* – or arguments and criticisms are a waste of time. Okay – I'll go for the first!
> We'll just have to agree to disagree. Nothing wrong with that. I just feel that if you want to be involved and successful in a collaborative business you have to go to where the action is. If you want to write novels, fine – you can do it anywhere, it's a very personal, secluded life. If I wanted to write novels I'd probably live in the west of Ireland and love it. If I wanted to be a rocket scientist I'd go and get a job with NASA at the Houston Space Center. If you love the movies and want to be a screenwriter – then first move to Hollywood. My opinion only.
> You say I'm living a fantasy. Maybe I am. If living out your

dream by deciding to be a screenwriter, then giving it 100 per cent of your time, is a fantasy – so be it. But if selling up and moving to Hollywood lock, stock and barrel and actually *doing* it is a fantasy, then my question is: where does that leave the other 99 per cent of the 'wannabe' screenwriters around the world who, in fact, do just dream about it? They have every conceivable excuse for not actually making the move and coming here and doing it – so where does that leave them? Whose is the fantasy?

I think that one of the things that surprised me most when you were over here was when you told me that, as a member of the Writers' Guild of America West, you were entitled to vote and attend the ceremonies of the Writers' Guild Awards held in Hollywood – the one big, huge prestigious annual event which is your great chance in the year to meet other writers, directors, producers and studio heads. You could make yourself known, meet old colleagues you have worked with, set up meetings and, almost certainly, get work! Most writers would die for this chance – yet you have passed it up! Each and every year! I think that really is a disgrace and, on its own and more than anything else, would explain your present poverty. It makes it completely self-inflicted. I mean – how in hell do you expect anyone in Hollywood to come calling for your services when you hide yourself away in the depths of the country? The next event is Feb '93 and I suggest you start planning for it now . . .

This letter may seem to contain a lot of criticisms, so be it – but I'm trying to encourage you to realise your full potential and so clear all your debts and become rich. I just can't believe that any screenwriter with Jeff Berg, the Chairman of ICM and 17th most powerful man in Hollywood, as his agent and a win at Cannes with his first film could be anything other than extremely rich. Working on rewrites at $100,000 per week etc. . . .

Contrast that with our friend Broderick Miller! I had breakfast with him last week. He's much richer and more successful than you or I! He knows everything going on in Hollywood, gets himself around, sees *every* movie in town (in the cinema, of course) and knows what's what. The result is he bought Greta Garbo's old house with the proceeds from *Wedlock* – apparently the most successful HBO Movie of the Week, and has bought a brand-new Saab convertible with just the advance on *Wedlock 2*. There's a lesson there somewhere!

Michael

16 February 1993

I hear from Lindsay that Sherry Lansing, now head of Paramount, wants us to make our sequel to *If . . .* I write a treatment, and post it to Lindsay.

17 February 1993

Lindsay rings. 'Your treatment is ridiculously long. Sherry Lansing isn't going to read seventeen pages. I'm going to cut it.'

23 February 1993

My seventeen-page treatment was vivid, funny – much better than the four-page treatment from Lindsay which I find in the post, but his letter to Sherry Lansing is good:

Dear Sherry Lansing

I was delighted to hear from my agent, David Watson, that you were intrigued by the idea of a sequel to *If . . .*, the film which I so so happily directed for Paramount in 1968. I have often talked with my friends David Sherwin (with whom I worked on the script of *If . . .*) and Malcolm McDowell, about the possibility of getting together again and showing what the years have done to us – and to all of us.

Sequels are often made now, I know, but I think that this one could really be unique, with the same characters, the same locations, and the same actors – taking advantage of the passing of time in a way that only the cinema could manage. So I'm sending you herewith the outline which David Sherwin and I have roughed out. I've not included 'flashbacks' in it (except one suggestion), though they would of course be tremendously valuable. I think there is a film here which would be like no other and saying some very important things. I do hope you'll agree, and let me know your thoughts.

With best wishes,
Lindsay Anderson

27 February 1993

A lunatic, aggressive letter from Mike Legge. He's gone mad in Hollywood like everyone else.

1 March 1993

Lindsay tells me his agent, David Watson, is asking £250,000 for the script. I tell my new bank manager, who is threatening to make us sell Cherry Tree House to pay the £21,000 overdraft. God, it's an up and down life.

I read Jean Rhys's last volume of stories, *Sleep it off Lady*. They are so simple and so powerful that they terrify me. She is my heroine. I identify totally with her.

27 April 1993
Cherry Tree House

Lindsay rings. Sandy wants to commit suicide, but won't discuss it. He got violent the other day and started screaming at Lindsay, 'You're dead – I'm alive!'

Both Lindsay's legs are agony. I ask him how he walks down three flights of stairs to do his shopping.

'Oh, I just hobble along.'

I feel dreadful. I ought to be in London looking after him, at Clanfield Cottage looking after Ma and Pa, who are both now 81, and here helping Monika.

1 May 1993

Mad letters and faxes from Mike Legge. At bottom he just wants the money.

11 June 1993

Malcolm calls from his home in Indian territory – Ojai, California.

'David! Listen – you and Monika need never worry again. I'm giving you the whole of my salary from my next picture to write *The Monster Butler*. You'll earn $200,000.'

'Just one question. Where will we work?'

'Oh, we've guest houses. Just bring that little typewriter of yours.

Lindsay's coming over. I want to spend four days with him and a week with you.'

'It'll take longer than a week, Malc!'

'Two!' says Malcolm.

'Have you seen the latest version of *The Monster Butler*?'

'No.'

'The one Lindsay and I did in February?'

'No. For God's sake, can you please express mail it to me,' asks Malcolm. 'It'll be terrific – just like the old days on *O, Lucky Man!*'

I am jubilant. $200,000. It's like the happy ending in *Garden Gnomes*. Monika and I rush off to Gloucester to buy clothes for California on the credit card.

16 June 1993

Malcolm phones. 'You won't be flying to California, you won't be earning $200,000, and you won't be writing *The Monster Butler*. My picture's off.'

'For Chrissake! Is Lindsay there?'

'Yes. Beside the pool.'

'Get him on the phone this instant.'

Five seconds pass.

'Hullo, Lindsay, how are you?' I ask tersely.

'Horribly hot. It's over a hundred.'

'Well, phone Sherry Lansing at once and get *If2* . . . set up.'

'I'll try,' he promises.

An hour later he rings back to say that he's seeing Sherry Lansing tomorrow.

17 June 1993

Lindsay phones. He is ebullient. He's just had an hour-long meeting with Sherry Lansing, *If2* . . . is on and I'm getting 'minimum dollars', whatever that is. I can't believe he actually got to see her like that so quickly.

'What was she like?'

'Oh, I don't know.'

'What was she wearing? What was her office like?'

'I never noticed. Everything was kind of beige. A beige office.'

'And you talked about *If2* . . . for a whole hour?'

'Of course not, you idiot. We gossiped for an hour. And then she said she'd do it for minimum dollars. So get cracking!'

Half an hour later there's a call from the BBC. They want to know all about *If2* . . . 'How did you hear?' I ask. 'I only heard a few minutes ago.'

'Oh, our Claire is very good.'

30 June 1993

A postcard arrives from Lindsay and Malcolm – a picture of three girls' bare bottoms. On the reverse side is written: 'Today I spent 40 minutes with SHERRY LANSING of Paramount who said she *loved If* . . . and her favourite film is *O, Lucky Man!* Yes LA is the world capital of bullshit, paved with gold! Love, L.' – 'For God's sake, write a bloody good part for *me*!! Paramount are going to *pay* for the script of *If2* . . . . Love Malcolm.'

24 July 1993
Fuchsia Cottage, Rustington

We think up a new ending for *If2* . . . At a Royal premiere of *If2* . . . itself the Queen Mother congratulates the characters on their fine work. We invent a new underground cell, based on rebellious Skye and her friends. The film is beginning to become real. Lindsay is 'chewing glass', always a good sign.

I limit our morning tours of the bookshops and groceries of Rustington to one hour at Gateways, my favourite supermarket. Time is of the essence.

25 July 1993

In the afternoon we visit Mary, Lindsay's elderly housekeeper, who has cherished and looked after Fuchsia Cottage for Lindsay, and before him for his mother. She is part of our Rustington life. Recently this summer her son, Andrew, died from undiagnosed cancer.

We visit her in her tiny council flat, bringing with us flowers, orange juice, a Kipling cake and fish fingers. She likes the flowers but can't eat. She's on antibiotics and can drink only water. She is close to tears for most of our visit. She tells us she wasn't meant to be on this earth. Her mother had her when she was 44. She wanted a boy. She told Mary things, lots of things over and over, which she doesn't like to remember.

Mary only moved here to be close to her family. 'My family is a mistake. They all hate each other. Karen' – Andrew's wife – 'well, I visit her because Andrew's dog isn't getting enough to eat. So I bring a tin of dog food. But they only want you when they want something from you. But Michael sometimes comes . . .' Michael is Andrew's son.

'NOW HE'S PRETTY HOPELESS,' says Lindsay, too loudly.

'No. I love Michael. He's his own person, like his dad . . . Andrew . . .' The tears begin. 'Oh, I miss Andrew so much. A jack of all trades, and good at them all.'

'DON'T YOU THINK HAVING THE TELEVISION ON IS VERY EXHAUSTING?' Lindsay shouts. 'I MEAN, SHOULDN'T YOU HAVE IT OFF? WOULD YOU LIKE A BOOK?'

'Oh, I'm into books. I don't like novels, but I like to read about other people's lives.'

'WELL, YOU'RE QUITE RIGHT. THAT'S VERY GOOD. DO YOU READ A PAPER?'

'Oh, no. Michael sometimes gets the *Observer*, but I don't read it.'

'WELL, YOU'RE QUITE RIGHT, MARY. IT'S A LOAD OF RUBBISH. WHAT A LIFE, EH? WHAT A BLOODY LIFE . . .'

'That's what I think. I shouldn't have been born . . .'

We make our sad farewell. On the drive back to Fuchsia Cottage, Lindsay points at Rustington's bland red-brick shopping parade: an Oxfam shop, a health-food store, a travel agency and Boots the chemist.

'You couldn't find that anywhere else in the world but England,' he says emphatically.

'. . . um . . . It's not so—'

'Well, could you? Has your brain gone?'

'No, but I hate stupid generalisations about the English. There's the North . . .' I say.

'No one gives a fuck about the North! When they talk about England they mean this, here, southern England.'

'If they do, then they're stupid. Look at America – people generalise about America, but it's a hundred different nations. Generalisations are stupid.'

'Generalisations aren't stupid. And I'm not talking about America. I'm talking about England. Your brain's really gone.'

'I'm more aware than I've ever been.'

'You definitely need a holiday.'

That night I dream I am being hunted to death by Saddam Hussein. Also the Ayatollah proclaims a holy war against me. Lindsay dreams that Patsy Healey, his ex-house guest at Stirling Mansions clinic, is shooting *If2* . . ., but gets it all wrong, and he tries to explain why.

28 July 1993

Lindsay makes one of his unannounced inspections. 'God, why do you always make your room look like a Palestinian refugee camp?'

He's right. There are suitcases full of newspaper cuttings, plastic bags of illegal beer and whisky, socks and pants drying on the radiator, and cartons of blackcurrant juice on the tobacco-flecked chest of drawers.

'Pack and hoover. It'll take two hours. God, a Palestinian refugee camp.'

10 August 1993

My father's eighty-second birthday. Sue drives Pa and Ma to Cherry Tree House for his party. I am shattered at how frail he's become. He has pains everywhere, and can only just hear. After they leave, my shoulders explode into two huge lumps.

I call the doctor. He says, 'My God, I've never seen anything like this,' and gives me antibiotics.

Is it cancer or stress?

I must spend as much time with my parents as possible.

10 October 1993

Another week looking after Ma and Pa. He sleeps in the sun looking like a dying Roman emperor. He wakes up to watch the horse-racing on TV, then becomes distraught because he's lost his bunch of keys.

'Don't panic,' Ma tells him.

'Don't be bossy. I must have my keys.' He finds them, dresses up in his best jacket and Homburg hat, and with his walking stick shuffles out into the mild October afternoon. He unlocks the garage and disappears inside. A few moments later his old Toyota emerges in reverse. He sits in it for a few minutes, then drives it back into the garage.

26 October 1993

Lindsay rings. The contract is here at last! We have to sign it in front of a public notary.

28 October 1993

I arrive at Lindsay's at midday exactly. He looks well, less florid, ten years younger. I tell him so.

'Well, you look pooped.'

Just as we are about to set off for the public notary, a large lamp overhanging the kitchen table comes crashing down on Lindsay's whisky, and smashes the tomato ketchup bottle. An omen?

29 October 1993
Cherry Tree House

Lindsay rings. 'Well, the money will take a week or two,' he says as we congratulate each other on having finally signed a contract for *If2* . . .

'The money is meaningless,' I say. 'It's the contract. I'm a real writer again.'

30 October 1993

I wake up early and get down to work. The opening sequence is of the old boys on the train returning to College. I let the characters' emotions carry the scene forward. Just as I turn to the next scene – the Chapel – the phone rings. It's Ma.

'The doctor's been round. He's ordered a thing to get Pa to hospital. Get over here. Come as you are.'

At Clanfield Cottage a neighbour redirects me to the Radcliffe Hospital where, after wandering down endless corridors, I find Pa lying in a bed with some kind of mask over his face. Ma sits beside him.

For about two hours, Ma and I watch Pa trying to breathe through his awful, cheap plastic mask. Every minute or so he flicks up a hand to the string round his ears, and tries to straighten the nose-piece.

'He's going to be fine,' the nurse says as we finally leave.
'Will we be able to take him home tomorrow?' I ask.
'That depends.'
Ma goes up to Pa, hugs and kisses him.
'We'll see you tomorrow.'
Pa takes my hand with his free hand. 'Very good of you to come.'
'See you tomorrow,' I say.
'Oh, wonderful. So glad.'

1 November 1993

Ma and I drive to Oxford. We buy a box of Swiss chocolates, a potted flower, and a Dick Francis novel in hardback. When we get to Pa's ward, a young sister takes us aside. 'He went for a walk just before lunch and had a fall. You won't find him his usual self.'

Pa lies exhausted, struggling to breathe through the plastic mask. As we come in, he tries to drag it away. 'Are you OK?' he says to Ma. And those are his last words. Ma cradles his head, stroking him.

'He's going,' she says to me calmly.

I love Pa. He will never leave me.

10 December 1993

At long last the first cheque for *If2* . . . arrives: £7,005.47p. Half the total. In Hollywood, 'minimum dollars' means minimum dollars. Eleven months ago, Lindsay's agent had been gaily talking of £250,000. My bank manager is not amused.

Once again I pack *If2* . . . into a shiny plastic suitcase and set off for Lindsay's.

Christmas Day 1993

New decorations hang bravely from the Christmas tree at Clanfield Cottage. Dear little Ma.

If only . . .

6 January 1994

I drive up to Stirling Mansions. Lindsay and I are going to work on *If2* . . . in Rustington. Lindsay goes to the Royal Free Hospital for a check-up. His heart is fine and he's told he needn't come back for a year.

7 January 1994

Patsy Healey comes to lunch. She and Lindsay have a huge quarrel about cooking. When I comment that they are like a dreadful married couple, Lindsay turns on me in fury. As he often says himself, he's an old curmudgeon now.

In the afternoon we pack everything and, after the usual last-minute hunt for Lindsay's spectacles, drive to Rustington.

We start work. I rewrite the opening scene and show it to Lindsay. He painstakingly copies out the whole scene, with his own changes, on to a pad. He is very slow. I tell him I can retype the scene with his changes in a minute.

'I'm going to write the whole script out by hand. It's the only way.'

'But it will take forever.'

'So long as Sherry Lansing likes it.'

Has he gone crackers?

12 January 1994

Dustin Hoffman pulls out of Lindsay's film of *The Cherry Orchard*. Lindsay is sanguine, but upset.

Lindsay cuts my scene of the old boys unwinding in the college library, which has been turned into a temporary dormitory for them. In its place he puts a very stiff scene in which the old boys and girls have tea with the housemaster. It's just one long procession of dull introductions, I tell him. 'You don't understand the cinema or how I'll direct it,' he replies.

14 January 1994

Lindsay cuts the scene of the old girls getting ready for bed in the college museum. For the first time in our twenty-eight-year partnership the problem of Lindsay's celibate homosexuality is ruining the script.

16 *January* 1994

Victory! 'Free', a rebel 17-year-old girl at the college, is allowed to have an affair with Gary, a revolutionary American.

20 *January* 1994

I'm typing away when Lindsay comes up behind me, his face covered in shaving foam.

'God, Lindsay, you're a ghoul!'

He chortles silently and reads through the scene with Free and Gary.

'Your favourite couple, I know,' and he chortles silently at my folly. His silent chortle is a new habit of his.

'Well, we could bring Bobby Phillips back,' I suggest, thinking of the pretty boy in *If* . . ., 'and have a big love scene with Wallace, who still fancies him.'

'Bobby Phillips was murdered some time ago on the New York subway.'

3 *February* 1994

We have a huge row over Lindsay's headmaster's speech to the Old Boys. I say it's cheap Monty Python. He says I'm drunk.

4 *February* 1994

I dream that I'm dead. But when I wake up, Lindsay admits that I'm quite right about the headmaster's speech.

21 *February* 1994

'The script is finished,' Lindsay declares. I point out that we've done no work on the highlight of the film: the headmaster giving a guided tour of the new twenty-first-century college, his beloved futuristic hothouse of spurious education.

'Sherry Lansing will never know it's not there.'

'Oh yes, she will. It needs another week's work.'

'No. It reads perfectly as it is. This is a very good first draft, David. We'll do the tour when Sherry Lansing gives you fifty thousand to write a second draft.'

With that I am foolishly dissuaded.

22 *February 1994*

Trevor Ingman of Yaffle Films comes over to pick up our manuscript. His girl-friend is going to type it for us. Trevor produced *Is That All There Is?* and has almost bankrupted himself trying to set up Lindsay's *The Cherry Orchard*. He's just had a rejection from Sky Television: 'Dear Mr Chekhov, Re *The Cherry Orchard*. Period pieces are not popular, but we would look forward to reading a contemporary subject by you set in the present.' Trevor is the nicest man in showbusiness but also has the stamina and total commitment needed for success in the land of 'bullshit and the rattlesnake'. We want him to produce *If2* . . . for Paramount.

24 *February 1994*
Stirling Mansions

It's my fifty-second birthday. From now on I'm going to have to be 49. Patsy Healey gives me a card with old sailing boats.

'Very Patsy,' says Lindsay.

'Very David,' I reply. 'I love sailing boats.'

A birthday dinner of Waitrose honey-roast ham, coleslaw and six cans of Guinness.

25 *February 1994*

A special meeting. Lindsay has arranged for Charles Drazin, a young editor at Hamish Hamilton, to come round to discuss the never quite dying *Great Advertisement for Marriage*. He's an invigorating mix of enthusiasm and criticism. He obviously likes the book or he wouldn't have written ten pages of notes on it, but he thinks it's too bitter and should have more poetry. As he is about to leave, Lindsay tells him I've also half-written a diary called *Going Mad in Hollywood* and I promise to send him a specimen.

14 April 1994

A postcard from Lindsay.

> Dear David, I did finally manage to get hold of and speak to Sherry Lansing last night, who was in the screening room. She seems to have rather changed her tune since she commissioned the first draft of *If2 ... Now* she says that a sequel to *If ...* is a *European* project, which will not be of interest in the US. I talked of further development of the script, but this plainly did not interest her. *Going Mad* submission hasn't yet arrived: I hope you are having fun with it! Sorry to be no longer HOT, but that's the way it goes. Remember – I'll be SEVENTY-ONE on Sunday!!
>
> Love, Lindsay

I phone Lindsay, who gives more details of his talk with Sherry. She thought the script lacked conflict. I tell Lindsay I agree with her – it does lack conflict, and 'European' is Hollywood for 'bad'. He chortles silently. I promise to send him the *Going Mad* chapter after the weekend.

15 April 1994

I go down to Ma's to start on the opening section of *Going Mad*. I have reread my eight volumes of diary from 1960 to 1969 over and over again and have the whole thing in my head. My impossible task is to fit a decade of adventures into a chapter.

18 April 1994

Thanks to some wonderful whisky and a manic energy, the first part of the diary is finished. I post it to Lindsay.

21 April 1994

Lindsay returns the diary with his comments marked in red Tempo. He likes the beginning, but thinks my first trip to Hollywood is a mess. And this is just the first chapter. In my caravan there are six iceberg lettuce boxes crammed with handwritten volumes of diary. Thousands of pages. It is an out-of-control monster.

8 May 1994

At 6.30 a.m. I'm awoken by Ma's cries for help. 'David! I can't breathe. Call the doctor. Quick. I can't breathe!'

The doctor takes one look at her and orders an ambulance. I summon my sister Sue from London and pack Ma's case.

9 May 1994
The Acland Nursing Home, Oxford

Ma's arms are like matchsticks. She hasn't eaten properly since Pa died. The heart surgeon arrives for his examination. Afterwards he takes me aside and says, 'Well, she has the will to live . . .'

The terse phrase is frightening. I spend all day with her. 'Talk to me, boy,' she keeps on saying. So I talk to her about horses, her favourite subject.

11 May 1994

Ma is off the danger list. As I've run out of horse gossip and she has a crew of visitors, I return home to tackle the diary. But I spend the entire day in a trance staring at Lindsay's words in red Tempo: 'The WHOLE Hollywood section a mess.'

My rock bottom

20 May 1994

A bad day. I slip and fall on the staircase and, as I put out a hand to save myself, smash the glass of our Victorian Methodist print, 'The Broad and Narrow Way to Heaven or Hell'. Lindsay has a similar print.

Monika curses me: 'You stink of alcohol. Drunken fool. Is the glass broken over Heaven or Hell?'

'Hell . . .'

'*I'll* clear it up,' she says. 'You'd cut yourself.'

I sit in my room, surrounded by the boxes of diary, bills, plastic carrier bags, bits of model planes, suitcases, and just stare at the horrible pink-dot Laura Ashley wallpaper. I sit there for hours. I write nothing, but just stare and drink and listen to the rain outside. I doze off and wake with a desperate craving for cheese.

I go downstairs to find my beloved print of Heaven and Hell covered up by one of Skye's paintings. I tear it down in fury.

Skye emerges. 'What are you doing, for Chrissake?'

After a huge row I order my wife and child to leave the house. I go back to bed.

21 *May 1994*

I awake early. As I lie in bed I overhear Monika on the phone to Lindsay: 'Yes, yes. It's the drink. Non-stop.'

She comes into the room. 'Lindsay's going to phone you in five minutes. Get up.'

The phone rings.

'Oh, hullo, Lindsay.'

'I suppose you're going to bluff your way through this?'

'No.'

'You can't go on doing this to Monika and Skye. You can't go on like this or you'll end up in the gutter. Phone those people who help alcoholics and ring me back in ten minutes.'

I do so.

'Someone's coming to see me on Sunday.'

'Pull your socks up, David. And good luck.'

23 *May 1994*

I meet my visitor in the caravan. I'm expecting him to ask me questions. Instead he tells me the story of his drunken life. I think he's on an ego trip until I realise he's describing *my* alcoholism: he talks about his rows, violence, inability to live without a drink, how he reeked of alcohol . . . My alcoholic history is no different – I need a beer to get into the bath, a beer to get out of the bath, a beer to clean my teeth, a beer to put on my clothes, a beer for everything. The times poor Monika cried, 'If only you could give up the drink and we could be a proper family.' I decide there and then to give up booze. But not today. I go back to my horrible room and finish the dregs of beer and whisky. Strange: I don't like the taste any more.

Then through the window I notice the two ponies careering round the side paddock attacked by wasps. I rush down. Amber is butting the side gate, trying to escape. I put a rope on her and lead her out.

Dizzy follows. I lead Amber up the lane, through the yard gate and into her stable. Dizzy stops to eat some grass on the knoll opposite. I unclasp the rope from Amber. In a flash she's trotted off to join Dizzy.

'Dizzy!'

But at my shout they both gallop off down Viney Hill.

I rush into the house to call Skye.

'You fucking deadhead,' she says. 'I'll get some horse mix. Mum will kill you for this.'

In terror I walk down Viney Hill. Not a sign of the horses. Cars speed by.

I swivel as I hear the sound of hooves. Dizzy and Amber race past me at full gallop, heading flat out for the deadly A48 at the bottom of the hill. I'm convinced they're going to be killed, and all because I'm such a drunk. But by a miracle a family at the bottom of the hill run out of their house and form a chain across the road. The horses peel off into their garden, where I catch them. Skye shoves the horse-pan at me and stomps off without a word. But a miracle has happened.

24 May 1994

A fine, sunny day. I'm free! Free of drink. A miracle. Freedom at last. I've found the perfect postcard to send to Lindsay: a line of police-men bearing aloft bottles of wine on trays as they jump over hurdles. I write, 'Lindsay, I'm off the booze. Thank you. All my love, David.'

25 May 1994

Malcom rings from Ojai. Lindsay has told him. 'I'm so proud of you,' he says.

29 May 1994

I've found a wonderful new drink – the aptly named 'Aqua Pura'. I spend the afternoon flying model aeroplanes with my closest friend in Lydney, Les Jones, a junior bank manager.

Lindsay calls in the evening: 'Are you still off the drink?'

'Yes, I had a wonderful day at the flying field.'

'I'm glad. You're my only ray of sunshine. I suppose depression is a fact. I'm depressed. You're my only hope. Stick at it.'

4 June 1994

'Have you heard about Jo Janni?' Ma asks.
   'What about Jo Janni?'
   'He's dead.'
   I'm appalled. Jo was terrified of death. He made me swear to come to his funeral. Jo Janni is dead.

28 June 1994

Charles Drazin sends me a copy of the proposal he wrote for his book on the British cinema of the 1940s with a postcard of advice:

> Dear David,
> Just in case this might give you some idea of what publishers mean by a proposal, I enclose the one I wrote for my intended book after asking the advice of the publishing director of Hamish Hamilton. He is commercially attuned and suggested the framework of introduction, outline, and conclusion (and in your case a sample chapter would be a very important accompaniment). He stressed the vital part of the proposal is for the author to explain why he thinks his book will sell and how he thinks it fills a neglected corner of the market. At this stage the important thing is to talk the publisher's language – i.e. stress the commercial.
>   I look forward to seeing the sample chapter.
>
> Best regards,
> Charles Drazin

Charles's proposal is beautifully written, and emotional in the best sense. I have no hope of writing a proposal as good. It's a pity he isn't a commissioning editor who can do deals – a BOSS instead of a workhorse. I write out his advice as slogans on A4 sheets and stick them on my walls: TALK THE PUBLISHER'S LANGUAGE ... THINK COMMERCIAL ...

2 July 1994

A perfect summer evening. I go with Monika to walk her jumping course by the Severn Estuary. We walk and walk, climbing over the obstacles. We are together. This is happiness. A gift from God.

4 July 1994

I parcel up a chunk of diary – one of many – together with the sample chapter, and post them to Charles. Good riddance to bad rubbish. Another weight gone.

Lindsay's shocked when I tell him. 'You can't expect Charles to edit your book.'

5 July 1994

Another letter from Mike Legge.

> Dear David,
> Please regard this more as an encouragement and call to arms on our two works in progress than a criticism of you, okay? . . .
> I just don't want *Chasing Dragons* to drag out any longer. The longer a project takes to complete, in my opinion, the worse it becomes. It loses all momentum. I don't want it to be another year in the making saga, which would guarantee its demise . . . It's already been two and a half years in the writing, which is totally ridiculous and quite unacceptable. You say it needs some 'thinking time'. Rubbish. We don't need thoughts, we need action, it needs to be got straight down onto paper and sent out, that's what it needs. I'm not going to let this drag out any longer or it will never get finished. You said you'd be over by the end of July. Fine. I'm now making a deadline for *Chasing Dragons* to have its final draft completed by the end of August, whether you come over here or not, and it's going out on that date in whatever state of readiness it's in. Then I am going to work, full-time, on the next scripts, for which I'm going to set myself short but realistic writing times. Around twelve weeks, start to finish . . .
>
> > All best wishes,
> > Mike

His *Chasing Dragons* is so awful that I decide a total rewrite by me is the only way it will see the light of day. I get a fit of manic energy and work through the night. Manic energy is an important part of my work. I'm glad I haven't lost it by giving up the booze.

8 July 1994

An enthusiastic call from Charles. He loves the diary. 'But it needs an editor.' He offers to edit it and find a publisher. I phone Lindsay, who says that Charles is obviously unique.

27 July 1994

Skye finishes her unpaid job at the Camphill Trust, where she has worked all year with the mentally handicapped. She loves them and calls them 'Fairy Folk', because they are simple and sweet in spite of occasional rages. She's also finished her Saturday job as a checkout girl at the Lydney Co-op. She was paid the slave wages of £1.99 an hour. Skye has an 'edge' to her, and, when she's not clomping up and down the stairs like Hitler, a fairy soul herself. She's off on Saturday for the holiday of a lifetime – in fact the first holiday she's ever had – sailing the Mediterranean with Monika's sister.

1 August 1994

I fax Mike Legge:

Dear Mike,
I've posted off to you my lengthy rewrite of the script today.
Many thanks for your letter and the extra script, which have just arrived.
I may be bonkers but I very much like Princess Fabrina and the last half – I've cut it drastically and rewritten a lot. A big problem (for me at least) is the construction from page 44 to 56 – which I've tried to solve. More work being done here.
The other problem, and it's a big one, is the 'style' of the descriptions. Sometimes they're not there. I've done work on this – I still have the script of *Milk Money* which I think is a classic of good description and dialogue (has it been made?!). You will see my changes to the last half and the end – but I 100 per cent think Princess Fabrina should end up with Max. We can't have the whole good stuff about her being sold like cattle – the huge build-up she has – the VG love scenes with Max – Robert falling for her – all great – for a deflation: they all let her go tamely off to this marriage after the whole script . . . look up William Goldman on how he killed a movie by letting the girl fall off that stunt plane at

the end. The audience hated it. They will hate it if Fabrina conforms to her father and Muslim lifestyle. I also apologise if my handwriting is difficult but I've numbered up changes like I used to do. Do send me the rewrite with your stuff as soon as you can and I'll post it on back. Yes – we will make the August deadline. I appreciate it's top priority!

David

10 August 1994

I ring Lindsay, but before I can utter a word he says, 'Something absolutely terrible has happened to me. I'm going to have a bath. I'll ring you back in twenty minutes.'

What's happened? His heart?

He rings back. 'I've got to do a play about Tolstoy with Vanessa Redgrave.'

'Lindsay! This is wonderful. Congratulations!'

'It's terrible. The writer's very bad and conceited, and Vanessa—'

'Brilliant, Lindsay!'

'And then there's something else that's terrible. When I get back from my travels we're going to start again on *If2* . . . now you're in really good nick again.'

'What are these travels?'

'First I'm going to Prague to show *Britannia Hospital* to a load of students, then I'm going on holiday with Lois in France, and then a film festival in Bulgaria.'

I'm worried. Lindsay has been unwell and depressed all year. I tell him, 'Be careful.'

'Onwards,' says Lindsay.

30 August 1994

At 6.15 p.m. Kathy Burke rings. 'Have you a chair,' she asks. 'You know what this is about . . .'

'Yes.'

'Lindsay died of a heart attack at Lois's three hours ago. I wanted you to be the first to know.'

31 August 1994

Phoning friends, getting calls from all over the world. My mind is a blur. I function with my notepad and the phone like a secretary. It's a mad circus, not a bereavement. Lindsay, in his death, has created the sequel to *Britannia Hospital*.

Remembering Lindsay

A letter from Broderick Miller in Hollywood, the production manager on Lindsay's film *The Whales of August* and writer of *Wedlock*.

Dear David,
My grieving has just begun, but I'm sure it's good therapy to write to someone who knew and loved Lindsay even more than I did. I am including a remembrance article which I today faxed to the *Los Angeles Times*. We'll see if they print it. I fear that one of Lindsay's enduring legacies will be the legions of Americans who are ignorant of his work.

You asked me to write a few words about the whisky flask Lindsay and I shared on several occasions. The first time Lindsay passed his personal flask of Scotch to me was during a particularly emotional moment at Monument Valley. Lindsay and I made a pilgrimage there to of course visit the ghosts of John Ford. We were sitting on a slab of red rock jutting out over the vast spectacle of Monument Valley, Lindsay quietly withdrew his flask, raised it in a silent toast to Ford, then offered me a drink. I will remember that reverent, holy moment for the rest of my life.

As you know, Lindsay and I shared a number of adventures in the States. And frequently a moment would arise necessitating a quiet drink together. Lindsay would pull out his flask and we would toast whatever muses were in the air at the time. These moments were precious to me, which is why I inquired about the flask. If no one feels especially partial to the flask, it would mean a great deal to me. It would bring back many, many happy memories, and would serve as a fitting memento of our long and fulfilling relationship.

Thank you so much, David, for all the trouble you've gone to in this matter. You are my most beloved link to Lindsay and I look forward to seeing you soon.

My love and thoughts to you,
Broderick

A letter from Ma, on holiday with my sister Sue.

My very dear David,
I can't tell you how shocked and sorry I was to hear the news of Lindsay's death – and not very old too, from my age level! It must be a great loss to you of a dear dear friend – there aren't people like that any more – and a great grief on top of a sad year with the death of Pa and Jo Janni.
We return on Saturday and I'll be in touch then.

With lots of love to all,
Ma

A tribute from Gary Sweet, Farmer's Creek, Texas.

I was at work when I heard the news. A friend of mine had called me at my office to tell me that Lindsay Anderson had died. I managed to keep my composure throughout the rest of the day but alone in my car I cried all the way home. I wasn't crying so much for Lindsay, however, but rather selfishly I was crying for myself for I was the one who had to carry on with the realisation that I could never contact him again. Luckily he had gone suddenly while enjoying himself with his friends – a lovely ending, really – and I am consoling myself with the knowledge that he was a great, special friend and now I have an angel. And you, David, were responsible for that friendship, for had you not penned those two classic films I'd never have met him.

Your relationship with Lindsay could have been nothing less than awesome, for you were not only friend and fellow artist but collaborator as well. But let me tell you about the Lindsay that I knew.

It was hero-worship, pure and simple, that changed my life so, but only after I had been given a *satori*, an awakening if you will, in a cavernous cafeteria at a Texas university dormitory, for that was where I first saw *If* . . . and *O, Lucky Man!* on Sunday afternoons, as part of a weekly series of 'fine art' cinema. The delight and amazement of seeing those two works, the ideas I had been forming in my own head, my attitudes, all thrown up there on the whitewashed walls, completely overwhelmed me. I couldn't get those movies out of my mind and I ended up in the library reading all about Lindsay Anderson. 'The single most influential figure in unsettling the complacency of the British film industry,' said the *Oxford Companion to Film*. Not only was Lindsay a radical film critic and editor of *Sequence* magazine, but he was also the guiding force of the Free Cinema movement in the Fifties (the last true documentary movement in Britain) with Karel Reisz, Tony Richardson, Walter Lassally and John Fletcher. The Free Cinema manifesto – entirely Lindsay's creation – demanded complete freedom for the artist, a close relationship between art and society, complete subjectivity, the expression of ideas firmly and forcefully stated, and (coincidentally?) alignment with the New Left. This manifesto was the basis for the rest of Lindsay's career. 'The artist must be a monster!' Lindsay told *Time* in 1973. On stage, too, he helped to carry on the revolution begun in 1956 by Tony Richardson and John Osborne at the Royal Court Theatre well into the 1970s. The Free Cinema Group influenced a flood of realism in British cinema which critics would sneeringly call 'Kitchen Sink'. In 1968 he and you turned the film world on end with the romantic, poetic allegory *If . . .* Lindsay was a master who crafted his wisdom into art. The fact that he made so few films and yet still managed to crack the facade of artistic apathy and gross commercialism is a testament to his purpose. To carve him down to basics, he was a genius. How could I not have been impressed?

I wrote to him and told him about the influence his work had on me and added that I didn't expect a reply, but reply he did, sending me a package of stills, books and a wonderful letter that mentioned, 'by the way, my address has changed, as above . . .', which I took to mean write again if you like. And a correspondence was begun which ended only with his death. At first I was the student and he the teacher, but when I was able to get his long-shelved film *The White Bus* into distribution at United Artists Classics I became an ally and later a friend. I attended the entire shooting of *Britannia Hospital* and all the rehearsals up to the opening of his stage production of *The Cherry Orchard*. I came to know Lindsay Anderson as a man.

What I found was one of the kindest souls on Earth and now, probably, in Heaven. He not only went out of his way for me, but for everybody else. Once, while walking down the London streets, a tourist asked me for directions. 'Sorry,' I told him, 'but I'm not from London.' Lindsay, who hadn't heard, asked what the man had wanted and when I told him, chased the fellow down the street and gave him his directions. As far as I could tell, he was the same with everybody who wanted his attention. And there were many who did.

His sense of humour tended towards the dark. I once pointed out a flaming red Ferrari parked kerbside and said, 'That's what you need.' Lindsay looked at the car and replied, 'At least it would be a quick way out!' On the other hand, one of my fondest memories is of singing church hymns with him in a pub.

While he was always firm in his opinions and steadfast in his convictions, he always tolerated opposite points of view – as long as you could state why you felt as you did. He had no tolerance at all if you couldn't back up your statements. Hero-worshipping fool that I was, upon our first meeting I tried to answer his questions as I felt he would want me to answer. He saw through that in about thirty seconds. It was only after I got braver and told him, 'I disagree because . . .', that I gained his respect.

Like any genius Lindsay was a very simple man.

When Lindsay came to Houston to lecture at Rice University, I drove him about. He kept wanting me to stop so that he could hand dollar bills to the beggars standing on the side of the streets holding their 'Will Work for Food' signs. I let him give one dollar away, but when he wanted me to pull over at the next corner I told him, 'Lindsay, you can't save the world.' He looked saddened and said, 'I suppose you're right.' Perhaps that was his tragedy. He had changed the world a little through his work, but he wanted to change it just a little bit more. He had more to say, but the money people wouldn't let him say it. His reputation as an artist had caught up with him and he knew it. If only he'd sold out like his old Free Cinema cronies. If only he'd made a *Tom Jones* or a *French Lieutenant's Woman* he might have been bankable. Instead he remained to the end an artist waiting to be commissioned. He told me that he made *Glory, Glory* for HBO to prove that he could be just another director, but that show, along with the television play *The Old Crowd*, all had the Lindsay Anderson stamp. He couldn't help himself. He had to remain true to his creed.

With Lindsay's passing, Free Cinema has gone. Its survivors have long ago abandoned it. But wait! There in the dark, on the screen is poetry, emotion and maybe even a carnival mirror reflection of life. The garish spectacle of *O Dreamland* is played out on the streets. *If . . .* still packs a colossal punch. *Britannia Hospital* is an indictment of us all. His films are with us still. As an artist, how like a god. But to those of us who knew him, loved him and were loved by him – what a piece of work as a man!

10 September 1994

Malcolm phones me after his return from Lindsay's cremation in France. It wasn't pleasant – the Anderson clique against Malcolm and his wife Kelley. But he took a photograph of Lindsay lying in his coffin which he's going to print when he writes his autobiography.

He is adamant that I should write Lindsay's biography. I think Gavin Lambert, his lifelong friend who started *Sequence* with him, would be better. Malcolm also tells me that Lindsay's death was a tragic mistake. Some idiot gave him Prozac, 'the happy drug', to cure his depression. One thing you never take with a heart condition is Prozac.

Malcolm is as adamant as I am that Lindsay's memorial should be at the Royal Court. Lindsay lived for the Court. Malcolm says he'll send me $2,000 as *If2 . . .* is sunk and I'm nearly bankrupt.

'I'll never let you go under, David,' he says, which lifts a grim worry from my mind.

12 September 1994

A fax from Mike Legge:

David,
Things and times certainly change fast, and when you least expect them and I don't just mean poor Kim [Mike's first wife, who died from a brain tumour, aged 45]. In no time at all I got painfully ill with infected kidneys, went to hospital ($700 in bills!), spent ten awful days on powerful and painful antibiotics, lost my job as an apartment manager, and had four days to vacate my flat!

Still, that was last week, I've now moved into a new place and all is temporarily well again. It's just a small studio flat, with bathroom and kitchen in an old 1927 Hollywood building.

Still, they say good things come out of bad and, as I lay in hospital, I became very clear-headed at one time and said to myself I must quit this job, for two reasons. First, it's too easy and I'm too comfortable now, I've few worries and, up to a point, less motivation. I have a luxurious two-bed, two-bath flat overlooking the Hollywood Hills and, as I loll in comfort, I try to remind myself I must get down to some writing. I'm behaving like I've sold a script whereas in reality I should be writing eight hours a day. Secondly it's an easy job, but I do get daily calls about leaky toilets and blocked drains, and when you're trying to write some dramatic scene these irritations buzz around your head like mosquitoes. I'll have to quit this job and get a small, cheap studio apartment and write. But of course I can't possibly afford to do that.

This option is now gone, I'm having to do just that and, provided I can find a small monthly income to pay the rent and bills, I'm probably better off.

It's just such a pity you didn't come when you could and should have. I kept calling you, I had plenty of room, I offered to put you up, pay half your air fare, everything. Can't you see, if you'd come in June as planned we'd have had *Chasing Dragons* finished and out by now, maybe have a deal if we're ever going to get a deal, be financially independent and you wouldn't have to be remortgaging your home. The only way we are ever going to get financial independence is if we sell a *commercial* script to *Hollywood* and we both know it, and all this continuous, non-stop procrastinating is so dumb.

What now? It's all so depressing. I can't put you up and I have no money for your air fare or expenses; you're on your own. What's going to happen to *Chasing Dragons*? If you don't come over very shortly I'm just going to have to take it back and try to complete it myself, yet again. Let me know soonest.

Michael

14 *September 1994*

I fax Mike Legge:

Dear Mike,
You have been through hell. Yes, I will cope with everything. You are now in a very good work environment but can't see the wood for the trees. What we do is stick to our life plan which is now much easier. I am fixing up cash with Halifax for my survival. You must right now work solidly on *Chasing Dragons* and send me your draft as per plan, which I will rewrite and post back soonest.

Remember with the script you also can't see the wood for the trees. Keep it as simple as possible and I beg you put in good descriptions because you KNOW THE DECOR, PEOPLE. And don't fuss about the end.

Second, the next script we must write together is about US and your apartment block. It will be a winner and be written from both our experiences, which is the only way to write.

My personal news. Reason for delays was that my mother was at death's door with a tumour then heart failure from March to August and my sister and I had to deal with that situation. Now under control. With me, family comes first. I know that sounds patronising after what you've been through with Kim and your family, and of course you are part of my family too. A bill for $150 follows in post. Just stick to *Chasing Dragons* and then we'll do the story about US, which will be a winner and which I'm mad keen on.

I am firing on all four cylinders – and it's all due to giving up the booze. To summarise – when I come out I want to be ready with *Chasing Dragons* and *Us* (a good title that – I'm registering it with the Guild).

So keep your pecker up. I'm here and we both still have a roof over our heads. I will be ready with the first draft of *Chasing Dragons* and the proposal for *Us*.

As Jeff Berg says, 'DO IT' . . .

And it certainly wasn't dumb not to come out earlier . . . It was just impossible. So please don't feel angry. I'm thinking of you.

David

21 *September* 1994

A fax from Mike Legge:

Dear David,
Thanks very much for your fax. It was terrific, encouraging, uplifting, positive and inspiring. Really, I mean it. Monika was right when she said you were now firing on all four cylinders, and I don't think it's just because you're off the booze. I think you've been liberated, unchained, set free. You're your own man now, you can do what you like with your life, and you don't have to answer to anybody. Well, except to immediate family, that is.

Lindsay may well have done a lot of good for you, especially at the beginning, but for the past several years I think he virtually enslaved you, tying you up in knots on projects that would never see the light of day, and, worst of all, taking all his hang-ups and insecurities out on you. One doesn't wish to speak ill of the recently departed, but I think he really treated you very badly. OK, when two people are involved in a difficult creative process, like writing, tempers do flare at times and we also have our ups and downs, but it is usually positive and we like and respect one another as well.

I agree I am now in a better work environment and I realise that the past couple of years were not as good as I thought they were for me. I was too comfortable, with no bills or expenses, no motivation and constantly on call in the building. I didn't write nearly as much as I should have. I was acting like I'd *sold* a script, instead of being nowhere near that stage. In the two weeks since I have been here, in my little garret room, I have written up a storm, all hours of the day, every day. There seems to be so much time and nothing else to do; the phone doesn't ring any more and nobody knocks on my door. I'm perfectly happy here now, just a bit worried about paying the bills. If I could get a writing job every month it would be perfect. I do answer every possible ad for writers in *DramaLogue*, the weekly trade magazine, which brings in some jobs, and I know many more people here now than I did when I first arrived. Which was on 1 October '91, so, in a couple of weeks, I'll have been here slogging it out for three years! . . .

I'm certainly interested in your idea about a script about us. It doesn't sound the sort of thing being made in Hollywood at the moment, rather too small-scale, but I'll wait to hear from you about it further, and if you're mad keen on it, then enthusiasm and motivation go a very long way.

I understand your reasons for the delays and wish you well with *Going Mad in Hollywood*. I'm delighted to see you might be out here sometime after November 20th! That's certainly not too far away, as we have a lot of work still to do on *Chasing Dragons*, and you on *If2* . . . and *Us*. Keep me posted. I do now have a comfortable camp bed and blankets here if we work late some evenings.

I'm glad you're coming out to see Sherry Lansing and some other producers, that's *exactly* what you need to do, it's great! Apart from anything else, with your reputation you could easily get many script doctoring and rewriting jobs here, which pay extremely well.

Looking around at many of the writers here, you shouldn't be broke, you should be seriously rich! Maybe now you will be. I mean, Broderick Miller seems to be working and selling his stuff all the time! He's just pitched a movie with actor Tom Arnold, Roseanne's ex-husband, based on an old 50s/60s TV show called *Highway Patrol*, which starred his godfather, Broderick Crawford, and for which he will, no doubt, be very well paid.

Sorry if this is a bit long! More material for *Us*? Hope it doesn't cost too much, perhaps you could rent a fax machine? That's all from here for now but I hope to see you soon.

Michael

1 *October 1994*

I fax Mike Legge:

Dear Mike,
Hope writing is outpouring. I'd leave *Chasing Dragons* if it is bugging you. For a while.

What I need – TOP PRIORITY for *Us* – is a fax about Kim and her death, and Nicola and your son's reaction. The episode. And of course your reaction.

My brilliant publishing editor took one look at our recent correspondence and said, 'Another film . . .'

Any money problems at your end, I'd try Broderick. He is a sweetie and seems about to sell something. Friends should support each other.

Incidentally, don't for Chrissake mention any small loan from me to you. Very sore point with Monika after my big loan to you as we're so broke. Our secret, Mike. And if you want to do your karma any good sometime, send me a twenty dollar bill in a card!

David

A fax from Mike Legge was waiting for me at Lydney Post Office:

Dear David
Thank you very much indeed for your card, and for the $150, which arrived in the middle of my hour of need! To say that it was much appreciated would be an understatement, it saved my life.

You said you wished it was more, but sometimes a small amount at the right time is equal to a huge amount at another time. I was down to loose change, but I had something coming to me in about a week or ten days – this bridged the gap. Thank you again.

I'm not sure what's going to happen to me now, but I'm going to hang on as long as I can. The idea of returning to England on the dole is too awful to contemplate, but I have to have an income or a sale, it's a fact of life, and both look remote right now. I can probably last until you come over in November, and I do hope you come, then we can talk. Sometimes I think that if I keep at it here, work hard and write more and better stuff, then something surely will happen. At other times, like now, and especially since I moved here, I despair that I'm an aging, unpublished, unbought, unproven, struggling starting-up wannabe writer, trying hopelessly to break into the movies in Hollywood like a million others, and I must be deluding myself . . .

Michael

In the evening I phone Kathy Burke. 'Kathy, it's ridiculous, but I don't have your address.'

Kathy gives it to me, sounding quite normal.

'Pinewood Road? That's a good name for your road. How are things back at the fort?'

'I'm afraid . . . My husband died.'

'Oh, Kathy, you don't deserve this.'

'No . . .' She bursts into tears.

'Oh God, Kathy, take care . . . you'd better go.'

I'd only met her husband, Jim, once – on the boat trip with the ashes of Rachel Roberts and Jill Bennett. Death is everywhere.

3 October 1994

Mike Legge has not been answering his phone or fax for a week and I'm worried he's committed suicide. I call my friend Broderick and ask him to go over to Mike's apartment to see if he's gassed himself.

4 p.m. Lydney Post Office ring. They have a fax from Mike Legge. He is OK, but broke. His phone has been cut off.

7 October 1994

I fax Mike Legge from Lydney Post Office:

Dear Mike,
A chance for you to sell an exclusive.

I rang my bank, Lloyds, in Ross on Wye, where I enquired about my $2,500 loan from Malcolm McDowell. I hadn't heard anything all week, and was wondering what had happened. I practically live in Lloyds Bank. They are terribly sweet people and terribly underpaid, since they handle millions but only take home about £200 per week. The sweet girl answered my call and said, 'Oh dear, all our computers are on the blink.' I said, 'What do you mean?' And she said, semi-exhausted, 'It's nationwide, the computers have been on the blink for two days and it won't come on again until this evening.' I immediately realised the possibilities for £1 million fraud and hacking. I rang Stewart Steven, the editor of the *Evening Standard*, but the paper had gone to press. Kelley McDowell says for God's sake sell the story, and I beg you to sell it for yourself.

David

The fax to Mike doesn't get through because his phone/fax is cut off. Excited by this mad story of Lloyds Bank being totally on the blink – nationwide – paralysed because of a central computer failure, I phone ICM in Los Angeles to get the story out. As I talk to a secretary, Jeff Berg suddenly cuts in, equally excited. 'Hi, David – I'll put you on to a stenographer!' Which he does. But no paper in America dares print the scoop.

The power of money. The only power there is, according to Mike Legge . . .

10 *October* 1994

A fax from Mike Legge:

Dear David,
This week I realise I've been here three years, and frankly I'm extremely disappointed at our achievements. Look at what they are: zero. Zilch. This week a new movie, *Pulp Fiction*, opens here too amid tremendous fanfare. Its writer/director, Quentin Tarantino, is, and I quote from today's paper: 'mugging his way across the pages of dozens of slicks and newspapers, holding court at festivals, in the trades, on radio, on television, the new indie boy wonder turned studio hire, a renegade, a player, the publicist's

wet dream and LA city's bright light . . .', etc. I mention this because when I arrived here *three years ago* Quentin was working in a video shop in LA, trying to get *his* first script off the ground. He did (*Reservoir Dogs*), it became a modest low-budget success, he then wrote and directed *Pulp Fiction* and it just won the top prize at Cannes. He's milking the hype and publicity brilliantly and is already rich beyond his wildest dreams, both financially and with the offers pouring in.

In the same time that Quentin wrote and directed his movies and won the top prize at Cannes, we wrote *Love and Madness* and I brought it over here. It went the rounds, I revised it, wrote another draft, then started on *Chasing Dragons*. You say it still 'needs work'. OK, answer me this: is something more likely to happen with a not-quite-ready script actually going the rounds, or by gathering dust on your shelf? If it 'needs work' when will you start on it? So PLEASE get it in to Channel 4, and anywhere else you can think *now*, as it is, ASAP, otherwise nothing will ever happen to it, ever. Which means nothing will happen, *can* happen, to improve our situation. You have made great comments and corrections on *Chasing Dragons* over the same three-year period, and now you are just 'ten days away' from being 'all mine'. Great! . . .

Michael

18 October 1994

Charles sends me a book called *Henrietta*. It's a memoir by Henrietta Moraes which Hamish Hamilton are publishing next month. The flyleaf reads: 'Born into a family of women (her Indian Air Force father tried to strangle her mother when pregnant and was never heard of again), Henrietta Moraes was brought up by a sadistic grandmother and sent to boarding school, where the girls took their baths in enormous cotton garments . . . Her first love was filmmaker Michael Law. They lived together in Soho: breakfast at the Café Torino, to the French Pub at opening time, a wine bar in the afternoons and the Gargoyle every night, the haunt of Cyril Connolly, Angus Wilson, Francis Bacon, Lucian Freud, Francis Wyndham . . . Henrietta Moraes married three times: to Michael Law, to John Minton's friend Norman, a bodybuilder and watchmaker, and to the Indian poet Dom Moraes, who went out one day for a packet of cigarettes and never returned. She then took up with a drug addict and developed a habit herself. Cat burglary became her hobby. In the late sixties, alight with the joys of acid and the hippy life, she dropped out with friends and took to the road in a gypsy wagon with a horse called Rizla. It took them four years to reach Wales.'

I read the book twice. It's pure poetry – original, shocking, fresh. It's the best memoir I have ever read. It would make a wonderful film.

19 October 1994

Skye reads *Henrietta* and exclaims, 'Dad! This is your chance for a comeback!'

3 November 1994

I go to Henrietta's publishing party in Chelsea. She has had a fall and broken her collar bone. She sits in a hospital wheelchair, signing copies of her book. I overhear one of her many friends saying, 'She writes even better than she talks!' It's a festive occasion. Charles toasts Henrietta, and Henrietta toasts her 'darling Charles'. It is a triumph after her years of suffering.

'I'd like to take you home with me,' I tell her.

20 November 1994

The big day has finally come: Lindsay's memorial celebration at the Royal Court. I nervously practise my speech. I've never ever performed in public, but what really scares me is my false teeth. If I don't wear them I'll be comfy, but may shock the entire audience. If I do, they may fall out in mid-performance.

We have a run-through in the afternoon, and then at six the show begins. All the people who are giving speeches sit in chairs on the stage. I'm surrounded by stars. Albert Finney, Tom Courtenay, Richard Harris, Alan Bates, James Bolam, Brian Cox . . .

David Storey begins the celebration, but I don't hear a word. I am hit by an overwhelming attack of tiredness and am suddenly near collapse. Panic on stage. I fumble desperately for my Ativan sleeping pills. Recently they've been having the opposite effect on me and keeping me up into the small hours. By the time it is my turn, I am wide awake. Malcolm introduces me.

I gaze out at the huge audience and improvise: 'I have to say the greatest gift, the greatest bequest that Lindsay gave me is he did get me off the drink. That is absolutely fantastic. I would like to talk to you about Lindsay's other home. Most of you know Stirling Mansions, which I called the clinic, but Lindsay had a second home, by the seaside in Sussex called Fuchsia Cottage, and when we went down to work there, he would unlock the door, open it, and everything in there had been preserved as it was when his mother died. That place was not just a haven, it was a heaven; and that is where we did most of our work from 1966 till last February.'

And then I read a comic account of the writing of *O, Lucky Man!* It feels like a public rehabilitation. I sense the audience is shocked to discover that I exist. That there was a writer who created Lindsay's films.

27 November 1994

I fly to Hollywood to work with Mike Legge on *Chasing Dragons*.

7 December 1994
Hollywood

I send a postcard of the Hollywood Hills covered in mock snow to Charles and his wife.

Dearest Charles and Dinah
Out here I realise for the first time that Lindsay is dead . . . awful . . . Mike Legge has just uttered the immortal words: 'There is no bullshit in Hollywood.'

My apartment is in mass murderer Charles Manson's old house, half destroyed by last January's big earthquake. Pure Barton Fink. There were two earthquakes yesterday. *Very* scary. I go to Malcolm's house in Ojai this weekend. He has 15 cars . . .

All best wishes
David

16 December 1994

Monika rings to say I've been invited to Jo Janni's memorial celebration in London on the 19th. As I won't be back in time, I send this fax:

David Sherwin

Dearest friends of Jo, Stella, Nicholas and family

I'm very sorry I can't be with you with morning to celebrate Jo
and his wonderful life. When I first heard of Jo's death I was
saddened – as Jo would say – BEYOND BELIEF. But I was over
the moon to read in his obituary that he had met his grandchild
for the first time and his eyes had lit up and twinkled. Jo had such
lovely eyes – and such a kind smile – so absolutely full of humour.
He was one of the most humorous and kind men I have ever met.
I well remember my first meeting with him. It was just after *If . . .*
had appeared. Jo and John [Schlesinger] were in terrible trouble
with *Sunday, Bloody Sunday*. It was February 1970. Shooting had
stopped for the script to be rewritten and the role of the doctor to
be recast. Recasting the doctor Jo did at a stroke – by asking Peter
Finch to step in, which of course he did brilliantly. Rewriting the
script was a different matter. It went on all of the spring and summer of 1970. John was so worried that he came up in huge boils
and was rushed off to hospital . . .

One evening, I was so exhausted that I fell down Sloane Square
Underground stairs and broke my wrist. Throughout everything
Jo was 'beyond belief' understanding and a pillar of strength. To
keep me calm and go over the script he would take me on the top
of a red London bus to travel all over – and especially to his
beloved fly fishing shop. 'David,' he would say, 'the answer to all
your problems with the script is to read *Country Life*, that is very
calming.'

In the summer of '75 a love affair of mine collapsed disas-
trously. Of course, one of the first people I went to see was Jo. He
immediately saw I was in trouble, sat me at the end of his long
table, asked me what the matter was. I just burst into tears. Jo
gave me a comforting copy of *Country Life* and a cigar.

I didn't hear from Jo again until the summer of 1986. A voice
from the grave – Jo's voice on the phone. 'David, I would like you
to write the film of a brilliant thriller, *The Boy Who Followed
Ripley* by Patricia Highsmith. It was bliss to hear from Jo again
and we met at his favourite inn in Burford, where we had very
good trout. Jo was fantastic in spite of his stroke and with great
humour and sadness told me the story of his collapse after *Yanks*
had finished shooting. From then on Jo was on the phone, often
three or four times a day, for two years. It was a marvellous way
of working, and together we produced a pretty good script. The

last time I worked with him was in 1990 when he asked me to write a black comedy about Stalin. 'It must be blacker than *If . . .* and funnier.' 'I'll have a bash,' I said. Two minutes later Jo asked, 'Did I say Stalin or Lenin?' 'Stalin, Jo,' I answered. And so the script *The Private Death of Joe Stalin* was born.

Every day, sometimes six or seven times a day, Jo would ring me with questions, ideas, and his own gallows humour jokes to gee me up. Every conversation began with detailed questions about the state of my wife's horses, for Jo loved the gentleness of horses and once owned a racehorse himself. 'David, tell me, how are the horses? They eat a lot better than you, I know.' I brought Lindsay Anderson in as director on *The Private Death of Joe Stalin*. And at our first meeting, in Jo's favourite fish restaurant, Jo gave a brilliant definition of his happy marriage. That day he wasn't only half-paralysed – he'd fallen over a loose rug in his house and broken his good leg. 'For heaven's sake, Jo,' said Lindsay, in his Lindsay Anderson fashion, 'throw away your rugs this instant.'

'I can't.'

'You must.'

'My wife likes the rugs.'

'What has that got to do with it? For God's sake, Jo, you may break your neck.'

'With wives, you never throw away the rugs – no matter what,' was Jo's reply.

Jo was a terrific story-teller and also a very modest man. One day, when I asked him about his Oscar for *Darling*, he said, 'I had completely forgotten about the wretched thing. Then one day some en came to take the old fridge to a tip and out fell my Oscar.' I never saw any signs of awards or ostentation in his house, but I always noticed his fishing rods standing ready behind the front door.

Dear Jo – the best producer in the world, friend, brother, hero – I salute you.

25 December 1994
Cherry Tree House

It's the first Christmas my family has known me sober. It's like the first Christmas I can remember. My family love me, and I love my family. This is God's greatest gift.

David Sherwin

March 1995

After Lindsay's flat has gone, Kathy writes to me.

Farewell Lindsay, Au revoir Jim.

I first met Lindsay Anderson in January 1977, having been recommended as a potential secretary by a mutual friend. My 'interview' was just a friendly chat over a cup of coffee. There was no test of typing or shorthand and very little discussion of salary; in fact there was more negotiation over the ashtray I would be allocated. A large green glass one was found for me and I started working for Lindsay a month or so later.

Life at Stirling Mansions was often chaotic. Particularly in the early years, friends came to stay, for short periods if they were passing through London, or longer ones if they had hit a crisis in their lives. The flat was christened 'the Clinic'.

Among the friends who came to stay was Rachel Roberts, and it was from Lindsay's flat that she returned to Los Angeles for the last time. Some months later her boy-friend, Darren Ramirez, delivered her ashes to Lindsay when he was passing through London on his way back to the US from Milan. They were in a small cardboard box inside a large glossy Versace carrier bag, where they stayed for many years until Lindsay made his documentary *Is That All There Is?* in 1992. In the closing scene Rachel's and Jill Bennett's ashes were strewn in the Thames.

The Versace bag returned to Stirling Mansions, but some time later, when moving it, I discovered that it wasn't quite empty. I didn't know what to do with the remaining ashes and left them and the bag where they were. So a small part of Rachel remained at Stirling Mansions.

Lindsay was always generous with his time and money, and many people had good reason to be grateful to him, but he could also be guilty of penny-pinching. He would be delighted if he found unfranked stamps on incoming mail; they would be carefully torn off and soaked for re-use. The Fire Brigade were called at least twice to the flat when he boiled up chicken bones for stock (rarely actually used) and went out to the cinema, leaving the pan to boil dry. On one occasion an antique barometer was badly damaged when the firemen forced entry to the flat, the front door needed extensive repairs and the kitchen walls were blackened, so it was an expensive economy.

I had lived in Swiss Cottage for nearly twenty years, but in 1983 my husband Jim and I started to look for a house in Bromley, Kent. I thought it only fair to warn Lindsay that I would be leaving, and he did interview a couple of prospective secretaries in a half-hearted way. A short while later he was going to America to do a theatre production in Washington and I offered to stay on until his return, as he would not want a stranger in the flat during his absence. He readily agreed and the matter of my resignation was never mentioned again. I travelled up from Bromley each week and was still working out my notice at the time of his death.

On Sunday 28 August 1994, Jim and I had spent the afternoon in the National Portrait Gallery. That evening Lindsay telephoned from France, where he was holidaying with his old friend Lois Smith. Jim told him that we had seen a photograph of him in the National Portrait Gallery amongst the theatrical greats. Lindsay was pleased and said he would seek it out next time he was there. He asked me to telephone Eva, his cleaner, and his friend Patsy Healey to let them know he was coming back on Wednesday. He sounded happy and relaxed, but was looking forward (as always) to getting back to the Finchley Road and Waitrose. As it was the Bank Holiday weekend, I did not make the calls until the Tuesday evening. I had barely put the phone down when I got a call from Lois to say that Lindsay had died an hour before. It was sudden and completely unexpected. Jim and I telephoned as many of his friends as we could track down to break the news to them so that they would not hear of it through the media.

Less than a month later, Jim too was dead. We had been together for thirty-five years. My life had been turned upside down in such a short space of time. They were both generous, honourable men and the world is a much sadder place without them.

Many of Lindsay's friends rallied round and were very supportive. We had to organise his memorial celebration and the flat had to be cleared, a mammoth task as Lindsay rarely threw anything away.

The last fortnight was extraordinary. People were coming and going all the time. Dr Sean Lewis and John Cartwright from the British Council, who had offered us some space to store files and papers, popped in to see what they were letting themselves in for. Representatives from the Cinema Museum and the Theatre

Museum were introduced to each other as they came to collect their bequests, stretching to shake hands over Mary Chapman of Fitzjohns Books who was sorting out books crouched on the hall floor. The furniture went off to Phillips to be auctioned, including my desk, so thereafter I operated from a card table. One day someone – I think it was Jocelyn Herbert – was looking for a bag to put something in. She spotted the Versace bag. 'What's this?' she asked, tipping it out over the carpet. 'That's Rachel,' I said, but she looked at me blankly. I don't think she understood.

On the last day, I thought I would be the only one at the flat to oversee the final clearance, but a few others arrived to help. Eva vacuumed each room as it was emptied, until finally the Hoover, too, went on the clearance truck, containing, presumably, the last remains of Rachel. At 4 p.m. all was done and I turned the key in the lock of 9 Stirling Mansions for the last time. Eva and I sat despondently on the stairs outside as I waited for my son to collect me.

When my mother died in 1989, Lindsay's was the first letter of condolence which I received. In it he said, 'These things change us and our lives are never the same again.'

30 August 1996
The Caravan, Cherry Tree House

My Dearest Lindsay,
Exactly two years ago, when Kathy told me you'd died, it didn't sink in. It has now. You're not coming back again from America, or Prague, or Australia, or anywhere. And I'll never hear your voice on the phone saying, 'Don't cough, I know you're lying. Just get on with it. You can do it. Constant communication!'

But I will carry with me to my grave the words you spoke at the beginning of *Britannia Hospital*: 'Only three things are real: God, human folly, and laughter . . .'

David

ONWARDS!